To Tame a Savage

By Emma V. Leech

****

Published by: Emma V. Leech.
Copyright (c) Emma V. Leech 2017
Cover Art: Victoria Cooper
ASIN No.: B079DGJVTV
ISBN No: 978-1986644525

All rights reserved. Without limiting the rights under copyright reserved above, no part of this publication may be reproduced, stored in or introduced into a retrieval system, or transmitted, in any form, or by any means (electronic, mechanical, photocopying, recording, or otherwise) without the prior written permission of both the copyright owner and the above publisher of this book. This is a work of fiction. Names, characters, places, brands, media, and incidents are either the product of the author's imagination or are used fictitiously. The author acknowledges the trademarked status and trademark owners of various products referenced in this work of fiction, which have been used without permission. The publication/use of these trademarks is not authorized, associated with, or sponsored by the trademark owners. The ebook version and print version are licensed for your personal enjoyment only.

The ebook version may not be re-sold or given away to other people. If you would like to share the ebook with another person, please purchase an additional copy for each person you share it with. No identification with actual persons (living or deceased), places, buildings, and products is inferred.

Table of Contents

Prologue	1
Chapter 1	9
Chapter 2	18
Chapter 3	26
Chapter 4	35
Chapter 5	44
Chapter 6	56
Chapter 7	64
Chapter 8	75
Chapter 9	84
Chapter 10	93
Chapter 11	100
Chapter 12	110
Chapter 13	119
Chapter 14	128
Chapter 15	137
Chapter 16	149
Chapter 17	157
Chapter 18	168
Chapter 19	177
Chapter 20	185
Chapter 21	193
Chapter 22	202
Chapter 23	210
Chapter 24	219
Chapter 25	227
Chapter 26	235
Chapter 27	245
Chapter 28	253
Chapter 29	263
Chapter 30	269
Chapter 31	279
Chapter 32	288
Chapter 33	298
Epilogue	307
Persuading Patience	314

Chapter 1	316
Want more Emma?	325
About Me!	326
Other Works by Emma V. Leech	328
Audio Books	331
To Dare a Duke	332
Dare to be Wicked	334
Dying for a Duke	336
The Key to Erebus	338
The Dark Prince	340
Acknowledgements	342

Prologue

"Wherein a young Lucretia Holbrook forces a friendship and dares the fates."

17th April 1809

At twelve years old, there were few things in the world Lucretia 'Crecy' Holbrook could endure less than a grown-up party.

She'd slipped away as soon as possible, leaving her big sister Belle to be the well-behaved one and stealing into the room where a lavish buffet had been laid out. Here, she picked at the best of everything she could find with two slightly grubby fingers, and finished off with a variety of cream cakes. Two of them were wolfed down on the spot, another carefully wrapped in a hanky and hidden in an increasingly sticky pocket within her voluminous skirts for later.

Crecy had also eavesdropped on several conversations. Most of them seemed to concern the latest gossip about a Viscount DeMorte. The voices that spoke about him sounded at turns angry, disgusted, intrigued, or utterly scandalised. One thing, however, seemed to link all these whispered voices together.

"He's mad, of course."

Crecy had stared with interest at an overly made-up woman in a startlingly orange gown. It was warm indoors as the spring sunshine fell upon the guests, and her make-up was beginning to sweat. Crecy narrowed her eyes, making her vision blur, and saw the woman's face distort, the colours bleeding and looking rather monstrous.

"Oh, undoubtedly," her companion said, nodding, her eyes alight with a strange kind of glee Crecy could not quite understand. If they spoke of a madman, why did they look like dogs salivating over a bone? And how did they know he was mad?

Young she might be, but Crecy had already formed the opinion that polite society was a kind of madness, everyone nodding and speaking of nothing while what they really thought was hidden behind a glassy-eyed expression of placidity. She suspected what polite society saw as madness was just a kind of outspoken honesty others did not appreciate nor understand, or perhaps were even afraid of. At worst, she thought it likely that they simply did not understand at all, and had no desire to.

Being *polite* was a skill that she had not yet learned to cultivate herself, much to Belle's distress. But Crecy found the world perplexing, and could not understand why people didn't see things like she did.

Why, for example, had that woman screamed and fainted when Crecy had showed her that lizard's tail? Crecy had thought it a fascinating thing. For the cat had been tormenting the lizard and almost eaten it, but the lizard had escaped, distracting the cat with its still wriggling tail, which it left behind. It had wriggled for ages afterwards, even with no body to move it. But when Crecy had explained, everyone looked at her like *she* was mad.

It was at that point she'd thought it prudent to make herself scarce. Now, however, she wanted to see the madman and see what she thought of him. She suspected she'd like him a great deal.

It took her a long while to track him down, but she felt her instincts had been correct, as he, too, had escaped the crowds and gone to sit, alone, staring out over a rather lovely lake. There were spring flowers all around, daffodils bobbing their jaunty heads and a sky so blue; it reminded her of Mary's cloak in the stained glass window of the church they visited.

She stared at his back for a while, admiring his hair, which was long and tied loosely back with a black velvet ribbon, which threatened to fall out, as it was half undone. His hair was messy, in fact, like he had run his hands through it, and so black it shone blue, like a crow's feather.

"You have lovely hair," she said to the back of his head as she made her way carefully down the bank he was sitting on.

The dark head turned to look at her and she was momentarily startled by a pair of intense, glittering eyes. Suddenly the sky didn't look so blue any more, not in comparison.

"It's like a crow's feather," she added, waving a hand at his hair in illustration.

Heavy, dark brows that matched his hair drew together and he looked away again. Crecy was undeterred by this, however. She liked to be silent sometimes, so his lack of reply didn't bother her. She sat down beside him and took out the cream cake. It was a little melted, and her hanky was in something of a state, but nonetheless, it *was* a cream cake. She began to eat it, trying with difficulty to keep her bites small and dainty, remembering her sister's recent scolding about her table manners.

She cast him a sideways glance. He was a young man, though a deal older than her, and he did have a rather forbidding expression. His shoulders were hunched and his glower was dark and angry.

"They're all talking about you in there," she said, wondering if that was what made him angry; she couldn't blame him if it was. Crecy hated people talking about her, too. Licking each of her fingers in turn, now that the cream cake was gone, Crecy got up and inched closer to the edge of the lake to rinse her hands and wash out her hanky.

"You'll fall in," he observed, sounding like he didn't much care if she did.

"Probably," she agreed, grinning at him. She crouched down, heedless of her skirts in the dirt. Leaning forward a little more, she rinsed her hanky and wrung it out again. Standing up, she went to turn, but slid on the mud and began to overbalance, her arms cartwheeling. With a startled shriek, she had a brief thought Belle was going to kill her for this, when a strong hand grasped her arm and tugged her forwards, sending her to her knees.

"Thank you," she gasped, looking up through the blonde curls which had tumbled into her face, up at the man who'd saved her. He gave her a dark look, heavy with irritation and said nothing.

Crecy scrambled back to her spot beside him, laying out with care her handkerchief to dry on the grass.

"Don't you have somewhere to be?" he demanded, and she smiled at the sound of his voice. It was a good voice, earthy and deep and rich. It did sound rather vexed, though.

"No," she said, leaning back on her hands and tilting her head to the sunshine. "Don't you?"

There was a grunt before he replied. "No." The word was curt and bitten-off.

"Why do they think you're mad?" she asked, looking around at him. "You seem fine to me."

He looked around at that, and if she had been a different kind of girl, she might have quailed at the look in his eyes.

"That," he said, sounding as though he wished her to Hades, "is because you are an empty-headed little fool. Now run back to your mother and leave me be."

"My mother is dead," she said, as matter of fact as ever.

"I suppose you think I should regret my words and pity you now," he said, sneering at her. "Should I tell you I'm sorry, too?"

Crecy frowned at him. "No, why should you?" she replied, sitting up and staring at him, her expression just as intense. "You don't know me, you never knew my mother, so why should you care? You're not the sort to care for someone unless you know them, are you?"

He stared at her, his expression a little perplexed, but that was nothing Crecy wasn't used to. "I care for no one," he said after a slight pause.

She nodded, pulling her knees up to her chest and leaning her chin on them. "I can understand that. People are hard to like. I prefer animals. Well, apart from Belle, of course, she's my sister."

She was rewarded with another grunt, this one slightly disgusted and, she suspected, rather disbelieving. She'd spoken true, though. Her father was a drunken fool, her only other relation an aunt who was beyond vulgar, and she'd always found it impossible to become friends with girls her own age. They were so ... dull.

"It's all right you know, I don't have any friends either," she said, wondering if the fact bothered him, as he did seem terribly lonely out here. "We can be friends, if you like," she added, brightening at the idea. "Then we both know there is at least one person in the world who thinks well of us."

He looked around at that, blue eyes outraged. "You're an annoying child, and I am not and never will be your friend. Go away, for the love of God."

Crecy accepted this without any feelings of hurt. She'd tamed a fox once, when they'd still lived in the country. It was injured and could no longer hunt, and its hunger made it desperate enough to approach her to accept the food she held. She'd nearly been bitten a dozen or more times before the creature had allowed her to stroke his head.

"Well, that's all right, I'll be your friend, at least. You can't stop me, you know," she added with a sympathetic smile, as if she knew full well her words would only annoy him further.

"Oh, God," he muttered, sounding as though any small amount of patience he might have had was fast disappearing.

They sat in silence for a while, and she watched him from time to time, wondering at the anger she could see as his dark blue eyes stared out, unseeing, over the water.

"When is your birthday?" she asked a little later.

He jumped a little and she realised he'd forgotten she was even there, lost in his thoughts as he was. The young man stared at her, incredulous, and for a moment, she thought he wouldn't answer, and then he frowned.

"Today."

"Oh!" she exclaimed, moving to her knees and staring at him. "Did you get any presents?"

He opened his mouth, staring at her before giving a snort of disbelief.

"I am considered a wicked and remorseless creature, black-hearted and mad. So, no, I did not."

"Are they right to think so of you?" she asked, her head tilted a little to one side as she struggled to see any signs of madness in him. He was angry, certainly, and she suspected he was generally bad-tempered, but, then, creatures in pain usually were.

"Yes," he hissed back at her, his eyes narrowed and intense.

Crecy nodded. "Well, it's still your birthday, you ought to have a present from your friend, at least." Quite unperturbed by his anger, she rummaged around in her pocket and drew out a beautiful feather. It was striped blue and black and quite the loveliest thing Crecy had ever seen.

"Here," she said, holding it out to him. "Happy birthday."

His expression was unreadable now, and she wondered if he would lose his temper entirely, but he said nothing. "Isn't it beautiful?" She twisted the feather in her fingers so that the colours caught the sunlight. "Still not as blue as your eyes, though," she added, grinning at him.

Those eyes rolled, looking revolted. "It's a jay feather," he said, the words a little reluctant, but then he added with relish, *"garrulus glandarius.* They're nasty, vicious birds that steal the young from other bird's nests."

Crecy shrugged, unmoved. "Well, they have to eat," she said, earning herself a look of surprise. "They're certainly noisy, always shouting and looking fierce, that's the *garrulus* bit, I suppose? But they seem shy to me."

She looked up as a slightly desperate voice called out her name, echoing across the gardens.

"I have to go," she said with regret. "But take your present first."

He stared at her, but didn't move, and she tutted. "I won't go until you do."

With a snort of annoyance, he snatched the feather from her hand and she grinned at him.

"I shall write to you," she said, smoothing down her skirts and seeing the mud at the hem with a sinking heart; Belle would be cross. Realising it was a lost cause, she looked up again. "As you're my friend now," she added with a tone that brooked no argument. "And next year I'll send you a present, too.

"Oh, for the love of God, please don't," he retorted. "I shall put any letters straight in the fire without looking at them," he growled, his words harsh.

Crecy stared at him, considering. "No, you won't," she said, and his eyes widened at her.

Belle spoke again, sounding a touch hysterical now.

"Bye," she said, picking up her still sodden hanky and moving away, and then pausing as she saw the black velvet ribbon that had secured his hair had fallen to the ground. With a grin, she snatched it up, clasping it hard in one hand as she ran away, holding her dirty skirts to her knees with the other as she went.

Chapter 1

"Wherein ... an invitation to Longwold."

*December 6*th, *1817*
St Nicholas Day

Viscount DeMorte
Damerel House
Gloucestershire

My dear friend,

I am to be your neighbour!

There is no need for despair, however, it is only for a few days, I assure you. By some stroke of good fortune (or misfortune, depending on your point of view), Belle has secured an invitation for us to attend the Marquess of Winterbourne's Christmas house party.

I know this news will vex you as your cousin is clearly not a man you hold any affection for, if what I read in the scandal sheets is to be believed? Are you really so very wicked as they imply? I wish you would tell me one day. You know by now that I do not believe you mad, though I strongly suspect you would not return the compliment to me, and perhaps you are correct after all.

I honestly don't know.

Shall we meet at last this year, as your estate is so close by? I intend to ride out and trespass if I get the opportunity, you know. Pray, don't shoot me!

I shall ask, as I do every Christmas, you reward my steadfast friendship by replying to this letter. Just one little reply would mean a great deal to me. However, after almost eight years of silence, I know you shan't; strangely, not even to demand I stop writing (yes, I am smiling a little smugly here), so don't imagine I shall be nursing a broken heart all the holiday, for I won't. No. I shall be having a grand time, providing I can escape the deadly dull parties (I know you would feel the same about it) and filling my time ghost-hunting. Such a place as Longwold must be stuffed to the rafters with them, surely?

Are there ghosts at Damerel? I shall discover it for myself one day, you know.

Your friend, etc.

Miss Lucretia Holbrook

***

"How impressive it is!" Crecy exclaimed, her excitement mounting as the huge, sprawling castle appeared. A frail sunlight sparkled upon the frosty landscape, a fine mist hugging the ground and bringing to mind every Gothic novel she'd ever read. "I wonder how many ghosts there are."

Her older sister Belle sent her an indulgent look and shook her head. Try as she might, Belle never could understand any of the things that held Crecy's interest, but at least she didn't revile her for them as most people did. Crecy tried to remember she must do her best to hold her tongue this time. Belle needed a husband, and this was their best opportunity. If she married well, they could escape their dreadful aunt and be comfortable. She could only pray Belle actually fell in love with a good man who would realise her worth.

"I wonder how much a man like the marquess is worth?" the very same dreadful aunt muttered.

Crecy glanced at Belle and saw her own horrified expression reflected at her. Oh God, if only they didn't need a chaperone. She stifled a snort of indignation. The idea that Aunt Grimble would keep them on a righteous path and far from sin was laughable. The first wealthy man to offer them a *carte blanche,* and she well knew the woman would be crowing with delight and urging them to take it.

Not that the idea of it was as troublesome to Crecy as it perhaps ought to have been. She knew well enough that Viscount DeMorte would never marry, after all.

It was strange, how her childish offer of friendship, which had been rejected at every turn, had grown into something far more serious, on her part at least. She had followed news of him as far as she was able, devouring the scandal sheets for any titbit of information. This had become easier once they'd moved in with Aunt Grimble after their father's death. The woman lived and breathed scandal, and for that reason alone, Crecy found she could bear with the wretched woman without throwing things. Aunt Grimble seemed to know everyone in the *ton*, and all of their dark secrets, and no one had darker secrets than Lord Gabriel Greyston, Viscount DeMorte.

Crecy had caught glimpses of him from time to time when he was in town, and in recent years her feelings had become more complex. Her offer of friendship to a creature she sensed was as lonely and misunderstood as she had been genuine, and she had held to it. She sent him letters once a month only, despite wishing to do so more often, for she lived in dread of boring him, and she sent him a birthday present every year on the seventeenth of April. She knew this was wholly inappropriate and dreadfully scandalous, but didn't much care. She never bought the gifts, after all, only ever sending such oddities that appealed to her own curiosity, and occasionally a small drawing or painting if she did something she felt would not shame her scant talents.

In a strange way, he had become a kind of confidant, even though he had never once responded and she knew not if he even read her letters, or if he threw them unopened on the fire as he'd promised. Nevertheless, he was someone to whom she only ever spoke the complete truth, and did not attempt to hide the quirks of her own nature. Whether or not this had given him a disgust of her, she had no way of knowing, but her instincts told her it had not. She hoped he was at least a little curious about her.

She was indeed a curious creature, after all, and one where she felt always out of step and strange amongst others. Not for the first time, she wished she'd been born a man, though that would have made her increasingly complex feelings towards DeMorte even more awkward. Crecy smothered a chuckle, pretending to cough as Belle gave her a curious look.

"You've not caught a chill?" Belle asked, her eyes filled with concern.

Crecy shook her head and assured her sister she was quite well as the imposing façade of the castle drew closer. If she had been a man, she could have travelled, she could have become an animal doctor or a scientist. No one would have thought her strange or morbid for wanting to draw a decomposing squirrel, or thought her fascination at the complex structure of bone and skin and sinew, anything out of the ordinary. As it was, they did, and she lived in dread of the next moment she would open her mouth and see her sister's horrified expression as it dawned on her too late she'd been utterly inappropriate.

Again.

Crecy sighed and banished such thoughts. Longwold drew ever closer and was every bit as rambling and forbidding as she had dreamed. The days of inconsequential chatter to come might be something of a horror to endure, but to search the castle's secrets and ghosts, and to ride out and set foot on Lord DeMorte's estate, perhaps even to see and speak with him ... that was a temptation which she had every intention of yielding to.

***

Crecy scowled at the snow beneath her feet. It was so startling in its pristine, bright purity as the winter sun gleamed down on it her eyes watered. She looked up, focusing instead on a vivid blue sky and the glowering walls of the castle. Belle marched behind her, struggling to keep up.

It was no surprise Crecy was in disgrace, again. Though it *had* been foolish to walk alone with Lord Lancaster, she knew that, really. Only she was bored to tears, and the idea of going out and discovering the snake skeleton he'd promised to show her was too great an incentive. Not only that, but the idea he seemed to share her curiosity for it was tantalising. Now she could see it had been nothing but a ruse to get her alone and kiss her - which he had, much to her disgust. She'd had the satisfaction of pushing him so hard he'd fallen in the snow, at least, and thank heaven Belle had arrived. Yet the disappointment lingered. Not only that, but Belle wouldn't even let her take the skeleton back with her, so it had been a complete waste of her time. It had been a beautiful thing, too, so perfect and delicate she had been afraid to touch it, but even Belle had grimaced and shuddered. Belle, who tried so hard to understand her strange and vexing sister.

Crecy sighed with remorse. If only she could be an ordinary kind of woman, then Belle wouldn't worry for her so. Belle had enough to worry about with her own situation without Crecy making it worse for her. She determined two things as she walked: firstly, she would try much harder not to embarrass her poor sister and give her cause to worry, and secondly, if it killed her, she would find an opportunity to ride out alone and get at least to the borders of Damerel.

If there was some disparity between these two vows, Crecy refused to see it.

She was so lost in thought that at first she didn't notice the towering figure of a man striding towards his waiting carriage. She glanced at the glossy black carriage and its equally sleek horses; four proud, black creatures, tossing their haughty heads with impatience. The heraldic device on the door was in white, gold, blue, and sable, and Crecy's heart leapt.

The coat of arms was unmistakable: two black crows, shot through the neck with an arrow.

Her head snapped around, and for the first time since that day by the river, she met the cool, blue eyes of Viscount DeMorte.

Crecy's breath snagged in her throat and she froze under the power of his gaze, simply staring back at him, unblinking. His hair was every bit as black as she remembered, still unfashionably long and tied back with a black ribbon in the style of the past century. His brows were hard and uncompromising as they drew together, obviously taken aback by her audacity in looking at him so directly. She knew he would tower over her, though he still stood some distance away, and the sheer size of him made something inside her quiver with a thrill of desire. It was hot and molten and threatened to consume her from the inside out.

He stopped, too, returning her frank gaze with one of his own.

He was perhaps not a handsome man in the conventional sense, at least. His features were too harsh; his eyes, though a stunning and deep, deep blue, were cold and forbidding, but, *oh my*, Crecy thought as her mouth grew dry … he was magnificent.

She was vaguely aware of Belle hurrying to her side and clutching at her arm, but Crecy was too lost in the viscount's spell to look away.

"Hello," she said, her voice low and breathless and far, far too intimate.

Those dark brows drew further together, and although his expression was harsh and contemptuous, she saw curiosity in his eyes.

"You have me at a disadvantage, madam," he said, his voice full of disdain.

Belle tugged at her arm, pulling her forcibly towards the castle doors. "Forgive us, sir," she said, whilst giving Crecy a sharp pinch that made her gasp. "We did not mean to disturb you."

Crecy moved away, knowing she could not acknowledge who she was to him, not in front of Belle, but she turned her head nonetheless, wanting to drink in the sight of him for as long as she could. He returned her gaze, watching her with an intensity in his dark eyes that made her heart beat hard and fast, crashing against her ribcage like a butterfly at a windowpane.

He turned as they entered the castle, getting into his carriage and driving away, but Crecy had seen him. She had looked into his eyes and seen everything she had dreamed of and longed for. Passion and danger and a soul so dark and wounded it would take everything she had to mend him, and still she might fail. He was everything she should fear and run from, and yet all she felt was exhilaration. Viscount DeMorte was the only man who had ever provoked such heady feelings within her, and she would not let them rest unheard.

***

By the time Gabriel reached Damerel House, the snow was falling again. He shrugged off his coat, handing it to his butler, Piper, as he brushed icy, white flakes from his black hair. Striding through the darkening hall of the great house, he made his way into the sanctuary of his study. No one disturbed him here, ever. Not if they knew what was good for them. Here, a fire was burning, the lamps lit, and he moved to the decanter and poured a small measure, smiling to himself. For one to whom the world believed lost in dissipation and vice, he drank very little. The idea of losing himself in drink was abhorrent to him, not least because of the lack of control. For Gabriel controlled everything with an iron will, and if his grasp slipped, he feared what remained of his sanity might crumble.

No, as tempting as it might be to be able to lose himself in a bottle, what followed as his control slipped and the ghosts forced past the walls he built ... it was not worth the risk. As it was, he was finding it harder to keep them at bay, to keep *him* at bay.

He shuddered, a clammy feeling prickling over his skin. *Pull yourself together*, he commanded, *you're not some snot-nosed child, afraid of the dark*. Taking a deep breath, he sat behind his desk, sipping at his drink, savouring the quality and the warmth of the fine liquor, and resisted the urge to pour another.

Fighting the desire for a drink, he reached instead for the paperweight that held some recent documents in place. It was smooth with wear, a natural stone, but strangely shaped, like a wolf howling, head raised to the moon. He rubbed his thumb over the length of the stone throat, a familiar and somewhat soothing gesture as his brows drew together. His visit to Edward had been amusing, if nothing else. Though he doubted his father would see it that way. He should have ended this long since, but he'd been too weak to strike the final blow that would have won him everything he'd been tasked with gaining. Accusing him of being pitiful and useless, an embarrassment to their ancient name, his father's voice echoed in his ears, though the man was long dead.

No different than in life, at least.

For a short time, Gabriel had been Marquess of Winterbourne, Earl of Clarendon, and a half dozen lesser titles, too ... just as his father had commanded him to be. For a brief and blissful period, the voices had begun to die down, the only one remaining pushing him to take the final step and marry Edward's sister.

To complete the destruction of his father's hated brother's line.

He had hesitated at that. Beautiful she may, be but she held no appeal to him; his skin crawled at the idea of her innocence. Bedding a virgin was not something he craved, taking a wife, less so, especially one that looked upon him as if he were a monster. Not that he believed her wrong, nor cared that she thought it. It was true and he accepted it, relished it in some ways. However, the desire to let the line end with him was a tangible one. The idea gave his soul some measure of peace, but only briefly.

His breath caught as skeletal fingers grasped his wrists. Gabriel closed his eyes as the memory came back to him, as cold and unforgiving as his father screaming in his face, giving him his instructions, to be followed to the letter or his sire swore he would haunt him until he found his own grave. He jolted, as he always did, as the remembered sound of the gunshot exploded in his mind, the bullet tearing through his father's brain and covering his only son in gore as the man took his own life before his eyes.

The empty glass slipped from Gabriel's fingers, clattering onto the desk as his breathing became harsh and uneven. *Get a grip, you bloody fool*, he cursed, clutching at the edges of the desk. *Think of something else*, he ordered, sending his erratic thoughts into free fall until they snagged upon the young woman outside the castle.

He'd never seen anything like her before, he thought, as his breathing began to steady. There had been something in her eyes that had seemed to call out to him, a look of such wanting he had been startled into silence. He'd been desired before; there were those who relished his brand of cruelty, after all, and the danger he brought to their dull lives. But never before had he received a look of such wanton desire from one who was so obviously an innocent. What the devil was the girl playing at? Her companion had been aware of the danger she courted, hurrying her from him as fast as she was able. The remembered terror in the older woman's eyes made him chuckle.

She, at least, had the right of it.

Chapter 2

"Wherein a wedding is planned ... quickly."

Crecy hid in the shadows of the ballroom. She'd only just managed to evade Lord Lancaster, whose tumble into the snow had apparently not cooled his enthusiasm. Worse still was a gloriously handsome man, a Baron Marchmain, by all accounts, otherwise known as August Bright.

With hair the colour of ripe corn and quite lovely green eyes, he was really something to behold. But Crecy did not want to behold him, and, try as she might, could not seem to get that point across, and she *had* tried. Belle had warned her he was a notorious rake and most certainly wasn't interested in marriage. As Crecy certainly wasn't interested in him, she saw little point in wasting the evening flirting with him, which she was no good at, in any case. So here she was, cowering behind a potted palm.

It was really rather lowering.

Biting her lip, as she knew Belle would be furious with her, she wondered if perhaps she might escape and find sanctuary in Lord Winterbourne's library. If Belle discovered she had gone off alone again, she'd be in hot water, but surely it was better than playing hide-and-go-seek with blasted Lord Marchmain. Crecy sighed and dared a glance from between the fronds of the palm to discover some kind of commotion at the far end of the ballroom. With a frown, she wondered what was going on and experienced a shiver of unease.

Belle had been acting very strangely tonight. Crecy had put it down to the fact it was their last night here and likely their only chance to snag a suitable husband. So here she was cowering in a corner whilst Belle ... Crecy had the uncomfortable sensation of growing suddenly very hot, and just as quickly doused with cold water.

Oh, Belle!

By the time she had forced her way through the excited crowd and found a familiar face, fear was clawing at her heart with sharp claws. Please don't let Belle have sacrificed her own happiness for her sake. Crecy couldn't bear the idea, but she knew Belle well enough to know she would do just that. With her chest so tight she could hardly speak, she saw the familiar figure of Lady Seymour Russell. The old woman was something of a tyrant and a towering figure among the *ton* despite only having married a mere Baron. She had a sharp tongue and a sharper wit, and had, for reasons neither of them could fathom, taken Belle and Crecy under her wing.

"Lady Russell," she cried out, by now breathless and anxious. "Have you seen Belle?"

The great lady smirked, an expression that did not ease Crecy's anxiety one bit.

"I should say so," she said, chuckling a little and leaning in to whisper in her ear. "Your sister is quite something, young lady." Crecy looked up at her, meeting the cool grey eyes with confusion. "Yes, she played that very well, indeed, and I think they'll deal admirably together."

"What?" Crecy shrieked in alarm. *"Who?"* Don't tell me she's accepted Lord Nibley?"

"Nibley?" Lady Russell repeated frowning for a moment. "Oh," she said, her face clearing as she nodded and Crecy felt like screaming at her. "You mean that academic fellow, always droning on about rocks?"

Crecy agreed that had been who she meant, growing ever more frantic and feeling as though she might cry. Where was Belle?

"No, not him," Lady Russell replied, shaking her head. "She's going to marry Winterbourne."

Crecy gaped at her, incredulous.

"Close your mouth, gel," Lady Russell scolded, looking so severe Crecy complied immediately. "Young ladies don't gawp."

"Winterbourne?" Crecy repeated, her voice faint. "The marquess?"

Gabriel DeMorte's despised cousin.

Lady Russell nodded, grinning at her with great satisfaction. "A fine match on both sides, if you ask me," she said. "Come along, find me some champagne, will you, I mean to celebrate."

***

Crecy dithered by Belle's bed. Her sister looked rather like she'd suffered a severe shock, only Crecy couldn't tell if it was a happy one or if the poor girl was terrified. She'd clearly slept little; hardly surprising after the furore that had ensued last night, and that Belle had instigated it ... well, Crecy admitted to being a little shocked. Her straight-laced sister setting out to snare a husband ... who would have thought it?

She moved forward, removing the breakfast tray Belle was clearly far too distracted to touch, and clambered onto the bed, the heavy skirts of her riding habit impeding her movements.

She simply couldn't tell what Belle was feeling, and her mumbled answers didn't help. Was she simply shocked?

"You do like him, don't you, Belle?" Crecy demanded, feeling a little desperate.

Belle looked up at her, as though she'd forgotten she was there at all.

"Oh. Er ... I ... I'm sure we'll deal famously together," she said after a moment, sounding quite certain of herself and much more Belle-like.

Crecy bit her lip, wanting to be reassured but still feeling uneasy. "But I thought you meant to have Lord Nibley?"

Belle nodded, flushing a rather violent shade of scarlet. "I did," she admitted.

"Then what …

Belle held out her hand, a look of desperation in her eyes. "Do you mind if we discuss this later? I have the most dreadful headache."

Crecy agreed with alacrity, though she did make sure to ask if Belle needed anything before she left. Though she knew she was selfish in the extreme, if Belle didn't need her, she had a whole day free.

And she meant to put it to good use.

***

It was a simple thing to ditch the groom assigned to chaperone her. Though she had experienced a qualm, and rather wondered if perhaps she'd lost her nerve for riding, as it had been some years since she'd last had the opportunity. But Crecy had always been a fearless rider, and, to her delight, nothing had changed. Riding had been one of her greatest pleasures, and she had never despised her own wretched excuse for a father more than when he'd sold her beloved horse to pay his gambling debts. It was at that point that Crecy had known those good men, nice men like her father, those charming men who smiled in your face and said all the right things … they were not to be trusted.

Far better a man you knew was set on ruining you and was honest about it, you could deal with that head on. You knew where you stood and what you had to lose. Far worse a man who crawled into your heart with pretty little lies and sweet deceits and whose promises were worth nothing but dust.

The morning and the countryside stretched out before her, full of promise and expectation. Longwold was situated high on the

Cotswold escarpment, and a vista of rolling hills and thick woodland spread out, all sparkling white under a crisp blue sky. She could see the Mendips, those limestone hills to the south of Bath, and remembered Lord Nibley at dinner one night. He'd grown *almost* animated whilst speaking of the carboniferous limestone that was found in abundance here. She had been briefly interested when he'd touched on the variety of Neolithic, Iron Age, and Bronze Age barrows to be found in the area, but sadly, these intriguing sites did not hold the appeal for him that a lifeless rock clearly did.

Leaning forward, she urged the horse on, revelling in the cold wind on her face, so sharp it made her eyes water. Her hair whipped about in the breeze, the jaunty green feather in her hat dancing madly as they flew across the thin covering of snow. She would need to make haste if she was to get to Damerel House and return before anyone noticed her gone.

***

Gabriel looked up as Piper came into the room, bearing a small silver tray with a letter upon it. The arrival of the post was the only exception to the *do not disturb* rule that was adhered to the moment his study door closed - unless it was a dire emergency.

"This arrived for you, my lord," he said as Gabriel reached for the letter. "It's early, isn't it? I hope there is nothing amiss with the young lady?"

Gabriel sent him a look that strongly urged the man to mind his own damn business and broke the seal with a frown. Waiting until his obviously concerned butler had closed the door, he opened the folded sheet with curiosity. Piper was correct, of course, she wrote on the first of every month, usually, with the exception of his birthday.

My dear friend,

 I am to be your neighbour!

Gabriel dropped the letter like it had scorched him, staring at the words as vexation burst to life. Blast the girl! What did she mean by threatening to seek him out? Was she utterly lost to propriety? Except she wasn't a girl any longer, was she? He had been aware for some months of a subtle change in the tenor of those letters. She must be twenty by now, twenty-one, even? He glared at the extravagant, looping writing, for once not crammed in to fill and cross every inch of space on the sheet. It had been written in haste, which meant ...

He got to his feet, taking a hasty step away from the letter as if it had the power to contaminate him somehow, to shatter his peace of mind ... and then he made the connection.

By God, the blonde outside Longwold, the way she had stared at him - as if she had a right to ...

That was Lucretia Holbrook?

Gabriel swallowed, a feeling of unease creeping over his skin. No, no, no. The last thing he needed was some pretty fool with ridiculous romantic notions about him trying to trap him into marriage. Though at this point, he had to admit the young woman seemed perfectly aware of all of his vices; she had never had the slightest hesitation in questioning him about them, after all. Sometimes the things she wrote, and asked, shocked him deeply. She clearly didn't have an ounce of shame, and even less good sense. Though his mouth quirked a little, involuntarily, as he remembered how some of those imprudent questions had made him smile. Nonetheless, unease prickled over his skin.

"Piper!" he yelled, refolding the letter with care and putting it in a large wooden box to peruse again later, when the coast was clear. For now, he needed to get away until the wretched woman had gone.

The butler appeared at his door, his face full of curiosity. Well, the fellow could keep his blasted nose out of Gabriel's affairs.

"There has been some kind of house party at Longwold. Do you know when the guests leave?" he asked, ignoring the man's disappointment at being kept out of the secret and refusing to let him know why Miss Holbrook had written him an extra letter.

"Yes, my lord, I believe they will be leaving today."

"Today?" Gabriel repeated, breathing a sigh of relief. So he only need make himself scarce for a few hours and he'd be in the clear. "Have Typhon saddled for me, I'm going out."

The butler nodded and retreated, leaving Gabriel to stare into the fire, trying hard to ignore an irrational surge of anger towards Miss Holbrook. He didn't want her here, didn't want to put a face to the strange and oddly intimate letters that arrived without fail each month. It was unsettling and ... out of the ordinary, and that was unacceptable. His life followed strict timetables, rules and rituals that kept the days ticking past and him on an even keel. Too many deviations from the norm, and he started to feel adrift and anxious and ... out of control, and that ... that made him angry.

He glowered at the flames, the rising heat fierce against his face. Well, she'd be gone soon, perhaps she'd already left, and then he could relax and concentrate on what next to do about Edward Greyston. For his father would not let him live in peace until he'd kept his promise and destroyed him.

**

Crecy rode hard, the powerful beast beneath her sweating and blowing clouds as she pulled up, her heart pounding with exhilaration and trepidation as a huge house came into view. It was built of squared and dressed limestone, like so many of the region, and dominated the landscape. From her position on the ridge and looking down, it had an H-shaped main body, with a projecting rounded porch and portico in the centre supported by paired Doric columns. It spoke of power and wealth, but Crecy cared not for any of that, all that mattered was it belonged to him. This was the home of Gabriel Greyston, the Viscount DeMorte, this was where he had been born and grown into a man. This place had shaped him, for good and for ill, and she wanted desperately to uncover its secrets. All of them.

Ignoring the prickle of unease at the back of her neck that told her that her presence was likely unwelcome, she urged the horse on again, moving at a steady trot now as she drank in the scene below her, committing it to memory.

A flicker of movement to her right caught her attention and she turned from the house and heard her own gasp as she saw a man on a powerful horse riding further along the ridge, heading in the opposite direction. Just before he turned and disappeared, the horse was checked, the man's head coming up and staring at her.

It was him! And he'd seen her.

Chapter 3

"Wherein our heroine is foolhardy."

Crecy held her breath, wondering what came next. Surely he had received her letter by now? Surely he must have guessed it was her who had been so captivated by him and stared in such a shocking manner? If he turned away now, all her hopes would shatter.

The moment seemed to stretch out, the distance between them growing larger as her heart beat in her chest, marking the moments as he made his decision. As the horse was urged into motion again, this time towards her, Crecy let go of a breath she didn't realise she'd been holding, though it didn't help her much. The freezing air seemed suddenly too thin, and no matter how she gulped it down, her chest heaving, she felt dizzy and unsettled. Some innate sense of self-preservation urged her to turn and flee, but she ignored it, drinking in the sight of him as he came nearer.

He drew up beside her, those dark blue eyes cold and angry, as she'd known they would be.

"Good morning, my Lord DeMorte," she said, relieved she didn't sound quite as breathless as she felt.

"What the devil are you doing here?" he demanded, his voice harsh as he glared at her, his displeasure at seeing her here only too evident. "This is private property, as I'm sure you are well aware."

"Of course I am aware," she said, grinning at him and feeling a rush of delight at being in his presence and speaking with him even though he was obviously furious. "I told you I was going to trespass, after all. Didn't you believe me?"

He paused at that, frowning as if he didn't quite know what to say to her next and was wondering why she wasn't terrified of him.

She wondered the same herself in the light of his rage, but discovered she was not the least bit afraid, only rather nervous. That strange, over-excited, nervousness that always accompanied thoughts of him.

"Are you going to shoot me?" she asked, her tone innocent as she quirked one eyebrow, knowing it would vex him and doing it anyway.

"No," he replied, the word curt and irritated as he gathered his horse's reins in large, powerful hands. "I'm going to escort you from my land and strongly encourage you not to return again."

"And if I do?" she asked with a sweet smile.

He glowered at her and she felt the strangest urge to laugh at the growing fury and the heated indignation in his eyes. *"Then* I'll shoot you," he muttered, gesturing for her to turn her horse.

Crecy sighed and looked down at the great house with regret. "I will see it one day, you know."

"Over my dead body," he snapped, his expression close to a snarl.

He trotted away and Crecy hurried to keep up with him.

"Oh, no," she replied with quiet calm as she drew alongside, perfectly serious. "That's no good at all. How will I discover all of those hidden staircases and dark secrets if the master is not there to point them out to me?"

He turned his head and Crecy could only stare at him, memorising every detail: the thick, black lock of hair that had fallen forward, the forbidding, hooded eyes, that cruel mouth that would change his expression completely if only she could induce it to smile.

"You really are insane, aren't you?" he growled, looking perplexed and really rather disturbed. He pushed the lock of hair from his forehead with one hand, a gesture she suspected he repeated often.

She shrugged at his question, giving him a frank, if slightly rueful, look.

"I don't know," she admitted, holding his gaze when he didn't turn away from her. "I know that ... that I'm ... *different* ... Odd, I suppose."

She watched him, wondering what he would say to that as he frowned, those dark brows heavy over his eyes. "You don't hear me disagreeing, do you?"

She laughed and shook her head, blonde curls dancing around her face. "No, I didn't expect you to, I promise."

He reached out and grasped her horse's bridle, pulling it to a sudden stop and staring at her, his eyes glittering and intense. "If anyone discovers you've been here, alone, you're ruined. Do you understand that?" he demanded, his cold eyes searching hers, clearly expecting her to look shocked and anxious.

"Of course," she replied, her expression placid. "I might be odd, but I'm not a fool."

For a moment, he gaped at her, obviously strongly disbelieving that statement.

"Don't you care?" he raged, letting go of the reins in disgust. "You'd never marry if you were to be seen in my company."

"I don't want to marry." Crecy saw utter disbelief this time, and he gave a snort, urging his horse on again.

"You damned liar," he threw at her over his shoulder.

"No, I'm not," she said, quite unruffled by the accusation as she moved her mount faster to keep up. "At least, I would marry you if you asked, *I think* ..." His horse was pulled to a sudden halt and Crecy followed suit. She kept her eyes downcast for a moment, aware of the weight of his gaze on, her but not quite brave enough to face it yet. Taking a breath, she ploughed on. "But I am well aware you never would, so there is no need to stare at me so. It's not like I'm hoping or angling for a proposal." She did look up then, and the expression on his face was one of such revulsion she almost laughed. "Well, you did ask, so I'm telling you," she replied, sounding a little indignant. "But frankly, well, there isn't another man in the world who would put up with me."

He blinked, silent and quite still, and she wondered what he was thinking. So many thoughts seemed to flicker behind those dark eyes, it was impossible to tell. But then they settled back to annoyance, that one was clear at least. "What the devil makes you think *I* would?" he demanded in outrage, settling his now jittery horse with light, masterly hands, despite his anger.

"Oh, nothing," she said with perfect sincerity. "But the thing is I think I *could* make you comfortable, if you would let me. You could be contented, even. I think we could deal famously together, actually."

He rode off without another word and she cantered after him, sparing a moment to admire the breadth of his shoulders, the powerful thighs, and the way he moved in perfect symmetry with the huge horse whose heavy hooves thundered beneath him.

They slowed as the terrain became rougher, conscious of their mounts sliding on the frozen ground.

"Shouldn't you have left by now?" he demanded after ten minutes of frigid silence. "All the other guests have, surely." He turned to look back at her, and she thought he looked wary, probably afraid she'd try and seduce him next, somehow trap him into marriage despite her assurances. The idea made her smile.

As if she'd have the slightest idea how to.

"We aren't leaving," she said with a smug smile, seeing the horror grow in his eyes with amusement.

"Why the bloody hell not?"

She gave a startled laugh at his exasperation which made him look crosser than ever. "Because, Belle ..." she began, and then stopped abruptly as she realised she didn't want him to know Belle was marrying his cousin. Not just yet. He'd find out soon enough, of course. "Belle has become good friends with Mrs Violette Russell, and she has invited us to stay for Christmas, too." It wasn't a lie, after all. "So I shall be able to deliver your Christmas present in person this year," she added with a merry smile before cantering off past him.

A rude word scorched her ears, something that ought never be uttered in the presence of a lady, and certainly not with such heat, but it only made her laugh all the harder. She pushed on into a gallop as the ground evened out, and then turned back, grinning madly, to see him spring his own horse, gaining on her with ease.

Crecy squealed, her heart hammering with excitement as they flew across the fields. The sun was growing warm now, hot against her back even as the cold air prickled at her skin and made her cheeks glow. She had never felt more exhilarated, more alive and vital, and despite the fact he likely wanted to wring her blasted neck, she felt happier than she'd ever known.

**

Gabriel watched her bolt across the fields, everything about her alive and vibrant, the sun on her hair glinting gold like a barley field. Yet all he could feel was fury. Damn her! Why did she have to come and provoke him so? He harboured concerns that perhaps she really was unstable. Good God, that was the last thing he needed. He was quite capable of courting scandal without any help from some strange young woman who ought to be locked up for her own safety. His thoughts strayed to the letters she'd written him, to the things he knew to be true about her. Things she had no right to confide to a complete stranger, certainly not an unmarried man. They had been sane enough, though, if a little ... *eccentric*, to say the least - certainly for a young woman.

He glanced at his watch, his temper flaring as he saw it was after midday. He'd never get back to the house before one o'clock now, which meant he'd be late for lunch. He ground his teeth as his shoulders tensed, his skin growing clammy at the idea. He needed to be back by one. He would not let this ... this *hoyden* ruin his entire schedule.

Urging his horse on, he galloped after her, Typhon eating up the distance between them with ease, though what he meant to do when he caught up with her he could not decide. He had never raised a hand in anger to a woman and never would. He'd hated his father for that very reason even before ...

Damn her, she was stirring everything up.

He forced the ugly scenes from his mind with no clear idea of what to do next. He just had to get her off his land and frighten her enough she would not dare return. Sadly, he got the feeling the chit didn't scare easily.

They were neck and neck now, the silly creature riding too fast, doing her utmost to outpace him. He turned and looked at her and she crowed with laughter, the delight and sheer joy in her voice a sound so utterly foreign to him he could not help but stare at her. But from out of the hedgerows, there was an explosion of birds as a dozen or more pheasants took flight, and her horse shied, rearing and dancing. To his astonishment, she held on, trying to calm the beast who refused to settle and bucked twice, finally unseating her.

Gabriel cursed; dammit, if the child had killed herself on his land ...

He threw himself down from his horse, running to her side to find her sprawled on her back in the snow, laughing hysterically.

"Oh, my," she said as her eyes glittered with mirth. "I can't remember the last time I had such fun! Wasn't it wonderful?"

Gabriel stared at her.

"No," he said, his tone short. "You're a blasted nuisance and deserve to have broken your silly neck."

She stuck her tongue out at him. "Pooh," she said with a dignified little sniff. "You're just cross because I ride as well as you do."

"I am not …" Gabriel retorted, only to realise he sounded like a five-year-old, and closed his mouth with a snap.

She grinned at him, which only increased his desire to throw her over his knees and give her a sound spanking. Except that image didn't help matters at all, and he forced it into a dark corner of his mind. There were plenty to choose from.

"Are you going to stand there all day staring at me then, or give me a hand up?" she demanded, folding her arms and raising one imperious eyebrow at him.

Gabriel swallowed a curse, though he imagined the look on his face was illustration enough as he reached down and grasped her arm, hauling her to her feet.

In retrospect, he'd been a little overzealous for a woman of her size, and she squealed, her boots sliding on the snow as her feet went from under her.

"Damnation," he muttered as he was forced to pull her closer, his hands at her waist to steady her. She stumbled into him, her hands grasping at his lapels to keep herself upright. The appalling creature looked up at him then, a shocking, intimate look from under thick, dark blond lashes, revealing the most startling pair of eyes he'd ever seen. They were a strange, violet grey, like a stormy summer sky.

Gabriel thrust her away, taking another step back, lest she should have any thoughts he was in any way interested in her. Turning, he saw her horse had finally calmed itself and was cropping the icy tufts of grass in a desultory fashion, a good three acres away. Muttering and cursing about devious females, he strode off after it.

***

Crecy watched the viscount as he walked to retrieve her horse. Her breath was still coming fast, partly from the race they'd just had, partly from finding herself at such close quarters with the man she'd been dreaming of for so long.

He was everything she had expected him to be. Suspicious and brittle and with such walls built around him he could not even conduct a simple conversation with her without growing angry. Although, to be fair, she *had* trespassed on his land and gone out of her way to tease him. Somehow, she doubted he was any different in any other circumstance, though. He was well known for being rude, abrupt, and downright insulting, and only got away with it because everyone was too scared to challenge him.

He might call them out after all, and his reputation as a crack-shot was legend.

But he couldn't call her out, and she wasn't the least bit frightened of him. Though she didn't know why, really. Except he had in no way made her feel physically vulnerable, quite the reverse, in fact.

She suspected he was afraid of her.

The idea gained merit as she watched him traipse about the field. She smiled, amused, as he looked increasingly like a big black storm cloud with his great coat swirling about him as he tried to get close to her reluctant horse. The poor dear, he wasn't having a very good day.

By the time he'd finally caught hold of her horse, he had a face like thunder, and she suspected she'd pushed him as far as she dare for one day.

"Thank you," she said, sounding rather contrite as he walked back to her. "I'm sorry for being such a nuisance."

"No, you aren't," he growled, and she could not help the burst of laughter that escaped her. She covered her mouth with her hand and tried to keep it in as she shook her head.

"No," she admitted. "I'm not. Not the least bit sorry." He glowered at her and she bit her lip. "I've had a lovely time."

"You ought to be locked up," he muttered, bending down and linking his hands together to give her a foot up. "For the safety of the general public," he added, his tone bitter.

With his help, Crecy vaulted neatly into place and arranged her skirts, before gathering up the reins.

"Oh, but I am sorry I've vexed you so," she said, her tone softer now. "But you need not come all the way to the border. I'll go, I promise. I expect you'll be wanting to get back now."

He frowned at her, looking rather more puzzled than angry all at once.

"You'll go?" he repeated, the suspicion in his voice quite evident.

Crecy nodded. "I will, I promise."

He let out a sigh that seemed to be really quite heartfelt and nodded, turning away from her.

"Lord DeMorte?"

He froze, his heavy shoulders sagging as if he'd known it was too good to be true. The unhappy figure turned to glare at her.

"What?" he barked, his heavy brows drawn over those blue eyes like thunder clouds in a summer sky.

"I'll see you tomorrow afternoon," she said, grinning at him before springing her horse and galloping away, before he could utter the curse that was so obviously on the tip of his tongue.

Chapter 4

"Wherein evasive action is required."

It was twenty past one by the time he returned to the house. The staff tiptoed around him, their voices barely a whisper as they were well aware how such changes to his plans affected his temper.

Gabriel sat down at the table, taking a moment to straighten the fork and tilt the napkin a little to the right. Out of the corner of his eye, he saw one of the serving staff send a panicked look in the butler's direction, but Piper merely took a step forward.

"Shall we serve now, my lord?"

Gabriel gave a curt nod, too angry to actually speak.

The food was placed in front of him and the staff retreated, leaving him alone. He reached for his napkin, unfolding it with care and laying it down with precision before he picked up his knife and fork. The plate was exactly the same every day. A cold collation of meat; beef, ham, and roast chicken. A platter of cheese sat at his left side, a pannier of bread on the right, a decanter of claret beside his glass.

He ate first the beef, then the ham, then the chicken, the same order every day, before reaching for the cheese and cutting one - *precise* - triangle from each before reaching for three slices of bread. One glass of wine was poured, exactly to the wing-tip of the little engraved bird that flew an inch below the rim.

The familiar ritual calmed him a little, and he tried to keep his eyes from the clock. He usually left the house at two o'clock, and he would need to hurry now to regain the lost time. Gabriel chewed, his face settled into a scowl. Damn the wretch for messing up his day, not to mention for having the audacity to tell him she'd return again tomorrow. Well, he'd just see about that.

Unbidden, the image her of sprawled on her back in the snow and laughing her silly head off flitted into his mind. His mouth twitched, just a little, but he suppressed his amusement with a reminder of his anger at her disturbing him and ruining his day. That she would be at his gates at every opportunity between now and Christmas was appalling enough to make him grind his teeth.

The girl was a danger to herself and a blasted nuisance. He could only pray his cousin had the good sense to send her packing as soon as possible.

***

The wedding between Belinda Holbrook and Lord Edward Greyston, Marquess of Winterbourne, was naturally a brief affair, but Crecy was disturbed by the stilted atmosphere. The groom looked ill and Belle resigned to her fate. Her sister seemed intent on avoiding her, though, and so there was little opportunity to reassure herself all was well. But Crecy felt Edward Greyston, her new brother-in-law, was a good man underneath that dour exterior. He had proved himself a hero in the war, he was clearly devoted and very protective of his young sister, and despite glowering at everyone and being generally antisocial, Crecy could detect no sign he would be a cruel husband. That he'd been scarred by the war was obvious, but if anyone could heal such scars, Belle could. She was patient and loving, and braver than she realised herself, in Crecy's opinion. So perhaps there were some hurdles to jump, but her instincts told her Edward and Belle would make a success of their rather impromptu nuptials.

Her own ambitions, therefore, were rather more to the forefront of her mind.

It was easier than she might have imagined to get away again that afternoon, as the rather odd atmosphere drove everyone to make themselves scarce. Her time was short, though, as she would need to be home for dinner, and she didn't want Belle fretting herself to death as she had the day before when Crecy had arrived home so late after getting herself hopelessly lost. At least she'd had a valid excuse for her disappearance, which didn't involve trespassing and aggravating Winterbourne's neighbour.

It was colder today, the sun less sure of itself and only giving tantalisingly brief glimpses between the thick clouds rolling in off the hills. The taste of snow was in the air as the temperature dropped, and Crecy rode hard, wanting to keep the chill from her bones as the freezing air bit at fingers and toes.

It occurred to her she wouldn't see him today. That he would take care to be out for the afternoon as she had forewarned him of her visit. Though she was much later than she'd intended to be, and it was almost four o'clock before she reached Damerel, and the countryside was already sinking into gloom. A shiver of apprehension rolled over her, perhaps she should not have come? Not that she was worried about seeing Lord DeMorte, far from it, but being lost again and in this weather …

But then she caught sight of his carriage and those four glossy black horses, rolling their elegant path back to Damerel, and she pushed her mount on, galloping flat out until she caught up with them. Riding beside the carriage for a moment, she glimpsed inside just long enough to see DeMorte's look of outrage, before riding off ahead to stand, awaiting his arrival on the doorstep of his home.

A rather elderly butler came out to greet her, his rheumy eyes alight with curiosity.

"I'm afraid his lordship is not here at this moment …" he began with a warm if rather anxious smile.

"That's all right, he's coming now," she said, sounding a little breathless as she slid from her mount. "And it's Miss Holbrook," she said, wondering if she had imagined the delight in his eyes at the sound of her name.

"Indeed, miss," he said, a flicker of mischief sliding into his expression. "Well, if Lord DeMorte is expecting you, won't you step inside for a moment?"

A look of understanding passed between them. It was quite obvious DeMorte neither wanted nor expected her after all, and both of them knew they would likely pay for this small act of rebellion on the butler's part, but neither of them gave a hoot.

Crecy beamed at him. "I am rather cold, *Mister...?*"

"Piper, Miss Holbrook," he said, leading her in through the grand front doors, "Just call me Piper."

Crecy had hardly caught her breath and even to begin to take in the magnificent entrance hall before the sound of wheels on gravel could be heard and Gabriel Greyston stalked in, eyes flashing with anger.

"What the hell do you think you're playing at?" he yelled, sounding so furious that even Crecy took an involuntary step backwards. Nonetheless, she put up her chin.

"I told you I was coming," she retorted, feeling that familiar sense of exhilaration that seemed quite normal in his presence prickle over her skin.

"And I told you to stay away, blast you!" He walked closer to her, towering over her, his blue eyes bluer than ever as they glittered with anger.

If he hoped to frighten her, however, he had misjudged, for the nearer he got, the harder Crecy found it to suppress the desire to reach out and touch him. She wanted to put her arms around him and rest her head on his chest; the urge to do so was so overwhelming that she blushed a little.

DeMorte's eyes darkened and he glanced up, a slight nod of his head to Piper indicating he should leave, *now*. The old fellow hesitated for just a moment, before making himself scarce. DeMorte watched him go, before turning his attention back to her.

Crecy's heart skittered in her chest, her stomach taut, and yet such longing beneath her skin she wondered if he could tell how much she wanted him.

"Do you want me to ruin you?" he asked. His voice was low and dangerous, his hooded eyes angry. He reached out and she gasped as his hand slid around her neck, not tightly, but there was certainly an unspoken threat behind his actions. His thumb tilted her head back, forcing her to look up into his eyes. "Is that it? Is that what you desire from me?"

Crecy was breathing so hard that for a moment she couldn't find the words, but then she met his gaze, suddenly certain that there was confusion behind his eyes and that, in truth, it was he who was more afraid. He was trying to frighten her away, but there was no violence in the hand that grasped her neck; in fact, his touch was gentle and she felt sure he would release her if she were to seem afraid of him. It was the fact that she wasn't that made him act so. She wondered if she *ought* to be more horrified by his words, if the fierce heat that uncoiled in her belly at the idea of allowing it to happen made her a vile and unnatural creature.

"I want to be your friend," she said, her voice soft and sincere.

He snorted, the sneer across his cruel lips ridiculing that idea. "I do not have *friends*," he said as though the idea was laughable, as though he'd descended beyond such ordinary human contact.

"I know," she said, her voice shaking a little now, but she refused to look away. "That's why you need me so badly."

He glared at her, and this close, she could see there were tiny flecks of gold in the blue, that his eyelashes were thick and as long as any girl's, and then her eyes dropped to his mouth. She wondered what he would do, just how angry he would be … if she tried to kiss him.

His hand fell from her neck and he took an abrupt step away, putting distance between them and turning his back on her.

"I'll have my carriage take you back to Longwold. If you come back here again, I'll have you prosecuted for trespass, and don't think I won't do it just because you can twist any other fool around your finger with those pretty eyes of yours, Miss Holbrook, because you'll soon discover your mistake."

Despite the seriousness of his tone, Crecy felt a smile creep over her mouth, and though she knew it would only serve to aggravate him further, she couldn't seem to stop it.

"What the devil are you smiling at?" he growled, moving backwards as she walked towards him. Crecy paused, her head tilted to one side a little as she considered him and everything she had learned of him so far. "You think it would be amusing to be prosecuted and have your name in the papers?"

Her face fell at the idea, now she really considered it, and she shook her head. "No, indeed," she admitted, thinking of just how distressed Belle would be if such a thing happened, and from the look in his eyes, he really did mean it. She felt suddenly dejected, wondering if the whole affair really was hopeless after all.

"Well?"

Crecy looked up, realising that he was still awaiting an answer. She smiled at him, but suspected it was rather a sadder expression now. "You think I have pretty eyes," she said, her voice quiet as she walked away from him and to the front door.

"Wait," he said, his tone as demanding as ever. She paused and turned back to see him watching her, looking puzzled. "You won't come back, will you?" he asked, sounding as though he was anxious she would still disobey him, though the anger had gone from his voice now.

"Goodbye, Lord DeMorte," she said, dipping a curtsy and going outside to his carriage.

***

The next day, Crecy stayed away, not being brave enough to push her luck that far. Besides, her sister needed her support. Belle's wedding night had appeared to be something of a non-event, her husband preferring to go out and get himself drunk and then freeze to death outside until Belle was able to persuade him back indoors.

Belle, however, seemed to have a new sense of determination about her this morning, and did not appear to need Crecy's demands she not give up. As she spoke, however, Crecy realised she needed to take her own advice.

"Don't be frightened off. If you don't interact with him, even if it's not exactly a positive experience, well, you've already lost," she said, urging herself on as much as Belle.

Belle frowned a little, but seemed to see the sense behind her words, and Crecy decided she must not give up herself. She was certain that DeMorte was a deeply lonely and unhappy man, wounded, somehow, but in a less obvious way than poor Edward. She needed to discover what haunted him so and find a way to exorcise whatever dark past seemed to shroud him with such pain. Certainty gripped her, and though she knew well it was the kind of certainty that would give poor Belle conniptions, she decided she would act upon it, come what may.

"You'll have to seduce him, Belle," she said, wishing she had the slightest idea of how to go about doing such a thing herself.

"Crecy!" her sister exclaimed with obvious horror, and Crecy couldn't help but smirk. Good Lord, if she knew what she was really thinking, she'd likely drop dead with the shock of it.

"Oh, Belle," Crecy replied, mimicking her shocked tone. "Do stop being such a goose. I know what happens between a man and a woman."

"You do?" Belle replied in alarm, looking as though all her fears had come to fruition at once. "How?"

"Oh, never mind that!" Crecy said, impatient, now, and not about to disclose that Aunt Grimble had educated her on a number of points she really ought not to have. "The point is that what does *go on* is powerful. If you can get him into your bed, you've a far greater chance of getting into his heart!" she added, her tone fierce, as much to convince herself of the truth of it as Belle. Belle, after all, was married; it was right and natural. Crecy was not and unlikely to be, and she had no evidence to suggest DeMorte wouldn't simply take what she offered and leave her in ruins.

But some stubborn piece of her heart had decided DeMorte was the only man she wanted, and Crecy was nothing if not single-minded. She would have him or … or live her days as an old maid. Either was preferable to living with a man who would never understand her and would always consider her a freak for her strange fancies and love of the dark and morbid. She felt a strange kind of assurance that this, at least, was something *her* Gabriel would never do.

***

The next morning, and much to Crecy's dismay, they left for Bath. From what Crecy could gather from her blushing sister, last night Belle had indeed seduced her husband and it had been something of triumph. This morning, however, she had discovered herself alone on waking, and was clearly unhappy about it, and rightly so. So Belle was leaving Winterbourne to his own devices to give him time to consider his actions, whilst she indulged in some long overdue shopping. Crecy was pleased to see her being urged on by Edward's sister Violette, who seemed determined to spend as much of her brother's money as possible.

In normal circumstances, Crecy would have been delighted by such a trip. Bath meant book shops and the theatre, two things which she did enjoy indulging in. However, Violette was eyeing up Crecy's wardrobe with as much disapprobation as she had Belle's, and Crecy felt sure she was going to spend the next four days being stuck with pins. It was not a happy thought, though perhaps worthwhile if it helped her catch DeMorte's eye.

Somehow, she thought it would take more than a pretty frock to do that, though. He was a wealthy viscount, after all, and despite his reputation, surely there must have been scores of women who'd tried to snare him? But his name had not once been linked to any eligible lady. In fact, it was well known he never dallied with innocents or even widows, preferring *houses of ill repute* and less reputable ladies for his entertainment.

Crecy glowered out of the window and wondered if she was kidding herself. He hadn't shown the slightest interest in her so far after all. He could have kissed her at least twice to date, after all, and he'd not taken advantage of that fact when any other man would have leapt at the chance. It was really very depressing. What was the use of being as pretty as everyone told her she was if she couldn't even get a man like DeMorte to take advantage of her? He obviously preferred more experienced women to silly little innocents, and she could little blame him for that. But somehow she must make him see there was more to her than met the eye.

Chapter 5

"Wherein fate takes a hand."

Gabriel breathed a sigh of relief as he set his foot down on the cobbles. It was raining in Bath and the streets were sodden and mucky with slush, but at least here he was free from the unnerving presence of Miss Holbrook and her strangely determined pursuit of him.

Why she had decided on him, he simply could not fathom. Surely, a young woman with looks like hers would be inundated with offers? Gabriel had to concede at this point that Miss Holbrook was quite astonishingly lovely. Certainly enough to make any *normal* red-blooded male overlook her lack of fortune. Though then her letters came to mind, and all the peculiar little gifts she'd sent him over the years, and he experienced a qualm of misgiving. That kind of behaviour, the subject matter of her conversations … none of that would be received well by any man of the *ton* that he could bring to mind.

Well, whatever. It was her future husband's problem, and not his, *thank God.*

Then he remembered her astonishing revelation she had no desire to marry - any man but him, that was. A more conceited man might preen a little at that, but the idea crawled beneath Gabriel's skin and prickled at him like ants on the march beneath his flesh. What was going on in the poor child's head that she should desire a man like him over … over *anyone?*

He shook his head, refusing to think about her a moment longer. He had visited the house of Mrs Wilkins and her exotic ladies yesterday, as was his usual routine, but even Mary's company had failed to relieve him of the vaguely unsettled feeling that was making him so on edge. The idea that Miss Holbrook could appear on his doorstep at any moment was unnerving, and though he was determined to prosecute her as he'd threatened, he found no delight in the idea.

So he had left.

Instead, he turned his thoughts to his cousin, in whom he was really rather disappointed. Edward believed him responsible for the attack on his sister's husband, Aubrey Russell, and yet he'd done nothing about it to date. At the least, Gabriel had been expected to be called out, but so far … nothing. That Edward was suffering, that his mind was unbalanced after his experiences in the war, all of that was well known, and Gabriel had hoped it enough to make sure the man would act rashly and come for his blood. But he'd been disappointed.

Not for the first time, the idea of him and Edward facing each other in a dual came to mind. Gabriel was by far the better shot and knew that he would fell his cousin, with no difficulty and fewer regrets. Yet the more tantalising idea, the one that kept him awake at night, was to allow his shot to go wide and to pray Edward was competent enough to kill him outright. It was such a peaceful idea that Gabriel almost longed for it.

Then it would be over.

He might have failed, but at least he would no longer care. Dead men couldn't be haunted after all..

Gabriel stared up at the imposing architecture of Bath Abbey and sighed. Well, now he was here and far from the wiles of a certain irritating young woman, but now what? He didn't have the slightest idea what to do with himself. That being the case, he did what he always did when at a loss and headed to the nearest book shop. He spent more on books than he cared to think about, but they were at least an escape from real life, and one which he need not relinquish control of his senses to enjoy. For that pleasure, he'd pay any price, and it wasn't as if he couldn't afford it.

The eyes of the rather obsequious owner of the book shop lit up at seeing DeMorte come through the door. Gabriel waved the man away like an irritating blue bottle and settled himself to perusing the shelves. He'd secured a room in his usual hotel where the staff were well aware of his peculiarities. His demand for punctuality, his need for absolute order, and for things just as he liked them was accepted as he paid well, and so he was reasonably content that a peaceful evening awaited him. It would be far more pleasant, however, with a good book to keep him company.

It wasn't as if anyone else would.

Gabriel was a little startled by the bitterness of that thought and wondered where it had come from. He didn't have to think too hard as Miss Holbrook's lovely face swam into his thoughts along with her breathless desire to *be his friend.*

Though he didn't doubt the authenticity of her words, Gabriel snorted with disgust at the idea. That might be what she thought she wanted, he muttered inwardly, remembering the desire he'd seen in her eyes. What she was likely to get if she carried on in such a manner was a man to take her in hand and show her what it meant to play with fire.

Except it was *only* him she played with.

The words were vehement, and he was a little startled by the revulsion he felt at the idea she'd act this way with anyone else. He squashed the idea. He knew her, knew she was genuine, if peculiar, and for some reason he could not fathom, she had settled upon him. He found himself strangely soothed by this idea, which was disturbing in itself. Once again, he pushed thoughts of her away from him with irritation, forcing a book back onto the shelves with rather too much vigour and earning himself a tut of reproach from a rather dandyish-looking fellow standing beside him.

Gabriel glowered and the man moved away with haste.

Dammit.

He'd come to Bath to escape the blasted woman and still she plagued him.

Gabriel picked up another book and flicked through the pages, settling on a description of the heroine and her *"fine eyes."* He scowled, remembering another pair of exceedingly fine eyes and trying to remember if they'd really been that strange shade of lilac grey they appeared to be in his mind's eye. Then he remembered the heat he'd seen in them, the way her heartbeat had fluttered beneath his fingertips whilst his hand had rested on her slender neck. He could have kissed her then, he could have plundered her mouth and she would not have resisted.

She would have welcomed him in.

He wondered if she would have made the slightest protest if he had taken her to his bedroom there and then. The idea that she would have accepted his advances with enthusiasm, that she would coil her lovely limbs around him and cry his name out was sudden and forceful, and left him rigid with desire.

He cursed, mortified at being so afflicted in a bloody bookshop, of all places!

What the hell was wrong with him? Virgins had never held the slightest appeal for him. What was the point in dallying with a woman who hadn't the slightest idea of how to please a man, and would likely weep all over him after the deed was done?

No, thank you.

And yet, the idea of teaching Miss Holbrook a thing or two made his mouth grow dry.

"Hello."

Gabriel jolted, horrified as his nemesis seemed to materialise in front of him. *Oh, good God.* He'd lost his mind completely. For surely she could *not* be standing in front of him now, here in Bath, in a bloody bookshop, and with him as hard for her as he'd ever been in his life before.

Please God, just let him be mad. It would be easier to deal with.

God, however – unsurprisingly - was not on his side.

"You can't prosecute me," she said in a hurry, her lovely lilac – yes, lilac - eyes just a little anxious. "I had no idea you'd be here, after all, and it is a public place."

Gabriel groaned and was thankful for the greatcoat he wore as it covered up his discomfort.

"My God, I'm doomed," he muttered, glaring at her and finding his temper flickering to life at the amusement in her eyes.

"Is my company such a dreadful fate to endure, my lord?" she asked with such an innocent lilt to her voice that he snorted.

"Yes."

He turned his back on her and walked away, deciding to look at the philosophy books instead, surely a young woman would not be interested in … He dared to glance up from the book he held to see her standing beside him, her nose buried in *The Phenomenology of the Spirit* by Hegel.

"You cannot be serious," he exclaimed, too incredulous at her choice of title to be provoked by the fact she'd followed him.

She wrinkled her nose in confusion, which he refused to find the least bit endearing and then she looked really a little annoyed.

"I've read it before," she said with cool dignity.

"You have not," he retorted, before good sense told him to keep his blasted mouth shut and move away.

She stared back at him, a challenging gleam in her eyes as she shut the book with a snap and handed it to him.

"The preface reads …" She cleared her throat and took a breath as she began to recite. "*'To help to bring philosophy nearer to the form of science – that goal where it can lay aside the name of love of knowledge and be actual knowledge – that is what I have set before me.'"*

Gabriel stared back at her, refusing to acknowledge that he was impressed.

"Go on, then," she said, waving an airy hand at him and looking appallingly smug. "Look it up."

He narrowed his eyes at her. "You could have just read that line this moment."

"I did not!" she exclaimed, looking as though she wanted to stamp her foot.

He believed her, of course. She was strange and annoying and always bloody *there,* but she was no liar. Gabriel chuckled and was immediately alarmed by the delight in her eyes, by the smile that spread over her sweet mouth like a dawning sun. Feeling quite revolted by his sudden romanticism, Gabriel thrust the book back at her and moved away again.

"Leave me alone, Miss Holbrook," he muttered as he discovered she'd followed him once more and was watching his perusal of the novels with interest.

"No, my lord," she whispered, moving a little closer to him.

Gabriel sighed and determined to ignore her. All he had to do was pick a book, any book, even if he already had the bloody thing, he didn't care. He picked one up at random and flicked to the first page. Miss Holbrook came closer and, to his astonishment, leaned into him, her hand covering his as she made him lower the book so she could see what it was.

"Oh no," she said, her voice low and intimate and rather breathless, as though she knew she was dancing around flames and was daring them to burn her. "Don't read that one. You'll be horribly bored. I was," she said, looking up at him from under her lashes once more. "And … I should hate to think of you sitting all alone tonight, and … bored."

He stared back at her.

Before he had actually thought about it, before the conscious acceptance of the idea had even flitted into his mind and been quite rejected because *it was Miss Holbrook and they were in a public place, for the love of God* ... he'd moved.

The book fell to the floor, quite forgotten as he grasped her by the wrists and forced her up against the bookshelves, his body pressing against hers, hard and unforgiving against her softness.

She gasped, but didn't shriek, didn't look appalled or shocked or horrified. No. The wretch lifted her mouth and stood on tiptoes.

Gabriel refused to kiss her. Refused to play this game she was intent on. He did not toy with innocents. He had no desire for them, he never had. Except Miss Holbrook was by now very well aware that this was a lie, so there was little point in voicing his indignation. She could feel his desire, as there wasn't a breath of space between them and it was hard to miss.

"Do you think of me, at night?" he asked, the words out before he could stop them, wanting to know if she was just a silly child with romantic dreams, or a woman who fantasised about what might truly happen between them if he was to allow it.

"You know I do," she replied, without hesitation or embarrassment, and with no trace of the virginal coyness or timidity that would have had him taking to his heels. She stared up at him, her gaze bold and enquiring. Watching him as if she wondered what he would do next.

Gabriel wondered, too.

"You want me to kiss you," he said, the words a fact, not a question.

She smiled at him and nodded. "Yes, please," she replied, all eager willingness. As though she were famished and he'd offered her tea and cakes.

"I'm not going to," he snarled, angry at her for tormenting him, for unsettling his life and interfering with his plans. He had no time for her, no need for her, no desire …

"That's all right," she said, her voice soft and amused. "I'll kiss you instead."

Before he could utter a retort, or better still move away, she had pressed her mouth to his.

***

Crecy wondered briefly if she'd finally run mad. Belle was somewhere in the shop, and kissing Viscount DeMorte in a public place was surely on the list of things a girl could be committed for?

It ought to be.

But then her mouth met his and she was startled by the softness of his lips. Somehow, she had not expected that. A rush of warmth shivered over her, heat and longing unfurling beneath her skin, and she pressed her mouth against his a fraction harder. She felt DeMorte suck in a breath, and she forced her eyes to open, to look up at him and see to the searing shock in his eyes as she pulled back a little.

He didn't move, nor speak. He looked rather stunned, actually, she thought with a touch of chagrin. Was that a good thing? She wished she could tell.

He moved as suddenly as when he'd grasped her wrists in the first place and dropped his hold on her, moving away, staring at her as though she was some alien creature that he'd never seen before.

"You're insane," he said, his voice rough and husky and sounding really rather unsettled.

"There, you see," she said, keeping her tone soothing though her heart felt like it was going to explode or expire if it kept thudding at its current, erratic pace. "I told you we were a perfect match.

He opened his mouth and she waited for him to speak, but nothing happened. Closing it again with a snap, he turned away, and she knew he would leave.

"Don't go," she said, the pleading in her voice quite clear. "Please." Crecy crouched down to pick up the book that he'd dropped. "You haven't found anything to read yet," she added, the words rushed but said with a smile as she stood again. "At least let me find you something." She turned back to the shelves, knowing that when she turned back, she'd likely find him gone, and listened for the sound of his footsteps moving away, but they didn't come.

She scanned the shelves, disregarding title after title until she settled upon one of which she thought he might approve. She smiled as she found *Tom Jones* by Henry Fielding, turning and offering it to him with smug grin.

He was still standing there, watching her with a look of deep suspicion in his eyes, like he was cornered by a savage animal that might turn on him and bite at any minute.

"Have you read this yet?" she asked, as his eyes moved reluctantly from her face to the book. He took it from her, still keeping her at arm's length as he reached for the book and studied the title.

He snorted, incredulous. "A long time ago, yes, but don't tell me that you have?" he demanded, those indigo blue eyes flickering with curiosity now.

Crecy flushed a little but held his gaze and nodded. She was well aware that the bawdy tale was shocking, and certainly not considered a suitable text for young ladies.

"Yes, I have," she said, raising her chin a little, daring him to chastise her for it. If he did, she would be sorely disappointed in him. "And ..." She swallowed, knowing if anything would shock him, this would, as the titles made Tom Jones look like a children's bedtime story. "I've read Fanny Hill too, and ... and de Sade."

His eyes did widen at that, and she could see that he was shocked indeed, but then curiosity seemed to override that immediate response.

"Which did you read by de Sade?" he asked, frowning at her now.

Crecy cleared her throat, aware that her cheeks were burning. "*Philosophy in the Boudoir*," she said, aware that she sounded defiant.

He gave a short, astonished bark of laughter. "Good God," he whispered. "And still you pursue a man like me? Did the story not give you enough reason to stay clear? What if I'm like the fellow in the book?" He paused, staring at her, his eyes hard now. "What if you're like the girl?"

Crecy flushed harder, but refused to look away or allow him to intimidate her. "I'm not like that girl," she said, her voice trembling a little. "And … well, yes, all right, I was deeply shocked, if you must know."

His mouth quirked a little, a smug smile at his lips.

"But I learned a lot, too," she added as DeMorte gaped at her and then cursed. He turned away, muttering under his breath, and then looked back just as fast. His expression suggested he hadn't the faintest idea what to make of her. "And you are not at all like him," she added, praying that that was, indeed, the case.

He let out a huff of laughter. "You have no idea if that's true." His voice was scornful, his expression a sneer as he dared her to believe he was anything less than a debauched monster.

Crecy nodded. "I know," she said, realising her hands were clenched tight, the material of her skirts bunched up and creased in her anxious grip. "But I believe it is, and … and until you let me know you better, I can only be guided by my feelings for you."

DeMorte looked faintly nauseated by this and grimaced. "And what," he barked in disgust, his words becoming a harsh whisper as he lowered his voice. "What if I allowed you to know me better?" The tone of his voice implied a very physical manner of getting to know him, and Crecy's breath caught in her throat. "What if I take advantage of your outrageous advances and ruin you as you so clearly desire ... and then you discover that I am every bit as dark and twisted as the characters in that book. *What then?*" His voice was low and hard and angry, and Crecy swallowed, knowing he was giving her fair warning. She might well be wrong, she might become a scandal, a fallen woman, a figure of ridicule and shame to everyone who knew her.

"At least I'll know," she whispered, feeling a lump in her throat at the idea she might never win this war for his soul, for his heart, this battle of wills. Perhaps she wasn't strong enough, brave enough. Perhaps she simply wasn't ... *enough?* "At least I'll have done something about taking my destiny into my own hands," she said, knowing that in this, at least, she was certain. "Instead of marrying a man who will own me and control me and never, ever *know* me."

DeMorte held her gaze, and she hadn't the slightest idea of what he was thinking. He looked away from her then, staring at the book in his hand.

"I liked this one, it was ... amusing. I don't own a copy, either."

Crecy nodded, trying hard not to smile and feeling as though she'd won a victory, albeit a small one. He looked up then, those eyes still full of suspicion.

"How the devil did you get hold of such titles?" he asked, his dark brows drawn together, though his expression was more intrigued than disapproving.

"After my father died, we had to pack up his library. Many of the books were sold, as we couldn't afford to keep them," she added with real regret. That had been a very dark time in her life. "But I found this secret box, and those books were there, and ...

well, we could never have sold them, in any case," she said, feeling a little indignant at the glitter of laughter in his eyes. "S-so I gave them new covers and ... and new titles and hid them in my bedroom."

She wasn't sure, but she thought she saw his shoulders shake a little.

"And what ... pray," he asked, pinching his nose and closing his eyes as though he feared the answer, "is the new title for de Sade's little masterpiece?"

Crecy gave a little, dignified sniff and pursed her lips. "*Songs of Innocence and Experience* by William Blake."

She watched the internal struggle behind his eyes with curiosity until it was clearly too much for him, and, to her delight, he burst out laughing. In that moment, he seemed transformed, his face alight with mirth, his eyes suddenly the blue of a hot summer sky instead of a glacial ocean. Crecy stared. She had the sensation that her heart had been somehow exposed, it felt raw and vulnerable and she knew in that moment that she had been right about him. The thought gave her courage, and she determined that Gabriel Greyston would be hers. No matter what she had to do, what risks she must take. She would give everything for the chance to save him from the darkness he so obviously dwelt in.

Chapter 6

"Wherein our heroine is suspected of witchcraft."

Gabriel was brought up short, the strange sound echoing around the high ceilings of the book shop. He couldn't remember the last time he had laughed. A real laugh, that was, one born of genuine amusement and pleasure, rather than the kind he reserved for those who thought to seek pity or beg for his understanding. That laugh he knew well enough. It was cruel and hard and unforgiving and summed him up quite perfectly well. If only this foolish young woman would open her eyes to the truth, she would see that in an instant. Yet those lilac eyes did not seem to have romanticised him. Indeed, the more she looked, that direct gaze piercing now, the more uncomfortable he became. He had the strangest sensation that she could see right through him. It was disturbing.

"You have a good laugh," she said, smiling at him. "I would like to hear it often."

His face fell back into its naturally taciturn expression, the brooding glower far more comfortable than the unnatural upturn of his lips, which felt foreign and strange and somehow false.

"I'm laughing at you, you ridiculous child," he said, knowing it was a lie, but needing her to leave him alone. He didn't want the unnerving young woman around him, unsettling him - making him laugh for no good reason.

Crecy snorted, and he found himself raising one eyebrow at the scorn she managed to convey.

"For such a bad man, you're a dreadful liar," she said, looking amused. "And I think you can tell ... I am no child." This was added with a rather smug look that dared him to try and pretend her obviously feminine curves were anything less than they were.

Gabriel felt his irritation climb another notch.

"Don't you have somewhere else to be?" he demanded, his voice harsh now. He was growing impatient, a strange and uneasy feeling beneath his skin that was disturbing. "Shouldn't you be at the assembly rooms or taking tea with friends or shopping or *anything else*, blast you?"

Her face fell, and for a moment he hoped he'd succeeded in offending her. But she just let out a groan and rolled her eyes.

"Oh, don't remind me," she muttered, looking really disgusted now. "I have to go for a fitting this afternoon."

Gabriel frowned, curious to discover that she did not enjoy such things. "Most women love spending money on new gowns."

She returned a scathing look, one elegant blonde brow arching at him. "I think we've already established, I am not *most* women."

Gabriel suppressed the desire to chuckle, keeping his lips from curving upwards with difficulty. She was amusing, this peculiar creature. Absurd and irritating beyond belief, but amusing.

"So what are you looking for here today?" he asked, gesturing to the shelves around him. "I don't think you'll find any de Sade on the shelves," he added with a smirk. To his disappointment, she didn't blush.

"No, I shouldn't think so," she replied, her voice even and quite unembarrassed. "I shall have to borrow yours."

The directness of her gaze, the bold manner of speaking to him - Gabriel knew anyone else would have been shocked, disgusted even. But she was … intriguing.

"In fact, I came to put in an order for a book," she said, her eyes suddenly full of enthusiasm. "I heard about it from a friend of the author and it sounds quite fascinating."

Gabriel watched her with interest. Vivacity seemed to light her up from the inside, a spark of joy glowing within her that was hard to resist. He would extinguish any such spark in little time if she continued to follow this dangerous path, though. Yet he wanted to hear her tell him about the book that had so captured her imagination.

"It's a retelling of the story of Prometheus," she said, taking a step closer to him. "It tells the story of a scientist and how he creates life itself. He takes bits of lots of different dead bodies and sews them all back together and creates a creature that actually lives and breathes and thinks!"

Gabriel blinked, staring at her in astonishment.

"Just imagine it," she said, sounding almost breathless with excitement. "A hideous, towering monster that goes on to hunt its creator when the scientist rejects him. It appears to be the story of the creation of a monster, but from what I can tell, the scientist is more monster than his creation."

Though he hated to admit it, Gabriel's curiosity was indeed piqued by this unnatural tale. "When will it be published?" he asked, hating that he was interested, but wanting to know just the same.

Her face fell and she gave a huff of frustration. "Not until the new year," she said, looking so utterly dejected that Gabriel almost allowed himself to smile again. "The only reason I know is that my friend is a relation of Mary Wollstonecraft. The book is being published anonymously, but in fact, it's her daughter who has written it." Miss Holbrook sounded quite evangelical by this point. "Just think," she said, looking positively gleeful. "How shocked everyone will be when they discover such a work as this - as it must create a furore - and it was written by a woman." There was such triumph in her eyes at this that Gabriel snorted with amusement.

"For my part, it doesn't surprise me in the least that a woman could create such a macabre tale," he said, his tone dry as he eyed her with distrust.

Miss Holbrook gave a delighted laugh and seemed to forget herself, stepping closer to him and taking hold of his hand.

"No, of course you're not surprised. You know me too well to doubt the possibility."

Gabriel froze as her warm fingers curled around his and he snatched his hand away.

"I do not know you at all, Miss Holbrook," he said, his voice cold and indifferent.

He had turned a little away from her, frowning at the book he still held in his hands and avoiding the openness of her expression. Nonetheless, he could feel the heat of her gaze upon him, as warm as her hand had been upon his skin.

"Yes, you do," she said, her voice low. "If you read my letters, you must do."

"I burnt them, every one of them," he snapped, turning back to her with a burst of anger. Who the devil did she think she was, anyway? What right had she to speak to him so intimately?

She stared at him for a moment and he forced himself to hold her gaze, knowing he looked angry and vengeful. To his consternation, after studying him for a moment more, she let out a breath of relief.

"No," she said, shaking her head and smiling at him. "You didn't. You read them, every one."

Gabriel gaped at her, a prickle of anxiety running over his flesh. The woman was a blasted witch. How could she possibly know that?

"I know you, Gabriel," she said, answering his unspoken question and bewildering him further still. The use of his name was shocking. That she should be so bold in the first place was astonishing enough, but to hear it spoken with such *tenderness* ... She reached out and placed a tentative hand against his chest and Gabriel resisted the urge to bolt. He was too curious to know how. How could she know him? "I know your soul," she whispered, stepping closer. "It belongs with mine."

Gabriel took a step back, every instinct telling him to get away from this strange creature, this beautiful temptress who threatened to know him, who implied she already did.

"It's all right," she said, her voice soothing as she dropped her hand and moved away, as if she was aware she'd pushed him as far as she could. "I must go now. But I'll be in the Sydney gardens tomorrow afternoon at two. At least, I will be if I can sneak away," she said with a devilish grin. "Will you meet me there? Please?"

"No."

She didn't say anything, her eyes searching his face in a way that made him deeply uneasy.

"Well," she said, shrugging. "I'll be there, by the bridge over the canal. I'll wait for you." She gestured to the book in his hand. "I do hope you enjoy it." With that, she gave him a last, dazzling smile and a look that spoke of regret, before turning and leaving him alone.

Gabriel simply stood there, rooted to the spot and wondering what in the blazes had just happened. He was still there, staring at the stupid book with a vacant expression when the shop keeper found him and asked if he could be of any assistance. Gabriel thrust the book at him without a word, paid the price given, and stalked back to his hotel room feeling thoroughly vexed.

***

Crecy tried to behave herself during the dress fitting and to show enthusiasm for all the lovely things she was shown. Indeed, Violette, who was most insistent that they spend as much of her brother's money in as short a time as possible, had exquisite taste.

That being the case, Crecy simply left herself in Violette's hands and allowed her to take charge of her purchases. This left her time to return to her conversation with Gabriel and daydream about that kiss.

If Belle thought it odd that she didn't complain or huff with impatience even once, whilst she was poked and prodded and pinned, then she said nothing. In fact, Crecy suspected she had never in her life been more docile and biddable, but she wanted to study every second she had spent in Gabriel's company, turning it with care in her mind's eye, reliving it.

My word, but he was afraid. Crecy knew that most people would laugh at the idea. That Viscount DeMorte, a man who was feared and reviled, that such a powerful man could possibly fear anything at all would seem a ridiculous thing to say. But to Crecy, it was obvious. She knew the rumours, knew he used blackmail and gambling debts to force others to his bidding. She could not condone his actions, but she could understand them. He was alone and always had been, from what she could tell. She knew that his parents had died young. His mother had committed suicide on the very same day that his father had shot himself, before Gabriel's very eyes. What must that have done to a young boy? The people who ought to have loved and protected him did that to him, leaving him all alone in the world, and in such a violent manner. Her heart bled for him.

That he was afraid, to trust, to hope, to live … that seemed a perfectly reasonable reaction to everything he had suffered. Crecy was no romantic fool, however. She knew well that the path she was set upon was fraught with danger. He was a grown man and his character not one that would welcome change. That he didn't trust her enough to let her in, well, that was quite clear. Yet she had sensed his interest, his curiosity, and she had certainly felt his desire.

She drew in a sharp breath, feeling herself flush. The young woman pinning a rather fetching blue carriage dress around her exclaimed in distress, believing she had pierced her skin instead of the gown. Crecy blushed harder and accepted her apologies with an anxious smile before returning to her thoughts. Though she had read all manner of things that a young woman ought never to set eyes on, she had still been a little startled by the physical evidence of his arousal. Not least by her own reaction to it. She had felt molten, as though a fire had been lit deep inside her and everything around it was liquefying, heating her blood, burning her from the inside out. She had longed for him to return her kiss, to pull her into his arms, to devour her. The strength and urgency of that desire was really rather terrifying, but Crecy determined to embrace it. She would have Gabriel, in every sense possible, and at least then, if she failed to capture his heart, at least she would have lived and experienced what it meant to love him for herself.

That evening, they went to the Theatre Royal on Beaufort Square. It was a sumptuous building, and Crecy was delighted that Violette's husband, Aubrey, had secured a box for them. From here, she could see everything. The walls were richly papered with a crimson-stamped cloth and an Egyptian pattern fringed with a gold stripe. The seats and edges of the boxes were likewise covered in cloth, and Crecy smoothed her fingers over the plush feel of it, revelling in the experience. The front of each box was painted the same deep colour, with four broad stripes of gold with golden scrolls at the centre. It was truly a magnificent building.

Such opulence and the chance to enjoy a really excellent theatrical performance would usually have been enough to have Crecy in raptures. Tonight, however, once the initial drama of her surroundings wore off, she found it hard to concentrate on the actors or their theatrics. She felt herself plunged into a far more dramatic tale in her own life, and her thoughts returned time and again to Gabriel, to the startled look in his eyes when she had kissed him, to the haunted, hunted expression that she had seen, albeit fleetingly, flickering behind the perpetual sneering, scornful mask he wore.

Crecy wondered if he would come tomorrow or if she was wasting her time. She must not be disappointed if he did not show, she told herself, even knowing it was hopeless. She was desperate to see him again, after all. If he did come, then surely there was hope, surely she had made enough of an impression to intrigue him a little? A small voice in the back of her head warned her that Gabriel would use her if she allowed it and drop her when he was done, but she refused to listen to it. She had made her choice now, decided to take the chance, so now, she must play her hand with the cards given her.

Chapter 7

"Wherein Gabriel is out manoeuvred."

"Wait," Gabriel barked, as his valet knocked on his bedroom door. It was barely five am but Gabriel slept little, retiring late and rising early. The job as his valet was unlikely to be considered an enviable one, though he paid well enough to keep from losing the fellow altogether. Changes to his routine were to be avoided at all costs, and breaking in a new valet too stressful to contemplate.

Gabriel removed such items that the hotel had put out for their guests use on the dressing table, picking each item up between finger and thumb and dropping it onto the chair beside him with a look of distaste. He found the idea of using things that may have been touched by any number of people before him revolting in the extreme, and took great care to always have his own things about him. He never journeyed unexpectedly, always ensuring that everything he needed would be at his disposal the moment it was required.

Once the surface was cleared, he withdrew a handkerchief and dusted the top of the table with great care, ensuring every inch of the wood was clean. The handkerchief was then removed to be placed with his dirty clothes for washing. Next, he moved to his travel valise and began to unpack the items required for his morning toilette. Each item was placed, straightened, and arranged three times, until everything had been laid out with meticulous care. He didn't doubt his valet had made himself comfortable while he waited, too used to what he suspected all of his staff considered their eccentric employer's *little ways* to be surprised by the interlude. Only when Gabriel was certain that everything was in its precise spot did he call for his valet to enter.

Though his attention to detail might suggest otherwise, Gabriel was not in any way vain. He cared little for his own appearance, beyond that it was neat and clean, and had no time whatsoever for fashion. His hair was too long, and a constant cause of distress to his valet, who implored him to cut it, to no avail. The idea of primping and coaxing his hair into some ridiculous style each morning was horrific. A thin black velvet ribbon kept it out of his way and reasonably neat, despite being dreadfully old-fashioned. Who cared what anyone else thought of him, in any case?

Besides which, Gabriel was well aware that his rather compulsive routines took up enough of his time as it was, and though he refused to let them become any more complex, it was a constant battle. Despite telling himself daily that the feeling of dread that swept over him - if he so much as considered leaving the room before every item on the dressing table had been put in its place and checked three times - was utterly ridiculous, he couldn't quite seem to shake off the desire to do it. If he tried, and he had tried, he'd get the strangest sensation as he walked away, a violent tingle crackling down his spine as his mouth grew dry, panic rising in his throat. He knew, too, that if he allowed it, such behaviour would creep into other areas of his life, but this, he fought, though it was an ongoing war. He knew his mind was determined to over set him, constantly undermining him and telling him he was worthless and a fool. Sometimes it won, and it felt then like his father was laughing at him, knowing he'd been right all along. So Gabriel fought. He refused to let his mind win, but each battle was hard-fought and left him increasingly exhausted.

Once he was dressed, his own items carefully packed away once more despite the fact they'd be needed again, and the hotel's items put back *exactly* as they had been, he was ready to leave. He had an appointment to keep. The idea that he had another appointment this afternoon drifted into his mind only to be stamped on. If Miss Holbrook thought that he would dance to her tune, she was to be sadly disappointed.

***

The air inside the Abbey was frigid. Gabriel sat still, though, not attempting to blow on his hands or stamp his feet. He stared at the stained glass in the eastern end of the building, admiring the vibrant design as the winter-white sky beyond the glass illuminated the colours. Such vivacity had his thoughts take an unwilling turn towards a certain, irritating young woman, and Gabriel tutted, checking his watch. He couldn't abide tardiness and his appointment was already two minutes late.

Behind him, there was the muffled thud of the Abbey door that echoed a little in the cavernous space, and a moment later, breathing heavily, a man took the seat beside him.

"Forgive me, my lord," the fellow said, sweating profusely despite the freezing temperature. He pulled out a handkerchief and mopped his face, pausing to wheeze and cough into it before stuffing it back into his pocket. Gabriel recoiled with distaste and shifted further away.

"Do you have it?" he demanded, without looking at the oily little man who made his skin crawl.

"N-not yet, my lord," the man stammered, and Gabriel shot him a sharp look to see an unwholesome creature whose skin was clammy and pale, his eyes red and bloodshot. "If you could just give me a day or two more."

"No more," Gabriel replied, getting to his feet. "You knew the arrangement. I shall instruct my lawyers to continue."

"But Lord DeMorte, *please!*"

Foolishly, the man reached out his hand, grasping Gabriel's arm, his expression pleading. The look in Gabriel's eyes made the fellow drop his hold on him like he'd been burned.

"Please, my lord," he said, his breath coming fast. "It's my home, it's all I have left."

Gabriel snorted, feeling no remorse for the pitiful creature. "You might have thought of that before you gambled away everything but the shirt on your back."

"But my luck will turn any day now, it's bound to ..." the fellow insisted, his eyes glazed with desperation.

"You damned fool," Gabriel spat, revolted by a man who could be so reckless as to lose everything he owned on the turn of a card and still believe in luck.

"But my mother," the man said, clasping his hands together in supplication. "At least give me a day or two to make arrangements. Where will she go? I can't afford to house her myself."

"To her nearest relation and far from you, I would imagine," Gabriel said with a snort. "I've no doubt it will be a relief for her to have you out of her sight."

With that, he got to his feet and strode away, leaving the man to consider his actions before God, if he believed in such things.

After a visit with his lawyer, which dragged on far beyond what he had allowed for, he only just made it back to the hotel for one o'clock. As arranged, a private parlour had been prepared for him, along with a plate of cold meat; beef, ham and roast chicken, a platter of cheese, a pannier of bread, and a decanter of claret.

Gabriel waited until the staff had withdrawn and then repositioned everything on the table, noting with irritation that there were four slices of beef instead of three as requested. He picked one up, scowling at it, before throwing it onto the fire. Once satisfied all was as it should be, he sat down. He ate first the beef, then the ham, then the chicken, before reaching for the cheese and cutting one - *precise* - triangle from each before reaching for three slices of bread. Once finished, he poured a glass of claret - to precisely one inch below the rim.

***

The clock over the mantle in the parlour chimed two o'clock, and Gabriel glared at it, irritated by the reminder that Miss Holbrook would be waiting for him. The staff had long since cleared away, and Gabriel had settled himself to read for an hour or so. He returned his attention back to the story, but found five minutes later, and to his frustration, that he had yet to turn a page. Try as he might, the idea that Miss Holbrook was sitting waiting for him in the freezing cold, while he was here, prickled at the back of his neck. It was an uneasy, uncomfortable sensation that felt a little like guilt and it was deeply aggravating. Gabriel did not feel guilt, nor remorse, nor care in the slightest for anyone but himself. It made life a great deal simpler.

Glowering, Gabriel returned his eyes to the book and determined to read to the end of the page, which he did. It seemed a rather hopeless accomplishment, however, when he went to turn the page and couldn't recall a word of what he'd just read.

Damnation.

It would serve the chit right if he did turn up, he thought gritting his teeth. If she was seen in his company, the talk would begin at once, the whispers about her and the kind of young woman she must be. He contemplated the idea. Perhaps he should go, at least to teach her a lesson. Perhaps if she discovered how vile and spiteful people really were, she would reconsider and give him a wide berth.

He sat still for another five minutes, fingers drumming on his thigh as irritation climbed up his neck. This was bloody ridiculous. As if he didn't have enough obsessions to cope with, without some eccentric, wide-eyed blonde returning the favour.

Fine, he muttered, getting to his feet. *Fine.* The word was savage, but there was laughter running through his mind, a sneering, taunting voice that mocked him for running when the girl crooked her finger. He tried to block the voice out, reassuring himself that he would be rude and unpleasant and as foul as only he knew how to be, and then she'd never want to see him again.

But the mocking voice still echoed in his head, telling him he was weak, a fool, a worthless fool.

By the time Gabriel got to Sydney Gardens, it was after half past two. He'd walked fast, his long strides eating up the distance as he hurried down Great Pulteney Street, but surely she'd be gone by now. There was a knot in his stomach at the idea, and he couldn't decide if it was relief or disappointment. With irritation, which seemed to be his prevalent emotion whenever thinking of Miss Holbrook, he realised that she had not given their meeting place as anything other than the bridge over the canal. The foolish chit had obviously never been there before, as there were several to choose from. It took him time to check each bridge in turn, but finally he saw her.

She was leaning over an elegant iron bridge, built in the Chinese style, and Gabriel had to pause for a moment to admire the picture. She was dressed in a dark blue pelisse, her bonnet lined with the same material, the inky velvet making her blonde hair shine like gold on a day that was bleached and white and devoid of colour. Gabriel could only think again of the stained glass in the Abbey, the colours singing against the icy chill of a December sky. For no good reason he could think of, his heart felt a little lighter. He watched as Miss Holbrook stamped her feet, burying her hands deeper into the muff around her neck, and he felt another, deeply unwelcome, stab of remorse for having made her wait.

He swallowed as she looked up, the voice in his head mocking him all the harder when his first instinct was to turn around and walk away from her, as fast as he could. But the smile that broke over her lovely face made him hold still, and when she raised her hand to wave at him, he felt his fingers twitch with the ridiculous desire to return the gesture. He clenched his fists, refusing to give in to such idiotic behaviour.

Gabriel watched as she ran across the bridge towards him, and glanced around, relieved to see that the freezing weather had kept more sensible people indoors. They appeared to be alone.

ladies do not run in public," he scolded, as she [...]ards him, holding her bonnet in place with a gloved [...] [ch]eeks were flushed and her eyes alight with pleasure [...] a laugh of delight. "Oh, give it up, do, Gabriel. Belle has been trying to cure me of it for years, and if she can't, you certainly won't."

Gabriel tensed, infuriated and unsettled as ever by her forwardness.

"You address me as Lord DeMorte," he growled, refusing to look her in the eyes. There was something so vivacious and alive about her it only made him feel dusty and dull in comparison. *Worthless*, the voice in his head muttered, and Gabriel pushed it away, only to hear it echoing over and over. He looked back at her, needing something else to think on, and grateful that she was speaking again.

"I didn't think you were going to come," she said, smiling up at him and looking so damn grateful that he felt positively nauseated.

"I wasn't going to," he said, the words terse.

Miss Holbrook slipped her hand into his arm and Gabriel tensed, torn between revulsion at her boldness and the desire to allow her to keep it there.

"I know," she said, grinning at him now, as though she'd won a victory of some sort. With reluctance, he had to acknowledge she was right. He was here, after all. "Why did you change your mind?"

Gabriel began to walk, it was far too cold to stand still, and Miss Holbrook was clearly shivering. "Because it occurred to me that you were foolish enough to freeze yourself to death if I didn't," he snapped, sounding deeply aggrieved.

There was a surprisingly deep chuckle and he looked down at her, struck by the colour of those unusual eyes all over again. Today, they looked more grey than lilac, and he fancied he could see the clouds reflected in them. Scolding himself for being nauseatingly fanciful, he pulled her forward.

"I am rather chilly," she admitted, as she quickened her steps to keep pace with him.

"It will serve you right if you catch pneumonia," he muttered, dragging her on. There was a chill wind cutting through his coat, and if she'd been standing on that wretched bridge for the best part of an hour, she must be frozen. There was nowhere they could go indoors without fear of being seen, so he headed for the grotto, casting furtive glances around to see if anyone was about.

"There's no one here, so you needn't fret about my reputation," she said, clinging to his arm and almost having to run to keep up with his strides. "No one is mad enough to walk the gardens in this weather except for us."

Gabriel sent her an unloving look before turning his attention back to the path. "I assure you, I couldn't give a damn about your reputation. Something you ought perhaps bear in mind, Miss Holbrook."

"Oh, do call me Crecy, please," she said, sounding a little impatient herself now, or perhaps she was just breathless with trying to match his pace? "After all, if I'm going to call you Gabriel ..."

"I never invited you to, *Miss Holbrook,*" he growled, feeling his temper rise. Damnation, if there was ever a more irritating female to walk the earth, he had yet to discover her.

"No, I know," she replied, her voice placid as he guided her around a large puddle. "But I'm going to anyway, so you may as well call me Crecy."

Gabriel lifted his eyes to the heavens and prayed for patience before the damp gloom of the grotto swallowed them up. It was no warmer in here, he realised with regret, but at least it was out of the wind.

"Oh, what a perfect spot," Crecy said, looking around at the moss covered walls with delight.

Gabriel snorted and shook his head. "Yes, a cold, damp cave on a freezing winter's day. I might have known you'd be thrilled by it."

The smile she shot him at that comment did something to his chest and he dropped his gaze, instantly wishing he hadn't as he noticed one of her buttons was not properly slid through the hole, but was only half visible.

Gabriel instantly reached out to correct this so that it matched the others before his brain caught up and stayed his hand. She was speaking again but Gabriel didn't hear her, all he could see was the button and the need to fix it buzzed in his head like a demented blue bottle. He breathed in, trying to override the feeling of alarm as his heart picked up and wrenched his gaze away, trying to focus on something, anything else. But even before he'd settled on something, his eyes were sliding back to that damn button.

"W-what did you say?" he asked, aware that she was waiting for a reply and trying to focus.

"I said, have you brought your lovers here before?"

The question was almost enough to jolt his attention from her pelisse, but not quite. He wondered what she would think if she knew the truth about him. People assumed so many things, after all. Though surely she knew that he didn't have lovers, not any more at least. He visited whores on occasion, an impersonal exchange that he felt able to deal with. At one time, he had dallied with those experienced widowed ladies of the *ton,* those who had an appreciation for his cruelty and lack of care, but he'd had too many instances like with this wretched coat. Moments that made those women look at him with curiosity - at first - but he'd known scorn and ridicule would follow soon after, so that had stopped. The whores were paid well, not only for what they did, but for keeping their mouths shut.

"Don't be ridiculous," he snapped, feeling suddenly breathless as his gaze slid back to the button once more. The desire to correct it, to slide it back through the hole was making him feel prickly and quite unable to focus on the conversation.

Crecy was staring at him now, though, her face curious. Good, at least now she'd know he really was out of his bloody mind, and would run a mile. Then he'd not be bothered by her again. Curiously, he found no satisfaction in the thought. He didn't want her to know about his ... difficulties, didn't want her to ridicule him, but she followed his gaze, dipping her head to her buttons to see what he was staring at.

"What's the matter?" she asked, clearly aware that he was uncomfortable and not understanding why.

Gabriel took a breath, trying to keep his breathing even. "That button," he said, gesturing to it with his hand and willing the words to sound reasonable and not like he was losing his damn mind. *But you are*, a snide voice whispered through his brain. He closed his eyes, ignoring it. "It isn't done up properly. You'll ... catch cold," he added, wincing inwardly as it sounded pathetic.

He opened his eyes again, expecting her to be looking at him with suspicion at the very least, but he found nothing but curiosity in her expression.

"It's bothering you," she said, voicing what was obvious even though no one else in the world would have done so. Anyone else would have politely ignored it and then sniggered behind his back.

He gave a curt nod and she stepped a little closer to him.

"Would you do it up for me, *please?*" she said, her tone soft.

Before his brain had even caught up, he'd reached out and slid the button through the hole. He let out a breath of relief, feeling suddenly lighter, as if he could relax and breathe easily again. His fingers still held the button, circling the circumference with his thumb. Finally able to lift his gaze from it he found himself staring instead into the eyes of the young woman before him.

"You shouldn't be here," he said, the words hard now, wishing that she would go as badly as he hoped she would stay. "I'll ruin everything. I'll do it on purpose." As warnings went, it was stark and to the point, and yet he should not have been surprised when she clutched at his lapels and stood on her toes, pressing her mouth to his.

Chapter 8

"Wherein ... a kiss."

He shouldn't have been surprised at all, not considering everything he knew about her, but he was, all the same. It was too far removed from any kiss he had ever known not to feel like he'd been thrown into hot water with no warning. Her lips were soft and sweet and gentle against his, and too many emotions slammed into him all at once. She should not be here. She should not be with him.

Worthless piece of nothing, disgrace to the name, weak, you're weak, Gabriel.

Anger struck at him all at once, the desire to shock her, to scare her so badly that she'd never bother him again. He'd found a way to cope with his life, a monotonous daily existence with one goal only in sight, destroying his cousin. He could live with that, *deal* with that, but now she was going to try her utmost to tie him in knots. Well, damn that, and damn her. So this time, he kissed her back.

His kiss was neither soft nor sweet, and certainly not gentle. He pushed her against the wall, forcing her mouth open as though he would devour her. His hands moved over her, falling to the soft swell of her behind, cupping and kneading hard as he pulled her against him. If she really wanted to be ruined, why the hell shouldn't he oblige, after all? Desire and revulsion crashed over him, the heated longing to take her to the cold, stone floor and lose himself in her warmth, vying against the need to let her go, to let her run from him ... while she still could.

He let her go.

Gabriel stepped away from her, turning his back and wiping his mouth on his sleeve as though she disgusted him, though the only revulsion he felt was for himself.

"You've got what you wanted, Miss Holbrook," he spat, sounding vicious and angry. "I suggest you go now before I take more than you're willing to give me."

He waited for the weeping to begin, the pitiful cries swearing he was a monster and she hated him, and was therefore somewhat wrong-footed when a perfectly collected voice spoke to him.

"Did you enjoy Tom Jones?"

Gabriel swung around, not quite sure if he was outraged that she wasn't outraged or ... or what?

"What? No! I mean ... Yes, but I only read a little," he began, seeing her mouth quirk with amusement and feeling his temper rise higher. "Damn you, never mind the bloody book!" He ran a hand through his hair, feeling as though Miss Holbrook was purposely trying to undermine what little hold on his sanity remained. "Why aren't you running back to your blasted sister, crying your eyes out?" he demanded, sounding ridiculously indignant that she hadn't. "Did you not care that I just ravished you in a nasty damp grotto, of all places?"

Crecy pursed her lips as though she was giving the question her full attention before giving him an apologetic smile. "Actually," she said, sounding a little rueful. "I was rather hoping you'd do it again."

Gabriel gaped at her for a moment as the desire to do as she'd asked warred with self-preservation. In the end, he threw up his hands, turning and going to walk away before changing his mind at the last moment and grabbing at her, his hands cupping her face and lifting it to meet his lips.

He was rather less harsh this time, though that wasn't what he'd intended. He'd intended to repeat his violent kiss, and then some. Yet the moment his lips had touched hers again, his anger had left him, and the desire to kiss her properly, deeply, had won out over everything else.

He felt her small hands sliding up his neck, felt the soft swell of her breasts pressing against his chest as he pulled her flush against him. She was all heated eagerness, pliant in his arms, and for the first time, he seriously considered taking her back to Damerel with him and teaching her everything she was apparently so eager to learn. God, but she felt good, too good, too sweet, too innocent ... What the devil was he playing at?

He let her go, refusing to regret it, and tried hard not to allow her glowing cheeks and swollen lips to have any effect on him. He looked away, knowing the vision of her flushed and dishevelled from his kiss was going to haunt him for the rest of his days, and regretted ever leaving the hotel at all. He should have let her freeze. Her breath fluttered against his mouth, desire burning so brightly in her eyes that it shook him.

"Go home, Miss Holbrook," he said, sounding a little unsteady and forcing himself to move away, feeling as though everything he'd ever clung to for sanity had just been rocked, the foundations still trembling with aftershocks. "For the love of God, go home and stay away from me."

"I can't do that, Gabriel."

Gabriel closed his eyes. There was something in her voice that told him she meant to make him care, and if he stayed here a moment longer, he had no idea what would happen. He had to get away from her. So he turned on his heel and left.

***

"Madam Chalon really is a genius, isn't she?"

Violette's excited chatter washed over her as Belle replied with a smile, nodding in complete agreement as she looked Crecy over with approval. Crecy gave the large feather in her bonnet a tweak and grinned at her before leaning back against the squabs of the carriage.

"Indeed, she is," her sister said, with a laugh, her voice warm, though Crecy could see there was worry in her eyes. No doubt wondering how Edward was going to react to her impromptu flight to Bath. Privately, Crecy thought he'd been well-served and that it had been the exact right thing to do, but she didn't doubt Belle was feeling a little trepidation at the idea of facing him again. She could well understand it.

Faced with an angry Gabriel in that dark grotto in Sydney Gardens, Crecy had almost lost her nerve, too, but she hadn't. She smiled, turning her head to hide it as she looked out of the window. The countryside rolled past as the carriage bore them back to Longwold and she watched tiny, fragile flakes of snow flit about on the icy breeze. It wasn't cold enough to settle, but the hot brick beneath her feet had long since grown cold, and Crecy longed for a warm fire to sit beside. As that was a good hour away yet, she returned her attention to Gabriel, and more importantly his kiss.

Warmth flooded her to her toes and she bit her lip to smother a grin, lest her sister notice and question her on it. My word, though … what a kiss it had been. The first time, he'd been angry with her, angry that she had taken what she wanted without it being bestowed on her. Women were not supposed to act in such a way, after all, it was wanton and lascivious. Crecy shrugged, wondering why women's emotions were supposed to be so far removed from what men felt. Why create a body that was capable of such passions and desires and then spend every waking moment repressing them? Obviously, some decorum was called for, nothing would get done if the world turned into some Bacchanalian orgy - she was forced to cough at this point to smother the burst of laughter that bubbled up unbidden as she imagined voicing the idea to Gabriel. Belle gave her a curious look, but carried on talking to Violette, too used to Crecy's odd ways to comment. But nonetheless, why should such feelings be ignored and shut away, as if it was in some way shameful? What shame was there in loving another human being and wanting to touch them?

Crecy sighed, knowing she was completely out of step, and that even Belle would be shocked if she voiced such opinions. Instead, she closed her eyes and relived the moments with Gabriel all over again. His hold on her had been fierce, his arms far harder and stronger than she had imagined beneath the heavy overcoat he wore. She had slid her hands over his chest, feeling the curve and cut of powerful muscle beneath her touch. Desire pooled deep inside of her, hot and needy as she wondered what his skin would have felt like if she'd dared slip her hands under his clothes. Oh, God, the longing to do so, to touch him again, was an ache beneath her skin, a longing so profound that she could taste it. The second time he had kissed her, that had been different. He had been different. He'd wanted to run, wanted to be angry, but in the end, he'd been neither. He'd given in and kissed her because he wanted to, and she shivered with pleasure as she relived the warmth of his mouth, the slide of his tongue over hers. Crecy swallowed, her mouth dry, longing to see him again.

She'd known she wouldn't see him again in Bath. Though she had hoped and visited both the gardens and the bookshop just in case, there had been no sign of him. But that was all right. He needed a little time to get used to the idea of her. She understood that and would not force him. Not yet.

***

Gabriel ran his hand over the cold stone of the wolf's head, his thumb moving back and forward over the throat, raised to howl at some distant moon. It was soothing, somehow, and he regretted not having taken it to Bath with him. If he'd had it, he might have been saved from some of the most ridiculous decisions in his entire life.

He gritted his teeth and concentrated on the feel of the cool stone, slate, in fact, long since rubbed smooth after years of wear. It was too heavy to slip into a pocket, sadly, though it was a satisfying weight in his hand, tactile. It had become a kind of talisman, and this a routine that calmed him when his temper rose to dangerous heights.

The irony of the fact that the young lady who was the cause of much of his ire had given him the stone as a birthday gift some years ago did not escape him. There had been a gift every year on the seventeenth of April, without fail. He had received a bird skull - with buttons for eyes and a garish combination of coloured feathers stuck on in a somewhat haphazard fashion, a piece of glitzy pyrite or fool's gold, a drawing of an exceedingly ugly dog with three legs, a rather dubious poem about a dead parrot, and all manner of things that anyone else would have thought revolting and utterly bizarre. That Gabriel had carefully stored every one in a drawer, arranged by year and placed with his usual precision, only showed the depths of his own idiocy.

At first, the letters and the gifts had irritated the hell out of him. What in God's name was the strange child up to, writing to him in the first place? But he figured that she would soon grow tired of such a one-sided game and give it up. Except the letters came each month, without fail, and little by little, he found he was amused by them and the bright, if rather twisted, mind that created them. They were original and funny and touched upon a life that was quite clearly anything but easy.

The years passed and Gabriel discovered a grudging admiration for the girl who would not be primped and moulded into a sweet little débutante. Instead, she was stubborn and wilful and strange and … well, downright peculiar at times, but Lord, who was he to judge? As the years turned, so the letters changed, using him as some kind of sounding board for all of her vexations and frustrations. He knew well her desire to learn medicine so that she could be an animal doctor, he knew that she hated her aunt, did not mourn the death of her father, and loved her sister with a devotion that was positively nauseating if laudable for one of her sex.

He knew she wanted to learn every detail of each dark and dreadful thing he had done in his life, just who had he blackmailed, had he really driven Lord Ruth to suicide, had he fought a duel and killed a man as they said he had? She was far too curious about his visits to *houses of ill repute* - were the ladies free to live as they wanted, to say and do just what they liked? – she'd asked with a disturbingly wistful tone. She wanted to know if he was truly responsible for trying to shoot his cousin, even though he hadn't pulled the trigger himself. In this, he had noted the first sense of chastisement and that she could not condone his actions, no matter how he hated his cousin. For Aubrey Russell had been shot by accident and nearly died in that ill-fated affair. But in the end, she had decided that he was not guilty of this crime at all, and had so convinced herself of his innocence that she begged him to say something to stem the rumours of his murderous command.

"It makes me furious to hear them condemn you without an ounce of proof, without any witness or demand that you account for your actions. No, they are happy enough to point the finger at you, but God forbid they confront you with it. Not one of them has the nerve to face you, Gabriel."

He snorted, turning the cool slate in his hand, over and over as he glanced at the clock. One more minute and the fellow would be late; his temper began to rise again, and he turned the wolf's head faster in his hand.

Gabriel got to his feet, replacing the chair so that it was exactly parallel with the desk, checking that the lamp, his pen, the black leather ledger, his diary, and the neat stack of correspondence that awaited his attention were all straight and parallel to each other. He kept the wolf in his hand, holding it in a firm grasp as he stalked to the door and wrenched it open.

"Where the hell is he?" he barked, just as Piper opened the door to the man in question. Paul Chambers was a tall, heavyset-looking fellow with strong shoulders on him, but he blanched at the sound of Gabriel's anger.

"Forgive me, my lord," he said, snatching the cap from his head and looking as though he was sweating. "I rode like the blazes to get 'ere on time. I'm only a minute or two late."

Gabriel swung the door to his study open without another word, and the fellow scurried through.

"Well?" he snapped, closing the door and stalking into the room behind him.

Paul cleared his throat, looking deeply uneasy, and Gabriel's stomach clenched.

"It's true, Lord DeMorte, Lord Winterbourne was married about a week ago."

Gabriel swallowed, panic rising in his throat. If Edward was married, then there might be a child, an heir to the marquisate. If that happened, everything was lost. There would be no peace for him, not ever, not in this lifetime. He was at least somewhat relieved to discover that there were limits to his depravity and that even he would baulk at the idea of killing an infant. His cousin was a grown man and he'd face him in a duel if only he could provoke him badly enough, but cold-blooded murder, no. Not even to silence his father's voice.

"Who is she?" he demanded, hearing the tremor in his voice and clearing his throat lest the fellow should believe he was troubled by the idea.

"I couldn't discover that, a closed-lipped lot, they are, up at the big 'ouse," he said, earning himself a look of disdain from Gabriel. "She's a nobody, though, that I do know."

Gabriel snorted, indicating that in his opinion the man knew nothing at all about anything.

"What I mean to say is ... she ain't no *lady* someone. Not from some grand family." The man's face became thoughtful and he shook his head. "Reckon there might be somethin' being hushed up, you ask me," he added.

"I am asking you, dammit!" Gabriel shouted, making the fellow jump out of his skin and flush, his sallow cheeks growing hot. "I pay you for information and this is all you get me? I could likely have discovered more from the scandal sheets."

"Ah, but you couldn't, my lord," the fellow objected, shaking his head and unwisely holding a hand out to stop Gabriel saying anything more. "Cause it weren't announced yet and no one up there will say a word about it, so ..."

"Get out!" Gabriel stalked to the door and wrenched it open once more. "Get out and don't come back until you have something to say."

He slammed the door behind the fellow and kicked it for good measure, breathing heavily as the urge to go back out and throttle the fool crept up on him. He held the wolf's head tightly, breathing steadily in and out and trying to calm himself. With a muttered curse, he tried to stall the need to return to his desk and check that everything was still as he'd left it.

"Of course it is, *of course it is,*" he muttered, feeling anxiety crawling up and down his spine all the same. Oh God, Edward was married. He was married and now he'd have a son and Gabriel was lost. He'd never have another moment's peace. The peace and calm that he longed for, hoped for, it was slipping away from him and there wasn't a damn thing he could do about it.

Worthless, pathetic worm. You're a disgrace, an embarrassment; you ought never have been born.

Unable to resist any longer, Gabriel returned to the desk, checking each item in turn before moving around the room, correcting every single thing he came across until everything was as he needed it to be. The wolf's head was still clutched in his left hand and his thumb moved over the throat, up and down, up and down as his breathing steadied.

God, he had to get out of here.

Chapter 9

"Wherein our hero takes a chance."

Gabriel rode hard, pushing Typhon faster, urging him on as though the Devil himself snapped at their heels. It didn't feel far from the truth. Everything was unravelling and his father's voice seemed louder than ever, berating him, mocking him. Any chance to be free of him, free of that hateful, taunting voice, seemed to be slipping through his hands. A part of him didn't entirely care; he was tired of fighting, tired of trying to hold on to a *normal* life. There were other ways out, after all, if things got too bad.

His stomach clenched at the idea, but he remembered his mother's face, almost peaceful in death as she had never been in life. It didn't look so bad.

He pulled his horse up, both of them breathing hard and Gabriel sucked in a lungful of cold air. It was brighter today at least, the sky blue and scattered with billowing white clouds though the ground was thick with frost.

With chagrin, he looked around and realised he'd ridden to the border of his land, to where it met Longwold. He hadn't noticed what direction he'd taken, just riding for the sake of it … hadn't he?

The idea that Miss Holbrook might be coming to find him flickered into his mind and he shoved it away. He had no desire to see her again, no desire to encounter a woman who did nothing but disturb and unsettle him. Yet he scanned the horizon nonetheless, looking for her.

He waited for a while, walking Typhon up and down so he didn't get cold, lathered up as he was, before turning him back towards the house. Gabriel refused to accept that the heavy sensation in his chest was disappointment. He had burdens enough to account for it without any sentimental twaddle over a foolish young woman who would do well to heed his words and keep clear. He had told her to, after all, demanded she go home and leave him alone.

"I can't do that, Gabriel."

Something caught in his throat as the words repeated in his mind. Soft words for once, kindly meant, given to him with affection. A longing to see her again crashed over him, taking him unawares and making him realise how damned alone he was. If he was honest, the letters she had written him had been the only things that had kept him alive when things had been at their darkest.

"We can be friends if you like, then we both know there is at least one person in the world who thinks well of us."

It was ridiculous, beyond pathetic, she had been a child after all when she'd spoken those words. She had no concept of what she was saying. And yet ... as the letters had kept coming, as it became clear that she did *know* him, or had at least guessed much about him, it had helped, knowing that there was one person in the world who thought well of him, no matter what. It had been a light in the darkness when there had been nothing else to keep him from falling into the abyss.

He pulled Typhon up again, a lump in his throat that threatened to choke him, and despite knowing he was a fool, he turned and looked again, and caught his breath.

He let out a startled laugh at the sight of her, cantering over the rise towards him as though he had conjured her up. Perhaps he had? Perhaps his mind had finally broken down and he was imagining her. He found he didn't much care.

"Hello, Gabriel," she said, sounding as bright and alive as she always did, a little breathless from her ride, her lovely cheeks flushed with the cold and exertion. Gabriel stared at her, finding his tongue suddenly nailed down, any reply lost as he remembered the last time he'd seen her, flushed and tousled for an entirely different reason.

He moved Typhon on, the big horse stepping out at a sedate pace with Miss Holbrook following beside him.

"How are you?" she asked, and for the first time in his life, he believed she really wanted to know the answer, had perhaps even worried for him.

He glanced at her and looked away, uncertain of how to reply to such an enquiry.

"You look tired," she said, and he could feel the warmth of her gaze on his face. "Don't you sleep?"

Gabriel swallowed. He didn't want to answer questions. Instead he turned to her and cleared his throat.

"Are … are you hungry?" he demanded, his voice sounding gruff and begrudging for no good reason other than he didn't quite know how to make it otherwise.

"Famished," she said, her eyes lighting up as she smiled at him.

He nodded and urged Typhon into a canter, glancing over his shoulder to make sure she was following, and led her back to Damerel.

Gabriel grimaced at the look in his butler's eyes as he led Miss Holbrook over the threshold and into his home.

"Miss Holbrook!" the fellow exclaimed, so astonished and wide-eyed that he might as well have been seeing Gabriel invite a fairy queen to lunch rather than a live flesh and blood guest.

"You'll need to set another place," Gabriel said, handing Piper his coat as Miss Holbrook divested herself of hat and gloves.

"Of course, my lord," Piper replied, practically beaming.

Gabriel scowled, now he'd have to put up with the staff gossiping about him. He kept the minimum of servants as it was; the fewer people aware of his *quirks,* the better.

Gabriel looked at his watch and checked it against the large grandfather clock. Ten minutes to one o'clock.

He put his watch away again and glanced at his guest, quite lost as to what to do next.

"Will you show me around, Gabriel?" she asked, taking a step closer to him. Gabriel scowled and shook his head.

"I eat at one o'clock, there isn't time," he said, his voice sharp.

Her face fell, clearly disappointed, but he refused to feel remorse for it. He glanced back at the hands of the grandfather clock and wished the bloody things would move faster.

"Well, afterwards, then?" she said, a hopeful tone to the question that was hard to miss.

Gabriel grunted, walking towards his study, unwilling to agree or disagree. She followed at his heels and he didn't know how to stop her, but he needed a drink. It wasn't usual for him to drink at this hour, but ... he had a feeling this was going to be an unusual day. He waited for the idea to send his anxiety spiralling, but caught the look on Miss Holbrook's face as she stepped into his study. She appeared enthralled, her eyes wide and delighted as she looked around.

"It's just as I pictured it," she said, sending him such a dazzling smile that he felt suddenly quite winded. She moved about the room, inspecting every surface, every picture.

"Don't touch anything," he barked, panic crawling up the back of his neck at the idea she might move something out of place.

She turned back to look at him, a little surprised, perhaps, but not as startled as he might have expected.

"All right," she said, her tone soothing as he looked away again and turned his attention to his desk. "I can see everything is very neat. You like order, don't you?" she observed as he moved his pen a millimetre to the right of his diary. He looked up, unaware that she'd been watching him.

"Yes."

He turned away and poured a small measure of brandy into a glass.

"May I have one, please?" she asked, moving to stand beside him.

Gabriel looked up with a scowl. "Young ladies do not drink brandy."

She quirked one eyebrow at him, a look of amusement lurking in those beautiful lilac eyes.

Gabriel sighed and poured another glass. "You are quite determined to be a scandal, aren't you, Miss Holbrook?"

He held the glass out to her as she gave a soft laugh.

"I'm going to be the most appalling guest if you don't give in and call me Crecy," she warned him, mischief lurking in her expression. "You'll never get rid of me."

She reached for the glass, and Gabriel repressed a shiver as her fingers touched his. The idea of keeping her here, with him, was suddenly not as unattractive as it had once been. What the devil had gotten into him?

"Very well, Lucretia," he replied, his tone begrudging as she rolled her eyes and tutted.

"Crecy," she said, shaking her head. "Repeat after me: kuh-ress-see." She sounded out her name as though he was a particularly slow child and he fought against the way his lips wanted to twitch upwards.

Instead he scowled at her again. "As you will, *Crecy,"* he repeated, sounding impatient, even as speaking the familiar form of her name sent a strange warmth uncurling in his chest. He looked up to see it was two minutes to the hour. Downing his drink in one go he returned to his desk, checking that nothing had moved.

Crecy watched him, obviously intrigued before raising her own glass and copying him. He raised an eyebrow as she spluttered a little, waving her hand in front of her face, her eyes wide.

"Well, that's warmed me up," she said with a gasp.

Gabriel tried to look revolted by such hoydenish behaviour, but suspected he failed as she simply chuckled and took his arm.

"Lead on, my lord," she instructed, giving him a look of such warmth that he was forced to look away.

He took her to the dining room where provisions for his guest had obviously sent his staff into a panic. He could understand their agitation. His own simple repast was not ideal for a female guest, and they did not want the lady to think badly of what had been offered. Yet any deviation from the norm would generally send their master into a towering rage. Thus it was that an extra place had been set beside his, an exact mirror image, and three servants dithered, holding plates that they had no idea what to do with.

"Just put the damn things down and get out," Gabriel snapped. Tension snaked down his spine, coiling tight, sliding around his throat and squeezing the air from his lungs. What in the name of everything holy had he been thinking? This was a disaster, a terrible idea ... He hauled in a breath, fighting for calm. It was just a meal, just food on plates, he could do this. *Get a grip, Gabriel.*

The servants did as he'd ordered and practically ran from the room. The moment the door was closed, Gabriel moved forward and rearranged the table. His mouth grew dry, a sour feeling climbing his throat until each item was arranged to his satisfaction. It took a little time, as moving one item often caused the need to go back and change another until it really was perfect and his chest unlocked with relief. Drawing in a shaky breath, he looked up, waiting to see the derision in Crecy's eyes, and wasn't sure what he felt when he found none.

"Still want to eat with me?" he demanded, his fists clenched as he waited for her to mock him. "You see tales of the mad viscount were perfectly accurate, only it's rather less romantic in the flesh, isn't it?" He sneered at her, bracing himself for her reaction.

Crecy moved forward, taking hold of his arm and reaching up, placing a kiss on his cheek. "May I sit down now, please, Gabriel?"

He stared at her for a moment before remembering what remained of his manners and pulling out a chair.

Gabriel sat himself and glanced at her. She was looking at the table with a little trepidation before the solution seemed to come to her. "Would you like to serve me?" she asked, a hopeful look in her eyes. "I like everything, so … whatever you're having would be fine."

Something inside him seemed to unwind, the tension twisted around his spine like bindweed, uncoiling and setting him free.

He got to his feet again, placing food on her plate until it matched his own, filling her glass to the wing tip of the little bird with a precision that had been given many years of practise. He sat again, moving his knife and fork a little before picking up his napkin and laying it in his lap.

They ate in silence, though strangely it didn't feel uncomfortable, and though he knew she watched him, he felt no judgement, no scorn, just curiosity, perhaps.

"What would happen," she asked once he had folded his napkin with care and replaced it where it had come from, "if I threw my napkin down on the table?"

There was no challenge in her voice, which was just as well, as the idea made tension snap down his spine like a whipcord.

"The house would fall down around my ears," he snapped, feeling suddenly enraged. Did she think him a fool?

She gave him an impatient look and tutted. "I wasn't suggesting you thought such a thing, I meant, what would happen to you, how would you feel?"

Gabriel got to his feet, breathless and irritated. "Just give it here," he said, snatching it from her hands and folding it himself, lying it beside her empty plate.

He moved away, heading for the door, and he heard her chair push back. He turned, relieved to see that she replaced it. "I only want to understand you, Gabriel, and I can't if you don't explain." She sounded so perfectly reasonable that he felt like an idiot, but he didn't want to explain, didn't want her know such things about him, didn't want her to think him weak.

"You wanted to see the house?" he said, changing the subject and holding the door open for her.

She slid her hand into his and squeezed. "Yes please, but don't think I won't get an answer from you, because I will."

Gabriel grunted and led her back into the hallway.

"What do you want to see?" he asked, sounding begrudging and bad-tempered but not releasing her hand. It was warm in his, far smaller and more fragile than his, own and he liked the feel of it. It was ... reassuring, somehow, a little like the wolf's head. He ran his thumb over the curve of her thumb, the gentle slope reminding him of the wolf's neck, but so much softer and smoother. He relaxed a little, repeating the gesture as they walked.

"I don't mind," she said, sounding a little breathless. He turned to look at her to find her staring at their linked hands, at the way his thumb caressed her skin. It was the gentlest he'd ever been with her, he realised. For a moment, the urge to tell her it was just a repetitive gesture that soothed him and she need not read anything into it hovered on his tongue, and was just as quickly rejected. He wasn't even sure it was true.

"Come along, then," he muttered, his voice gruff now. "I'll give you the tour."

Chapter 10

"Wherein horrors of the past come to light."

Crecy followed Gabriel as he led her around the house, and as much as she had been desperate to see it, as enraptured as she was to familiarise herself with his home, nothing could take her attention from the way his thumb was stroking her hand.

It was such a tender, loving gesture that emotion settled in her throat, making it hard to speak to him. So she didn't, sensing that he preferred quiet, in any case. Somehow, she thought that he had taken a big leap today in allowing her to eat with him, and she was anxious about pushing him too far, too fast.

Though she had sensed from the outset that he was a man who needed to be in control, she had not realised to what extent this control had turned around and begun to control him. She had read articles about the mind and its workings before; some had seemed reasonable, others utter twaddle, but she felt sure his need to control and check must stem from the horrors of his childhood.

The desire to question him about it was tangible, but she did not relish the thought of upsetting him, especially as she had no intention of leaving without being kissed. As it happened, however, the subject raised itself.

"What's down there?" she asked, as he hurried her past a corridor they had not investigated on the first floor.

He paused, and she noticed his eyes did not stray in that direction.

"Those were my parent's rooms," he said, tugging her on, but Crecy dug her heels in.

"I should like to see them, please," she said, sounding a little stubborn, but she was intrigued to see if she could gain any deeper understanding of the son from what his parents had left behind.

"You want to see the scene of the crime, you mean?" he said, his tone accusing, eyes narrowed with suspicion. He dropped her hand, his posture changing as he became tense and wound tight before her eyes. "Is that why you came?"

Crecy stared at him in horror before rushing forward and taking his hands in hers. "Oh, Gabriel, no. I'm so sorry ... I ... I didn't know. I swear I didn't."

He scowled at her, suspicion still lurking in the blue of his eyes, though he didn't withdraw his hands. "You didn't know they killed themselves?" he retorted, sneering at the idea.

"Yes, I knew that, of course," she said, keeping her tone even and soothing, moving closer still and stroking his hands in the same manner he had done with her. "But I don't know the circumstances or ... where it happened. I would never have asked if I'd known, honestly, I wouldn't. We needn't go in if you find it upsetting."

He was still for a moment, and she got the feeling he was fighting some kind of battle as he turned his head to look down the corridor.

"Why not," he said, a tone to his voice that she could not like as she looked up and saw a muscle leaping in his jaw. He walked forwards suddenly, keeping hold of one of her hands and grasping one of the door handles, wrenching it open.

It was dark inside. A musty, unused smell filled Crecy's nose and she shivered at the cold. This room had been dark for a long time. To her surprise, Gabriel let go of her hand and moved forward, snatching at the curtains and pulling them open with a savage air. Light flooded the room, suddenly too bright after the darkness, illuminating a large bedroom, decorated with a pretty, feminine hand.

Crecy looked around, fighting the urge to sneeze as the dust kicked up by the curtains tickled her nose. Gabriel was standing by the windows, staring outside, his large hands braced on the sill, shoulders hunched. Crecy looked around and caught her breath at the portrait that hung on one wall. A lovely woman with jet black hair stared down at her. She looked rather frail, ethereal, almost, with a delicate heart-shaped face, but such a familiar slant to her dark blue eyes that Crecy suppressed a shiver. She looked sad, too, rather desperate, in fact, something about her expression that the painter had perhaps not realised he'd captured, or else he'd have changed it.

"I found her here."

Crecy jumped a little, the oppressive atmosphere of the room working on her nerves in such a way that Gabriel's voice startled her.

"She was in her bath," he continued, the words so matter of fact that the hairs on the back of her neck lifted. "I'd never seen so much blood."

Crecy swallowed, moving back to him and sliding her hand into his. She said nothing, not wanting to give him words that would seem meaningless. Instead, she waited for him to speak again, if he wanted to.

"My father had been away on business. That was unusual, as he rarely left her alone. She took the opportunity to have an affair with Lord Winterbourne," he said, his eyes never leaving the view outside of the window, though she felt he was seeing something else entirely. "Edward's father."

Crecy suppressed a gasp as so many things she'd wondered suddenly became a lot clearer. She leaned into him, holding his hand within both of hers now.

"What was your father like?" she asked, and he snorted.

"He professed to love my mother, beyond anything she could possibly comprehend, beyond reason. He seemed to think of himself as some great, romantic hero." He fell quiet and she waited, watching the rise and fall of his chest. "It took me a long time to understand that it wasn't love at all, it was control. He would not allow her to leave the house, not allow her to have visitors, friends. He was too jealous of anyone spending time with her. She was completely isolated."

Crecy looked up at his face, seeing no emotion there, but sensing the turmoil raging behind the façade.

"And then you arrived," she said, guessing that this would have been a strain upon an obviously difficult relationship.

He tightened his hold on her hand and she wondered if he knew he'd done it, as his expression did not change.

"He hated me from the outset. He started hitting her. He was jealous, you see, jealous that she loved me better than him." His throat worked for a moment before he looked down at her. "She did love me," he said, the words sounding almost defiant.

"Of course she did," she said, fighting the urge to weep for him, sensing that he didn't want that from her, that he would revile her pity. "How could she not? I bet you were a gorgeous little boy."

He snorted, shaking his head. "I hated her for a long time for what she did, for leaving me, but … but now I understand. She just couldn't take any more."

There was something in his words that sent a shiver of foreboding thrilling down her spine, and she clutched at his hand. "You're not alone, Gabriel, not like she was."

"She wasn't alone, either," he countered. "She had me."

He let go of her hand, moving to pull the curtains back into place, twitching them until they were even, before leaving the room and closing the door behind them. They moved to the next door and Gabriel hesitated, his hand reached out and dropped again before it touched the handle.

"Let's go somewhere else," she said, but he shook his head, stubborn now.

The door swung open without the faintest squeal of protest from the hinges, and this time Crecy hurried ahead of him, throwing open the curtains and allowing the daylight to chase away the worst of the ghosts, except it didn't work. She could see them still, lingering in Gabriel's eyes.

"Father found out about her and Winterbourne, of course," he said, lingering in the doorway. There was a portrait of his father in this room, and she felt he stayed where he could not see it. He was obviously a big man, like Gabriel himself, and that cruel set to his mouth was familiar, but his eyes were not Gabriel's and his hair was a sandy blond.

"You favour your mother," she said, looking away from a man whom she had hated on principle, but now loathed for good reason.

"Not as much as you might like to think." His eyes glittered, as though daring her to think of him as a good man, a man in need of love or understanding. He believed himself to be every bit the monster his father had been, that much was abundantly clear. But was he? She knew he had done some terrible things, but was that truly him? Was that the only man he could be, or could he change, if only someone would give him the chance to be something else?

Crecy looked around her, the dark walls aggressive, somehow, as if something of the room's former occupant still lingered. Well, she had come to Longwold, desperate to see a ghost, but she'd found them here instead at Damerel, and they were anything but silent. Their voices still stretched out across the decades to torment their only son. Well, she'd see about that.

"What happened then?" she asked, turning back to Gabriel. "When he found out?"

Gabriel shrugged, though she felt he was anything but nonchalant as he answered.

"He brought her back. I ... I remember her screams as he dragged her upstairs by her hair. He just went ... mad," he said, meeting her eyes. "There is no other word for it, I think. He raged and wept and screamed, he beat her so badly that I thought ..." He stopped as the words grew ragged, and then cleared his throat. "I tried to stop him, but ... I think he must have knocked me unconscious. It seems that when he'd had enough of beating her, he returned to Longwold to confront Winterbourne, and the man called him out." Gabriel laughed, though it was full of bitterness. "I think that rather shocked him, that her lover should object to him beating his own wife to within an inch of her life. He didn't understand it, saw her only as property. He *owned* her." Crecy heard the revulsion behind the words and knew, *knew* she was right to trust him. No matter what happened after this, no matter how long it took, she would fight for him. "Father agreed to meet him, at dawn, but when he got home, mother was dead, she'd cut her own wrists."

"And you found her?"

Gabriel nodded. "When I came to, I remember ... everything was so very quiet. I was afraid of it, and then I saw the room, her room, it was such a mess from father's rage. He had destroyed everything, everything scattered around, broken ..." She sensed his agitation growing as he remembered the scene and ran back to him, holding his hand within both of hers. "I remember thinking that ... that if I could only put everything back as it was ..." He choked, the sound turning to callous laugh as he pulled his hand away from hers. He moved into the room, never looking at the wall that bore his father's image, and closed the curtains, his movements quick and precise, before turning and leaving the room. She ran out ahead of him, the sound of the door slamming shut echoing around the still house.

How did he live like this? Alone in this big, empty mausoleum? Even Longwold, though it was bigger and grander still, seemed to have more life, more warmth to it than this place. It felt as though Damerel had never seen the sun before.

He stalked back through the house, hurrying down the stairs, and she realised the tour was over, he would reveal nothing else, not now, not today. In all honesty, Crecy felt relief at that. Everything he had told her had horrified her and made her heart ache for the little boy that had lived through it. Good God, was it any wonder his outlook on life was so … so dark?

"You should go," he said, as he reached the bottom of the stairs, walking away from her and into his study without a backwards glance. "Piper will have your horse brought around."

Piper appeared at this moment, sympathy in his eyes as he regarded her, looking a little lost in the vast hallway as Gabriel slammed his study door shut.

"I'll fetch your belongings, Miss Holbrook," Piper said, moving to turn away.

"No," Crecy replied, her tone determined as she walked to the study door. "I'm not leaving yet."

She squared her shoulders and ignored the panic in the butler's voice as he exclaimed from behind her.

"*Miss Holbrook!* I really shouldn't …"

But Crecy had already gone through the door and closed it behind her.

Chapter 11

"Wherein Crecy gets what she wants."

Crecy's heart was thudding hard as the door clicked shut, but she wasn't about to leave. Not yet.

Gabriel spun around, his face so incredulous that she almost laughed, though happily she stopped herself in time. She suspected he would find her laughter neither amusing nor appropriate.

"I told you to go," he barked, his body rigid with tension, his hands clenched. He held something in one hand, she noticed, and stepped closer, wondering what it was.

"But I don't want to go yet," she retorted, giving him a direct look and carrying on as he opened his mouth to rage at her. "You haven't kissed me yet, Gabriel, and I'm not going until you have."

That seemed to have spiked his guns, she thought with satisfaction as a new light entered his eyes. This one hotter and fiercer.

"Oh, yes," he said, his tone mocking now. "I'd forgotten how eager you are to fall from grace. Was that your purpose in asking to see the house? Should we have lingered in the bedrooms? Was it my room you were hoping to see?"

Crecy nodded, amused by the shock in his eyes and refusing to let him fluster her. "I was hoping to see your room, as it happens. You can tell a great deal about people from their bedrooms, I think. Though I wasn't considering spending any great time there with you," she carried on with perfect candour. She saw no reason not to be honest with him after all. "I will," she added, avoiding his eyes now as a blush stained her cheeks. "One day soon, I hope, but not yet, I want to know you better first, but ..." She looked up now, meeting his eyes and hoping he could read the sincerity there. "But

I would very much like to kiss you again, to feel your arms around me. Last time was rather wonderful."

He looked quite adorably perplexed now, not sure whether to continue being outraged by her, or to just give in and kiss her. She felt sure he wanted to, no matter how he acted towards her.

She moved closer to him, aware of the tension singing through that powerful body. His expression showed her nothing but confusion, and she didn't know whether he would storm off in a rage, kiss her with as much anger and violence as in the grotto, or simply ignore her request with a look of contempt. Crecy reached out, placing her hands on his chest beneath his jacket, feeling the warmth of his body radiating through his shirt and waistcoat. How strange, that a man everyone else feared and reviled should make her feel nothing but safe. She lay her head on his chest, hearing the steady thud of his heart. He didn't move, didn't speak, and she stayed where she was, aware that there was some kind of war being fought in his mind and waiting to see who won.

It seemed a long time later that his hand raised, lifting to touch her hair. His touch was tentative, as if he wasn't quite sure what he was about, and she lifted her head to look up at him. He looked tense, still and uneasy, but his big hand moved from her hair to cup her face, his thumb caressing her cheek. She turned into it, lifting her own hand to cover his and pressing her mouth to his palm. Crecy heard his breathing hitch and smiled, her mouth curving against his skin. Reaching down, she caught his other hand, intending to kiss that too, but his fingers were curled tight around something and her eyes widened with recognition as she saw the wolf's head.

"I gave you that," she said, smiling up at him and feeling her heart swell. He had kept it, which meant he had read her letters. It must do. "You kept it."

"I did," he admitted, his voice rather gruff.

He allowed her to take it from his hand, watching as she smoothed her fingers over it and then placed it down on the mantelpiece with care. Crecy raised his other hand to her face, nuzzling it and kissing the palm. He moved then, cupping her face between both hands and staring down at her as if she was a puzzle he had no idea how to solve.

"Stop thinking so hard, Gabriel," she said, her voice quiet and intimate. "Kiss me."

Her breath caught as his head lowered, his lips just as soft as she remembered. Crecy opened her mouth to him, knowing how this worked, now, and mimicking the slow glide of his tongue over hers. His hands dropped to her waist, and then around her, and she closed her eyes, lost in his kiss.

There had been a part of her that had expected him to kiss her roughly and then push her away, but it wasn't like that at all. He was tender with her, kissing her as though it really meant something, as though he cared, and Crecy held nothing back. She wanted so badly for him to trust her, had been certain that this loving man was there, beneath the scars of his past. She knew that she would do anything, anything at all, to set him free.

His lips left her mouth and she sighed as they trailed along her jaw, tracing a delicate path down her neck.

"Gabriel," she whispered, the sound of his name joyful and reverent as she slid her hands into his hair. He paused for a moment, and she saw anxiety in his eyes but she pressed her lips against his once more.

"Don't stop," she pleaded, the words breathed against his mouth.

He was still for a moment, and then she gasped as he reached down, lifting her with ease and moving to the chair by the fire.

He sat down with something of a thud as her weight overbalanced him, and Crecy laughed, delighted to be here, to have come this far, but her laughter was cut short as his mouth captured hers again. She sensed the change in him, sensed he was fighting to keep his desire in check and wondered at it. If he had pushed the issue, she knew she had no resistance to him, she wanted him and she wouldn't hold back. He knew it, too, she felt sure of it. But she was nervous yet, in truth, and wanted to wait a little longer, wanted to understand him better, to know him more fully. Yet if he was really such a decadent man, so lost to propriety, why did he not seduce her now, when he had her in his arms, why not take everything he could have?

Unless he cared for her.

The idea bloomed in her chest, a warmth that lit up her heart and made her smile even as he kissed her. He pulled back, frowning a little.

"What are you smiling about?" he asked, still sounding rather fierce, which only made her smile all the more.

Crecy reached out and stroked his cheek, realising as she stared into those troubled indigo eyes that she loved him, so much that she felt her heart might burst from trying to contain it. She couldn't tell him that, though, not yet, sensing that this admission might be enough to spook him and send him running.

"I'm smiling because I'm happy, Gabriel, because you make me happy."

He looked really perplexed now and she laughed, moving forward to cover his face with kisses.

"Oh, my, you're adorable when you're puzzled, my love." The endearment slipped past her lips despite her intentions and he reached up and grabbed hold of her hands, moving them from his face. He looked deeply troubled, now, and she realised she'd still said too much, moved too fast, but she couldn't regret it.

"You'll come to a bad end," he said, his voice stark now, but Crecy would not allow him to spoil the moment. She just nodded, her expression placid.

"I know," she said, sounding quite accepting of the idea. "At least others might think it bad, but as long as I get what I want, what I need … then I'm happy to take the consequences."

He huffed and got up and Crecy slid to the floor, but refused to move away from him, though he'd released her hands.

"You'll not get back to Longwold before dark if you don't make haste," he said, and she felt sure he was trying to sound as if he didn't give a damn and was failing miserably.

She reached up and slid her hands around his neck.

"One last kiss and I'll leave, I promise."

"For God's sake, just go home," he growled, but she tugged at his neck and he came to her, kissing her hard and fierce for a moment, his arms locked about her, before releasing her so fast she stumbled, regretting the loss of his warmth as he walked away.

He moved to the mantelpiece and picked up the wolf's head, holding it a little behind him and not meeting her eyes.

"I'll see you again soon," she said, feeling ridiculously pleased.

He grunted and walked to his desk, moving each item in turn just a little, keeping his eyes from hers.

Crecy walked to the door and opened it, pausing in the doorway and quite unable to keep the stupid smile from her lips. "Goodbye, Gabriel."

**

As it turned out, Crecy would not get to see him again for some days. Regret at that fact and a desperate longing for him was a constant pressure in her chest, but there was nothing to be done about it. Belle needed her, and she could not abandon her sister.

She had hoped that Belle's relationship with Edward had been growing closer, and to her eye, it seemed as though it was. Edward was quite obviously falling for her, in Crecy's view, but Belle seemed still uncertain of his affections, and disbelieving if Crecy voiced her opinion. This morning, however, something had happened which had sent Belle into a panic, and Crecy's plan to visit Gabriel had to be abandoned.

Crecy shivered, cold seeping into her boots and making her already frozen toes ache harder. It had snowed again and the landscape around them was white with hoarfrost, the snow frozen and cracking beneath their feet.

"Edward!" Belle's voice, desperate and full of fear rang out across the fields once more, but there was no reply. Crecy took her sister's arm and squeezed as Belle fought back tears. "Why can't the idiotic man see it was an accident?" she said for the fifth time in as many minutes. "It was my fault entirely; I should never have tried to wake him when he was having such a terrible nightmare."

"He'll see that, too, Belle, when he calms down. He's just horrified at having hurt you. That shows he cares, doesn't it?"

Belle nodded, sniffing, and they set forward once more. Poor Edward was a troubled man, his experiences during the war had scarred him deeply, and he was prone to flashbacks and violent nightmares. He'd lashed out at Belle, perhaps believing her the enemy as she tried to shake him from his dream, and she'd fallen from the bed, hitting her head. It was a minor scratch, in truth, but the sight of her blood had sent Edward spiralling into the dark, and he'd disappeared.

Crecy sighed. It was too easy to draw parallels between Edward and his cousin, for her, at least. But Edward was a hero, his wounds inflicted by the war, and so his rudeness and sometimes appalling behaviour was forgiven and excuses were made for him. That was as it should be, of course, he should be treated with patience and understanding. The people who cared for him should support him and care for him and ensure he knew that he was loved and not alone.

But who had cared for Gabriel? His trauma was no less devastating, and he had been only a child. Edward had chosen to go to war, the decision of a full grown man. Gabriel had seen his parents die in a brutal manner before his very eyes, and then he had been left all alone. From what Crecy could gather, he'd been alone ever since. There had been no family member willing to take him in, and after the scandal, it was unlikely that his uncle, Edward's late father, would have adopted him. So Gabriel had been left to be raised by whom? The staff, she imagined, wondering just how long Piper had served him and what he could tell her of his master. And now that Viscount DeMorte was a wealthy and powerful man, full grown, no one cared about what he had suffered, what it had done to his soul, his heart. They saw only the man it had created, not why he had become that man - because no one had cared enough to stop it happening.

Crecy swallowed hard, blinking back her own tears. Well, they would find Edward, and Belle would continue to work her magic. It was obvious to Crecy that they were made for each other, and she felt confident that they would make it work in time. And as for Gabriel …

Crecy sighed, smiling as she remembered his kiss, the puzzled look in his eyes when he discovered she was happy, that *he* had made her happy. She hoped he wasn't too disappointed that she hadn't come today. Not that he would ever admit it if he was. But she began to wonder if he would worry, if he would believe that she hadn't wanted to come. Slowly, it dawned on her that this was exactly what he would believe. Frowning, she tried to figure out how she could get a message to him as she tramped through the snow. It wouldn't be easy.

An hour later and Crecy was shivering in earnest.

"You two should get on back inside, it's freezin'," Edward's rather unusual if devoted valet, Charlie, said with concern in his eyes. He was met with a predictably irritated expression from Belle, who had heard him say the same thing every half hour since they'd begun, and ignored him every time. "Look 'ere, Lady Winterbourne, ye sister is freezin', take 'er 'ome, at least."

"I'm fine!" Crecy shot back, indignant at being used as an excuse, though, to be honest, she was frozen to the core.

"No, you're not," Belle said, admitting defeat though she was clearly disappointed. "We're never going to find him, are we?" Crecy took her hand as poor Belle sounded so heartbroken it made her want to cry.

Charlie shrugged, but his expression wasn't encouraging. "The fellow grew up 'ere, knows every inch of this vast estate. I reckon we won't find 'im if he don't want t' be found."

Belle swallowed down a sob of despair, and Crecy pulled her into a hug. Charlie's face softened. He came closer and laid a hand on Belle's arm. "I'll keep lookin' once yer back 'ome, so don't you fret so. He's tough as old boots, is Eddie. Bit o' cold ain't enough to do for 'im, I promise ye that."

Belle nodded, giving a smile that didn't fool either of them. "Come along, Crecy. Charlie is right, of course, and I can't be responsible for you taking ill."

"I told you, I'm perfectly fine, Belle," Crecy grumbled, though she realised her assurance was rather spoiled by the fierce way her teeth were chattering.

"Humour me," Belle said with a smile, taking her sister's arm. "We'll keep looking on the way back."

Crecy sank back into her own worries about Gabriel as they trudged back to Longwold. Perhaps she could bribe one of the maids to put a letter in the post. Only everyone was so devoted to Edward, and loathed Gabriel so much, she wondered who on earth would take her up on it and not tell Edward or her sister. Perhaps the young man who was supposed to accompany her on her rides. When he was supposed to be with her, he slipped away to see his sweetheart so he had no idea where she went to, and as much as she would have to trust him with her secret, so he was trusting her with his. It was a risk, but she had little choice.

A distressed, squawking sound made her jump and she looked around, wondering where it had come from. Letting go of Belle's arm, her sister made a sound of protest but did not bother trying to stop her as she headed into the woods.

She heard Charlie demanding what she was up to as she ducked her head and pulled at her pelisse, which was snagged on a bramble. The cry came again and Crecy pushed on, heedless of the damage to her clothes as she saw a large bird, hopping and listing to one side as it tried to move away.

"Hush, now, hush, it's all right," she said, keeping her voice soft and soothing as she moved closer. The magpie squawked and tried to fly off, but the brambles overhead impeded it and it hit the ground again in an undignified flurry of feathers. Crecy rushed forward and scooped it up, wincing as the bird pecked at her fingers with its sharp beak. "It's all right," she soothed, holding it against her and stroking the top of its head. "I'm not going to hurt you, I promise."

Whether it was just admitting defeat and giving itself up to be eaten or whether it truly understood she was no danger to it, she didn't know. But to her relief, the pecking stopped. She emerged from the undergrowth with bits of twig and leaf in her hair, and Belle greeted her with an affectionate, if long-suffering, expression.

"It's a magpie," she said, grinning at Belle, who rolled her eyes. "The poor fellow has broken its leg, I think."

"Poor devil," Charlie muttered, giving the bird she held a leery expression. "Give it over, Miss Lucretia. I'll take care o' the wretched blighter for ye. Musn't let 'im suffer, eh?"

Crecy glared at him in fury, revolted by the idea. "No!" she exclaimed, holding the bird a little tighter and moving away from him. "I can mend his leg. He'll be fine in a few weeks."

Charlie grimaced at her and shook his head. "An' whatcha gonna do with the poor bugger 'til then, 'scuse my French?" he added, obviously remembering who he was speaking with. "Things probably crawlin' with fleas, and ... *ugh.*"

"I don't care!" Crecy flung back at him.

"Be kinder to put the thing out o' its misery," Charlie grumbled at her as Crecy moved further away, just in case.

"Would you put me down as fast, Charlie?"

They all started in surprise as Edward appeared, looking dirty and dishevelled as though he'd slept in a ditch. Crecy moved away to give Belle some privacy, but turned around a moment later as Edward's voice rang out. "Don't touch me!"

Belle jumped away from him and Crecy's heart sank. She watched as Belle called him back, but Edward just stalked away from her. Crecy returned to Belle, finding Charlie with her, talking to her softly.

"You're a good friend to him, Charlie," Belle said, her voice so sad and yet so full of gratitude that Crecy's heart clenched. Charlie blushed a little at the compliment and touched his fingers to his hat before striding off ahead of them.

"You can't let him push you away, Belle," Crecy said, her voice low as she stroked the head of the bewildered-looking magpie.

Belle smiled at her sister and nodded. "I know that, Crecy, and believe me, I have no intention of letting him succeed." Crecy nodded, smiling at her, and they walked back to the house. Both of them had challenges ahead, that was for sure, but Crecy felt sure that Belle would win her battle. It remained to be seen if her own advances were of any significance, and if there was hope for her, too.

Chapter 12

"Wherein darkness takes a hold and a spark catches."

Gabriel turned Typhon for home. The sun was sinking and he was chilled to the bone. She wasn't coming. That was clear enough. Worse, he was acting like a bloody fool. What in God's name did he expect? She'd likely gotten what she wanted, bearded the lion in his den and won. She was probably gloating. Right now, she was probably laughing her head off with her blasted sister and bragging how she'd had the terrifying Viscount DeMorte eating out of her hand.

His gut clenched, an unfamiliar ache spiralling out from his heart that he refused to acknowledge.

You're a fool, Gabriel, a weak, pathetic fool. The girl used you, Edward probably sent her. They're probably all laughing at you now. You've messed up again, you worthless excuse for a man. Can you do nothing right?

He rode harder, Typhon thundering across the fields back to Damerel House. The wind rushed in his ears, the cold stinging his skin and his eyes, but nothing could drown out his father's voice.

The next days were bad. The little sleep he usually managed evaded him as thoughts of Crecy slid into his mind and refused to be pushed away. He remembered every detail, every touch, every remembered sensation. If he closed his eyes, he could feel the silk of her hair against his fingertips, see the tiny freckle on her right cheek, recall the gentle touch of her hands against his face. He remembered the way she had run to hold his hand when he'd told her something of his past, rushing to comfort him as no one had ever done before, and the way she had said his name … like it actually meant something. Every moment was relived in tiny detail, played over and again in his mind with obsessive accuracy. Oh God, as if he needed another obsession.

He was clinging to normality by his fingertips - or his idea of what passed for it, at least. It took him twice as long to leave his room that morning, driven to check and recheck the items on his dressing table until he wanted to scream with frustration, to rage and shout at the young woman who had forced her way into his life when he hadn't wanted her to, hadn't given her the slightest encouragement. Why the hell did she do it? What in the name of God could she possibly get out of tormenting him?

"I'm smiling because I'm happy, Gabriel, because you make me happy."

Liar.

He went to his study and sat down behind his desk, determined to leave thoughts of her behind. The stack of correspondence at his elbow beckoned him, and he forced himself to straighten the items on his desk - no more than usual - before reaching for the first letter from his lawyer. It should have been answered before now, but he'd been too distracted. Anger bit hard, along with a scalding rush of embarrassment at himself for allowing such a forward slip of a girl to get under his skin. Scanning the missive briefly, he reached for paper and pen and scribbled a reply, his writing less legible than usual. He had always thought it strange how someone like himself, who strived so hard for perfection and order, could have such sloppy handwriting. One of the ironies of his life.

Gabriel.

The sound of his name on her lips stilled his hand and he closed his eyes. He'd thought the echo of his father's voice was torment enough. Foolishly, he'd thought there could be nothing in the world that could torture him more than that.

"She was just toying with you, you bloody fool," he muttered, signing the letter with an angry sweep of his hand before reaching for the pounce pot and shaking it over the letter. With the greatest care that none of the fine dust should cover his desk, he lifted the letter and sifted the excess back into the pot. Satisfied that that the ink was dry, he folded it with his usual precision and melted a seal on the join, pressing his signet ring into the soft wax.

The next letter was reached for and the process repeated, all the while with Crecy's soft voice lingering at the back of his mind while his father's voice mocked him for it.

He sealed the next letter, adding it to the first, and concentrated on breathing deeply, bracing his elbows on the table and covering his ears, as though that would make it stop. Gabriel breathed in and out, trying to keep the breaths even and to not allow the dark clouds gathering in his mind to swallow him up.

A knock at the door brought his head up, and he barked a demand for Piper to enter. The blasted fellow was grinning - actually grinning - as he hurried forward and presented the tray to Gabriel. The letter was addressed in a familiar, extravagantly looping handwriting that made his breath catch. He snatched for it, avoiding the man's eyes. Getting to his feet, he turned his back on Piper, too aware that his reaction was revealing.

To his relief, he heard the door close as Piper left him alone, and he broke the seal, refusing to acknowledge that his heart was thudding harder than usual. Too hard.

My dearest friend,

I am so sorry that I have not been able to visit you, but my sister has been rather out of sorts and has needed my company. She has borne with me and my strange ways with such devotion over the years that I cannot abandon her, not even for you, though it is far harder than you perhaps realise for me to stay away.

I miss you. I miss you so much, dearest Gabriel, and I count the minutes until I can see you again. Did you think it otherwise? Did you think I had deceived you and tricked you into playing some twisted game?

I know you, Gabriel. I know you like I know my own soul. You belong with me and I won't let you go.

If you believe nothing else, believe this: I am thinking of you, every moment of every day, and I won't be able to breathe freely again until I am with you.

I will come to you as soon as I am able to.

Yours, ever,

Crecy

Gabriel sat down, the letter still in his hands as he read it over and again. There was a tightness in his throat as the words sank into him, sliding under his skin and finding their way into the cold, dark depths of his heart. Something lit there, a spark in the bleak expanse of nothingness that had swallowed up his ability to feel, to understand, to empathise. It was frail and tentative, but it was there, a living thing that threatened to blaze and illuminate all the darkest corners of his soul.

It was terrifying.

A part of him wanted to snuff it out, to extinguish it before it had the chance to take a hold of him and blaze like a forest fire, raging out of control. His father's voice urged him on in this, telling him she was only tricking him further, snaring him tighter in her clutches so that her victory would be all the more complete when she revealed her true nature and laughed in his face. But Gabriel wouldn't let it happen. He shielded the spark that she had struck, like a match flame against the storm of his father's ridicule, against his own self-destructive nature. She would come to him again. She would.

And perhaps he was the biggest fool alive, but he would be waiting.

***

Crecy looked at the drawing in her hand with a critical eye. She had no great confidence in her skill with a pencil, but she thought that perhaps it was a passable likeness. It was the best her limited skills could achieve, at any rate. Turning it over, she tried to think of the words she needed, the pencil hovering over the paper with indecision. How to tell him everything she wanted to without scaring him off was becoming a dilemma. She just wasn't sure how far he could be pushed, and how fast. For her own part, impatience was her own cross to bear. Thoughts of spending all of her days with him, and more significantly all of her nights, were becoming increasingly hard to ignore.

Crecy had done her best to keep Belle company, throwing herself into decorating the vastness of Longwold for Christmas with all the enthusiasm she could muster. But her thoughts were never far from Gabriel, all alone in that big, empty building he called his home. She didn't think for a moment that there would be Christmas decorations there, that anyone would visit him and wish him merry. She felt as though her heart was bleeding from an open wound whenever she thought of it, and knew she would grab the next chance she had to see him, no matter how risky.

As it turned out, it was easier than she expected. Belle was preoccupied herself and had been spending time with her guest, Lady Falmouth since she and her husband had returned for the Christmas period. So no one noticed when Crecy disappeared for a long ride early on Christmas Eve. Her love of riding and being in the fresh air, no matter the weather, was well known by now, so it didn't seem at all strange.

She waved to Jack Crowther, the stable boy, as they parted ways, him to visit his sweetheart, Crecy to her own. She had paid him well for delivering the letter to Gabriel, and he had spent it on a gift for his girl. The idea pleased her.

Crecy rode hard, her eagerness to be with Gabriel making her more reckless than usual. By the time she crossed the border onto his land she was flushed and breathless, her heart pounding wildly, but it beat harder still when she drew her horse to a halt.

He was waiting for her.

Crecy gasped, joy a living thing beneath her skin as she took in the sight of him, a towering, dark shape against the brightness of the clear, winter sky. He looked like a fallen angel, a devil, even, a vengeful god, with those cold, blue eyes and his long black hair tied back from that hard face. His lips were cruel, and if anyone but Crecy looked upon him, they would shrink from the harshness of his expression. As it was, Crecy could only smile.

She watched as he dismounted, his great coat swirling about him as he left Typhon to crop the frozen grass, and strode over to her. Crecy could not read his expression as he stood beside her horse, looking up at her. His face was too guarded, too shuttered up, but he was here. He had come to her. It felt like a gift.

She reached out her hand, laying it against his cheek, and felt her heart squeeze as he closed his eyes and turned his face into it.

"Oh, Gabriel, I've missed you so much."

Before she knew what had happened, a strong pair of hands had caught her about the waist, hauling her down and into his arms. She stumbled, laughing as she braced herself against him. Crecy looked up into indigo eyes that gave nothing away. She would need to push him a little to discover what she wanted to know.

"You're supposed to say that you missed me, too," she said, her voice quiet as he stared down at her. She pursed her lips, considering his expression in the light of his silence. "Unless you di--" she began, only to have the words devoured as his mouth captured hers.

Crecy melted into him, a bizarre mix of frost and lava as she coiled around him. She was chilled to the bone from her early morning ride, her toes and fingers and face frozen, but Gabriel was everything that was heat and warmth. His mouth was hot against hers and she burned beneath her skin at the sensation of being in his arms again. He surrounded her, encompassed her, and she had never felt so content, so certain of the rightness of it. Her whole life, she had been wrong somehow, out of step, an odd puzzle piece to which there was no picture to fit into. Until now.

He let her go and she let out a sigh of deep contentment, her eyes still closed in case it was a dream that she had no desire to wake from. In the end, she forced herself to peek, to look up at him from under her lashes.

"Does that mean you did miss me?" she asked, her mouth smiling around the words. "Just a very tiny bit, at least."

He grunted, a flicker of amusement in his eyes that felt like another small victory. "Perhaps ... a very tiny bit." The words were gruff and a little begrudging, but Crecy didn't care. She beamed at him.

"Oh, I wish it were summer and the ground wasn't all cold and wet," she said with obvious regret, and her meaning showed clearly with the desire in her eyes.

He let her go, the movement rather abrupt.

"By God, woman, don't say such things. Do you have any idea how close you are to being compromised?"

He sounded really rather angry with her, which only served to make her happier. He cared. He did. He must.

"Surely the dreadfully wicked Viscount DeMorte doesn't care for something like a foolish young woman's reputation?" she said, teasing him gently. She took his hand, looking up at him with a smile to ensure he knew she wasn't taunting him in earnest.

But the look in his eyes was grave and not the least bit amused.

"Do you really know what you're doing?" he asked, the words harsh now. "Have you really considered? Do you think to force my hand? Do you expect me to marry you?"

"No," she replied, the word easily said, though she had lost sleep enough over the reality of what it would mean.

"Don't you want more than this?" he barked, his eyes cold now, and she knew there was a part of him that was angry at being here, angry at being made to care at all.

"I just want you, Gabriel," she said, whispering the words and praying that he could hear the sincerity behind them. "However that happens, whatever it means."

"You're a bloody fool," he snapped, letting go of her hand.

"Perhaps," she said, her tone placid as she captured his fingers again, stubborn to the last. "Don't be cross." The words were cajoling and soft, and he reluctantly allowed his fingers to curl around hers once more, though his face was still a mask of indifference. "It's Christmas Eve, after all, and I have a present for you."

She hid her smile as his eyes slid back to hers, a flicker of interest there that she delighted in. Talking to Gabriel was like deciphering smoke signals on a cloudy day. If you didn't watch hard, the clues to his feelings were so fleeting and well camouflaged that you could miss them, but every one captured and recorded was another revelation, a tiny step closer to knowing him.

He made a noise deep in his throat, somewhere between a grunt and a laugh, and he led her back to her horse, linking his hands together to give her a foot up. Crecy vaulted neatly into place, watching with admiration as his large figure moved back to his own horse that he mounted with ease. Without waiting for him to give any indication he was ready, or that he was, in fact, inviting her to accompany him, she took off.

She gave a cry of delight as her horse galloped away from him, knowing he would consider her a hoyden and yet not think the worse of her for it. She glanced back, certain that she saw a smile cross his lips as he sprang his own horse, Typhon surging forward in pursuit.

Crecy laughed, her heart light as Gabriel thundered after her, knowing he could catch her with ease, yet she did not having the slightest intention of escaping him.

Chapter 13

"Wherein games are played."

Piper's expression was one of such pleasure at seeing her that she wondered at it. Gabriel caught his look, too, glowering at him. Piper hurriedly rearranged his features to something more sombre, but there was still a pleased glitter in the old man's eyes that was hard to miss. What kind of relationship did he have with Gabriel? He certainly treated him with deference, as was normal for a butler, but bearing in mind Gabriel's reputation as a brute and a bully, it seemed strange that he show any pleasure in the fact that his master had a guest at long last. She suspected that the old man saw through Gabriel as she did, and that he was glad that someone was finally trying to break through the thick walls that the isolated viscount had built around himself.

Once they had handed over coats, hats, and gloves, and Piper had withdrawn, Gabriel hesitated. He looked tense, unsure of what to do now, how to treat a guest in his home.

"The parlour, perhaps?" Crecy suggested, her tone gentle, not wanting to create the impression that she was trying to give orders herself. "And some tea would be nice," she added.

Gabriel gave a curt nod, and she jumped as he bellowed across the great entrance hall. *"Piper!"*

Piper reappeared, looking not the least bit surprised at being summoned in such a manner, so she imagined he was used to it.

"Tea. In the parlour," Gabriel instructed.

Piper nodded and went to withdraw, but Crecy felt the need to add, "Thank you, Piper," shooting a reproachful look at Gabriel, who only glowered harder.

"A please or thank you doesn't cost anything, Gabriel," she said, aware that she was scolding him, but feeling that someone ought to.

Gabriel snorted, giving her a look of disgust. "You seek to tame the savage beast, is that it? Give the monster some manners? Good luck with that." He strode away from her and she hurried after him, catching hold of his arm and tugging him to a halt.

"You're neither beast nor monster, Gabriel."

He looked down at her, his expression as cool and unreadable as ever.

"Whatever your reason for being here," he said, the words somehow ominous as he reached out and touched her cheek for the briefest moment before letting his hand fall away again. "Don't fool yourself on that point."

He moved away again, tugging his arm from her grasp and holding open the door to the parlour for her. Crecy sighed, knowing that this was going to be a long and hard-won battle before walking through into the parlour.

It was a lovely room, if rather faded and a touch tired at the edges. She suspected his mother was responsible for the décor here once more, and wondered if Gabriel had made any changes at all to his home since his parents died. The answer seemed obvious, and the idea made her feel unsettled, as if the ghosts of his past were still among them, watching them. How did he exist, in this self-imposed exile with reminders of his parent's violent lives and deaths surrounding him at every turn? But then, that was all he did, wasn't it – *exist*. He hadn't the slightest idea what it meant to have friends, to talk about nothing in particular just for the pleasure of speaking, to have fun. She wondered if he'd ever had fun in his entire life. Did he even know how?

She looked up as Piper returned bearing a tray with the tea things and a golden pound cake, which made Crecy realise that she was actually famished. Piper placed the tray down and straightened up.

"Would you like me to pour the tea, my lord?" he enquired, apparently fighting to keep his mouth from curving into a smile.

Gabriel gave a curt shake of his head and Crecy glared at him. He glowered harder.

"No. That will be all, Piper ..." The silence stretched on. *"Thank you."* The words were obviously begrudging and bitten off, but they had been spoken nonetheless.

Crecy looked around to see Piper staring at the viscount with something close to astonishment before remembering himself. He nodded at Gabriel and removed himself, still looking somewhat startled as he closed the door on them.

"There, see," Crecy said, knowing she sounded far too pleased with herself. "That didn't hurt a bit, did it?"

Gabriel grunted, which seemed to be his default response for anything he didn't want to answer, and waited until she sat by the tray before taking a seat on the chair to her left. He did have some manners, then, she noted with amusement. Crecy turned her attention to the tea.

"Milk and sugar?" she asked, and then paused as he nodded, lifting one eyebrow just a little as he gave no further response.

Gabriel rolled his eyes. "Yes, please," he muttered. Crecy returned to her work and felt his eyes on her. She wondered if it was her he was studying, or if he simply wanted to rearrange the tea-tray. She flattered herself that this time it was her, but wasn't entirely sure.

"One lump or two?" she asked, sugar tongs suspended over his cup.

"Three ... *please."* He smiled at her, though it was more a snarl, in truth, a sarcastic baring of teeth.

She snorted and shook her head. "A sweet tooth, who would have thought?" she murmured. She passed him his cup before returning her attention to the tray.

"Cake?"

He shook his head and she shrugged, cutting a generous slice for herself. She bit into it and sighed with pleasure. Moist and buttery, it melted in her mouth, and she found herself relieved that he ate well, at least. They drank their tea in silence, and Crecy did nothing to try and make polite conversation. Gabriel would hate it, and she was content just to be in his company. The tea finished, Gabriel replaced his tea cup, and she watched with interest as he turned the teapot, milk jug, and both cups so that the handles all pointed in the exact same direction.

"Do you have any games?" she asked as he sat back down, earning herself a look of complete surprise this time.

"Games?" he said, sounding as appalled as if she'd asked if he had horns and a tail.

"Yes," she replied with a nod, determined that he should be taught to have some fun. "You know, entertainments."

"I have cards and dice," he replied, his tone dry. She looked at him, his large frame filling the chair he sat in. Outwardly, he looked relaxed, one long leg crossed over the other, his huge shoulders leaned back, but there was something in his eyes that told her he was still all on edge.

"I don't mean gambling, Gabriel," she said, tutting at him and sounding a little cross. "I mean parlour games … for fun."

"Fun?" he repeated, sounding somewhat revolted. "I'm a grown man, Crecy, you do understand that?"

"Oh, for heaven's sake, Gabriel, I'm quite aware, I assure you," she replied with an arch tone that was somehow rather flirtatious and not quite what she'd intended. His eyes darkened a little and she felt a responding flutter of excitement in the pit of her stomach, but refused to be diverted. "You must have something?" she pressed.

Gabriel gave a huff of impatience, but seemed to consider the question for a moment before getting to his feet. He crossed the room, opening the doors of a rather elegant cabinet and crouching down, searching through the contents.

"Well, I'll be damned."

Crecy got to her feet at the soft exclamation and ran to look at the box he'd retrieved.

"Oh, perfect!" she said, bouncing on her toes with delight.

"I can't believe it's still here," he said, staring at the box as though it had appeared by magic, or possibly witchcraft, going on the uneasy look he was casting it.

Crecy ignored that and took the box from his hands.

"Move the tea things, please, Gabriel," she said as he followed her back to the table.

Gabriel looked like he was biting his tongue against whatever retort was fighting to get out, but did as she asked. Crecy sat on the floor beside the coffee table and opened the box, getting out the board and remarking on the beauty of the painting and the carved wood teetotums instead of dice - that was too close to gambling to be allowed in a family game. "Come along, then," she said, looking up at him with impatience as he hovered over her.

He glowered some more, indignant and intimidating, a big angry man with a forbidding scowl. "You can't be serious?"

"Perfectly serious, sit down, please," she instructed, ignoring his obvious antipathy towards the idea and patting the floor space beside her.

"On the floor?" He sounded rather outraged now.

Crecy scowled at him. "Well, really, Gabriel. Don't tell me you're too top-lofty to sit on the floor with your friend?"

Gabriel opened and closed his mouth before muttering under his breath and getting to his knees. He cast Crecy a deeply aggravated look as he endeavoured to manoeuvre his large body into a position beside her. He ended up sitting cross legged, arms folded with obvious irritation, and wearing a rather mutinous expression.

Crecy read out the rules to the Game of the Goose while Gabriel muttered, "This is ridiculous," under his breath.

"You're just worried I'll beat you," she said, the words tart as she took the first spin of the teetotum. With a crow of delight, Crecy spun a double six and moved her white goose the twelve places to land on a field with a goose in. "Ha!" she exclaimed, picking her goose up again. "I get to double the number." She moved on to the twenty fourth space, which was over a third of the way around the board. "Your go," she said, turning back to give him a triumphant grin.

Gabriel returned a long-suffering look but picked up the teetotum and spun a one and a three.

"Oh, bad luck," she said, in such an exaggerated manner that it was clear she was taunting him.

Gabriel snorted and picked up the black goose, moving it four spaces.

Crecy took her turn. Another double six. She gave an excited burst of laughter and moved her goose on again. Gabriel narrowed his eyes at her and picked up the teetotum once more. A five and a four made him glower a little, but he moved his piece, looking up at Crecy as she tutted and gave a sad shake of her head.

"Oh, dear," she said with a sigh. "You've landed on the inn."

"So?" he demanded with such suspicion that she had to bite back her laughter.

"Well, it's a very good inn you see," she explained, struggling to keep a straight face as her explanation made him look ever more indignant. "And all that good food and wine has made you sleepy, so you miss a turn."

"That's ridiculous," he growled, staring at her hard. "Are you sure you're not making this up?"

"I'm not!" she retorted, snatching up the sheet of instructions and waving it under his nose. "See for yourself."

Gabriel took the sheet from her, reading it and casting it aside in disgust before he returned to the game, grumbling about the stupid rules the entire time. Crecy spun the teetotum again. Double six. She bit her lip and turned to look at Gabriel with trepidation.

"Are you cheating?" he demanded, looking really rather cross.

"No!" Crecy flushed, feeling rather indignant herself. How dare he? "I would never do such a thing. Besides," she added with a sniff, "there's no need."

Gabriel narrowed his eyes once more. "I've never seen anyone spin three double sixes in a row," he muttered, still sounding suspicious.

"Well, perhaps it's witchcraft," she teased him, widening her eyes and waggling her fingers in a spooky manner. "Or maybe I'm the devil in disguise."

Gabriel snorted. "That, I can believe."

"Yes, I know," she said with perfect seriousness as she moved the goose around the board. "I don't doubt that's exactly what you tell yourself the moment I'm out of your sight."

He fell silent, and she knew she'd struck too close to the truth. He hadn't enough belief in himself to understand why she should want to know him at all. The only explanation he'd understand was that she was up to something.

"Oh, bother."

Gabriel sat up at her despondent tone to look at the board. "Ha!" he exclaimed, not sounding the least bit chivalrous as he noticed that she'd fallen in the well. "You lose two turns."

Over the next ten minutes or so, it dawned on Crecy that Gabriel was rather competitive. She looked up at him, realising that he was utterly absorbed in their silly game, and felt her heart ache that there had never been anyone to be silly and childish with him before.

"Your go," he said, and Crecy returned her attention to the board. They were neck and neck now, each having to spin an exact number to land on field sixty-three and win the game. Crecy bit her lip as the counters hit the board.

"Damn!" she cursed, banging the table top with frustration.

Gabriel gave a bark of delight. "Prison for you, my girl. I told you you'd come to no good."

"Well, there's no need to crow about it," she said with a huff, only to exclaim once more as he made a two and a four and landed neatly on the last field.

"I win!" he said, eyes glittering with triumph.

"Well, really, Gabriel," she said, folding her arms. "I think it positively monstrous of you not to let me win. I am your guest, after all," she added with a pout. She didn't mean it in the least, of course, but she was so enjoying his pleasure in his triumph over her.

"That's what you get for cheating," he said, looking far too smug.

"I did not!" Crecy said, rising to the bait, even though she knew he was teasing her. "You take that back!"

"No," he said, grinning at her in such a fashion that her heart did a strange little leap in her chest, thudding in a rather uneven manner.

"Fine," she said, folding her arms and putting up her chin as she pouted at him. "Then I won't let you kiss me."

He was quiet for a moment, and she refused to look at him, her head turned away in an imperious sulk.

"Yes, you will," he replied, a smooth, dark tone that did something to make her insides feel like they were melting into a puddle. Crecy gave a little sniff and looked back at him.

"Whatever makes you think so?" she demanded in her haughtiest tone.

"Because you've been dying for me to kiss you ever since you got here."

She flushed a little, as it was perfectly true, but held his gaze, arching one eyebrow.

"Then what the devil are you waiting for?"

Chapter 14

"Wherein the winner takes his prize."

Gabriel's expression was unreadable for a moment, and she held herself still, expecting any moment that he should move towards her to take his kiss. But then she saw a rather wicked look creep into his eyes that made her shiver with expectation.

"No," he said, holding her gaze. "I won. I'm the victor. You should kiss me."

Crecy felt desire surge beneath her skin and looked away from him, taking a moment to rearrange her skirts while her heart thudded in her ears. "For someone who didn't want to play, you're awfully proud of yourself."

"And you're a bad loser."

She looked up at him then, scowling a little. "Am not."

Gabriel shrugged.

"Come here, then," she said, hoping to keep the upper hand, as she was feeling hot and nervous and a little like things could get quickly out of control if she wasn't rather more careful than usual. But he just shook his head, a slow back and forth movement as those indigo eyes studied her.

"You wanted to play this game," he said, and suddenly she knew he wasn't talking about the Game of the Goose.

She sucked in a shaky breath and got to her knees, shuffling forward a little towards him. Gabriel never took his eyes from hers, and she wondered why she felt so much less courageous this time. Gabriel held perfectly still. Watching. He didn't move an inch. Didn't lean forward towards her or make it any easier. He was still sitting cross legged, and she moved until her knees bumped against him. She leaned forward then and pressed a brief kiss against his mouth before drawing back.

"Is that it?" he said, amusement glittering in those cool, dark eyes. "Don't tell me you've lost your nerve?"

Crecy wondered if he was right for a moment, but it was only a moment, as his hand reached out and grasped the back of her neck, pulling her back to him. He kissed her this time, and the heat Crecy had felt melting her from the inside out seemed to explode through her veins. She leaned into him, bracing her hands on his wide shoulders as his hands settled on her waist. Gabriel shifted, unlocking his crossed legs and pulling her forward into the space. Crecy tried to move as he wanted, but found her skirts impeded her, and fell forwards against him as they caught under her knees, crashing against him with a startled exclamation.

Gabriel caught her against him, but her weight pushed him back, and she fell with him, lying between his legs in such an intimate manner that her breath caught.

She watched as he regarded her in return, perhaps waiting for her maidenly sensibilities to kick in and for her to scream in outrage. As it was, her breath caught as she felt the evidence of his desire, hard - and a little daunting, truth be told - pressed against the softness of her belly. With more instinct than thought, and without really considering what she was doing, Crecy shifted her weight a little, pressing back against him. Gabriel's breath hitched, and she felt a rather wicked smile curve over her lips as she watched his eyes darken in response.

"Little devil, indeed," he growled before turning, shifting her onto her back in one smooth movement that had his big frame hovering over her. He stared down, watching her with a mixture of curiosity and unease. He was waiting for permission, she realised, and reached up, linking her hands behind his neck and tugging with impatience. His head lowered, then, and captured her mouth, and Crecy was lost in the pleasure of it. Kissing Gabriel was far beyond anything she had ever known, such a combination of contentment, fierce desire, and utter bliss that she quite lost her head the moment his lips touched hers. The desire to know what else there was, what more could be experienced with him, was both a burning need and a quiet terror in her heart.

His mouth left hers, trailing kisses over her jaw and neck, as though she had spoken her desire to learn more aloud. One large hand moved over her, sliding up from her waist to cup her breast. Crecy gasped as pleasure spiked within her, somehow linking the heat of his hand on her breast to somewhere even more intimate. His thumb circled the peak, pinching her a little as he squeezed her nipple through the fabric of her dress. Crecy heard a decadent sound of pleasure in her ears, and it took a moment to realise that it had been her that had made it. She looked up, feeling suddenly bolder as she saw the intense quality of Gabriel's expression, knowing he was just as affected by this as she was. The need in his eyes only made her burn hotter, and she arched beneath his touch as his hand slid lower once more. He moved slowly, too slowly, when she felt instinctively that she knew what his goal was.

"Is this what you've been wanting?" he asked, his voice low and every bit as seductive as his touch. She closed her eyes as his hand slid between her legs, the intimacy of his touch at once stunning and everything she'd known it would be.

"Yes, Gabriel," she said, her voice spoken on a long exhale as pleasure crashed over her like a wave. He kissed her again, his body a weight that would crush her if he allowed it, but now was only a warm solid presence that she clung to like an anchor. Crecy moved beneath his touch, an unfamiliar, impatient feeling thrumming in her blood. Her breath came faster as he caressed her, slow and even, though the feeling it created was demanding, compelling, clamorous in its desire for more.

A low, masculine chuckle rumbled over her, through her as it vibrated from his chest. "Stop chasing it," he scolded, sounding amused as he dropped warm little kisses over her face and neck, over the curve of her breasts as her chest rose and fell with each urgent breath.

"I don't know ..." she began, feeling really quite desperate and unsure of what it was she wanted. "I don't know how ..."

"Yes, you do," he replied, his voice sure and soothing now as his clever fingers continued to caress her through the gown. "Look at me." The voice was a command, if a gentle one, and Crecy looked up, feeling the strangest sensation of security as those usually cold eyes stared down at her with such warmth that she felt it in her bones. "Let go now, I've got you."

And he did.

She knew that he did. Gabriel would not hurt her. Perhaps that was not true for other people, but it was for her, and she trusted in it. Her breath grew faster as that demanding sensation swept her up again; it was the oddest mixture of tension and expectation, the feeling of rushing towards some unseen destination. But Gabriel was with her, the weight of his gaze hot and soothing all at once, and she let go, trusting in him to guide her, and crying out as the force of it took her by surprise.

"So beautiful."

The words were whispered against her skin, so soft and Crecy so lost that she almost missed them, almost didn't hear the reverence with which they were spoken before she was lost in the pleasure that rolled over her in delicious waves, jolting her body like a marionette on strings, quite out of her own control.

Gabriel soothed her, murmuring words that she could not take in, and she knew she would regret not knowing as she felt her body melting into the thick rug beneath her. She felt languid, her bones heavy and unwilling to move, as sleepy as a cat in the sun as she let out a sigh of content.

"Oh, my," she breathed, quite pleased that she'd managed to say anything coherent at all after such an experience. She opened her eyes, feeling a little shy all at once on finding Gabriel staring down at her still. His expression was a little more guarded now, she felt, but she smiled, reaching up to touch his cheek. "Thank you," she murmured, feeling like anything more than that was too great an effort.

Gabriel snorted and shook his head.

"You'll thank me for taking your maidenhead, too, will you?" he asked, and there was once more a harder quality to his voice.

Crecy sighed inwardly, knowing that this would be the way of it with Gabriel. She would win a small victory from time to time, but the war was far from over.

"If it's anything like that, I'll be a puddle at your feet," she retorted, pleased when he gave a sudden burst of laughter. It was all the more pleasing, as it was quite obviously unwilling. He didn't want her to charm him, didn't want to be made to care, she knew this, but she couldn't let him back away.

"You are a strange creature," he said, sounding perplexed, but the words were warmer this time. She smiled at him, reaching up to tug his mouth back to hers once more, but stilled as she heard the grandfather clock chime out in the entrance hall.

"Oh my!" she exclaimed. "I have to get back."

Gabriel glowered a little, shaking his head. "How did I just know you were going to say that?"

She gave him a sympathetic look, pulling him down for a kiss and then shoving him away again when it became clear he wasn't inclined to stop. He grumbled a little, but moved away from her, getting up and helping her to her feet.

"I'm sorry," she said, hoping he could hear from the regret in her voice just how sorry. "I'll make it up to you."

He stilled then, tension running through him.

"You should not come back," he said, and for once the words weren't barked out with anger. "You know where this will lead you."

Crecy wondered if it occurred to him that he didn't have to be the man he'd become any longer, not if he didn't want to, not if he wanted to change badly enough. But she knew it was too soon to try and get him to see that. She could only hope and pray and trust her instincts.

"I know," she said, moving closer and smoothing her hands over his chest. "I've told you before. I don't care. I want to be with you, Gabriel, nothing else."

His face grew colder, his eyes full of mockery. "And what happens when I grow tired of you? What happens when I'm done and you've nowhere to go?"

Crecy jolted, a little shocked by the starkness of his words, which was of course what he intended. He was warning her off by showing her everything she was risking, trying to frighten her away as he did everyone else. But Crecy saw through his threats and knew that, in truth, it was him who was afraid. He was protecting himself because he still didn't trust her. It was incomprehensible to him that he could be reason enough for her to keep coming back. But if she didn't persevere, if she didn't teach him that he was worth loving, then no one would. He'd be forever alone, and he deserved better than that.

She reached up her hand, smoothing her thumb over his mouth, surprised all over again at how soft it was. "Then I shall have to make sure that you never grow tired of me, won't I, Gabriel?" The words were flirtatious, somewhat teasing, even, but she thought he heard the determination there, too. He stared at her, those dark eyes watchful, and then took her hand, pressing his mouth to the palm and kissing it, closing his eyes as he did so. It was such a tender gesture, and so revealing that Crecy caught her breath.

"You'd better go," he said, sounding his usual gruff self as he released her and turned away, the moment gone just as abruptly as it had arrived.

Crecy nodded and moved to retrieve her reticule, and then remembered his Christmas present.

"Oh, I almost forgot," she said, tugging the little drawing out and handing it to him. She blushed a little as he took it, curiosity in his eyes. "Merry Christmas," she added. He stared at it and she studied his face, trying to decipher his reaction, but he seemed to be holding himself very still, and it was impossible to read him.

"It's a good likeness," he said after a while, still looking at the drawing and not at her.

"Well, the best I could do at any rate. It's not much, I suppose, and perhaps … a … a bit presumptuous," she stammered, aware that she was rambling, but feeling foolish all at once. "I wrote on the back," she added, as if that made it any more worthwhile.

He turned it over and she felt like her heart was in his hands as he read the words. She watched, wondering if he would repay her in kind, if he would gift her with some small word of affection or encouragement, but he said nothing. But then his thumb moved over the words, as though touching them with a caress, before he frowned, remembering he was being watched, and tucked the small image into his inside pocket.

"Thank you," he said, looking a little awkward.

"You're welcome."

It was strange, how they could go from such startling intimacy to polite distance in the space of a few moments. Well, he could. She moved closer to him and reached up, kissing him full on the lips.

"Merry Christmas," she said again. "I'll come back as soon as I can."

She walked away from him before he could respond, aware that she'd be horribly late if he returned her kiss, as she hadn't the will power to leave him if he asked her to stay. But he said nothing, just shadowing her as she returned to the hallway. He called for Piper and her things were brought for her. She thanked his butler, who smiled at her and bid her good day as he retreated and left them alone again.

Gabriel watched, his expression intent as she tied her bonnet and did up her buttons. Crecy stood still as he moved forward, knowing that he wanted to rearrange her. She smiled at him as he tweaked the bow under her chin and touched each button in turn, frowning a little as he checked that each one was properly fastened.

"Thank you," she said, aware of the bemused look in his eyes.

"You'll come tomorrow?" he demanded, returning his gaze to her buttons rather than look her in the eyes. She hid her smile, knowing that he wanted her to come and desperately didn't want to admit it.

"Not tomorrow," she said, with real regret, which deepened as she saw his face shutter up again, expecting to be rejected. She reached out and took his hand before he could withdraw completely. "It's Christmas, Gabriel. I won't be able to get away, no matter how much I want to."

He scowled, his face darkening, but then he looked up at her. "I ... I could meet you. If I rode onto Winterbourne's land, to the edge of the woods where it meets the lake at Longwold. It would only take you an hour to get there and back again."

Crecy felt a lump in her throat. He was admitting to wanting to see her, so much that he was prepared to trespass on his despised cousin's land, and even put himself out to do so.

"I don't know what time I can get away," she warned him, praying he'd say it didn't matter. "But I'll find a way, if ... if you don't mind waiting a while?"

Gabriel shrugged as though it mattered little. "I don't have any other pressing engagements tomorrow," he said with a sneer that only served to show Crecy how desperately alone he was. "Besides," he added, sounding his usual gruff self again. "I owe you a gift now, don't I?"

She smiled at him, absurdly charmed despite the gracelessness of his words. "You don't owe me anything, Gabriel. I didn't give it to you to get anything back. I just wanted to make you smile, to make you as happy as you've made me."

He snorted, clearly believing that she was madder than he was.

"It's true," she insisted. She put her hand on his shoulder and kissed his cheek. "I doubt it will be much before four o'clock, but I shall get away as soon as I can, I promise."

He nodded and accompanied her outside to her horse, waving the groom away as he approached with the mounting block, and helping her up himself.

"Take care," he said, the words hard, as though they'd been dragged from him unwillingly.

"I will," she said, accepting them as the gift she knew them to be. "You, too." She blew him a kiss, not caring that the groom was watching with wide eyes, and rode away, feeling as though her heart were floating with the clouds, somewhere way above her head.

Chapter 15

"Wherein something precious is stolen."

That night was torture of a different kind. Gabriel lay in bed, so far from sleep there seemed little point in staying there. But he closed his eyes, pretending he was making the attempt, when really he was indulging in a fantasy. Not that he had thought of anything else all day, not since the moment she had ridden away, blowing him a kiss as she went.

In his mind, they were together again, Crecy laid out on the floor, her eyes on his, trusting in him as he gave her the first taste of the pleasure to be found between a man and a woman. It had been humbling, that trust in him. His body grew taut as it remembered the feel of her body beneath his hand, the soft sounds of her pleasure. Longing swept over him, such need that it overwhelmed him, terrified him. He knew that this was not simply desire, this was not simply an urge to satisfy a base, physical demand. It was about her and her alone. He wanted her with a yearning that threatened to overpower him. Yet he could not deny it, could not push it away or consign it to some dark corner of his mind. It was too strong.

He knew he could have taken everything, right there and then. He could have indulged his desire and she would not have stopped him. But he hadn't. Gabriel refused to dwell on that, refused to study his reasoning. For surely, ruining one of Edward's guests should give him pleasure. Knowing that someone staying under his roof, someone whose family Edward perhaps cared for, had been seduced by him … that should be a small triumph in this war they fought. But he couldn't do that when she said his name and clung to him, giving herself into his hands.

Oh God, this was a madness all of its own.

Although he'd promised himself he would not, he began to imagine what lay beneath the gown she wore, imagined stripping each layer from her and laying her down on his bed, taking her body along with everything else she was offering him.

He groaned in the darkness, so hard it hurt. It had been a long time since he had reached to touch himself. Control over every aspect of his life was the only thing that kept him somewhere close to sane, and no part of his existence was unaffected by that compulsion. But this need was greater still, the burning for her too fierce to be ignored.

It didn't take long, not after spending every moment since she'd left him aching and unsatisfied. He came so hard it shocked him, fear churning in his gut as he realised what power she had over him already. What wouldn't he do to see her again?

Self-loathing washed over him, and he cleaned himself up with disgust. He was weak. A vile creature who had no business touching a young woman like Crecy, much less indulging in sick fantasies of what he wanted to do with her.

But she wants me, she cares for me.

The voice was faint, if hopeful, but he crushed it. There was no point in hoping for such things. She must have a reason for pursuing him, and sooner or later he would discover it. He'd be a fool to believe otherwise, for what in the name of God could she possibly see to care for when she looked at him?

Power? Money?

No.

No.

He would not believe that of her. It wasn't true.

Despite everything, that fragile spark she had lit in his heart refused to be snuffed out, and Gabriel slept at last, dreaming of impossible things.

***

The next morning dragged so slowly, Gabriel thought he really might lose his mind for good. Every half hour found him in front of the large grandfather clock in the entrance hall, checking it against his own watch. This naturally drove him to check every clock in the damn house, even venturing into rooms he hadn't set foot in for years, to wind and set clocks that had long since fallen silent. It passed the time, at least, he thought with an ironic laugh.

As it was, by one o'clock, he was so agitated that he could barely eat, forcing himself to finish his meal, driven by compulsion rather than hunger. By twenty past one, and with no other business to distract him, he could wait no longer, and rode out for Longwold, despite knowing she'd warned him that she would not get away before four, and that he would have a long wait in the freezing cold.

It was a strange feeling, riding through Edward's land, trespassing. He wondered what the man would think if he knew Gabriel was so tangled in Crecy's toils that he'd been driven to sneaking about in such a fashion. The old Gabriel would have flaunted such a conquest, rubbed his cousin's nose in it. Yet he couldn't do that to her.

So instead, he consigned himself to linger in the shadows; that, at least, he was used to, scanning the surrounding countryside and hoping she had understood where he meant to wait for her. Gabriel tethered Typhon, slipping the big horse a lump of sugar as reward for having to stand around in the cold for him. He stroked the creature's heavy neck, realising he'd never before felt any real depth of affection for anyone or anything, other than Typhon. Not until now. And no matter how many times he told himself it was simply a natural masculine desire to get the woman into his bed, yesterday had proved that whatever it was he was feeling, it ran deeper than that.

Gabriel paced, the cold biting harder as the time passed. It was colder still in the shadows of the woods, but he felt conspicuous sitting in the sunshine, even knowing how unlikely it was that anyone but Crecy would come past. They would all be celebrating the day with their families - visiting church, eating together, exchanging gifts.

Heat crawled up his neck as he reached for the small parcel in his pocket, his gift to her. He had spent forever dithering over what to give her. His first instinct had been jewellery, something expensive and beautiful, but at short notice, all he had was his mother's jewellery and for some reason, that didn't sit well with him. When he gave her jewellery, it would be for her alone. Not something passed from a woman who had been so unhappy in life. The idea that this - whatever this was - would continue and he was thinking of buying her jewellery in the future was something he refused to dwell on. Instead, he wondered for the hundredth time if he had been foolish in his choice, if she would laugh at the idea. He wouldn't blame her, but … but some instinct had guided him that it would be what she'd prefer.

It was four-thirty when he caught movement on the horizon, and he was startled by the way his heart seemed to leap in his chest. The sun was getting low, the day already growing gloomy, and he knew they would not have long. At least there was a clear sky and a full moon to help guide her home again.

Gabriel watched as she rode towards him, the horse galloping flat out and Crecy urging the creature on. He felt an unfamiliar surge of pride in her; she was quite a horsewoman, and utterly fearless. She'd have to be in order to spend time with him, after all. He felt the strangest desire to smile at the idea, an urge which only grew as she brought her horse to stand in front of him, launching herself from the saddle into his arms.

"Gabriel!" she cried, hugging him tightly.

Gabriel pulled her close, finding he couldn't speak, not yet, he was too consumed by the feeling of her in his arms.

"I was afraid you would have gone," she admitted as he looked down at her, taking in the flush in her cheeks, the sparkle in her lovely eyes. By God, but she was beautiful.

"I said I would wait for you." He knew the words sounded gruff and ungracious, but she didn't seem to care, reaching up and peppering his cheek with kisses.

"Thank you, thank you, dearest Gabriel," she said, burying her face against his chest and holding tight. "I couldn't bear to be another moment without seeing you."

His breath caught despite his best efforts. How did she say things of that nature with such ease? Was it because it was untrue, perhaps, or was it simply like breathing to her, to give her feelings to another without a second thought?

Gabriel had the sudden desire to tell her that he had longed to see her, too, but he knew the words were beyond him. Instead, he swept her up into his arms, earning himself a startled shriek of laughter as he carried her, and then another kiss on his cheek as she wrapped her arms around his neck.

"Are you going to carry me away to your lair and eat me, Mr Wolf?" she said, her voice low and breathless in his ear.

Gabriel snorted. "Don't tempt me," he muttered, wondering if she had the slightest idea how close he was to doing just that.

"But I want to tempt you." The words curled around him, sliding over his skin like a caress and making his body grow impossibly hard.

No. He would not take advantage of her in the freezing cold, on Winterbourne's land, for the love of God. No. No matter how much he wanted her.

Instead, he carried her to the large stump of a felled tree and sat down, arranging her on his lap and luxuriating in the feel of her in his arms.

Crecy sighed, smiling down at him. "I so wished you were with me today," she said, holding his face between her hands and stroking his cheeks. "The mummers came this morning, and it was the funniest thing, Gabriel. You would have laughed so. I think the dragon had been exceedingly well lubricated by the previous wassail cups," she said, the delight in her eyes at telling him her tale quite visible. "He barely made it to the end of the performance. I think he passed out just at the moment he was supposed to be slain, the timing was impeccable." She laughed, everything about her vivacious and alive and so full of joy. Being with her was like a kind of drug, a high which he could only reach in her presence. He had no idea how to do it by himself, but with her … he felt perhaps it was possible to … to know what it was to be happy.

"It sounds as though you had an enjoyable day," he said, wishing there hadn't been such obvious reproach in his voice. Why should she not have fun without him? God alone knew she'd not get it with him.

She paused, stroking his cheek again, staring into his eyes in a way that made him feel exposed, like his soul was laid out for her inspection. He closed his eyes, turning his face into her hand, and she sighed, pulling his head against her until it rested against her chest.

Gabriel could hear her heart beating beneath the softness of her breast, could feel her hands stroking his hair, and had the absurd desire to never want to move from this position again.

"I have thought of nothing but you since the moment I woke," she said. "I even dreamed of you." Her words were hypnotic, drawing him further under her spell even as the dark voice in his head scoffed at the idea, refusing to believe she could be as desperate for him as he was for her. "I could think of nothing else but how it felt to be with you, of how it felt when you touched me."

"Stop it," he said, his voice harsh as he pulled away from her with regret, but God in heaven, didn't she know what she was doing to him?

"But it's true," she insisted, her lovely face frowning now as she spoke. "I ... I have barely been able to concentrate on a thing, and ..." He looked up with interest now, aware that she was blushing deeply.

"And?" he pressed, feeling rather breathless all of a sudden, needing to know if she felt as frenzied and out of control as he did, wanting to hear the words so badly that he wanted to shake them from her.

"And ... I ache, Gabriel," she whispered, the words hesitant as he held his breath, the strangest sensation burning in his chest, expanding and filling him up as desire leapt like a flame beneath his skin. "I feel ... impatient and..." She stopped again, and he looked up at her, seeing the confusion in her eyes, the desire to explain it to him. "It's like ..."

He felt like he might die of impatience himself, waiting for the words to come. "It's like...?" he repeated, his voice rough and sounding rather desperate now, as something that might have been joy unfurled in the barren landscape of his heart.

"Like I need you, need to touch you to ... to be whole again," she said, the words raw and honest and the greatest gift that anyone had ever given him.

"Yes," he said, the word every bit as raw as her own, wrenched from him before he could consider the implications. "Yes, exactly that."

He kissed her, then, and she met him with all the passion he had heard in her words, clutching at him, wanting them to be closer than the cold and too many layers of clothes would allow for. Sanity of a kind reasserted itself before Gabriel was too lost in desire to think about the fact that it would soon be dark and that she was shivering with the cold already.

"You're freezing," he said, shrugging out of his coat and wrapping it around her.

"No," she objected, putting it back over his shoulders, but then burying beneath the folds of it. "I'm not cold," she objected as he raised an eyebrow at her.

"You're shivering."

"Not from the cold," she said with a rather devilish smile.

Gabriel groaned, the situation not helped as she wriggled on his lap, trying to get closer to him. "Crecy, sit still, you little wretch, you're killing me."

Her laughter was a delighted and rather naughty sound that made his heart lift, and he felt suddenly absurdly happy. She had laid her head on his shoulder now, her bonnet long since abandoned and her curls tickling his neck. One arm was behind his back, under his coat, and the other toyed with the buttons on his waistcoat.

"I'll come early tomorrow," she said, and he turned his attention from her fingers on his chest and back to her face.

"You will?" he asked, anticipation at seeing her again so soon making him quite unable to disguise his impatience.

She nodded, smiling. "I'll spend the day with you. I can pretend I went too far and got lost. It wouldn't be the first time," she added with a chuckle.

"You got lost?" he demanded, the idea of her riding these hills in the dark and freezing temperatures of the night clutching at his heart and making terror roll over him. "When?"

Crecy paused, apparently aware of his concern from the warmth that lit her eyes. "The first time I came to you," she said, her voice soothing. "Don't worry, I know my way now. It won't happen again."

Gabriel looked up and noticed with regret that the sun was sinking fast now.

"You must go," he said, though it was the last thing he wanted. He would have stayed with her here, in the cold and the dark all night if he could, and wasn't that just bloody ridiculous?

"I'm not going yet," she said, shaking her head and looking rather defiant.

"Oh?" he growled, torn between delight that perhaps she didn't want to leave him, either, and the desire for her to get home to Longwold before darkness fell.

She pouted at him, and he gasped as a cold hand slid inside his shirt. He glanced down, realising that she had undone the buttons on his waistcoat while they were talking and found the gap in his shirt to slide her hand though.

"Crecy," he said, his breathing uneven as her fingers slid over his chest and found his nipple. She caressed it and then gave it an experimental little pinch, rather like he had done to her. "Don't!" He snatched her hand away, regretting the anger of his outburst as she jumped in shock, but he was terrified that his self-control would not last much longer. "You can't tease me like that," he said, trying to keep the words from sounding so harsh. "Not unless you want to find yourself on the frozen ground with your skirts around your neck." The words were crude, perhaps, but he needed her to be aware of what she toyed with, yet when he looked up, all he could see was a blazing desire that matched his own.

"Oh God."

He got to his feet, letting her slide from his lap.

"Go home," he instructed, dragging a shaky hand through his hair and wondering what would happen tomorrow if they really were to spend the day together. He didn't think he could take much more of this torment.

"No, not yet," she said, stubborn little devil that she was.

"Why not?" he demanded, unable to resist as her hands slid around him once more.

"Because you promised me a Christmas present," she said, putting on a sulky tone and looking up at him with big eyes.

He snorted, refusing to consider how it made him feel to have someone to tease him, to play these ridiculous games. "So I did." He felt nervous again, wondering if he should have brought jewellery after all, something expensive. That's what women expected, after all. Wasn't it?

"Well?" she demanded. "If you don't give it to me, I shall have to search you. I know you've brought me something." True to her word, her hands began to roam over him, dipping into pockets and tickling him as they went. Gabriel gave a bark of startled laughter as her hand deliberately quested under his armpit and he picked her up, dumping her a foot away from him and holding one hand out to stop her.

"Behave," he warned, scowling at her, though, somehow, it was an effort to do so now. "I'll only give it to you if you keep still."

Crecy folded her arms with a huff, but did as he commanded, and Gabriel reached into his pocket. He withdrew the little parcel, suddenly plagued with doubt.

"It ... it isn't much, I mean ..." Before he could say anything further, she had snatched it from his hands with a delighted whoop and begun to undo it.

Gabriel stilled as she looked inside, waiting for her to scowl and look up at him with an indignant expression at the admittedly whimsical gift.

Instead, she beamed at him, eyes glittering a little too brightly as she held the lock of his black hair to her lips and kissed it.

"Thank you," she whispered, and then ran to him, wrapping her arms around him again.

"I should have given you jewellery, something pretty," he said, his voice gruff and laced with regret, but she shook her head.

"I wouldn't have been able to wear it," she said, with no trace of condemnation, though he winced inwardly as the reason for that was obvious. "But this …" She looked up at him and gave him a smile that hit him square in the chest. "I shall keep this close to my heart." Good as her word, she undid her pelisse, and Gabriel watched with his heart thundering in his ears as she tucked it beneath the bodice of her gown, against her breast.

Gabriel hauled her back to him again, wanting nothing more but to slip his hand under her gown and hunt for his gift again. It took every bit of his iron self-control to stop it from happening.

He let her go, savouring her sigh of content and the dreamy look in her eyes as she smiled up at him.

"Lovely," she whispered. "I shall sleep with it right where I put it, you know," she added, an amused lilt to her voice that implied she well knew she was tormenting him.

Gabriel groaned, burying his face in her hair. "Don't push your luck," he grumbled as she chuckled. He busied himself with doing up her buttons, trying to keep his thoughts from the warm place his gift had been hidden.

"Gabriel," she said, her voice soft as she watched him trace a finger over each button in turn, checking it was fastened properly. "I have a confession to make." Though good sense told him she was still teasing, the words made his blood run cold. He looked up, regarding her with his heart thudding again, but this time it was a sickening feeling.

"Oh?" The word was hard and suspicious, and covered up the terror that was rolling over him, but Crecy only nodded.

"Yes," she said, amusement lingering in her eyes. "I'm afraid I stole something from you?"

Gabriel let go of a breath he didn't realise he'd been holding. He didn't care what she'd taken, she could have anything she liked. Anything.

He reached down, his fingers grasping her chin, trying to keep his expression grave, and failing, too relieved that it was only theft and nothing that would hurt him. "Oh? And what was that, my little villain?"

"A black velvet ribbon." She tugged at his hair, grinning at him. "I stole it from you the first time we ever met. Do you remember, by the lake?"

For a moment, he struggled to recall it, that strange child and this extraordinary young woman had seemed separate things in his mind. It was bizarre to think that it was really the same girl. "I remember," he said, wondering at how different he sounded when he spoke to her now.

"I've kept it with me always. It's my bookmark," she admitted, blushing a little.

Gabriel found there were no words he could say, and, at a loss, simply pressed his lips to hers once more.

"Go home, little thief," he said with his forehead pressed against her. The words were still gruff, but far softer than anything he'd said before. "I'll be waiting for you to return."

Chapter 16

"Wherein chances are taken on all sides."

Crecy awoke at some ridiculous hour of the morning, the darkness surrounding her like a blanket. She was hot, her skin tingling and over-sensitive, and it didn't take her long to realise she'd been dreaming about Gabriel. With a sigh of despair, she knew that any chance of sleep had long gone. Reaching inside the bodice of her nightgown, she withdrew the lock of his hair. It was warm from its position close to her heart, and she trailed the silky strands back and forth against her lips, eliciting a shiver of desire.

The idea of spending the day with him tomorrow was as delicious as it was nerve-racking. She knew that both of them were on the edge of what could be endured. She wanted him so badly that she could hardly think of anything past what it would be like to lie with him, to feel his skin against hers. The idea brought a wave of heat and desire crashing down on her, and she groaned, muffling the sound in her pillow with despair.

Trying to turn her mind from such heated thoughts, she considered other matters. At the Christmas dinner last night, Belle had interrogated everyone about what charms they'd received in the Christmas pudding. To Crecy's delight, Edward had received an anchor. It seemed the perfect end to her sister's eventful Christmas, for surely Edward had found his safe harbour. The adoration that was now so obvious to see between them gladdened Crecy's heart, but only made her long all the more for Gabriel.

She slipped her hand under her pillow and took out the charms she'd found in the pudding herself. A shoe for travel, and a thimble - another year single. She swallowed, knowing what it was telling her, yet torn between desperate excitement and abject terror. Could she really do it? Could she run away with him, forever cut herself off from polite society ... bring shame upon her sister?

Yes.

Yes.

The answer was dreadful and shocking and so inevitable that she didn't bother considering any other option. She had always known this was how it would go, after all. Gabriel had warned her often enough, as if she hadn't figured it out for herself a very long time ago. If she wanted him, she would have to prove that she was prepared to give everything up, that he was worth more to her than her reputation, than a world where people wouldn't gossip about her, than her own flesh and blood. But it was the only way he would ever accept that he was worth anything at all, let alone being loved. She would have to trust in him and risk everything, or she'd lose any chance she'd ever had.

The idea that there was a lie that sat between them even now, threatening everything she had dreamed of, made a knot tighten in her belly, though, and a rolling shiver of cold washed over her. She felt hot and cold and clammy all at once, for she had still not admitted to him that her sister had married his cousin, that she was now a member of the Winterbourne family. She was too afraid. Everything between them was too new and fresh and fragile, and she didn't dare risk the anger that she felt would arise when he discovered it. But he would, sooner or later, he would, and if she didn't tell him herself, he would think the worse of her. She must tell him, before anyone else did.

***

The next morning, Crecy got away early as she'd promised. Gabriel was waiting for her, Typhon thundering beside her as they raced back to Damerel. Crecy whooped from the sheer joy of being alive, of riding hard and fast with the man she loved at her side, him casting her looks that made her skin heat as they rode neck and neck together.

He was laughing as he pulled her down from her horse, the sound of it so extraordinary that Crecy felt her eyes fill with tears as she tumbled into his arms.

"And what have you come to steal today, little thief?" he demanded, the words hard and harsh, though there was warmth and a glittering amusement in his eyes.

"Nothing less than your heart, my lord," she said, the words whispered back to him. He stilled, and she felt the tension singing through his body and wondered if she'd said too much. He leaned down, giving her a brief kiss, but his expression was grave now.

"You can't steal what has never existed," he said, taking her hand and leading her indoors.

Crecy smiled despite the sadness she felt at his words. The idea that he had no heart was so ridiculous to her that she wanted to rage against it, to shout at him for even thinking it. But she said nothing, not yet. She would prove it to him, sooner or later.

Piper greeted them, and Crecy saw warmth in the old man's eyes as he took her coat, but there was something else, too, worry - worry for her. He knew the risks that she was taking, just as she did. She returned a smile, wondering if he could tell what she tried to convey with her expression. Perhaps he knew what she was doing and understood her desire to save Gabriel, to love him, or at least realised that she took these risks with her eyes wide open.

Gabriel led her to the parlour and she laughed, delighted as she saw the Game of the Goose had been set up ready to play.

"Ha! I knew you enjoyed it," she taunted, clapping her hands and bouncing on her toes.

Gabriel snorted, shaking his head. "No such thing," he said, denying the obvious with a cool tone. "I'm merely indulging your foolish notions of entertainment and giving you the chance to try and beat me again."

Crecy stuck her tongue out at him, more pleased by his attempt to make her happy than she dared express. She wanted to tell him she loved him, loved him with all her heart, that she would do anything he wanted if he would only keep her near to him. She knew better than to say the words, though.

He watched her as she sat on the floor beside the board, standing with his hands clasped behind his back and still looking a little awkward, despite the fact that it had been his idea. Crecy smiled and reached out her hand to him. After a moment's hesitation, he moved forward and took it, and she gave his arm a little tug. With a sigh, he sat on the floor beside her and Crecy thought her heart might actually melt at seeing him do so, simply to please her.

They played twice, Crecy winning the first round and Gabriel the second. There was tension between them, though, and Crecy could feel it grow as each game progressed. They both knew this was merely an interlude and that what came next would change everything. Anticipation and fear mingled in her blood, making her blush easily and stammer some of her words as her nerves leapt beneath her skin. Every time his hand brushed hers or he cast her a look from those dark blue eyes, a shiver ran over her and it was all she could do to concentrate on the game at all.

They both looked up as there was a knock at the parlour door, and Piper informed them that lunch was ready.

Gabriel nodded and began to pack the game away as Crecy watched him. Each piece was put carefully in place and checked several times over.

"Can I help you?" she asked, curious as to how this compulsion to check and recheck affected him.

"No." The word was hard and a little sharp, and he paused with his hand over the box. He glanced up at Crecy and then back to the game, putting the counter in place. "No, thank you," he amended, and Crecy's heart squeezed in her chest.

Gabriel put the box away and then sat down as Crecy stood, getting out his watch. Crecy looked at him in surprise, expecting them to go into lunch now. He cast her an uncomfortable look, frowning a little. "It isn't one o'clock yet," he said, showing her his watch, which read three minutes to the hour. She thought he looked faintly embarrassed despite the scowl, which she suspected served to cover up his discomfort.

Crecy put out her hand and he looked at her with suspicion before he took it. She tugged a little and Gabriel got to his feet, looking reluctant.

"Come along," she said, her voice soft but firm as she led him from the room. Crecy could feel his unwillingness to follow her; the tension practically vibrated down his arm, and she saw the anxious looks he cast the grandfather clock as he crossed the entrance hall to the dining room. By the time they stood on the threshold, he looked like he wanted to be sick. Crecy stepped in, watching the desperation to yank her from the room flicker in his eyes. She held out both hands to him. "Nothing bad will happen, Gabriel, I promise."

He looked down at her hands but didn't move, so she reached out and took his, pulling a little, though he didn't budge.

"Please," she said, staring into his eyes and willing him to trust her. "For me."

With obvious resistance, and looking like he was going to be seriously unwell at any moment, Gabriel stepped into the room. Crecy beamed at him, throwing her hands around his neck and kissing him hard.

"See, nothing bad," she whispered. The clock chimed a moment later and Gabriel exhaled.

Once he had arranged the table, Gabriel seemed to relax a little. Crecy had not pushed him to stop, or to leave things as they were. She sensed that he had already made a big effort in his attempts to please her today, and she did not take that lightly. If she wanted him, wanted to understand and help him, she would need to be patient. So she smiled as he poured her wine, and they began their meal.

After the cold meat had gone, Gabriel cut her three pieces of cheese before putting three identical pieces on his own plate. They had eaten in silence so far, which Crecy hadn't minded in the least. She was often silent herself, lost in her own thoughts, so she never begrudged it in anyone else. Now, however, she looked up as Gabriel cleared his throat.

"Did ... did you have a nice Christmas?" he asked, looking faintly nauseated. Crecy bit back a smile with difficulty and reached out, covering his hand.

"You don't need to do that," she said, curling her fingers around his. "I know you don't like small talk, and I have no need of it." She smiled at him, then, squeezing his hand a little. "You can tell me anything, Gabriel, speak about anything you wish to, whenever you want to. But you do not need to speak if you don't want to. I am happier to be silent with you than to be sat talking about anything to anyone else."

He let out a breath, frowning at his plate. "I don't understand you," he said, his gravelly tone sounding so utterly perplexed that she couldn't help but laugh a little.

"I know," she said as he looked up at her. "We shall just have to do our best to understand each other, to learn how to make each other happy."

He snorted, sounding revolted by the idea but there was curiosity in his eyes all the same.

"You've done a wonderful job so far," she added, watching that curiosity morph into something that might have been pleasure, but he looked away too quickly to be sure. Gabriel withdrew his hand and they finished their meal in silence.

***

A letter arrived for Gabriel after lunch, and Crecy followed him into his study, looking around the room as he wrote a reply. She could hear the scratch of his quill as he wrote, but felt his eyes on her all the same. There were many artworks in the room, mostly small pieces, but of exquisite quality. This room seemed the only one in the house which truly belonged to him, though she hadn't seen his bedroom yet, of course. The thought sent a jolt rushing through her and a blush to her cheeks, and she turned away from him to study the bookshelves so that he couldn't see it.

"No de Sade," he said, sounding amused. She turned back, but he was looking down, sealing the wax on the letter with his ring.

"Not on display, at any rate," she retorted, earning herself a low chuckle that did something strange to her insides.

"True enough," he said, leaving the letter in the exact centre of his desk before getting up. "Would you like me to show you where they are?"

He moved towards her, an intensity in his eyes that made her heart feel as though it were skipping in her chest. Crecy swallowed and reminded herself that she had made her choice long ago; there was nothing more to consider.

"Yes, please," she replied, holding his gaze. He paused in front of her, staring at her as though weighing her determination, waiting for the moment she ran from him. *I'm not going anywhere, Gabriel.* She wondered if he could see her answer reflected in her eyes, but, just in case, she took his hand and raised it to her lips.

Gabriel cupped her face, his expression troubled.

"You should run from me." There was no inflection to his voice, no force or anger or judgement, just a flat statement of the facts.

"I can't," she said, turning her face into his hand and kissing his palm again as she held his gaze. "I won't." She moved forward until their bodies touched. "I don't want to be anywhere else."

He leaned down, pressing a soft kiss against her mouth, so sweet and tender that she could only smile as he moved away, looking a little anxious.

"Show me these scandalous books," she urged, feeling like she'd won a huge victory as a smile tugged up one corner of his mouth.

"You have a one-track mind, you dreadful creature."

Crecy nodded, her expression solemn. "I know," she said, following that with a dramatic sigh as he led her from the room.

Despite knowing that this was what she wanted, what she dreamed of and longed for, despite knowing that there was no other way … Crecy was still sick with nerves as she climbed the stairs in Gabriel's wake. But soon enough, they were stood before a bedroom door, one she had not seen behind before.

"Is this your room, Gabriel?" she asked, hearing the breathless quality of her own voice.

"It is."

Crecy swallowed, staring at the door for a moment and knowing that she was about to leave behind any possibility of the kind of life her sister had dreamed of for her. She looked up at Gabriel, finding him staring at her in turn, his gaze cautious, watchful.

"Well, are you going to let me in, then?" she asked, hoping she sounded as confident and determined as she'd hoped, and not like she was trembling, which was much closer to the truth.

He regarded her for a moment longer before reaching forward and allowing the door to swing open. He waited, then, and she knew that stepping inside was going to be entirely her decision, he would not encourage her.

So Crecy took a breath and stepped into the room.

Chapter 17

"Wherein love is mentioned."

Gabriel watched as Crecy walked into his room, and tried to tamp down on the unruly emotions surging through him. At every moment since she had arrived, he had waited for her to change her mind, to tell him that if he wanted her they must be married or that he must give her whatever financial amount she had decided she was worth for a *carte blanche*.

Loathing hit him like a wave as she stepped into the room, putting herself totally into his care. How could he have believed it of her? Yet it was too extraordinary. What in the name of God did she see in him? Why was she here? As if she'd heard the thoughts in his head, she glanced around, then, the look in her eyes so loving and full of trust that his breath caught. It was impossible. Ridiculous and impossible. Yet the spark of hope that she had lit within him flamed, a rush of warmth beneath his skin, the like of which he had never before known.

She moved towards the bed, one hand trailing around the heavily carved wood of one of the four posts.

"I don't see any books?" she said, a teasing tone to her voice that made him want to give in to a smile.

He looked away, for some reason unwilling to let her know that she made him want to smile. For if she knew that, she might realise how tightly he was caught up in the spell she had cast over him. She might know that losing her had become something he feared more than any other sensation of dread that he had ever known, even as its inevitability loomed over him, stealing his breath.

He moved to a large glass-fronted cabinet, which was lined with red silk to protect the books inside from the daylight. Gabriel unlocked it and opened the doors, which swung back to show some of his collection. In fact, there were many more, but his favourites resided here, along with those that were shocking enough that he preferred the staff didn't stumble across them by accident.

He didn't turn, but knew that Crecy had come to stand beside him.

"Did you think I'd lied to get you up here?" he asked, immediately regretting the accusation behind the words. He hadn't meant to sound so aggressive; it was simply a hard habit to break.

"Of course not." Her voice was soothing, smoothing down any anxieties as she laid her hand on his arm. "I don't really want to see the books, anyway, Gabriel." Her admission was quiet, her voice trembling a little, and any suspicions or cynicism that remained melted away as he realised that she was dreadfully nervous.

He frowned, turning a little to look down at her, but finding he could not meet her eyes. "Are you afraid of me?" he asked, hardly daring to hear the answer, but holding himself very still. He forced himself to look her in the eyes, and the smile that dawned over her face made his breath catch.

"Don't be silly," she said, and once again the realisation that she trusted him hit him hard and fast. It was on the tip of his tongue to tell her she was a bloody fool, that it wasn't worth it, *he* wasn't worth it. But he was a miserable, selfish bastard, and he wanted her so badly that he wasn't altogether sure he wasn't trembling with nerves, too.

He reached out a hand, touching her cheek.

"I won't hurt you," he said, cursing himself as the words sounded harsh and impatient rather than reassuring. But nonetheless, she stepped closer to him.

"I know that."

Gabriel swallowed, panic sliding over him as he realised he didn't know what the hell to do now. His body was well aware what came next and was clamouring that he bloody well get on with it, but this was different. For starters, he'd never been with an innocent before. The women he favoured knew well what they were about and what they'd get if they dallied with him. He was neither tender nor kind. Exchanges were harsh and crude, as fast as he could manage, and totally impersonal. He didn't want names, didn't want to know anything about them, and he certainly didn't hang around after the act itself was done. The idea of cuddling some woman after sex had always appalled him. He'd never cuddled anyone in his life, for the love of God. He was simply not the kind of man young women fell in love with, dammit.

But this was Crecy, and she trusted him.

Before he could give himself a stern talking-to and demand he *get a grip, you damn fool,* Crecy had taken his hand and was leading him to the bed.

Gabriel dug his heels in. This was the outside of enough. He was *not* going to be seduced by a virgin. His ego was fragile enough without adding that to his list of failures. He could hear his father's mocking laughter and forced it away with an effort. No. Not here. *This is mine.*

"Gabriel?" Crecy's voice was quiet and unsure of itself, and he hated to hear it so. Crecy was nothing but vibrancy and determination and everything good in life.

"Sorry," he said, the word sounding awkward and rusty on his lips. "I ..." He let out a breath with the slightest huff of laughter. "This is ..."

"You don't normally bed virgins," she said, cutting to the heart of thing as she so often did.

He looked down at her and saw the trepidation in her eyes, the fear that he didn't desire her in this way, and wanted to cut his own heart out for putting that doubt there.

"No," he said, trying to keep his voice softer. He tugged at her hand and she moved back to him. "I don't know how to be what you want me to be." The admission was honest, at least, he owed her that much. "But if you are thinking that I don't want you ..." He put his free hand to her waist, pulling her close, pressing her body hard against his so that his arousal was blatantly obvious to her. She looked up, eyes dark with wanting, and he captured her mouth, his arms holding her tight, too tight, probably, he realised. He eased his grip a little, pulling back as Crecy clutched at his shoulders.

"You are exactly what I want you to be, Gabriel," she said, her voice fierce now, any trace of anxiety or timidity suddenly vanishing. "Don't, I beg you, try to be anything else."

He took her at her word, too desperate to taste her again to hold back, in any case. By the time he felt able to let her go, she was flushed and breathing hard. The lush swell of her breasts pushed against the confinement of her clothes, and he could not wait any longer. He needed her naked and in his bed, and he needed it right now.

Gabriel put his hands on her shoulders, turning her around so that the ties to her dress were before him. He tugged each one in turn, trying not to rush, not to be impatient, but finding himself cursing under his breath as one caught in a knot. He was all fingers and thumbs, and by the time the dress slithered to the ground, he was breathless with impatience and desire. A strange and not altogether welcome surge of possessiveness swept over him, shocking him rather as she withdrew the lock of his hair from under her bodice and gave it to him to put to one side. The rest of her underclothes were summarily disposed of, no seductive unveiling here, he thought with a grimace, and then he looked at the prize he'd finally managed to unwrap.

Crecy turned back to him, eyes downcast, shivering a little, her arms clutched around herself.

Gabriel caught his breath, feeling himself at one and the same time to be the worst kind of monster and the luckiest man on the planet. He wanted to tell her that. He wanted to explain that he had never seen anything so beautiful as her, that he was humbled, honoured, that he would kneel at her feet if she demanded it, but no words came.

Instead, he reached out a hand, tracing a finger along the soft curve of her cheek as she looked up at him.

"Come here." His voice was rough and scratchy, so taut with desire it was a wonder he'd managed to say that much, and when she did as he'd asked, any possibility of saying more vanished.

He kissed her, his hands sliding over skin, finer than any silk, warm and soft and giving and ... *his*. It was easier than he'd imagined after all, to treat her with reverence. He wouldn't hurt her, it was impossible, he could not. His lips brushed over hers, toying a little with her tongue, the movements soft, delicate, as he held back his own desire with a will of iron. How strange, he thought, for he'd never enjoyed kissing before, and avoided it. It had always seemed an unpleasant intimacy, too messy and unrewarding, but no longer. Her mouth was so sweet, so welcoming, and the soft sounds she made as his hands explored and stroked were enough to set him alight.

Gabriel drew back, knowing even his encompassing need for control could not hold back his own desire for much longer. He led her to the bed, taking a moment to strip the covers back before kissing her once more.

"Lay down," he said, the words breathed against her mouth. This time, at least, the words had been gentle. She did as he asked, lying down on the white cotton as Gabriel shrugged out of his jacket. Usually, everything had to be carefully put away, folded or hung up, but his desire outweighed his need for order in this moment, and he contented himself with hanging his jacket on the back of a chair and throwing each remaining item on top of it.

His mouth grew dry as Crecy sat up, watching him with obvious interest as he undressed. To his surprise, and as something of a boost to his masculine pride, her eyes grew wide and round as a slow smile curved over her lush mouth.

"Oh, my," she said, looking him over with such obvious desire that Gabriel wondered how the hell he was going to last long enough to make her first time painless. He wasn't sure he could wait. He wanted only to find his place inside her and claim her as his own, with no provision for tenderness or patience. He needed and he wanted like he'd never known before, had never come close to, and he didn't think he could hold that back.

Yet as he lay down beside her and was welcomed into her arms, with no hesitation, no reserve or false blushes, he was aware that he still wanted to be tender.

Crecy reached out, touching a tentative hand to his chest. Her fingers trailed through the coarse dark hair, and then she surprised him by pressing her face against his chest, kissing him and rubbing her head against him like a cat. He grinned, the unfamiliar upwards kick of his mouth feeling less strange than usual. Much more of this, and he might even become used to it.

"Gabriel," she said, the smile behind his name almost visible even before she looked up at him. "You're so ..."

Gabriel quirked one eyebrow, waiting for what on earth the dreadful creature would say next.

"Big."

A guffaw of laughter caught him unawares, as her wide eyes made him laugh until his shoulders shook.

Crecy flushed, though her eyes sparkled with amusement. "I didn't mean *there,*" she scolded him, her voice tart. "I meant ..." She waved her hand to encompass the whole package as Gabriel struggled to rearrange his face. "Everywhere else."

"Oh?" he said, hearing the teasing tone to his own voice and not recognising it at all. "Is *that* part of the package not up to expectations, then?" he demanded as her cheeks went a quite remarkable shade of scarlet.

"Now, you're just being crude," she said, pursing her lips and looking a little indignant.

"Yes," he murmured, catching hold of her hand. "I am, and I will be. Do you mind?"

"Of course not," she replied without hesitation, mischief glittering in her eyes.

Gabriel stared, a strange feeling growing and expanding in his chest as he gazed at her. "Just as well," he said with a smirk as he guided her hand to the part of him that was most desperate for her attention. His breath caught as her fingers wrapped around him and he guided her as to how to touch him.

"Certainly meeting expectations so far," she murmured, eyes wider still, and Gabriel found himself smiling against her skin. He'd never done this before, never enjoyed a woman's company for any other reason than the obvious, and it was new and strange, and he didn't know quite what to expect of her next. He kissed her, deciding that he was safer if he kept her quiet, preferably speechless, as right now his heart felt unguarded and most definitely at risk. He took her hand from his flesh, interrupting her intimate caresses with regret, but it was too distracting, in any case. It made him want to seek his own pleasure instead of seeing to hers, and he was damned if she'd leave his bed with the ability to walk a straight line, let alone string a coherent sentence together.

He kissed a trail down her neck, wondering at her boldness as she tilted her head back, her hands tangling in his hair as he nuzzled the soft valley between her breasts. One hand continued down, smoothing over the soft curves of her waist and hip, caressing her thigh as his mouth captured one delicate, pebbled nipple. Her husky cry sent a jolt of desire through him, his body taut and aching with need as she arched beneath him.

Gabriel dared a glance up, catching her eyes and seeing such emotion there that he was forced to look away. He couldn't believe in that look, it was too … It was impossible. Wasn't it?

He returned his attention to the physical; that, at least, he could manage. Though somehow, the physical and emotional had become tangled up and were impossible to keep apart. The harder he tried to hold something of himself back and concentrate on wringing those soft, feminine cries from her lips, the harder it became not to realise that he worshipped this strange, wonderful, extraordinary woman.

Sliding one hand between her thighs as he caressed her, he remembered the first time he had done this, with far too much clothing between them. Not a problem now, though, as he slid one finger inside her, hearing her gasp of shock and wondering if he'd gone too fast. Crecy was always ahead of him, though, and merely opened herself to him further as he spiralled out of control.

Urging her legs further apart, he took his place there, he couldn't do this, couldn't wait any longer. He wondered then if she would hate him for it, for not taking more care, and began to move away again, but she wrapped her legs around him, pulling him towards her.

"Yes, yes, please, Gabriel. I want you … like this."

He stared down at her, seeing his own need reflected in hers and wondering at it, but she urged him on, gasping with pleasure as he nudged inside of her.

Her murmured words came faster and less comprehensible as he sank deeper, feeling her hands grasping at his shoulders, holding onto him. He tried to slow, aware that he was about to hurt her, after promising he wouldn't. Even though every instinct demanded that he sink into her now, this minute, he held himself back, easing into her with care.

"It's all right," she said, stroking his back, and he looked down, startled to be the one receiving assurances. "Don't stop, Gabriel," she begged. "I want you."

There was simply no way of denying her, even as her words slid under his skin and he realised just what danger he was in. As he sank into her, soothing her past the sharp intake of breath as he took her innocence, he was welcomed into her warmth. She gave him everything she had with no demands, no ultimatums, and he realised that there would never be another like this. There would never be anyone who made him feel this way, who accepted him and made him feel ... whole. He gasped, desire and emotion overwhelming him. Somewhere in the distance, fear was lurking in the darkness, waiting for him, but this was too bright, too dazzling to pay any heed, not now.

For the first time in his life, he felt someone cared for him, cared enough to take a chance, to risk everything. It stole his breath and made his chest hurt, making him more attentive in his loving, wanting to give her everything he could in return for her trust in him. Crecy tugged at his neck, pulling his head down, demanding he kiss her even as her breathing became harsh, her body growing taut.

Words crowded his brain, words that she deserved to hear, but he was too afraid to voice them, and then it was too late. She cried out, her body tightening around him, and Gabriel could think of nothing, consider nothing past his own pleasure, crashing over him like a wave as he shook with the force of it. A harsh, guttural cry ripped from his throat, too late to consider that the servants might have heard them as his body convulsed, spilling himself inside of her.

He collapsed, aware that he was likely crushing her, but was utterly boneless, too sated and exhausted to move an inch. Little by little, however, his breathing steadied, and the first rush of recrimination hit him. Loathing began to wash over him, a filthy tide determined to destroy any pleasure he might have found, and then ... Crecy began to laugh.

From somewhere, he found strength enough to prop himself up on his elbows and look down at her, torn between astonishment and indignation.

"What the devil are you laughing at?" he demanded, sounding terse and not in the least lover-like.

Crecy bit her lip, apparently trying to hold her mirth back, but it bubbled over and she chortled, covering her mouth with her hand.

"Well?" he pressed, starting to feel anxiety crawl up his neck.

"Oh, oh," she gasped, shaking her head as tears rolled down her cheeks. "I ... I don't know, only ..."

"Only?"

She took a deep breath, apparently gaining some control and smiling at him with such joy that he felt like his emotions had been turned inside out and upside down in the space of the last few seconds.

"Only, I was so nervous, and it was so ...so ... wonderful," she said, reaching up and touching his face with a sigh. "Oh, Gabriel, I do love you."

Gabriel froze.

He didn't know what to do, to say ... to ...

Crecy's face fell.

"I'm sorry," she whispered, making him feel like a real bastard now for chasing the happiness from her eyes. "I ... I didn't mean to say that, not yet ... not ... I know you don't want to hear it yet," she added, sounding so contrite that he wanted to rage about it, but he didn't know why. He didn't know if he was angry with her or not. Was he angry because she'd said it, or angry because he didn't believe it, *couldn't* believe it. Which meant she was lying, which ...

"Gabriel."

"Gabriel!"

He looked down, startled by sharp the tone of her voice.

"Stop thinking, Gabriel."

She tugged at his neck, pulling him back for a kiss, and for once, Gabriel did as he was told.

Chapter 18

"Wherein plans are made and too quickly shattered."

"I should go."

Gabriel frowned, not liking the idea of Crecy leaving the warmth of his bed one bit.

"No."

She chuckled, the sound burrowing inside of him somehow, making him feel lighter. They had been here for hours and Gabriel could hardly credit the fact, but he didn't ever want to move again. He glanced down at her as she turned in the circle of his arms. One hand reached up, her finger tracing the outline of his lips as she sighed.

"I don't want to, believe me. But they'll send out a search party if I'm too late."

Gabriel glowered harder and tightened his hold on her. The idea that he could keep her here if he so chose was like a maggot in his brain. If he married her, she would belong to him. No one could ever take her away. He sucked in a breath as the enormity of that idea hit him. The idea of letting someone else into his life, of working her into the precision of his ordered world, it was terrifying. Crecy wasn't ordered, she was the closest to chaos he had ever been. There would be forever books and clothes and jewellery and whatever strange thing she had most recently found scattered about his room, about the house. She would be late for meals, she would try and change him, she would probably make him talk to people. The thought made his chest tight, and yet the idea of letting her go back to Longwold and out of his life made him feel strangely hollow; alone in a way he never had before.

It was like being presented with what you wanted and being told it was on the other side of a mountain range that looked nigh on impassable.

Yet he wanted her to stay.

"Thank you for today," she whispered, her words a soft breath tickling over his skin as her fingers trailed over his chest.

He snorted, feeling bitter all at once. "Well, I did say you'd thank me for ruining you, it looks like I was right."

Crecy sat up, staring down at him, her face rather stern all at once.

"Stop that, now."

He glanced up at her, frowning. "What?"

"Stop turning something wonderful into something dark and hurtful. I know you'll do it the moment I'm gone, that you're doing it even now." She sounded really angry, and Gabriel watched her with interest, intrigued in the light of her fury. No one got angry with him, ever. They wouldn't dare. "I can't stop how you'll make this look in your mind, but you hear me now. You didn't seduce me, you didn't ruin me, and I didn't take anything from you that you didn't want to give, you just remember that. We like each other, we like each other's company, and that's all right. *It's allowed.* You are allowed to be happy. Everyone is allowed a little happiness, Gabriel, even you."

He said nothing, too perplexed to know what kind of answer to give. Silence seemed safer.

Crecy shook her head and sighed before turning and clambering off the high bed. He watched as she moved about, gathering her things together. He felt unsettled, uneasy. Crecy brought change, she brought things that he did not want, and yet watching her prepare to leave his house made him want to throw things. It wasn't her fault she had to go, he reminded himself, the words sharp in his head.

She didn't look at him, and the idea that she was hurt or angry with him was even worse. It was like ants crawling under his skin, an uncomfortable feeling that made him want to … to say something - to make it better, but … He scowled and got out of bed, snatching up a dressing robe and putting it on with sharp, angry movements. Damnation.

Crecy sat at his dressing table, trying to create some order in the tangle of unruly curls that had fallen about her neck, and Gabriel watched her pin it back into place with regret. He had liked it like that, loose and abandoned, framing her lovely face. Once satisfied, she reached behind her neck with both hands, struggling to do up the fastenings on her dress. Gabriel moved forward, avoiding her gaze in the mirror as he approached.

"Stand up," he said, not sounding the least bit like a man in need of forgiveness and wanting to bite his tongue off for it.

Crecy did as he asked and he tied each fastening in turn. He finished the last one at her waist and she began to move away, but he stopped her with a hand on her hip. She turned, gazing up at him, an expectant look in her eyes.

Gabriel huffed out a breath and hung his head, avoiding that look that demanded something from him.

"I don't want you to go." *Oh, very eloquent*, he muttered inwardly. *You don't sound the least bit like a sulky five-year-old.*

He glanced up to see her face had softened, and she smiled at him, and though he knew he didn't deserve it, the tightness in his chest eased a little. She tugged at the cord holding his robe closed and he moved forward.

"I'll come back," she said, her voice so full of certainty that it seemed impossible to doubt her, not now, at least. Not in this moment. "You know that I will come back. You have my heart, Gabriel, like it or not. I can't very well go on living without it, now, can I?"

He stared at her, words crowding in his head, fear making his chest tight all over again. Why did she insist on spoiling everything by ... by making him doubt her with such ...romantic nonsense.

Crecy lifted onto her toes and kissed him. Only once, a brief touch of her lips that made him feel at once cherished and scolded. He wanted more. So much more.

"I have to run now," she said, moving to the door.

"Wait," he demanded, needing to delay her, at least a little. "I'll dress and see you outside, at least."

She gave him a smile, so full of understanding that he felt rather winded. "I don't have time, my love. It's all right. I can manage perfectly well."

Gabriel felt his jaw tighten, knowing how long it would take him to dress and quite unable to contradict her. "Will you come tomorrow?"

She frowned for a moment, her blonde brows drawn together as her face fell. "Oh, damn it," she cursed. Gabriel found himself amused at hearing her swear, so unladylike, but then he realised that meant she wouldn't come, and he felt like saying something far more obscene. "Belle has ... I mean, we are supposed to be visiting someone tomorrow, I think? I'm not sure I can. But the next day, I promise. Early as I can," she added, hearing the clock chime downstairs as her eyes widened. "Good Lord, I have to run. Goodbye, Gabriel." She blew him a kiss and closed the door, the sounds of her footsteps flying down the stairs echoing around the quiet house.

Gabriel stood in the middle of his room, finding that it seemed suddenly empty, devoid of colour, of life ... of her.

He sat down on the bed as the realisation hit him that unless he did something, she *would* leave him. Perhaps not right away, and perhaps not willingly, but someone would discover them, someone would take her in hand - God knew someone needed to. A young woman of her astonishing beauty going about the countryside all alone, heaven alone knew what could happen to her. He couldn't breathe for thinking about it - and then gave a bitter laugh as he realised that the worst had already happened. He had taken that which none but her husband had the right to. Not unless *he* was her husband. The idea rang in his head again, louder, more insistent, demanding to be heard.

He should marry her.

He should.

He would.

Gabriel grasped the bed post, feeling his heart squeeze so tight in panic he thought he might actually die. No. No. No. He repeated the word over and again as his breathing steadied. He wouldn't die if he married her ... but he might if she left.

He dressed for dinner, taking his time, hoping his rituals might sooth him a little, to push back the panic that his decision had created. It hovered about him still, though, like a monster he could see out of the corner of his eye. If he didn't confront it, perhaps it wouldn't strike, after all. So he ignored it, pretending he hadn't made the most momentous decision of his entire life, and carried on as usual.

He went into the dining room and sat down to his meal as the servants came and went. Gabriel looked up as Piper spoke to him.

"Will that be all, my lord?"

Gabriel knew he was by far from the most perceptive of beings when it came to fellow human emotions, but it didn't take a genius to figure out that Piper was angry with him from the terse tone to his voice.

He nodded, watching Piper as he turned and left, the old man looking stiffer and more on his dignity than he ever had before. For a moment, he felt bewildered, wondering what the devil the old fellow's problem was, and then it dawned on him.

Crecy.

Piper knew. He knew what Gabriel had done, dammit, the whole bloody staff probably knew. A creeping sensation of heat prickled over him, accompanied by a wash of guilt, and for one horrific moment, he actually considered calling Piper back and explaining.

He took a large swallow of wine and composed himself. He was damned if he was going to explain. But they'd see. Tomorrow, he would make the arrangements for the wedding. A special licence would be required, of course, he needed to get this over with as quickly as possible, needed to re-establish some kind of normality in his life as fast as he could. The idea that he also needed to have Crecy with him with all possible haste was so obvious that he didn't bother denying it.

He finished his meal, determined to go to his study and make a list of everything that needed to be done, the things his wife would need ... He stilled in the middle of folding his napkin, the word so foreign that he had to think about it again.

His wife.

For a moment, he didn't realise he was smiling.

Gabriel got to his feet, leaving the dining room and heading to his office to start his list, but looked up as he heard voices and realised Piper was speaking to someone at the front door.

"I have news, my lord." Paul Chambers, the man he used to spy on Winterbourne here in the country, strode towards him, looking pleased with himself. For a moment, Gabriel frowned; he had completely forgotten about Edward, about his vendetta. "I know who she is, Lord Winterbourne's wife."

Gabriel gestured for the man to enter his study, finding to his surprise that he would just as soon tell the fellow to come back another time, he had more important things to deal with, after all.

"Well?" he demanded, feeling terse and impatient and wanting the fellow gone already.

"Well, I got the story from Lady Scranford's maid," he said, beaming at Gabriel. "Apparently, they've hushed it up at the big house, but there were two sisters at this party of Lord Winterbourne's, and the both of them fortune-hunters. They both tried to get Winterbourne, by all accounts, but the older one set a trap for him. Apparently, her and his lordship was caught in a delicate position in the fellow's library. Lady Scranford was there, saw it with her own eyes as she was one of the party that walked in on them, and she said it was obvious the marquess had been caught right and proper. He had no option but to offer for her."

Gabriel snorted, amused by the idea. Edward had always been such a ladies' man, a popular and beloved fellow who knew just what to say to make a woman fall into his arms. You'd think he'd have been awake to such tricks. More fool him.

"So who are these enterprising young women?" Gabriel asked.

Chambers fished about in his pocket, pulling out a crumpled piece of paper. "Oh, nobodies, like I said. Not a farthing to their name, apparently, and a vulgar aunt in tow, too. Let me see, now. Oh yes, here it is, Belinda and Lucretia Holbrook."

It was strange, how everything was so still as that name was spoken. How quiet the house seemed, when in truth, it was crashing down upon his head. He was silent for a moment that seemed to stretch out until fury hit him, hard and hot and overwhelming.

"You're lying."

The words were quiet but said with such white rage that Chambers's eyes widened, fear draining the colour from his face in an instant.

"N-no, my lord, I ... why would I?" Gabriel moved towards the man, who backed up, holding one hand out in front of him. "It's the God's honest truth, you go and ask Lady Scranford, she'll tell you herself."

Before Gabriel could consider anything else, he found his hands had clasped the man about the neck, and the desire to squeeze the life from him was all-encompassing. He didn't hear or think or feel anything else but the desire to drain the life from the man who had destroyed everything.

Chambers clawed at his hands, hitting him as his eyes bulged and his face grew purple, and Chambers might be a big man, but Gabriel was out of control. Chambers wasn't going to escape. The door to the study flew open, and suddenly Piper was there with one of the lower footmen, both of them shouting and trying to prise his hands from the fellow. The shouts drew other servants running, all of them begging him to stop before he murdered the man.

Gabriel let go, just wanting them gone now, turning on them and screaming at them to get out, get out and don't come back.

There was a terrific buzzing in his head, his breath short and hard to snatch at, and pain, such pain that he felt he would die of it, he prayed that he would.

Fool, fool, you pathetic bloody fool.

I told you.

His father's voice rang in his ears, louder and stronger and more strident than ever. *This is what you get, Gabriel, this is what happens when you ignore me. You can't survive without me, you're too weak, too desperate. She got you good, didn't she?*

No. No.

She tied you up in her games, made you believe she cared about you. You? Who in their right mind would want you? She wants your title, your money, that's what she wants - not you, you miserable excuse of a man. She nearly got you, too, you damned halfwit. She crooked her finger and lifted her skirts and you were actually going to marry her!

Gabriel let out a howl of rage, of pain, sweeping everything from his desk with one furious movement. Satisfaction at seeing everything crash to the ground made his anger grow, and he repeated it across every surface, sending everything hurling to the floor until it was all scattered. He staggered backwards, surrounded by destruction, by the ruins of everything he had, the pitiful life he had carved for himself destroyed by a pretty face. Gabriel leaned against the wall, suddenly exhausted, hollowed out, empty.

He slid to the floor as a strange emotion clawed at his throat, clogging it up, making it hard to breathe. Gabriel sucked in a breath, trying to hold it back, he would not ... would not ... But he could not stop the tears, tears that he had never cried for the loss of his parents, that he had never cried for being alone and unwelcome, unloved and unlovable. But now they would not be held back, and Gabriel put his head in his hands and wept.

Chapter 19

"Wherein sorrow and despair take hold."

It was the early hours of the morning when Gabriel finally stirred himself to move. He looked up and saw with revulsion the destruction surrounding him. It felt like his guts had been sucked out of him. He was nothing but a hollow, dried-up husk. His father's voice berated him, but he was too numb to even acknowledge it now. Seeing everything in such disorder was enough to make him want to retch, though, and he knew he had to put things straight.

Memories of another night came back to him in a rush as he bent to pick up the broken pieces. That, too, had been a night full of violence and terror and regret. His stomach roiled and he moved more quickly, feeling that the memories might go away if only he could tidy things and put everything back as it had been. His skin was clammy, everything slipping through his fingers, and a prickling sweat broke out over his flesh, and his breath came fast as his anxiety grew.

It was hard to get everything just right, as his hands were shaking, and over and over he cursed himself for being so bloody weak. He picked up every broken shard, heedless that he'd cut himself until he bled over the pages of a book and he was forced to throw it in the bin, too, along with the evidence of his shocking lack of control. Those pieces seemed to burn as bright as a dozen candles despite the dim light of the room, and in the end, he was forced to take the bin downstairs to the kitchens and throw the entire thing in with the household refuse. He buried it under a mountain of food scraps, revolted by the filth on his hands but needing to bury the shame of it out of sight. He washed his hands again and again, but the sun was beginning to dawn before he was satisfied, and he hurried back to his study before the staff saw him and realised their master really had run mad at last.

Not that they didn't already know it. If they hadn't guessed it long since, then any doubts would have been put to rest by last night's performance. At least he paid them well enough and they feared him badly enough to keep their bloody mouths shut. He did not need to worry about his humiliation becoming the next story in the gossip sheets. They simply wouldn't dare. They knew too well what he was capable of. They knew he was a monster.

Gabriel closed the study door behind him and went to reach for the slate wolf's head, pausing before his hand could close over it. She had given him that. He snatched his hand back and turned away from it. There was no *she*, no her, no woman. She had been the figment of a deranged mind, nothing more. He had seen what he'd wanted to see, not the truth. The truth was a grasping young woman who had hoped to get what she could from him, and had failed.

There was a small voice inside of him that protested, that reminded him of everything that young woman had said and done, but he stamped on it. He would not think of her. He would not.

He would go away. His property in France had sat empty for too long, and his affairs there had long since needed his attention. He would go away, and by the time he got back, the woman would be gone, probably long since married to some other rich, titled fool who had fallen for her lovely and all too willing charms.

The thought hit him in the gut like a fist, and he swallowed down a well of misery. No. It was a lie, a mirage. She was not what he'd thought. She never had been. But he would endure. He would endure and he would have his revenge.

Perhaps you've had it already. That cold, hateful voice echoed in his mind. *Even now she could be carrying your bastard. Wouldn't that be a fitting end to this affair? If Winterbourne was forced to raise your bastard child. I might even feel proud of you.*

Gabriel ran from the room, flinging open the door and running across the entrance hall, barely making it outside before he retched, heaving over and over as he began to shake.

No. No. Not that.

The idea that he might have given her a child was …

He leaned against the wall, watching as the sun rose on the horizon. It blurred as he blinked, the startling orange growing ever more vivid and colouring the dramatic clouds that had begun to gather, and hung low in the skies, promising storms would be coming soon.

He closed his eyes against the beauty of it, too full of pain to take any pleasure in anything anymore. He must get away from here. He must go now.

Before he proved to everyone just how weak and pathetic he really was.

***

Crecy saw Damerel house come into view with a surge of happiness and no little relief. It had been two days, two whole days since she had seen Gabriel. They had visited friends the day after her last visit, as she'd told him, but the weather had closed in and they had been forced to spend the night. Their hosts were so welcoming and delighted by their visit that it had been impossible to leave until after lunch the next day, and so any wistful ideas of visiting Gabriel had been taken from her.

She hoped he wouldn't be too angry with her for breaking her word. Not that it had been her fault, and he needed to understand that, but she felt she had begun to understand the way in which Gabriel undermined himself, how he sabotaged any hopes for his own happiness. It stemmed from a lack of self-worth, that much she was certain of. No one had ever taken the time or the trouble to get to know him, to understand him, and so he believed himself not worth the attempt. It was why he trusted her so little, and why something like leaving him alone for an extra day would immediately be accompanied by dark thoughts and speculation about her motives. Still, she would cross that bridge when she got to it.

Leaving her horse with the groom, she hurried to the door, a little surprised that Gabriel hadn't come out to meet her. Of course, he couldn't have known that she was coming. With regret, she realised that he might not even be here. Perhaps he had business in town?

Her fears grew as Piper opened the door to her. There was sympathy in the old man's eyes and a look that made her heart grow cold.

"Hallo, Piper, is … is Lord DeMorte not at home today?"

Piper's face was grave as she walked into the house and he closed the front door.

"Would you come through to the parlour, Miss Holbrook?" he said, his voice so gentle that anxiety curled around her heart and began to squeeze.

"What is it, Piper?" she asked, following him into the parlour. To her surprise, the butler closed the door, and she realised that he was trying to keep the other staff from overhearing what he had to say.

"He's gone, miss," he said, such regret in his eyes that Crecy did not have the luxury of misunderstanding him.

Her breath caught and she sat down. A rush of cold seemed to cast over her in a wave and she clasped her hands together, finding them clammy. "Gone where?" she whispered.

Piper hesitated, and then his face softened. "France, I believe."

Crecy swallowed. The urge to burst into tears was so strong that it was almost overwhelming, but she would not embarrass the poor butler with such a scene. He had always been kind to her, and it wasn't like she hadn't known the risks.

"Do ... do you have an address?"

Piper shook his head. "His lordship has always been cagey about his property abroad. I believe he considered it wise to have a bolt hole that no one else knew of, in case ..." He hesitated and Crecy nodded.

"I understand, Piper, you need not explain." She knew well enough that Gabriel played many dangerous games. If things went awry, it would be just like him to have a safe place to retreat to. "Is there anyone who might have the address? Someone he trusts, perhaps?" The idea that he might trust anyone at all was slim but she had to ask.

Piper looked torn for a moment, loyalty to his master warring against his desire to help her. In the end, he sat down, his voice confiding as he leaned towards her.

"His man of business, he has an office in Bath, but ..."

Crecy snorted and shook her head. "Yes, I can imagine the likelihood of him giving out Lord DeMorte's address to a single female of my ilk." She looked down at her feet, knowing she could not hear the answer to her next question and hold back her tears if Piper was nice to her.

"Did he say when he would be back?" There was at least a little hope that he had gone to cool off and would be back in a week or so, but her hopes were short lived as Piper shook his head.

"No, miss, but ... I was given to believe he would not be back before the summer."

"Oh." Crecy concentrated on breathing. It seemed a remarkably hard thing to do. The idea that she would need to keep on doing it, keep on forcing herself to breathe in and out for six months, at least, before she would have the opportunity to even try and explain. It was too painful to contemplate. "Why?"

Piper was quiet for a long moment and she looked up, wondering if he was angry with her for asking.

"A man came to him. Lord DeMorte had charged him with ... discovering who it was that his cousin, the marquess, had recently married."

Crecy gasped, knowing that this was all the explanation that she needed. She covered her mouth with her hand, trying so hard to hold on to her dignity, but a tear over-spilled despite her best efforts, and was quickly followed by another.

"I'm afraid that the information came from Lady Scranford," Piper continued, his voice grave.

"Oh, no." Crecy didn't need him to say more. Lady Scranford had hated her on sight, and things had gotten progressively worse over the period of time they'd been guests at Longwold. The woman had hoped to get Winterbourne herself, and had embarrassed herself in the attempt. Crecy could only imagine the story that had been given to Gabriel, but she doubted it was flattering, and that she and Belle and been painted as unscrupulous fortune hunters, she had no doubt at all. "This is my own stupid fault," she said, wiping her tears with the back of her hand. "I should have told him myself, I should have explained. I meant to, you see," she said, looking up at Piper, who ought to be revolted and scandalised by her, but who only seemed to be compassionate of her plight. "I was going to, only ..." She blushed, then, wondering what Piper knew. He hadn't treated her any differently when she had come downstairs after ... *after*. But she didn't doubt that he had guessed she had been compromised. "Only it had been such a perfect day, and ... and I was afraid," she admitted. "I was frightened he wouldn't believe me, and I thought, if I could only have a day or two more to convince him of my feelings ..."

She buried her head in her hands and was surprised a moment later when Piper moved closer to her, laying a fatherly hand on her shoulder.

"Perhaps ... perhaps it's for the best, miss," he said, his voice grave but full of kindness. "I've known his lordship since he was twelve years old, and ... well, I've tried to guide him, to ... to be something of a father figure, I suppose, but … Well, I never did succeed, put it that way." The old man shook his head and gave her a sad smile. "Perhaps if I'd known him before his parents did what they did, but he'd been alone in this blasted house two years before I got here, and I don't think anyone had really done anything more than feed and clothe him, and make sure he was educated befitting his station. I don't think he'd had a kind word from anyone before I got here, and by then, well he was aloof, to put it mildly."

Crecy cried harder, shaking her head. It wasn't for the best. It couldn't be. Hearing everything she had always suspected put into words was heartbreaking. To know that Gabriel was now more alone than ever, and believed that she had lied to him for nothing more than avarice … She couldn't bear it. With her best efforts, she had struggled to convince him of her loyalty, of her love for him, but with someone pouring such poison in his ears … she didn't stand a chance.

"May I write him a letter, please, Piper?"

"Of course, miss," he said, getting to his feet again. "Only, I know his lordship spent some time informing all of his business associates that he would be away for several months, and that they should correspond via his man of business. Usually, he would send someone every few weeks to collect any mail and deliver it to him, but … in the circumstances …"

Crecy nodded, but she had to take every possible chance to reach him.

"Well, surely he'll send someone sooner or later?" she said, trying to smile and appear hopeful so that Piper wouldn't keep on looking like he was worried to death for her. She was strong, she knew that. She had always been single-minded and determined, and now she must be strong for both her and Gabriel. Sooner or later, she would see him again, and when she did … She drew in a breath and composed herself before tears overwhelmed her again.

"I shall bring you pen and paper, Miss Holbrook."

"Oh, no, Piper, I know I ought not ask you, but … but may I write it in his study? I …" She let out a breath and gave him a smile that she knew must look pathetic, indeed. "I know it's foolish of me, but … I would like to sit in his study, just for a moment."

Piper gave her a smile of such understanding that it was nearly her undoing, but he nodded. "Come along then, miss. I'll take you there."

Chapter 20

"Wherein life goes on, regardless of broken hearts."

Piper led Crecy to Gabriel's study and showed her where she might find ink and writing equipment.

"Is there anything else I can do for you, Miss Holbrook?"

Crecy shook her head, hoping she could last until he closed the door before the tears started again. Piper turned to leave when she realised she couldn't let him go without knowing one last thing.

"Piper?"

"Yes, miss?"

"What ... what happened, when he found out?"

Piper's face became grave and he walked back towards her, lowering his voice.

"It was bad, miss. I've seen him lose his temper, many, many times. We all know when to tread carefully around him, you see, but ... Well, I don't think any of us have seen the like of it before."

Crecy swallowed hard as her eyes burned.

"He tried to kill Mr Chambers, that fellow who brought him the news. Took five of us to stop him, and then ... he went wild. Smashed this room to pieces."

She covered her mouth with her hand, stifling a sob. Looking around, she realised that there were many small items missing from around the room, things she had noted on her previous visit.

"You must have had a lot of clearing up to do," she said, feeling appalled at the devastation she had caused by not being honest with Gabriel sooner.

Piper looked saddened and shook his head. "Oh no, miss. His lordship always clears up his own mess. More than your life's worth to try and help him do it, believe me, I know." He paused, letting out a breath, his expression thoughtful now. "I've always thought he did it as a kind of penance. Punishing himself for having lost control in the first place."

Crecy gave him a frail smile. "I think you are very perceptive," she said, feeling as though the life had been drained out of her. She wanted to sit down in the dark and curl up in a ball until Gabriel came back to her. But that wasn't going to solve anything. She wasn't going to allow herself to wallow in self-pity when this situation was of her own making. Gabriel needed her to be strong, whether he knew that or not.

Piper left her alone, then, and Crecy sat staring at the sheet of paper with despair. How on earth was she going to put into words everything she felt, everything that was true, in language that Gabriel would listen to? In the end, she could do nothing more than say what she felt.

My dearest friend,

You cannot imagine my devastation as I write this letter. Knowing that it is in great part my own fault only makes it far worse.

I meant to tell you, Gabriel. You must believe that. I meant to tell you when we were last together, only I was so happy, and afraid that my words would spoil things between us.

I don't know exactly what you've heard, but if the rumours came via Lady Scranford as I am informed, then I can well imagine. Oh, Gabriel, surely you know enough to realise that woman is vain and selfish and empty-headed? She hated me on sight for being prettier than her! Can you imagine a more ridiculous reason for hating someone? As if I can do anything about it? But then she tried to flirt with Winterbourne, and he gave her the cut direct - *in full view of the whole party. Can you imagine her feelings towards Belle and I now?*

As for that. It is quite true, Winterbourne was trapped into marriage. Belle intended to trap Lord Nibley, in actual fact. He is a sweet-natured, if dull, fellow, and sorely needs looking after, so it didn't seem such a terrible thing. But Winterbourne discovered Belle's plan and went to stop her, with the results you now know. But Gabriel, dearest Gabriel, you must not think badly of my sister. We were on the edge of ruin. My aunt had told us that if we hadn't married or at least found a man to keep us, then she would turn us out. She was trying to sell me to the highest bidder, and Belle, my beloved sister, was prepared to sacrifice her own happiness to save me.

The funny thing about it is that the two of them are now very much in love and so very happy together. I can't help but feel that perhaps fate was looking after them, guiding them together. I only wish it had felt as kindly towards us.

Gabriel, I am sitting here crying my heart out, as the smudges on this letter will surely attest to, but in truth, I am very angry with you, too. How could you believe such a thing of me? I have told you time and again that I would not insist on marriage. If you would only give me your address, I would come to you now, this instant. I would leave everything behind and bring scandal and shame upon my poor sister, if only you would give me the chance to prove my loyalty to you. Belle has plans to send me to London for the season and has overridden my every objection. She wants to believe I can find a man to make her as happy as she is, and I cannot tell her that I already have. If you don't send for me, I shall be forced to go with Lady Russell and endure endless dances and socialising, and Gabriel, I swear I will die. I cannot do it. And don't you <u>dare</u> go thinking it is my perfect opportunity to snare a wealthy husband, for if you do, I swear I shall throw something at you the next time we meet.

I will never, ever marry, that much I swear to you. I will have you, my love, or die an old maid. It is your decision. I will wait for you, Gabriel. Please don't let it be forever.

I love you,

Your friend,

Crecy.

She was sobbing in earnest by the time the letter was done. Wiping her eyes, she folded it carefully and looked about the desk for the wax to seal it. Seeing nothing obvious, she pulled one of the desk drawers open and caught her breath at what she discovered. The next one was opened in turn, and she gave an unsteady laugh as hope rekindled in her heart. In each drawer, arranged in date order and carefully laid upon thick green baize, was every strange and quirky gift that Crecy had ever sent him. In the third drawer, and arranged with equal attention, every single one of her letters.

"Oh, Gabriel," she said, feeling her heart clench in her chest. She reached down, trailing her fingers over years and years of one-sided correspondence, every one of them opened and then stored carefully in the place he spent most of his time, every day. She closed each drawer in turn, realising as she closed the second one that there was a space. The wolf's head. With a lurch of hope, she wondered if he had taken it, knowing that he often reached for it in times of stress. She moved to the mantelpiece and her hopes snuffed out as she found it still there. Picking it up, she held it to her lips and determined to keep it with her. She would give it back to him herself.

A further search of the office turned up the wax and she sealed her letter, leaving it on his desk and praying that it would get to him soon. Taking one last look about the room that kept so many secrets about the man she had lost her heart to, Crecy turned and walked away.

***

1st April, 1818

Gabriel glanced at his watch and put his head in his hands. An hour. He'd been ready for an hour and he still hadn't managed to leave the damn room. Anxiety clawed at his throat, and he looked back at the dressing table. *It's fine. It's all fine. Just leave it alone, you bloody madman.* He clenched his fists, a shudder running down his spine as nausea roiled in his stomach. It had been a long time since things had been this bad.

Damn her.

Damn *her*.

Don't think of her. You must not think of her. But it was a forlorn hope. He thought of little else. Every conversation they'd had, every touch they'd shared. Everything was examined and turned over and seen in a new light, or rather, without any light at all. He was cast into darkness, and he could see no way out.

The trip to his property in France had been an unmitigated nightmare, and he wondered that his valet, John Allen, hadn't deserted him entirely, for surely, even after fifteen years of Gabriel's strange behaviour, the man had been tested to the limits of his patience. Gabriel had compensated him handsomely for his troubles, and, to be fair, John had never uttered a word of reproach. He probably didn't dare, Gabriel thought with a snort. Who knew what a madman would do? He might try and strangle the life out of the poor devil, like he had with Chambers.

But even John had begun to try and coax him from the room, and by God, wasn't that humbling?

"Please, my lord, won't you come downstairs now?" John said, his placid voice as calm and as unruffled as ever, despite having said the same thing twenty times already. "I believe the gentleman you dispatched to retrieve your correspondence arrived late last night. Worn to a thread, he was, a terrible crossing, by all accounts. Still, after waiting over a week for a crossing at all, I expect he was glad enough to get one."

Gabriel looked up, meeting the fellow's eyes and cursing himself for hoping.

"There's post?"

"Yes, my lord." John's eyes were too full of sympathy, and Gabriel looked away. He'd be damned if he'd have his bloody staff pitying him. They could fear him by all means, but not pity.

"Is there much?" *Stop it, you bloody fool. You don't want to hear from her.*

"No, I don't think so, my lord. He has brought some important documents from your lawyer, I believe, as Mr Bainbridge did not wish to consign them to the post and waited to put them in his hands. I believe there is also one letter. That one came from Damerel House."

Gabriel caught his breath as sweat prickled down his spine. Hope and anger and fear, all of it coiling in his gut and making him want to retch. He waved John away, wanting to be alone for a moment. He would not run downstairs and tear the bloody letter open. He would not.

John went to the door, but paused, turning back to him.

"May I speak plain, my lord?"

Gabriel looked up in surprise. John rarely spoke at all. It was one of the things he appreciated most about the fellow. He was quiet and discreet and he never appeared to be judging him, though he didn't doubt his long suffering valet thought him perfectly insane.

He nodded, too curious to tell John no.

"I was engaged to be married once, a long time ago," John said, an uncharacteristic blush staining the fellow's cheeks. "A lovely girl, she was, sweet and pretty as a daisy. But then, someone told me something about my fiancée … he made *allegations.*"

Gabriel felt his humiliation deepen as the man spoke. For the love of everything holy, it was bad enough they all thought him mad, but to think they knew a woman had tipped him over the edge. It was too much.

"Well, my lord, it turned out the fellow was jealous. He wanted my girl for himself, and he got her, too," he said, his voice turning bitter. "By the time I realised what a blasted fool I'd been, it was too late." John cleared his throat, looking exceedingly uncomfortable. "I've regretted that a long time, my lord." With an awkward nod, he excused himself and left the room.

Gabriel sat, considering John's words. Was the fellow actually trying to defend the woman - he would not say her name - after everything she had plotted?

If she had plotted.

Don't pin your pathetic hopes on more lies, Gabriel. What in the name of God would a woman like that want with you? She's beautiful, she could have anyone. She probably already has. She'll be hunting bigger fish now, opening her legs to other more inviting prospects. Maybe she's hooked herself a duke?

No. Stop it. Shut up.

Though he kept telling himself to burn the damn thing, he reached for the pocket inside his jacket and withdrew the small sketch she had given him. Try as he might, he hadn't been able to consign the wretched thing to the flames. Her lovely face stared back at him, making longing sweep over him. Why did he keep torturing himself like this? Just burn the damn thing. He stared at the flames, knowing he wasn't strong enough to do it, and tucked the picture back out of sight as his father mocked him for it. He got to his feet, needing to block out his father's voice. The letter. He would go downstairs and read the letter.

***

By the time he had dismissed the fellow who had brought the post, after hearing lengthy and unnecessary tales of the man's appalling voyage, he was close to breaking. Finally, however, he was left alone and reached for the papers, casting them aside with little care and less patience as he searched for the letter.

There it was. The sight of her familiar, looping handwriting making his breath come short.

Burn it. *Burn it.*

Gabriel stared at it, desperation a searing pain in his chest. He got to his feet, tipping the chair over in his haste, snatching the letter up as he went. Striding to the fireplace, he held it out over the flames, but try as he might, he could not let it go. If he couldn't burn her picture, what hope was there for the letter he had longed for and dreaded in equal measure?

"Just do it," he muttered, knowing that talking to himself was likely not a good sign. "End this."

He couldn't do it.

Sitting down heavily beside the fire, he stared at the letter for a moment before breaking the seal.

My dearest friend,

You cannot imagine my devastation as I write this letter.

Gabriel read with his heart in his throat. His father's voice was raging at him, chastising him for being a damn fool, a pathetic worm who wanted to crawl beneath the woman's skirts. But her words curled around him, and he remembered again the things that she'd said, the manner in which she'd said them, the way it had felt to be close to her. As much as he could not believe that she loved him, could not trust in her … he still hoped, still wanted.

His father was right - he *was* pathetic … but he had to see her again.

Chapter 21

"Wherein a shark scares the pretty fishes."

12th April 1818

Crecy sat down, as far into the corner of the room and out of sight as she could manage. Perhaps if she stayed with the wallflowers, she'd be safe. The room was too hot and she was exhausted. Thoughts of her bed were only too appealing, and she swallowed hard as a wave of dizziness overcame her.

"There you are," a rather smug, masculine voice said, startling her enough that she jumped. "Hiding your light under a bushel as usual, eh?"

"Oh, August," she said, sounding impatient. "Thank heavens it's only you."

The ridiculously good-looking man in front of her sucked in a breath before tutting at her. "Crecy, love, you are terribly hard on a fellow's ego, you know."

Crecy snorted, glaring at him. "Oh, I think you'll bounce back," she said, her tone dry. August Bright, Baron Marchmain, had been one of her most ardent admirers and had pursued her relentlessly for the first month of her time in London. Eventually, however, she had finally gotten it into his stubborn head that she was the owner of a broken heart and would never marry. What was more, she certainly wouldn't be having a love affair with one of London's most notorious rogues. Since then, he'd given up his pursuit of her, and actually became a rather unlikely ally, shielding her from the worst of her admirers whenever possible. This had naturally sparked rumours, but there was little to be done about it. August was incredibly charming, and despite her gloom could even manage to draw a real smile from her, rather than the fake ones she reserved for such occasions as these. He seemed curious rather than startled about the odd or outspoken things she was prone to say, though even they had become less as she withdrew into herself. She was far quieter and more subdued than she had ever been before, her naturally outspoken nature somehow choked by misery. In that, at least, August was a breath of fresh air, keeping her from descending too far into depression, though soon even his friendship would likely wane. But for now, August was a cheerful friend and rather impossible not to like. Unlike a certain, brooding, ill-tempered, emotionally unstable viscount who was never far from her thoughts.

She sighed as longing made her chest tight. It had been nearly four months since he had left, and she'd had no word. She had given Piper her address in London, hoping against hope, and whilst the dear old fellow had written to her, as yet, he'd given her no news of Gabriel.

"Penny for them?"

She looked up and cast August a weary smile. "You shouldn't waste your money."

August frowned and reached over, patting her hand in a comforting manner. "Still pining over this wretched fellow that broke your heart, I suppose?"

"I suppose so," she admitted, looking away from him as a new set of dancers arranged themselves on the dance floor.

"I'll bloody kill him if I ever lay my hands on the fellow," August muttered, folding his arms and scowling harder.

Crecy bit back a smile. She wondered if he would be so glib if he knew who it was she was aching for. Not that she doubted August's courage, but Viscount DeMorte was too notorious and dark a figure to be faced with equanimity.

Her amusement faded as a wave of nausea hit her, and Crecy sucked in a breath.

"I say, Lucretia, are you quite well? You look positively ill."

"Dear August, you're dreadfully hard on a girl's ego, you know," she quipped, though it was a rather breathless and half-hearted attempt at humour, as she felt like she might pass out at any moment.

"Crecy, I'm not joking. Shall I take you out of here?" he demanded, his green eyes filled with anxiety for her.

"What, and have every scandal sheet in the city talking about our sudden departure? I think not." She sat back and closed her eyes and tried to concentrate on breathing in and out. Dear God, please let Belle have got her letter and allow her to come home. She didn't know how much longer she could carry on like this. "Be a dear and go and fetch me a glass of lemonade, please."

August didn't budge, staring at her with concern. "I'm not sure I should leave you."

"Oh, do stop fussing, August," she snapped, immediately repentant as she saw the hurt look in his eyes. "Forgive me," she said, suddenly feeling on the verge of tears. "I ... I'm not feeling well, if you must know, but I'm sure I'll feel better if you get me a drink. It's just so very hot and noisy in here."

He gave her a rather direct look that was somewhat unsettling, but nodded. "I'll be right back," he said, hurrying off to fetch her drink.

Crecy let out a sigh of relief and closed her eyes. One hand slid protectively over her stomach and she tried hard to hold back the tears that would come if she allowed herself to think of the future. Gabriel would come back. He had to come back. Surely, she hadn't brought such dreadful shame upon poor Belle for nothing. Yet it hadn't been for nothing. Short as it had been, it was everything she'd known it would be, and she could not regret it. But she needed to get out of the public eye, and soon. She would have to keep August at a distance, too, she realised, lest people speculate that he was responsible for her delicate condition. To make matters worse, she had begun to fear Lady Russell suspected something. Her chaperone was sharp-eyed and up to every trick, no matter her age, and the old woman had dropped some subtle but enquiring questions of late that had made Crecy's heart pound. It was pounding now, and Crecy tried harder to calm it. Panicking would not do the least bit of good. Now all she could do was endure.

***

Gabriel stared around the crowded ballroom, every instinct demanding that he turn around and leave, now, this minute. He despised London, could not abide the crowds and the dirt and the bloody gossip. His hostess had looked like she'd been about to pass out when she saw who had crossed her threshold, but there was no one brave enough to deny him entry, despite his lack of invitation.

He'd arrived two days ago, sending his London house into utter chaos as he'd given them no warning, and his visits were so rare that he kept the bare minimum of staff in residence.

Finding his room unprepared for him was not something he could grumble about in the circumstances, but it little helped his temper or his state of mind. Frankly, it was a wonder he'd managed to leave the house at all, he thought with disgust. But seeing Crecy again had become as much as an obsession as any of his other compulsions, and that desire had overridden everything else.

He shut out the whispers and gasps and the looks of outrage as he moved among the cream of the *ton*. He always felt like a shark at these events, every eye watching him with fear for what he might do or say. Strange, really, as he had never made a public scene at such an event, unless being forced to meet his apparently dead cousin in full view of the world counted. That, however, had been Edward's doing, not his. He'd rather admired his cousin for that move, in fact.

Edward was far from his thoughts, now, though, as he scanned the crowds. He lingered in the shadows, behind the huge marble columns that stretched this side of the ballroom. From here, he could see the dancers and …

His breath caught, pain making his chest grow tight as he found her among the throng. God, but she was lovely. She was dancing with a handsome young officer, who looked dashing and heroic in his regimentals, and Gabriel stamped on a surge of jealousy before he forgot himself enough to cross the room and murder the fool in full view of everyone. Crecy looked up as her partner addressed her and smiled at his words.

See, I told you. You're long forgotten. She's moved on, casting her lures for another pathetic fool who can be seduced by her charms.

Gabriel felt the words hit him like a barb caught in his heart, but he didn't move, stubbornly holding his ground when his father would have him just turn and leave.

Something had changed - she was different.

Now that he really looked, it was obvious. She danced with as much elegance as he'd imagined she would, and she smiled, clearly charming everyone around her, but she wasn't the same. All the vivacity, the energy and joy that she had seemed to carry within her had gone. She looked pale, her face drawn, and the smile she gave did not reach her eyes. She looked … sad.

He stared across the ballroom as she left her partner and hurried away, and he moved along the outskirts of the throng, tracking her movements as she found a quiet place among the wallflowers. Gabriel watched, frowning as she sat down, closing her eyes and pressing gloved fingers against her temples. She was tired, and she didn't want to be here. The desire to cross the room and sweep her up, to take her home with him, was so overwhelming that he had to force himself to keep still. As he continued to study her, his temper flared as he noticed Baron

Marchmain approach her; she looked startled but not displeased to see him. Damn the bastard. August Bright was everything that he was not. Charming, well liked ... sane. By God, but wouldn't they make a dazzling couple? The idea made him want to retch. Either that, or go and break the handsome lord's damned nose. That might put a dent in those golden looks.

To his relief, however, Crecy didn't look as though she was flirting with him, though seeing Marchmain reach out and give her hand a brief squeeze did not make him feel the least bit charitable towards him. *Take your bloody hands off her.*

It was clear, however, that Marchmain had noticed that she was out of sorts; he was looking at her with obvious concern, and Gabriel could only smile as it was clear Crecy had given him an impatient set-down. She would hate being fussed over. Marchmain left, and Gabriel hesitated.

If he approached her in full view of everyone, it would set tongues wagging all over London. He never singled out young women. Ever. Frustration gnawed at him as he wondered how to get her alone, when some idiot's drunken drawl reached his ears.

"Bet you fifty pounds I can have her before the season is out."

"You're a bloody fool, Tony. She's already turned down about three marriage proposals that I know of. One of them was the Earl of Clayton. If you think she's going to accept a *carte blanche* from you, you've got rocks in your head."

"I will have Miss Holbrook, on her back, before the season is out, Charlie," said the obnoxious voice as a burst of rage hit Gabriel, so intense that he felt like his head might burst. "Do you accept?"

Gabriel did not think. He did not consider that he was in a crowded ballroom, surrounded by the cream of the *ton*. He simply reacted.

Before his brain had even had a chance to catch up, he had turned and smashed his fist into *Tony's* face, feeling a rewarding crunch as he broke the fool's nose. There were screams and shouts, but nothing registered, he was solely focused on his victim, who had staggered back and crashed against two other men, sending all of them to the floor in a tangled heap. Gabriel wasn't done, though, and he advanced on the man, who actually screamed and tried to scramble away, but Gabriel reached down, lifting him by his preposterous cravat and twisting it in his hand until the man gasped for breath.

"How dare you speak her name," Gabriel said, his voice low enough that only the fellow trembling and choking in his grasp could hear. "You will never, never, speak it again. You will tell no one what or who this disturbance was about, only that it was a matter of honour, and you will name your seconds."

He released his hold on the young man, who collapsed, falling to his knees and looking utterly terrified.

"B-but, I meant no insult to y-you, my lord," the young man, whom Gabriel now vaguely recognised as a Mr Anthony Bellinger, sputtered. His father had been a fool, too. Gabriel had relieved him of a rather large sum of money some five years ago. It looked like his son had inherited his bad manners and stupidity, not to mention cowardice.

"No," Gabriel retorted, his voice mild, though he was well aware that his face looked murderous, to say the least. "You did not mean to insult me, because you would not dare. You reserve your slander and disrespect for those who cannot defend themselves, you gutless pup."

"Forgive m-me …" Bellinger stammered, clearly out of his wits with terror. "I'll never mention it … h-her … again."

"No. You won't." Gabriel replied, staring at him with contempt. "But you will meet me. Hyde Park, the ring, at dawn."

Gabriel turned and strode away, and the crowd parted, everyone staring at him like a monster had appeared in their midst. He didn't look at them, he never did. Who cared what they thought of him? Nothing new, that was for certain. He didn't regret what he'd done, not even slightly, but he did regret leaving without looking Crecy in the eyes. He had wanted to see her reaction to his arrival, to judge if any of what he'd believed of her before his hopes had been dashed had been true. But she would know he was here now, he thought with a grim smile. The gossip columns would ring with this story for weeks. He would just have to see what she would do about it.

***

Crecy stared at nothing, visions of a happier past and a rather bleak future jostling for space in her crowded mind. The idea of never seeing Gabriel again, and of having to go home and confess to Belle what she'd done, was too terrible. If she'd felt ill before, that idea was enough to make her quake in her satin slippers.

Her troubled thoughts were interrupted, however, by screams and shouts, and she got to her feet, her own problems momentarily put aside by curiosity. Moving further into the ballroom, she saw the source of the disturbance as the crowd fell back, away from the scene. A fight! Goodness, how shocking, an honest to God fight in the middle of a ballroom. Crecy almost smiled at the looks of absolute horror on the faces around her, that such ungentlemanly behaviour had been foisted upon them. And then she saw the two men involved.

One was Anthony Bellinger, who seemed to have been on the receiving end, as blood streamed from his nose and he appeared to be pleading for his life. Good. He was a revolting, insinuating man who had rather frightened Crecy. He'd made some unpleasant and wholly inappropriate remarks to her, and was forever trying to get her alone. Rightly or wrongly, she could not help but feel a surge of pleasure in seeing him finally get his comeuppance. The man who held him in his powerful grasp was clearly in control of the situation, he was a big man and …

Crecy's heart stuttered, hope and joy and a terrible anxiety growing in her chest.

"DeMorte's called him out," a scandalised voice said as Crecy's blood ran cold.

"Bellinger's a dead man, then," came the reply. "He killed Lord Aston outright. Bullet to the brain. Right between the eyes, I heard."

"Oh, no, Gabriel," Crecy whispered. Not that she gave a damn for Bellinger, but she could not let Gabriel make himself into the monster he believed himself to be.

She moved forward, pushing through the crowd with difficulty as they strained to get a front row view of the scandal that would keep their jaws wagging from now until the end of the season. Crecy saw Gabriel turn, stalking away as people fell back to let him pass, and she hurried after him.

Thankfully, everyone was too intent on discussing the momentous event with each other to be watching the doors, and Crecy slipped out of the ballroom. He had almost reached the outer doors by the time she managed to catch him.

"Gabriel!"

Crecy held her breath as he stopped in his tracks. If he carried on walking, she would know she was on her own, but maybe, maybe if he turned, there was still some hope for them.

Time seemed to stretch out and Crecy could hear her blood pulsing in her ears.

"Gabriel," she said again, softer this time, pleading ... and he turned around.

Chapter 22

"Wherein ... a reunion of sorts."

Crecy ran forwards, wanting nothing more than to wrap her arms around him, but halted as she saw his posture stiffen. He stood staring at her, perfectly rigid, his face a mask.

"Hello," she said, uncertain as to whether she wanted to cry and rage at him or just fall at his feet. She was smiling, though, her heart alight with hope. Surely, there was hope? There had to be.

Gabriel said nothing, his eyes wary now.

"You shouldn't be out here," he said, his voice hard and curt. "If you want any chance of catching yourself a husband, you'll regret getting caught here with me."

Crecy felt her smile fall away, but she found she could not be angry with him. He was staring at her as though she was a threat now, as though she posed a danger to him, and she knew how badly he'd been hurt.

She moved closer, slowly, as if she was approaching some wounded, wild creature, and she smiled a little as she realised that it was exactly that.

"I will tell you now what I have told you before, Gabriel," she said, keeping her voice soft. "And I will keep on telling you until you believe it. I will never marry. I will have you or no one, and if you want to walk back into that ballroom right now with me on your arm, then I am ready to do it."

His gaze was fierce for a moment and then he looked away, folding his arms. "Come over here before anyone sees you," he said, his voice gruff and rather begrudging as he nodded towards a more secluded corner. At least he still seemed to have some care for her.

"Why did you attack Bellinger?" she asked, wondering what had riled him badly enough for such a violent outburst.

"Why?" he asked, the sneer in voice clear enough. "Was he one of your beaus?"

Crecy felt a burst of fury with him and struggled to tamp it down. "No," she said, the word brittle and angry just the same. "He's a revolting, ill-mannered libertine, and I was never more pleased to see anyone brought to his knees. I wanted to cheer you on, if you must know," she added, folding her arms to mirror his defensive stance.

Gabriel looked a little startled, and then his face darkened further.

"Did he touch you?" he demanded, his arms falling to his sides as he walked closer to her. "Did he hurt you?"

Crecy melted all at once, utterly undone by the concern and fear in his eyes.

"No," she said, smiling at him and wanting to reach out and touch his dear face so badly it was an ache beneath her skin. "No. He made me very uncomfortable and I dislike him intensely, but nothing more than that."

He seemed to let out a breath, and yet that stiff, cool look swept over him again.

"Don't meet him, Gabriel," she said, her voice pleading as she dared to take another step forward. "Please, don't."

"Why?" he demanded, his eyes glittering with anger now.

She reached out a tentative hand and laid it on his sleeve, feeling the hard muscle beneath the fine cloth, perfectly rigid with tension.

"Because I'm frightened, Gabriel." She dared to move a little closer, staring up at him and feeling the tears prickle in her eyes. "Even a fool like Bellinger could get lucky, and even if he doesn't, it will hurt *you*, Gabriel. Killing a man simply over angry words is foolish and will leave a mark on your soul. Please, my love, don't do it."

An uncertain expression slid into his eyes and he looked down, away from her gaze.

"I've issued a challenge, now, there is no backing down." His face grew cold once more and he gave her a rather unpleasant smile. "It's a matter of honour."

Crecy swallowed, knowing her voice was going to tremble but needing to get the words out. "You have more honour than you know, Gabriel, certainly far more than most of the people in that room."

He snorted, incredulous. "You can say that?" he mocked, shaking his head and removing his arm from her grasp.

"I knew what I was doing," Crecy said, feeling suddenly worn and exhausted. She no longer had the energy to battle him so hard, to battle the ghosts of his past that were forever whispering their vile words in his head. "I have no regrets."

He looked around, perhaps hearing the change in her demeanour. He looked concerned all of a sudden, and that, at least, warmed her heart.

"What is it?" The words were an imperious demand. He would know what was wrong. She smiled at it, knowing his harsh tone hid anxiety, but only shook her head. She would cry if she said more.

"Tell me," he insisted as he moved back to her. He touched her face, a fingertip lifting her chin so he could look down at her. "You're pale," he said, hiding his growing concern with a gruff voice. "You're not sleeping?"

She shook her head, which only made things worse as a wave of dizziness hit her and she was forced to hold onto him.

"Crecy!" he exclaimed, real concern audible now. "Are you sick?"

Crecy swallowed hard, what remained of her self-control dissolving in his presence. "N-not sick," she whispered as her eyes began to fill, but forced herself to hold his gaze.

Gabriel stared at her, uncomprehending at first, but she saw the moment her words sank in.

He gasped and shrank back, and she wondered if she'd made a terrible mistake, and then his jaw tightened.

"Whose is it?"

For just a moment the pain of his words stole her speech, or any ability to react at all, but not for long. She slapped him. Crecy put everything she had into that one strike and the burning pain of it seared her palm, making her eyes water and the tears spill over.

"How could you?" she said, though she was more hurt than angry now. It was too much. She could not face any more of his anger and hurt, not now. So Crecy began to walk away.

"Crecy!" She was halted with a large hand on her arm, though his grip was gentle. She paused, looking back at him with tears running down her face. "I ... I should not have said that."

"No," she said, with as much dignity as she could find as she tried to dash the tears away with her gloved hand. "You shouldn't have."

He was quiet for a long moment, his hand still holding her arm, but his presence was reassuring now, hopeful.

"You're sure?" he asked, his voice low and a look in his eyes that she could not quite read, but she thought that he looked afraid.

Crecy nodded, knowing she would simply crumple if she tried to speak. Gabriel let out a breath, running a hand through his hair.

"We cannot discuss this here," he said, glowering now, and she sensed his frustration. "Can you get away?"

"Yes," she said, though in truth, it was hard to do. She felt sure Lady Russell didn't trust her an inch.

Gabriel nodded. "Go to Hatchard's. I'll have a carriage pick you up outside and bring you to me, tomorrow morning, at ten?"

Crecy nodded, smiling again now, and the tears that she was trying desperately to hold back were of the happy variety now as she felt her faith in him had been justified. She wasn't out of the woods yet, but if he would speak with her, surely she could win him around?

"Yes," she managed, her voice a little uncertain. "But what about Bellinger?"

Gabriel tutted, looking angry and disgusted in an instant. "Oh, for the love of God. Fine! I won't kill the blasted fool, if it's going to make you weep all over me."

Crecy laughed, a startling sound as it was so long since she had heard it herself. "Oh, Gabriel, I do love you, whether you want it or believe it."

For a moment, there was a flash of something in his eyes, something warm and hopeful, but it was quickly hidden. He grunted but said nothing, and Crecy reached out, clasping his hand and raising it to her cheek.

"Promise me you'll be careful."

He glowered a little but gave a curt nod.

"Tomorrow, ten o'clock," he repeated, avoiding her gaze.

"I'll be there, Gabriel."

***

Gabriel waited in the damp mist of an early April morning at The Ring in Hyde Park. It was chilly and murky, and he'd much rather have been in his own bed, but he was damned if he'd let a nasty jumped-up jackanapes like Bellinger get off scot-free. Especially after Crecy's words. The longing to put a bullet in the fellow was tantalising. Happily, there was not a soul in sight apart from his opponent, who had gone to throw up his guts behind a tree, and the idiot's friends. The last thing he needed was for the law to get wind of it.

Gabriel looked up as Bellinger's second approached him, looking very much like he wanted to make use of his friend's tree as soon as possible.

"My lord," the man said, barely able to meet Gabriel's eyes. There was some satisfaction in being thought a monster after all, Gabriel mused, smiling inwardly. "Mr Bellinger is truly sorry for having slighted the young lady in such an abominable manner and would like to offer his sincere apologies."

"I'm quite certain he would," Gabriel said, with what he was very sure was a most unpleasant smile. "I, however, do not accept. Mark the points and let us get this over with."

His friend blanched and gave a stiff nod, and Gabriel watched with a keen eye as the ground was paced out, a sword struck into the ground to mark the firing positions for both parties. Once this was done, Gabriel rapped on the carriage door to indicate to the doctor that his services may be required. He had also blackmailed an indignant Mr Rufford - who owed him a large sum of money - to stand as his second, and this gentleman now bore Gabriel's pistols off to Bellinger so the fellow could inspect them and make his choice.

This done, Rufford presented the case to Gabriel, who took the remaining pistol. With a twisted smile, he realised that Bellinger had taken the one that his father had used to blow his own brains out. You could tell, as there was a slight nick in the fine, polished wood of the butt. Wouldn't that be ironic, if Bellinger got lucky as Crecy feared, and he was killed with the same gun? Almost poetic. If it hadn't been for Crecy's revelation last night, he would probably have hoped for it. But his thoughts on the matter were too tangled of yet, and he needed time to decide what was to be done.

Rufford gestured for him to come forward, and he stared hard at Bellinger, who walked to his position, ashen-faced and looking like he might cry. They stood back to back, and then, as the signal was given, they walked away to their firing positions. Gabriel reached his and began to turn as the sound of a gunshot ricocheted across the empty park. Gabriel turned fully to see that Bellinger had fired on him while his back was to him, and had missed by a mile. The fellow looked like he was about to bolt, his second obviously feeling the same as he shouted at Bellinger to hold.

Gabriel took his time, raising the pistol and taking aim. It would be an easy thing, to rid the world of this unpleasant creature, but Crecy would not be pleased with him – to say the least. He deloped, firing the gun into the ground before handing it to Rufford and giving Bellinger one last look of disgust.

"I suggest you stay out of my way in the future, Bellinger," he said, watching with contempt as the man sat heavily down on the damp ground and put his head in his hands.

Once he'd returned Rufford to his home, Gabriel returned to his own to pass the interminable hours until it was time to send a carriage for Crecy. He would not send his own carriage, as his coat of arms was far too distinctive, so a hired carriage would have to be arranged. At least he had time enough to dress and prepare himself if he started at this ungodly hour.

He began his ablutions with his thoughts in a tangle. The idea of Crecy carrying his child brought such a terrifying range of emotions that he simply didn't know how to deal with them, and all the time he could hear his father's instructions to him.

Throw her out, send her back to Edward, let him raise a DeMorte bastard. That's almost as good as destroying him, Gabriel, it will ruin his reputation, make him a laughing stock when you live on his own doorstep. It's our revenge!

"Yours, not mine, Father."

He would have to call you out for it ... we can finally end this.

Oh, God, the idea of an end to this torment, to this living nightmare, that was sweet indeed. But could he do that to Crecy? Could he really turn her away?

His chest grew tight, pain radiating out from his heart. Could he do that to his own child? He racked his brain, trying to think of a way he could have everything.

"Edward might get rid of the child, she might not be given proper care, she could lose it. I can't risk that," he countered, knowing it was just an excuse, but clinging to it anyway. "Better I keep her close, at least until the child is born. Then I'll take her back, with the babe in her arms. Edward won't have any choice then."

His father was silent on the matter and Gabriel considered it a victory, or at least ... a temporary reprieve.

Chapter 23

"Wherein Crecy must keep her own counsel."

By a quarter past ten, Gabriel was pacing the parlour of his London town house with his guts in a knot. His father's voice was still ringing in his ears and all of his own anxieties were simply piling one upon another until he felt like he might buckle under the weight of it. What if the child was like him, like his own father? What if it grew to be mad and wicked and dangerous?

And then he heard voices at the door, and she was there.

Gabriel held his breath as she was shown into the parlour, and he dismissed the butler with a curt nod. The man, who Gabriel had decided he disliked intensely, gave a disapproving scowl at him for being alone with a young lady, but moved somewhat quicker when Gabriel's expression rather outdid his own.

The door closed and Gabriel wondered what Crecy would do. Would she run to him? She had wanted to last night. He was sure of it. He had wanted her to. But now she hovered just over the threshold, looking a little anxious and uncharacteristically unsure of herself. He didn't like to see it.

"I'm so glad you're safe," she said, the sincerity in her voice matched by her expression, though her eyes grew troubled and she took a step forward. "You're not hurt, are you?"

Gabriel shook his head, refusing to admit he was touched by her concern. She let out a breath. The two of them stood staring at each other, but of course it was Crecy who spoke first.

"I'm going back to Longwold this afternoon," she said, glancing up at him and then away again. "I haven't told Belle about … about anything," she said, her voice quiet. "But I won't be able to hide it much longer, so I asked if I could go … go home."

Nearly four months, he realised, she was close to four months pregnant.

Gabriel nodded as plans began to form in his mind. It would be far easier at Longwold. He'd wondered how to get her away from everyone without being seen. Though it wouldn't take long for the story to break if she ran away with him. The idea of people gossiping and speaking ill of Crecy made an unfamiliar feeling of protectiveness flame up inside of him. They'd regret it if they did.

But wasn't that what he wanted, to shame and discredit the Winterbourne family, to tarnish their good name as his own had been tarnished by them? To do that, Crecy would have to be sacrificed. He scowled.

"Don't … don't you care at all, Gabriel?" Crecy's voice was faint and hesitant, and Gabriel braced himself against the flood of emotion that hit him. He didn't want this, couldn't do it. He didn't want to hurt her, but he couldn't help her either, not how she deserved to be helped. Dammit, why had she thrown herself into his life?

"Did you mean what you said?" he asked, feeling too raw and exposed to answer that particular question.

"I meant everything I've ever said to you," she replied, moving to sit down as Gabriel realised he should have invited her to do ten minutes ago. She looked tired and frail, and some unfamiliar feeling in his chest made his heart contract. "Was there something in particular?"

Gabriel nodded. "You said … you said that you would come away with me."

He watched, curious and astonished as a weight seemed to lift from her shoulders. For just a brief moment, she closed her eyes, and then she smiled up at him, a real, proper smile that lit up her face and made him remember exactly what the days with her had been like, what seemed like an eternity ago.

"Yes, Gabriel. I meant it."

Gabriel felt the same amount of relief shudder over him and struggled to keep it hidden, but Crecy's eyes were on him. Why was it that he felt like she saw straight through him? Gabriel turned his back on her, feeling too exposed, and went to stand by the fire. He distracted himself by rearranging the items on the mantelpiece.

"We'll go on the sixteenth. I'll bring the carriage to the end of the driveway at Longwold to meet you."

"I can ride to Damerel," she offered, but Gabriel shook his head.

"No." If she fell in her condition ... He felt cold and panicky just thinking about it. "You won't be able to bring anything, but I will provide everything you may require," he said, hating himself for sounding as though he was negotiating a business deal rather than running away with his lover.

"Very well," she said, and he could feel the weight of her gaze between his shoulder blades. He should turn around, he should say ... *something.* He should tell her he was sorry, that ... that he'd missed her. He *had* missed her.

He clenched his jaw. No, he hadn't missed her, he thought with a burst of anger. Missing her implied a wistful desire to see someone again, and it hadn't been that. It had felt as though someone had carved his heart out with a dull blade and packed the void with salt. It felt like losing his grip on the world - on himself. It felt like dying forever with no hope of peace at the end of all the suffering.

"I can't stay long, Gabriel." The regret behind the words was obvious, and he did turn then. "Lady Russell suspects, I think," she said, laying her hand over her stomach. The sight of that protective gesture stirred something in Gabriel, some desire long since abandoned to know what it was to have a family, a place he belonged, maybe even a place he was loved.

Don't be so disgustingly sentimental. No one could love you.

He looked away, feeling like he was being split in too many different directions at once. He no longer knew who he was, what he was supposed to do. Before Crecy had come into his life, it had been simple enough. He was hated and reviled, he had no one but himself, and that was the way he liked it. But now ...

"I'm so sorry, Gabriel."

He was startled by the apology, wondering what on earth she was apologising for.

"For not telling you. I should have done. I know I should. I'm so sorry I hurt you."

Gabriel felt a blush stain his cheeks and turned away, walking over to the window. It was on the tip of his tongue to refute her, to sneer and say he hadn't cared a bit, but it would be too obvious a lie. She would see right through him, and that would be more humiliation than he could bear.

"What time shall I meet you?" He realised she was trying to save him any further awkwardness by changing the subject, and he took a breath, turning to face her. Yes. Best to stick to details. He could make arrangements, that much he was good at, at least.

"When can you get away?" he asked, wondering what she would do if he walked over to her and took her in his arms. Would she be as willing as before? Would she slap him, or be cold, reproachful? He could hardly blame her.

"After breakfast, I suppose, say, ten-thirty, to be on the safe side. I don't want to keep you waiting if I get held up."

He nodded his agreement and Crecy got to her feet. She hesitated for a moment and he felt a flicker of hope that she might come to him. It grew as she took a few steps closer, but she was so hesitant that it made him ache with regret for the damage he'd done. Gabriel closed the distance, thinking he owed her that much, and she reached up, giving him a soft kiss on the cheek.

Gabriel closed his eyes for the brief moment her lips touched his skin, memories of other, passionate kisses only to easy to recall.

"Goodbye, then," she said, and before he could find anything to say of any value, anything that he ought to say after everything he'd done ... she had gone.

***

Crecy waved to her sister, giving her a bright smile and wishing she didn't feel like such a traitor. After everything Belle had done for her, to do this to her was so unfair. But she could not, would not, give up on Gabriel. Belle had Edward who would protect her from anything the world could do or say. Here at Longwold they were protected from the worst of it anyway. Neither of them cared much for the world outside of the gates of the huge castle, and soon there would be another, joyful distraction to stop them from fretting over Crecy's terrible behaviour.

Belle was pregnant. Crecy was sure of it, and the desire to confide in her sister had been so hard to deny. Belle had been a mother to her when Crecy's own hadn't cared, and then for the years after the woman's death. That they shared different mothers had never mattered a jot to either of them. They were sisters, and they had always looked out for one another. But if Belle found out about the child, she would want Crecy to accept one of the marriage proposals she'd received with all haste, to ensure her safety - and that she could not do. So she must deceive her sister and dearest friend, and the idea of Belle's pain when she discovered the truth was enough to reduce her to a snivelling wreck. So she didn't think of it. She had no more choices. She had put her faith and trust and all of her hopes in Gabriel, and she would not doubt him now.

It had occurred to her, however, that he might doubt her. So she was on her way to the village under the guise of sending a

To Tame a Savage Heart

parcel to Lady Russell in thanks for her kindness, but in truth to send a letter to Gabriel. It was just a note, assuring him that she was ready to leave and that she would meet him as arranged. Tomorrow, she would place herself entirely in his hands. Crecy could only pray he wouldn't let her down. Her last meeting with him had been hard. She'd wanted so badly to run to him, to hold him and tell him she forgave him, that she would never leave him, but she sensed he wouldn't believe such declarations. He needed to come to her, in his own time, and she needed to give him the space to do that, to learn to trust her. But it was dreadfully hard to do.

By that evening, Crecy was all on edge, her nerves convincing her that everyone knew she was about to do something dreadful and was watching her every move. As it happened, however, Belle had her own concerns, as she'd rowed with Edward, who had done another disappearing act.

"He'll be back soon, Belle. He's so much better than he was, anyone can see that." Crecy gave her sister a sympathetic smile. "He just needs to calm himself, you know that. Once he's settled down, he'll be back here begging forgiveness."

Belle smiled at her and nodded, but didn't look very reassured.

"Come now," Crecy said, seeing how pale Belle looked and feeling only too sympathetic. She gestured towards the untouched bowl of soup in front of her. "Eat up. You must keep your strength up."

Crecy's mouth twitched a little as she spoke, knowing what she was insinuating, and Belle narrowed her eyes at her.

"What do you mean by that?" her sister demanded.

Crecy smiled, looking down at her own soup and not feeling too much like eating it, either. "Belle, I know you better than I do myself. You've never had a fondness for peppermint tea, and you've always loved roast pork and lamb. Especially the fatty cuts." Crecy snorted with amusement as Belle swallowed convulsively. "I'm so happy for you," she added with a broad grin, though sorrow stabbed at her heart. Would she ever see Belle's child? Would their children grow up together, play together? Of course they would, she scolded herself. There was no doubt in her mind that Belle would not abandon her, no matter what happened. The thought lifted her spirits a little. "I hope it's a boy," she added with a wicked glint in her eyes. "I shall teach him to play in the dirt, and tell a badger's skull from a fox's, and how to tame a magpie."

"Have mercy, Crecy, love," Belle said, looking a little alarmed as Crecy reached out and took her hand. "And besides," her sister added with a sniff, "it's probably a girl."

Crecy pursed her lips. "Actually, that's even better," she added after a moment's reflection. "I'll teach her all the same things, and then she'll be a sight more interesting than all the other simpering débutantes when she's grown." Crecy gave a dark chuckle as she looked back at Belle. "You love me, really," she taunted, sticking her tongue out at Belle until she gave in and laughed. She let go of Belle's hand and wondered how far she was about to test that love. She needed to compose a letter and try and to explain, at least a little, so that when they discovered her gone, they would not worry too much.

Crecy forced her thoughts from her own troubles and back to Belle.

"Does Edward know?" she asked, her voice gentler now.

Belle shook her head. "I've wanted to tell him, but I'm afraid how he'll take it, and after today ..."

Although Edward's morbid thoughts were growing fewer and more manageable as he grew to trust Belle and let her in, more and more of them included Belle herself and revolved around his fears for her. As if the fears that stemmed from his experiences in the war had transferred to fears for his wife as she grew more important to him. Crecy could well understand that Belle was worried about revealing her pregnancy to him.

"You mustn't say anything," she said to Crecy, who glared at her, rather hurt that Belle would even suggest it.

"As if I would!"

Belle sighed and nodded. "Forgive me," she said, looking tired and worried and rather worn out. Once again, Crecy wished she could confide in Belle, to tell her she knew exactly how she felt, but that was impossible.

A knock at the door startled them, more so as Garrett and the other staff usually made a scratching sound, which Edward said was easier on the nerves.

A moment later, Edward's butler, Garrett came through the door, looking uncharacteristically ruffled. "Forgive the intrusion, my lady, but I must beg leave to go and help in the south barn. It's on fire, and with the wind blowing as it is, it could catch the castle, too, if we don't act fast."

"Oh, my word!" Belle exclaimed, setting down her spoon with a clatter.

"Please, my lady," Garrett begged, looking appalled at having frightened her. "There is no need for concern. I took the liberty of sending to the village for help, we'll have it under control in no time."

"And Lord Winterbourne?" Belle demanded as Crecy rose and crossed around the table to take her hand.

"We've not yet seen his lordship," Garrett replied, but he was obviously eager to be gone, so Belle sent him on his way with a plea to take care.

Crecy put her arms around Belle, hugging her tightly. "He'll be fine, Belle. You know he'll be hiding out in the woods somewhere like he always does."

Belle nodded, agreeing, but Crecy could see she was terrified.

"The south barn is full of hay," Belle said, her eyes on Crecy. Neither of them said anything. They both knew how fast that could burn if the fire took hold.

"I can't sit here imagining," Belle cried, getting to her feet. Crecy nodded and the two of them hurried to fetch their pelisses before rushing outside.

Chapter 24

"Wherein a disaster strikes and too much is revealed."

"Oh, my," Crecy exclaimed as they stared upon the frightening scene, and she clutched Belle's hand.

The air was full of acrid smoke that caught at the back of your throat, and Crecy was startled by the noise of the fire. The crackling flames leapt high into the night sky above them, sparks shooting upwards and soot falling in soft, dark flakes all around them.

There were people everywhere and shouts as orders were given. The inhabitants of the village had turned out in force, determined to help. Crecy couldn't help but wonder if they'd have run to Gabriel's aid so quickly. She somehow doubted it. Buckets of water were being filled and thrown at the blaze, everyone working their hardest, men with their shirt sleeves rolled and sweat on their foreheads, but it seemed an impossible task, as the flames simply leapt higher.

They searched the crowds, desperate to see Edward and know he was safe.

"Have you seen Lord Winterbourne?" Belle asked over and over, each time receiving a disheartening shake of the head from a weary, soot-smudged face.

Crecy turned as a voice called out behind her. "He's in the barn."

Belle span around in horror as Crecy clutched her hand tighter.

"What?" she exclaimed as the young lad pointed thankfully at the smaller barn and not the one beside it that was blazing like an inferno.

Crecy looked at the blaze and felt her heart grow cold. The smaller barn would catch any moment now.

"Why?" Belle cried, moving forwards. "What's he doing?" Crecy could hear the fear in her voice and they both looked around as Edward's butler, Garrett, ran up to them, looking extraordinarily dishevelled.

"He's sawing through the truss, my lady. They're going to use the horses to pull the roof down so the fire can't take hold." Belle gasped and Crecy clung to her, praying that everything would be all right. Belle had sacrificed too much, had tried too hard to make their marriage work. It would be too cruel to lose the man she loved now. "Now you stay here," Garrett instructed, sounding surprisingly authoritative. "Or his lordship will worry, and I'll be dismissed if I let you go another inch," he added, his tone brooking no argument.

"But Garrett!" Belle pleaded, staring at the smoke billowing from the smaller barn with horror. Crecy could feel how badly Belle was trembling and could only cling to her, offering what support she could, but Belle began to move forwards.

"No, my lady," Garrett said, his voice firm and his grip upon her arm even firmer. "It's not just you to worry about now."

Both sisters stared at the butler in astonishment, and Crecy noted a fatherly light in his eyes.

Before they could remark on Garrett's rather startling sixth sense, there was a roar that hurt Crecy's ears, and a blast of heat so intense that her skin prickled and grew tight. The south barn collapsed in on itself, throwing flames and sparks and debris high into the sky. The horses screamed in horror, surging forward. The big fellow who had been holding them still was carried along, digging his heels in and pulling with all his strength. But the mighty shires were too strong, even for one built like an ox himself, and they lumbered forwards, ears flat back and eyes rolling with fear.

"Edward! *Edward!*"

Belle's cries were horrified, and Crecy's heart broke for her sister as she saw the terror that her husband had been inside the building. The butler tried to hold her back, to restrain her, but Garrett could not keep her from running towards the man she loved as fear gave her strength. She ripped her arm from his grasp as Crecy screamed for her to stop, running forwards as a sickening crack split the air like a gunshot. Crecy ran after her and then stumbled to a halt as a plume of dust and smoke and splinters exploded through the open doors of the barn as the roof caved in - and in the midst of it, a figure emerged through the doors, scrambling on the wet cobbles to get clear as the roof crashed to the ground.

"Edward!" Belle screamed as Crecy wondered if either of them would ever breathe again.

Belle launched herself into her husband's arms, almost knocking him flat against the cobbles as he fell to his knees. He was breathing hard, coughing and choking, but he was alive.

"Belle," he said, grinning at his wife as though he'd won some kind of prize. "Belle."

He pulled her close, rocking the two of them together as Belle sobbed into his shoulder, one minute scolding him and pounding at his chest with fury for putting himself in danger, and the next running her hands over him, begging him to assure her he was unhurt. Crecy sighed, closing her eyes with relief and moving away to give them some privacy.

She wondered how she would have felt, knowing that Gabriel had been in that barn and fearing he might not come out again, and experienced such a rush of emotion that she had to lean against a wall. Crecy pushed the thought from her mind. She couldn't lose him, that's all there was to it. She'd never recover.

"Eddie!" Crecy turned to see that Edward's devoted valet, Charlie, was running out through the smoke, waving his hat and

rushing up to his master, his narrow chest heaving. "Damn me," he said, gasping for air and bracing his arms against his legs to catch his breath. "When ... when I saw that building collapse and they said ye was still inside ... Lawd, ye gave me a bleedin' fright."

Crecy smiled and made her way back towards them. She looked up at Edward with admiration. "How brave you are, Edward," she said, smiling broadly and feeling very proud of him. He truly was a good and kind man, and he'd made Belle so happy that she could not but look upon him with approval.

Edward looked a little awkward at such fulsome praise and cleared this throat to avoid answering.

"Yes, well, that's enough of my husband's heroics for one lifetime," Belle replied, her voice firm now that her terror had passed. "So, enjoy it while you may," she added, glaring at Edward, who simply grinned at her.

"Any ideas how it started?" Crecy asked, wondering how such a dreadful blaze could have begun. They all turned to look at the devastation, relieved to see that at least the blaze was under control now.

"Probably someone smoking around the barn, though, damn me, I've told them until I'm blue in the face," Edward muttered, looking irritated now. "I thought I'd got the point across, but perhaps not."

"You sure about that, my lord?" Charlie asked, a dark look in his eyes. "It was a close-run thing the castle didn't catch, eh? If we 'adn't a noticed it so quick, an' you 'adn't thought to bring that roof in… Well ... could'a been a sight worse, is all I'm sayin'." The man's voice was so ominous that Crecy stared at him in alarm.

"Do you mean to suggest someone did this on purpose?" Belle exclaimed, clearly horrified by the idea.

Charlie gave Edward a significant look and Crecy saw him frown. She felt a chill run down her spine, afraid that she knew what he was insinuating. "He means my cousin Gabriel, Viscount DeMorte," Edward said.

Crecy felt a rush of anger so intense that she wanted scream.

"Why do people always do that?" she demanded, knowing that she ought to say nothing, ought not to give herself away, but she could not allow them to defame Gabriel so. It seemed like every bad thing that happened could be laid at his door without any scrap of proof.

Belle, Edward, and Charlie looked around at her, staring in shock at her outburst, but Crecy was too angry to be prudent.

"Once someone has a bad reputation, no matter if they deserve it or not, it's a stick to beat them with, isn't it?" she shouted, her fists clenched so hard she could feel her nails digging into her palms.

Belle gaped at Crecy, quite obviously appalled and astonished by her outburst.

"But Crecy," she said, staring at her sister as though she'd never seen her before. "DeMorte tried to kill Edward, he almost killed poor Aubrey when he stepped in to save him."

Oh, God. If she'd been angry before, this was the last straw. She felt wild with fury, her need to protect Gabriel overriding any scrap of common sense that told her she need to close her mouth. Now.

"And you have proof of that?" she demanded, staring at Edward with such fury that he looked every bit as alarmed as Belle. "Did you see him pull the trigger?" she shouted, feeling like she was on the edge of doing or saying something really dreadful and far too revealing.

"No," Edward said, frowning at Crecy. "In fact, it wasn't him who pulled the trigger. But Aubrey saw DeMorte speak to the man who *did* then shoot at me right before he left Almack's. Whoever he was, he was waiting for me outside."

This explanation did nothing to calm her, but she tried to moderate her tone, finding she only sounded even more furious as she bit the words out.

"So now a man is guilty of attempted murder because he's spoken to a man who did attempt it?" she flung back. Belle took a breath, astonished and appalled by her sister's outburst.

"There is a little more to it than that," Edward said, his tone careful, and Crecy could tell he was trying to be diplomatic, trying to calm the hysterical woman. It only made her all the more furious.

"Why do you defend him so, Crecy?" Belle demanded, cutting to the heart of it, and Crecy blushed, knowing she could say nothing that wouldn't ruin her plans. "What is there between you and Viscount DeMorte?"

"Nothing," she said, hating the lie, hating the fact she was denying Gabriel, but knowing she would never make it out of the house if they knew what she truly felt.

Belle staggered a little, clutching at her husband's arm, and Crecy could see she was exhausted by the drama of the past hours. She experienced a rush of remorse at having made things far worse.

"Belle?" Edward said, sounding anxious as his arm went around her. "Come along. Let us all get out of the cold and this dreadful smoke. I think there has been enough excitement for one day." He turned his attention to Crecy and she quailed a little under that piercing gaze. A lump rose in her throat and she struggled to keep the tears from coming. "We can talk about this later," he added, not unkindly, but with a tone that suggested Crecy would have questions to answer. Her stomach flipped as she knew she had said too much, revealed too much, but at least she would be gone before they could get to the truth.

***

Since he'd last seen Crecy, Gabriel had lived in something of a daze. His desk was stacked with lists - albeit tidy ones, neatly arranged - and he must have written a dozen letters.

The amount of things a young woman - particularly one in a delicate condition - needed to get through a day was quite astonishing. Gabriel had sent out orders for everything from clothes, to toiletries, and such things as a Crecy might prefer to eat beyond his own, rather limited diet. He had written enquiring for information about the best doctor to be found in France, arranged a lady's maid and sent instructions to his French house that preparations must be made for their arrival immediately.

It had, at least, kept his mind occupied, and his father's voice had been blessedly quiet. Now he sat, pen in hand, trying to cudgel his tired brain into going over it all again in case he'd forgotten anything. Try as he might, he didn't have the slightest idea what would be needed for a newborn beyond a cradle, clothes, bonnets, and linen clouts. Here, however, his imagination deserted him, and he decided they had time enough to discover what was required when the doctor attended Crecy. That was the priority and must be dealt with as a matter of urgency.

Thoughts of the child itself insinuated themselves into Gabriel's mind at odd moments, and he had found himself considering a small girl with golden hair and unusual violet eyes like her beautiful mother. At this point, he would experience a surge of terror and push the image away as fast as he could.

Just focus on today, Gabriel. He put his head in his hands and tried to breathe as the image of the child kept creeping back behind his eyes. Dear God, what if she was like him? The idea made him want to be sick. The Greyston family had long been known for instability. There were numerous anecdotes of ancestors who had been strange at best, some so disturbed that they'd been locked up. Too many years of inbreeding, no doubt. How could he have done such a thing as create a child? Of all the wicked things he'd done in his lifetime, this had to be the foulest.

He'd been so careful until Crecy, and had denied his own pleasure rather than risk the possibility of leaving a bastard behind him. But with her, all sense had escaped him, he'd been so caught in her spell, so wholly lost in her that the thought had never even occurred to him.

Thoughts of his own father came to mind and he shivered with revulsion. Well, this child would not suffer that, at least. Edward was a good man. Gabriel had hated him for so long that it was hard to admit it, but he knew at heart that his child would be safe and loved at Longwold. It was small comfort, but there was little enough of that in his life to be satisfied by it. One thing was for sure, Gabriel was not fit to be a father. Thoughts of what could happen if he lost his temper or if the child made a mess made fear crawl up his throat until he felt he would choke.

No. He would see that Crecy and the child were safe, that they had everything they needed, and then they would never see him again.

Chapter 25

"Wherein Crecy runs away."

Crecy was more than relieved to discover that Edward and Belle had slept in after the drama of the night before. So she was able to eat breakfast alone, without any difficult questions to answer or anyone to notice how badly her hands were trembling.

As it was, her appetite had deserted her, and she simply drank some weak tea and nibbled the corner of a piece of dry toast in the hopes the nausea she had come to accept as part of her pregnancy would subside. She realised as she glanced up at the clock that she hadn't even thought to ask Gabriel where they were going. Not that it mattered. As long as they were together, she didn't really care about the details, but she had to admit to a little curiosity.

For a moment, she allowed herself to daydream about it, about a place where she could go to sleep in Gabriel's arms and wake with him beside her. The thought brought a rather dreamy and wistful smile to her mouth. Despite her nerves, her guilt at leaving Belle in such a deceitful way, and all of her fears for the future, she felt hope that things were going to be all right. She would do all she could to bring Gabriel to trust her. Surely, with all the love she had in her heart for him and her dogged determination, surely that could overcome anything?

Her breakfast finished, Crecy returned to her bedroom. At least there was nothing for her to pack, and though she regretted some of the things she must leave behind, she hoped that it would not be forever. Belle loved her too well to never see her again, no matter the shame that she was about to bring down upon herself and her family. She swallowed down the sadness that idea gave her and reached for the letter that she had hidden in her bedside drawer, leaving it tucked just out of sight on the mantelpiece. It was addressed to Belle, and hopefully they would find it when she was still missing by dinner time. After last night's outburst, she doubted it would be such a surprise as it might have been, but she didn't doubt at all that Belle would be horrified.

She had tried to convey in the letter just how wrong they were about Gabriel, but she knew in the light of the fact she'd run away with him with no offer of marriage, that it was likely her words would fall on stony ground. She hadn't even mentioned the child. Not yet. That was too much for Belle to take in all in one go. She could not be so cruel. But she would have to tell her. When they were settled, she would write again and explain everything, as best she could, at least.

Crecy took one last look around her bedroom before putting on her pelisse and bonnet. It was her favourite one, which she had bought whilst in London, and she wanted Gabriel to see it, for she knew it suited her. A bright, cerulean blue velvet, it made her feel hopeful as it put her in mind of blue skies and sunny days. The carriage dress below it was the same colour, though in India muslin, and Crecy felt sure that Gabriel would like it. That he wouldn't say so was a thought so obvious that she didn't consider it. Gabriel said very little at all, but that he felt a great deal was something she had always known. It was just a case of figuring out what was going on in his head, and she felt she was perhaps becoming more accustomed to that.

Crecy was early as she walked down the long, winding driveway from Longwold to the village. She had forced herself to walk slowly as she left the house, so as not to raise suspicion, but now that she was out of sight, she lengthened her strides, looking over her shoulder with anxious glances. She would not fail at this late stage.

To her relief, Gabriel was already there waiting for her, his glossy black carriage and horses gleaming in the spring sunshine. He got down from the carriage, looking serious and not the least like a lover running away with his mistress, but Crecy didn't care.

His black hair shone blue and he was as large and stern and imposing a figure as ever, and it took all of her self-control not to pick up her skirts and run to him. But she had promised herself to take things slowly, not to push him, and so she just took his hand, smiling up at him as her heart lifted. Suddenly her guilt and fears were gone. This was right. She knew it was.

"Hello," she said, quite unable to keep the smile from her voice.

"Good morning."

Gabriel looked tense, awkward, and so she thought it best they get going as soon as possible.

"Shall we, then?" She grinned at him, gesturing at the carriage.

"You're very perky for a young woman running away from home," he muttered, frowning at her.

Crecy allowed him to hand her up into the carriage, and sent him an arch look as he sat down opposite her. "If you haven't discovered by now that I am a strange and contrary creature, I do despair of you, Gabriel," she said, sounding rather tart, though her eyes must be filled with laughter.

Gabriel snorted and banged on the carriage roof, and the conveyance lurched forward a little, swaying as they moved off.

Crecy caught her breath as she realised she was really doing this. Good Lord, she was unmarried, almost four months pregnant, and running away to God knew where with her lover. Being every bit as contrary as she'd just stated, she could not but help the smile that curved over her mouth.

She looked up to find Gabriel watching her, his eyes curious, and her smile only grew.

"Shouldn't you be weeping into a handkerchief or something?" he grumbled, looking perplexed. "You do realise what we are doing?"

Crecy chuckled, finding herself thoroughly entertained by his chagrin. "Of course. I've been telling you from the start that I would run away with you. It's you that doesn't believe a word I say," she replied, shaking her head as she stripped off her gloves. It was a lovely spring day and really quite warm behind the glass of the carriage window. She gave him a direct look. "Would you prefer it if I cried, Gabriel? I can try if you would like me to?" Crecy struggled to keep her face straight, but managed to make the words sound perfectly serious.

"Good God, no," he replied, looking perfectly revolted by the idea, but as he turned away to look out of the window, Crecy thought she saw a smile tug at his lips, and felt satisfied that she had amused him.

"Where are we going?" she asked, drawing his attention back to her again.

"I wondered when you were going to ask that," he said, his tone dry. "For all you know, I'm going to cart you half way around the world with me."

Crecy shrugged. "I don't care, as long as I'm with you."

Gabriel sighed, looking exasperated. "Well, you should care," he snapped, folding his arms in a way that looked like it put his coat under remarkable strain as his powerful arms bulged. "You're carrying my child."

Drawing her eyes from his impressive musculature with difficulty, Crecy just smiled at him. "I'm in perfect health, Gabriel, please don't worry."

"Have you seen a doctor then?" he demanded, those dark, indigo eyes flashing as Crecy realised that he really was frightened for her.

"Of course not." She tried to soften her words as she understood his concern, but surely he well knew she hadn't seen a doctor. How could she? He was merely being sarcastic to make a point.

"So how the devil do you know you are in perfect health?"

Crecy drew in a breath and remembered that she was going to be patient with him. "Because pregnancy is not an illness, and apart from the dreadful sickness in the mornings I feel perfectly fine."

"You didn't look fine at that ball," he persisted, his voice a growl of discontent. "You looked pale and ill and like you might pass out at any moment."

She sighed and leaned back in her seat, staring at him with a fond expression. "That's because I was utterly wretched without you," she said, quite unable to give him anything but the truth. "I feel much better now."

He frowned and cast her a puzzled look from beneath his dark brows before grunting and looking out of the window. Crecy smiled. *I'll get you yet, Gabriel, just you wait.*

"You still haven't told me where we're going," she said, watching as he glanced back at her.

"France," he said, offering nothing more in the way of information. "We're going to France."

***

They made Bristol by precisely five minutes to one o'clock, and Crecy could only smile at Gabriel's organisational skills. Lunch was ready for them the moment they arrived in the private parlour of a neat little inn. The meal was identical to that which he would have eaten at home, and she wondered just how precise the instructions he had sent ahead had been.

By the time Crecy had freshened up and returned to him, Gabriel had the table arranged with military precision and was staring at the clock with irritation as it now showed three minutes past.

"Forgive me," she said, leaning over and giving him an impulsive kiss on the cheek before picking up her knife and fork.

Gabriel glanced at her but said nothing, turning his attention to his meal. Crecy discovered that her appetite had quite returned to her and that she was utterly famished. She devoured everything on the table with gusto and quite happily accepted the serving girl's offer of apple pie and cream. This was so good, in fact, that she ordered a second helping. She'd just taken her first mouthful, feeling rather gluttonous and very contented, when she looked up to see Gabriel watching her with amusement.

She chewed and swallowed, raising her eyebrows at him. "What?"

"Hungry, were you?" he asked, his mouth twitching a little.

Crecy gave a haughty little sniff, smoothing out her napkin in a dignified manner before picking up her spoon again and scooping up a generous mouthful. "I am eating for two, you know," she returned, before digging in with relish and with a twinkle in her eye. Crecy returned her attention to her bowl because it really was extremely good, and then looked up with a start of surprise as Gabriel chuckled. She could not help the heartfelt smile that curved over her mouth. Everything was going to be all right.

After their meal, she was rather surprised when there was a knock on the door and a rosy-cheeked, plump young woman came in at Gabriel's invitation.

"Good day, my lord. I'm Beth Dean." Crecy looked up as Gabriel rose and the girl bobbed a curtsey.

"Thank you for coming, Miss Dean." He turned and gestured towards Crecy. "This is Miss Holbrook, whom you will be working for." The girl looked Crecy over with wide eyes, barely suppressing what looked like an *ooh* of astonishment as she looked over Crecy's stylish London outfit.

Crecy blinked in surprise. When Gabriel had said that he would make all the arrangements, it had never occurred to her that he would make *all* the arrangements. She wondered what on earth else he'd arranged, especially as the *Miss* Holbrook had appeared to give the girl a moment's pause.

Crecy got to her feet and greeted Beth with a smile. "Hello, Beth, I'm very pleased to meet you."

Beth returned the smile, relaxing as it became obvious Crecy wasn't going to be the snooty kind of mistress who would barely acknowledge the existence of a maid.

"I'm right happy to be here, Miss Holbrook," she said, looking like she meant it. "I hope you'll be pleased with my work."

"I'm sure I shall be," Crecy replied with a reassuring smile. She found she meant it, too. The girl had an open, pleasant face and kind brown eyes, and Crecy thought they should get along splendidly, providing the girl didn't shock easily.

"They've shown you to your room?" Gabriel enquired, sounding as gruff as ever. Crecy hid a smile as Beth shot a rather anxious look in his direction. She nodded and stammered a reply in the affirmative. "We leave at seven AM, sharp," he continued, making the girl pale further. "The tide is at eight fifteen and I have no desire to be late."

"Yes, my lord," she said, still staring at him and quailing a little. "I'll make sure everything is ready in good time."

Gabriel nodded his acceptance of her words and Beth curtsied again, then hurried from the room.

"You've thought of everything, haven't you?" Crecy said, looking at him with obvious admiration. Gabriel looked a little awkward.

"I don't like disorder," he said, sounding rather grumpy, as though he'd been caught out in caring for her and looking after her needs.

"No," Crecy said, giving a serious nod and holding back her smile. "I know."

They went for a walk around Bristol after lunch, and Crecy thought she had never felt happier, her hand on Gabriel's arm as they strolled around the shops. A book shop was an obvious magnet for both of them, and Crecy quite startled Gabriel by giving a crow of delight when she laid her hands on a copy of Frankenstein.

"I thought you'd ordered a copy?" he demanded as she waved the book under his nose with a triumphant expression.

"I did," she said, frowning. "Only I never got to Bath to collect it. I suppose I shouldn't buy two copies," she said, looking at the horrific price of the book and knowing she was being dreadfully extravagant.

Gabriel tutted and rolled his eyes. "Oh, give it here," he muttered, and added it to his own selection, which quite made Crecy's day.

The only fly in the ointment came at bedtime. Crecy glared at her bed with a mutinous expression before flinging back the covers and removing the warming pan. She had expected Gabriel to be warming her bed tonight, but apparently he was prepared to run off with her but not debauch her until they got to his home.

So with a frustrated sigh, Crecy flounced onto the bed and sulked until she fell asleep.

Chapter 26

"Wherein a long journey, a welcome arrival, and a home are discovered."

Crecy got into the carriage at *Le Havre* with a sigh of relief. The past two days at sea had been wearing, to say the least. Gabriel was clearly not at his most relaxed whilst travelling - to put it mildly - and did his best to save her from this by avoiding her entirely. As it happened, Crecy did not complain, as the seas were rough, compounding her morning sickness until she felt like she would die from it. Even now, she was certain she could feel the swell and roll of the waves beneath her, though the carriage wasn't even moving. She swallowed hard and tried to ignore it.

It was barely eight o'clock. The boat had made port in the early hours of the morning and Gabriel was clearly keen that they reach their destination as soon as possible, as he'd insisted everyone was up at the crack of dawn. Not being a morning person by any stretch of the imagination, this had not helped her disposition. Crecy strongly suspected that Gabriel had not slept at all; otherwise in his present state of mind, they'd have been waiting for him until lunchtime. He'd probably begun getting ready instead of going to bed. The idea saddened her, but she was determined to help put him at his ease once they were settled.

Beth, at least, was a godsend, and had already earned Crecy's undying gratitude. She had been sympathetic to her mistress' distress without fussing, and when Crecy had decided that she'd best tell her about her condition at once and before she guessed, the girl had barely blinked.

"That's all right, miss," she said, barely looking up as she unpacked a very pretty nightgown from the surprisingly comprehensive chest of items that Gabriel had provided for her comfort. "I helped my eldest sister deliver two of hers. I know what's what."

With that little drama over without so much as a blink, Crecy felt her last hurdle had been successfully cleared. But that had been before the boat set sail.

Crecy opened her eyes as Gabriel got in the carriage and it swayed into motion.

"Are you feeling better?" he asked, sounding rather anxious. "Miss Dean informs me you have been quite poorly."

"Oh, Gabriel, please don't talk about it," Crecy said, shaking her head and putting her hands to her stomach as another wave of nausea hit. To her surprise, Gabriel moved, sitting beside her. He turned her head to look at her more closely.

"You're very pale," he noted, sounding more unsettled than ever.

Crecy sighed, knowing she must try and be well, for he'd only fret her to death with his worries if she wasn't.

"I'm fine now, tired is all," she lied, smiling at him. "It was just that dreadful boat. I didn't get a lot of sleep."

"Well, then, you must try and rest now," he said, his voice firm and authoritative. "Dr Marchand will attend you during the next week to make sure everything is all right. From what I can gather, he's the best doctor in France. I have sent someone to fetch him and bring him to you. He will stay close by until after the birth."

"But you can't possibly have had a reply from him yet," she said, realising that Gabriel in his usual way had simply demanded the doctor attend her and expected his orders to be carried out. "What if he doesn't want to? What if he has other patients?"

Gabriel gave her a curious look that suggested the idea had never crossed his mind. "He will come," he said, looking mutinous, and folded his arms. Crecy held back a curse, as she didn't want some fancy French doctor, in any case, but couldn't help but hope that this Marchand fellow would do as Gabriel wanted, for the doctor's own sake.

She sighed and decided she didn't have the energy to argue about it, and in truth she was deeply touched by his care of her and the lengths he had gone to in order to ensure her comfort, and more importantly, she suspected, her health. Crecy smothered a yawn, feeling sleepy all at once.

"You should try and rest," he said, his voice surprisingly soft.

Crecy nodded and untied her bonnet, casting it to the other side of the carriage whilst she curled her feet up on the seat beside her. Gabriel was watching her with a curious expression until she tugged at his arm, indicating he should lift it up. This, he did, scowling a little, and Crecy laid down, suspecting he was utterly scandalised as she laid her head on the surprisingly hard surface of his large thigh. She shifted a little, until her head was more comfortably positioned on his lap and dared a glance up to see Gabriel staring resolutely out of the window. Biting back a smile, she pulled his arms back around her, gave a sigh of content, and went to sleep.

***

By the time the carriage had drawn up in front of the *Manoir du Lierre,* it was late in the afternoon. They had stopped briefly for a lunch, which had put Gabriel in a shocking mood and had also informed her of the fact that he spoke perfect French. At least, it sounded so to her untrained ear, and he certainly had the staff jumping to do his bidding with alacrity. The meal had not met with his approval, however. Crecy had once again eaten like a starved pig, and then returned to her comfortable position on Gabriel's lap and had an untroubled, deep sleep, while he seethed and muttered about the irritations of foreign travel.

Crecy awoke to the sound of the wheels rolling over gravel, and looked up, blinking sleepily at Gabriel, who was still looking a little tense.

"We're here," he said as the carriage swayed to a halt, and Crecy sat up all in a rush, putting on her bonnet as quickly as she could and smoothing out her wrinkled clothes before having to face the staff. She wondered if they would disapprove of her and be unfriendly, not that she'd understand a word of anything if they were rude, as she didn't speak any French at all past *bonjour* and *merci*.

Gabriel got down before turning and giving her his hand. Crecy put her hand in his and her foot on the step, and then stopped as she caught her first glimpse of the property.

"Welcome to the *Manoir du Lierre*," Gabriel said, looking rather nervous.

"Oh, Gabriel," Crecy breathed as her heart lifted. "It's beautiful."

Glancing back at him as she stepped down from the carriage, she knew she had said the right thing as he seemed to relax, pleased by her comment. It had been important to him that she like the place, and she felt relieved that there was no need to pretend. It was charming.

Built of granite with a grey slate roof, it was at once stern and imposing, but age had softened its edges, and a profusion of ivy that scrambled up the front wall gave it a rather fairy tale feel. It was far smaller than Damerel, but still grand, with a tower to one side of the main building, which looked like it had started life as a medieval hall.

"It was built in the early sixteenth century, though parts of it are older," Gabriel said, and she smiled as she heard something that sounded like enthusiasm colouring his voice. He also hadn't let go of her hand, she noted with a little surge of pleasure. "I inherited it about a decade ago. It belonged to some ancient great uncle I didn't even know of, but I never saw it until a couple of years ago," he said, looking at the house with an almost fond expression. "I thought perhaps Napoleon would have destroyed it beyond repair, but the damage wasn't too extensive."

Crecy watched him with interest as he put her hand on his arm and led her toward the front door.

"I had the roof repaired and one of the chimneys, but really, it was just the interior. That was in a shocking state," he said with a grimace of such distaste that she could well imagine how he'd hated seeing it so run down and disordered. "It took a lot of work to get it back into a habitable state. Especially as I don't get here as often as I'd like to."

She paused and he looked down at her, a question in his eyes. "This is your house, isn't it, Gabriel?" she said, knowing it was true as a slightly guarded look came into his eyes. This was why he protected it so carefully, keeping the address a secret and any chance of anyone finding him here to an absolute minimum. No one knew him here. No one knew about the scandalous and dreadful reputation of Viscount DeMorte, and as he would not socialise, no one likely would. He would be free. "Damerel is the place you were born and it belongs to you like the London house, but this ... this is your home."

Gabriel didn't answer, but moved her on again.

"Come along," he said, not looking at her. "I'll show you around."

***

By dinner time, it was clear that the staff here were as used to Gabriel's rather precise ways, as everything in the house ran like clockwork and the meal was identical to that which was usually provided, with one notable exception: Crecy's meal was different.

She looked up at Gabriel in surprise, but he was concentrating on rearranging the table with even more determination than usual, and was ignoring her.

"Gabriel?" she said, laying her hand over his to stop him fussing any further. "Thank you."

He didn't look at her, staring at the water jug which had been next on his rotor to adjust for at least the fifth time. Crecy wondered how long it would take him to relax here, but determined that she should begin to help him as best she could.

He didn't answer, but frowned a little, still staring at the jug and looking increasingly agitated.

"For allowing me a different meal," she added, to be sure he understood the reason for her gratitude. She didn't doubt it disturbed his need for symmetry, so she was doubly grateful.

He frowned a little harder. "The doctor said you needed a ... a lowering diet in your condition."

Crecy opened and closed her mouth in surprise. "Which doctor?"

Gabriel looked increasingly uneasy, his hand clenched beneath hers. "I consulted a doctor in London before returning to Damerel," he snapped, sounding really impatient now.

Crecy blinked in astonishment. The idea of Gabriel seeking advice from a doctor for her pregnancy ... Providing a good doctor was one thing, but she could think of no other man in the world who would have lowered himself to do something as outrageous as becoming informed on the subject. Pregnancy was for women and doctors alone, and men stayed well clear of knowing anything about it. But not Gabriel. She released his hand and he moved immediately to straightened the jug again.

"That's enough, Gabriel," she said, her voice firm, wanting to speak to him further on the subject, but not feeling able to until she refocused his attention.

Naturally, he ignored her.

"I said, that is enough," she repeated, not unkindly but with enough force that he turned and glared at her.

"Of course it's enough," he snarled, his eyes glittering with fury and embarrassment. "Do you think me an imbecile? I know it's enough, dammit."

Crecy sighed and got to her feet, she put her arms around his neck and leaned down, kissing his cheek. "I think ... you are quite the most caring and wonderful man, and as far from being an imbecile as it is possible to be. But I also think you need my help to stop you behaving in this manner because it makes you very unhappy." She paused, pressing her cheek against his as he sat rigid under her touch. "Now, please pick up your knife and fork and eat your dinner. The table is perfect, as you well know." Crecy took a breath, not liking to blackmail him, but not finding any other solution. "If you do not, I will go straight to bed without eating a morsel."

"You can't do that," he snapped, sounding really furious as he turned to glare at her. "It's bad for the baby."

"Yes," she agreed, her tone placid. "But I shall do so nevertheless, Gabriel, because this behaviour is bad for you, it makes you unhappy, and that makes me unhappy, and *that* is far worse for the baby."

Crecy straightened and returned to her seat, and watched with interest as he scowled in fury at his plate, and then snatched up his knife and fork and began his meal. With a quietly smug smile of satisfaction, Crecy ate her own with pleasure.

The rest of the evening passed pleasantly enough. It was apparently Gabriel's usual routine to sit in the library and read after dinner, and Crecy was more than happy to do the same. The library here was a wonderful room. It was a very masculine space with mahogany bookshelves lining every available wall space. As it was, Gabriel's books had naturally been arranged with precision, and Crecy was only disappointed that so many of the titles were in French. The fire was blazing and the deep green brocade curtains closed against the chill of the evening. With the lamps lit and casting a soft warm glow about the room, it was cosy and welcoming in a way that none of the rooms in Damerel were.

"You've done a wonderful job with this place, Gabriel," she said, an hour or so later as she put her book aside. In truth, she'd barely read a word, as eager as she was to read her new book, as her thoughts were too consumed by the man opposite her and the coming night. "Why have you never made Damerel your own in the same way?"

He didn't look up from his book, but she could tell he was considering the question. After a while, he looked up her. "It has never felt like mine, like ..." He stopped and Crecy waited for him to find the words he wanted. "I've never felt able to," he admitted.

Crecy nodded and got up, going to sit down on the floor at his feet.

"Perhaps when we go back there next, I could help you?" she suggested, seeing a look of interest spark in his eyes before he turned away.

"Perhaps," he muttered, sounding non-committal, though Crecy had been sure he'd liked the idea. He got to his feet and reached down a hand, helping her up. "It's late and you've had a long day, I'll show you to your room."

Crecy stared at him in horror. *"My* room?" she repeated, eyes wide.

Gabriel looked uneasy, but nodded. "Your room," he said, his voice firm.

Folding her arms, Crecy knew that this was one fight she had to win. If she had any chance at all of gaining any emotional intimacy with this stubborn man, she had to share his bed.

"Gabriel, you've been everything that has been kindness and consideration," she said, her words careful as she tried to keep a lid on her frustration. "And for dressing and preparations of that nature, a room of my own is a good idea as I won't risk disturbing your things. However," she added, her voice becoming a little strident despite her best efforts. "If you think I'm not sharing your bed at night ... well, you've got another thing coming!"

Gabriel huffed out a breath, looking irritated. "The doctor also said that ... that the intimacy of ... *the act* was not good for the child."

Crecy stared at him in utter horror. "The man's an imbecile!" she exploded, feeling horrified at the idea of not being able to touch this infuriating, gorgeous man before her for another six months. Oh, no. That was *not* going to happen.

"The man is a respected physician," Gabriel shot back at her, looking like he wanted this conversation to be over right now.

Crecy muttered a rude comment under her breath, but refrained from saying any more. "Very well," she said, thinking that if she could just get into his bed, she could deal with this foolish idea in her own time. "But that is no reason that we cannot share a bed together."

A tinge of colour crept into Gabriel's cheeks as he shook his head, and Crecy was relieved to discover that he felt there was an extremely good reason.

"Crecy, I ... If you're in my bed ..." he began, trailing off and looking as though he'd rather die than admit how much he wanted her.

Walking closer, she took his hand, looking up at him and smiling.

"Can't keep your hands off me, hmmm?" she said, teasing him a little.

Gabriel snorted, giving her a dark, glittering look that made something deep inside her clench with anticipation. "That's how we got into this damned mess in the first place," he growled with frustration. "I never usually ..." Gabriel clamped his mouth shut, but Crecy could guess the rest.

"You never usually leave your seed behind?" she asked without so much as a blush.

Gabriel tutted. "Good God, woman, is there nothing you won't say?" he said with a huff, looking appalled by her outspokenness.

Crecy chuckled and shook her head. "Probably not, my love, so you'd best get used to the idea."

He made a noise which might have been amusement ... or frustration, or possibly both, she wasn't sure.

"Can we go to bed now, please?"

Gabriel sighed as she tugged at his hand and he rolled his eyes in defeat. "Come along, then," he grumbled and led her up the stairs.

Chapter 27

"Wherein Crecy is stubborn and takes Gabriel in hand."

Gabriel showed her to her room so she could get ready for bed, and she entered with start of surprise at how pretty the room was. It was all done in a rather deep blue, which reminded her strongly of Gabriel's eyes and so naturally found favour with her. The rest was white with a few touches of a rather bright yellow here and there in the furnishings, which gave the room a rather joyful, sunny feel, even on a chilly spring night. That Gabriel was responsible for it was yet another revelation about the man she was coming to know.

Beth was waiting for her in the adjoining dressing room, unpacking a huge trunk that Crecy had never seen before.

"Goodness, what on earth is in there, the lost city of Atlantis?" Crecy said with a laugh as Beth returned a puzzled look.

"No, miss," she said with all seriousness. "But there's more dresses and the like than I ever saw in all my born days, and that's the God's honest truth." She gestured to the walls of the room, which revealed dozens and dozens of dresses of every type and colour imaginable. Crecy gaped in astonishment. Moving to a large wardrobe, she opened it to find rows of shoes and boots, gloves, stockings ... so much it made her head spin.

"That ain't all, miss," Beth said with a grin. She tugged at Crecy's hand, pulling her to the far side of the room where Crecy's breath snagged in her throat and tears pricked at her eyes. It was a crib. Beautifully done, it was made of walnut and designed to swing. Crecy touched it, watching as it rocked gently, and felt her chest tighten. A smaller chest beside the cradle was opened but not yet unpacked, and Crecy bent to run her hands over the tiny items. The bonnet was delicate and ridiculously small, tiny with lace trim, and she had to swallow hard to stop herself from sobbing.

"Did his lordship order all of this?" Beth asked, looking at the carefully packed chest of miniature items with as much reverence as Crecy was.

Crecy nodded, quite unable to say a word.

Beth gave a wistful sigh, smiling at her. "He must love you very much, miss. If you don't mind me remarkin' it?"

Wiping an errant tear from her cheek that had escaped despite her best efforts, Crecy gave a choked laugh. "Yes," she said, nodding. "He really must."

Once Beth had left her, Crecy took one last look at her image in the looking glass and pronounced herself satisfied. The nightgown was so fine it was almost sheer, and it was trimmed about the neck and cuffs with a beautiful lace, which gave her a deceptively virginal appearance. Her hair had been brushed and fell in heavy golden waves about her shoulders, and after a good meal and a quiet evening, the colour had returned to her cheeks. Indeed, she thought she had never looked better, a healthy, wholesome look to her skin that she had not seen for some months. She bit back a smile as she wondered how hard Gabriel would try to resist, her and then paused as she remembered her promise to let him come to her. Damnation. Well, there was nothing to say she couldn't tempt him a bit, at least.

Crecy made her way to the adjoining door, which Gabriel had indicated led to his room, and knocked. She heard the muffled sound of Gabriel dismissing his valet, and a moment later, the door opened.

Gabriel filled the doorway. Large and masculine and virile, Crecy had to force herself not to launch herself at him.

"Hello," she said instead, quite unable to keep the silly grin from her face.

Gabriel stared back at her, his expression unreadable as he looked her over, but that was telling enough. The harder it was to read him, the stronger he was trying to hide his emotions. Crecy decided that was good enough and moved past him without waiting for an invitation.

She looked about the room with interest. It was indeed a more masculine room than her own, done in a much darker blue and with heavy wooden panelling around much of the walls where hers had been painted white. The space was dominated by a massive bed, hung with luxurious brocade curtains of the same deep blue, shot through with gold thread, and with gold tassels along the edges. It was surprisingly opulent and indulgent. Crecy cast Gabriel a mischievous look, undid her wrap - throwing it at him as she went - and then ran to the bed, jumping on it with all the glee of a naughty seven-year-old.

Gabriel shook his head and began to fold her wrap with his usual care. "You're pregnant for heaven's sake, have a care, Crecy."

"Oh, pooh," she said, sticking her tongue out at him. "That doesn't mean I shall let you wrap me in cotton wool, so you may as well give up on the idea." She watched with impatience as he put her wrap away and then did the same with his own, before turning towards the bed. "Come along," she said, stripping the covers back further on his side and patting the space that was his.

Gabriel let out a long-suffering sigh. "Remember what I said," he muttered, the warning behind the words unmistakable.

"Mmmmhmmm."

He gave her a suspicious look, but got in beside her, pausing only to blow out the candle. Crecy wasted no time in wriggling beneath his arm and laying her head on his chest.

"Crecy," he said, sounding irritated.

"Oh, come along, you can't deny the mother of your child a cuddle, at least," she said, a distinctly whiny quality to her voice that she was rather pleased with.

She could practically hear him grinding his teeth, but he said nothing more, and she counted that a victory. Content, for now, Crecy discovered she really was dreadfully tired and went to sleep happy.

***

Gabriel stared into the darkness and wondered how the hell he was going to get through the next six months. Could you die from desire, he wondered with a touch of desperation? He couldn't help but hope so. It would make things a deal easier.

Crecy was warm and soft, cuddled as close to him as she could manage, her hair a silky curtain falling over his arm as the faint scent of lily of the valley drifted up to him. The delicate huff of her breathing fluttered over his chest, sending goosebumps chasing over his skin, which did not help matters in the least. He could tumble her onto her back now, this minute, and she would be only too pleased to welcome him. The idea was like a maggot in his brain, wriggling in his conscious mind until he knew he wouldn't sleep a wink.

He was hard and aching, and the object of his desire was only too close and as far from unwilling as it was possible to get. He sighed, suppressing a groan and consigning himself to a night of utter torture.

***

Crecy woke, a sensation of peace and happiness stealing over her. She wriggled her toes in the warmth of the bed and realised that the heat source making her so cosy was Gabriel. Without opening her eyes, she registered the feel of him under her hand, the tangle of coarse hair on his chest and the surprisingly silky skin beneath. With a deceptively sleepy sigh that might fool him into believing that she was still asleep, she stirred a little, allowing her hand to drift lower. The already tense body beside her seemed to grow tauter still, and he sucked in a breath as her hand covered a rather impressive show of arousal.

"Crecy!" he growled, though his voice sounded more desperate than angry.

She looked up at him, blinking and giving him what she hoped was a beguiling look, as her hand firmed a little, caressing him through his nightshirt.

"Yes, Gabriel?" she replied, her tone one of innocent enquiry.

She moved her hand over him, eliciting a deep groan that made her own body spring to life in response. To her chagrin, Gabriel put a dent in her enthusiasm by grasping hold of her wrist.

"I told you no already," he said, lifting his head to glare at her and sounding very much as though he was talking through gritted teeth.

Crecy pursed her lips and shook her head. "You told me that ..." she hesitated, finding that even she baulked a little at being too expressive. "That *the act* was forbidden, but ... and I know I have no experience of such things, Gabriel, but I suspect that does not cancel out every aspect of pleasure?"

Gabriel stared at her in outrage for a moment and then capitulated. His head hit the pillow with a thud and he released her hand. "Fine, fine ... just ... *please* ..."

Crecy grinned, feeling rather smug. That had been easier than she'd anticipated. With every indication of enthusiasm, Crecy returned to her work, wasting no time in pulling the infuriating shirt out of the way. That would *have* to go. She pushed it up, revealing Gabriel in all his glory, and making her feel all the more smug and not a little possessive. He sat up, stripping the shirt off and throwing it to the floor with impatience. Crecy took a moment to admire that impressive chest and the scattering of dark hair that trailed below a hard stomach to regions she had every intention of becoming better acquainted with. She hesitated, though, eyeing the shirt on the floor and wondering if he'd insist on tidying it. But he was staring at her with a rather frantic look in his eyes, and didn't seem the least bit concerned with the shirt.

Intrigued, Crecy returned to the even more interesting work of familiarising herself with Gabriel. He sucked in a breath as her hand returned to him, and she ran her fingers up and down the hard length, watching with interest as he shivered.

"Like this, remember?" he said, his voice hoarse as he took her hand and showed her how to go about the business of pleasuring him. Crecy repeated his instructions, watching closely as Gabriel shut his eyes.

Crecy knelt beside him, using her free hand to smooth over his skin, and noted with interest the moisture that gathered, allowing her hand to slide more easily as his breathing became deeper and faster. She bent lower, quite unable to resist the urge to kiss his stomach, pleased by the hitch in his breath as her lips met his skin. She shifted around a little, moving between his legs and bending again, this time to nuzzle her face against his thigh. Her lips continued their exploration, mapping the rough hair of his thighs and the intriguingly soft skin at the apex. She wondered if the skin she held in her hand was even silkier, as it felt like it was, and she paused her attentions for a moment. Gabriel raised his head, looking a little indignant, just in time to see her duck down and press her lips to the head of his arousal.

"Oh, good Christ." The words were said in a rush, and Crecy decided this was something that pleased him, and continued, discovering that trailing her tongue over his flesh drew quite a remarkable sound from him. With no real idea of what she was doing, but guided by the increasingly agonised sounds from the far end of the bed, Crecy alternated her attentions between mouth and lips and tongue until Gabriel was clutching at the bed covers.

"Stop, stop," he said, and Crecy looked up as he took himself in hand and his body grew taut, every muscle straining with exertion as pleasure overcame him and he found his release. Crecy watched, fascinated and burning with desire for him. She wanted him to make love to her so badly that she thought she'd go mad if he didn't, but she suspected her opportunity to persuade him this morning had been lost. Still, she knew it didn't do to push Gabriel too hard. She would just have to be patient.

She sighed inwardly, never having felt less patient in her whole life. Still, he had already shown her there were other ways to bring her pleasure, too. Sitting up, she stripped off her nightgown and used it to clean him up.

"Crecy," he said, still breathless and a little dazed, by the sounds of things. "For the love of God, you don't need to do that."

"But I don't mind," she said, giving him a curious look. "I want to." Her lips quirked as she looked down at him, noticing the moment when he registered her nakedness. "Besides," she added. "It's my turn."

***

Gabriel wasn't sure his heart - or any other part of him, come to that - could stand much more.

He felt raw and exposed in more ways than simply being naked before her. She was digging so deeply into his heart, it was terrifying, and he didn't know how to stop it happening. And now, there she was, demanding that it was her turn.

He didn't know whether to thank God or curse the devil.

Before he could consider the options further, his body had decided it wasn't worth the effort of further thought, and he'd tumbled her onto her back as he'd been dreaming of doing all night. Though he would never have admitted it to Crecy, he cursed the bloody doctor who had advised him, and decided he would seek a second opinion - just to be on the safe side. For now, though, he was going to take his time and give a little retribution.

Gabriel moved over her, bracing his weight on his elbows and kissing her, quite unable to disguise his feelings on the matter. With Crecy's arms wrapped over his shoulders, holding him tight, and her body as inviting and welcoming as ever, there was no greater happiness than this. He could not help but show it, kissing her slowly, tenderly, and with such reverence as he felt for her, this strange and wonderful woman who was mad enough to care for him.

But there were other inviting areas to attend to, and Gabriel made a thorough exploration of all of them, smiling as his lips closed over her breast and she gasped, clutching at his hair, and fighting back the absurd desire to laugh as his mouth trailed over her stomach and lower, and she squealed and gasped and arched beneath him.

When he finally reached his destination, the sounds he drew from her were even more pleasing. He decided that he was glad the walls were so damn thick, or the servants would not be able to look them in the eye in the morning, as Crecy did nothing by halves. Hearing his name cried out in such a desperate manner as she came, clutching at the bed covers and writhing beneath him, had him hard and nursing the violent desire to bury himself inside her. He was definitely going to consult Dr Marchand on the matter. The moment the fellow got here. Good Lord, surely a Frenchman would be sensible?

Gabriel knelt back, surveying the devastation he'd wrought with satisfaction. Crecy was gasping, her arms akimbo, hair a tangled mess against the bed covers, and her skin deeply flushed. She had never looked more beautiful, and Gabriel could no longer deny the feeling that seemed to push at his chest, needing more room than he had to give to physically contain it. It was too vast, too overpowering … too frightening, but it was real.

He loved her.

Chapter 28

"Wherein Crecy confronts the devil."

The months that followed were idyllic, as far as Crecy was concerned.

Perhaps not quite perfect, as the stupid French doctor had confirmed his English counterpart's ideas on lovemaking whilst pregnant. But discovering other options was a rather delightful way to pass the time. Gabriel was at his most wonderful in these moments. His ability to love and care for her was something which continued to astonish her. That a man who had received so little care in his life was capable of such tenderness towards her was something she felt humbled by, and extremely fortunate to experience.

Not that everything was easy. By no means. Gabriel's obsessive behaviour had not diminished as much as she had hoped, and indeed, as her pregnancy progressed, she sensed it worsening. She had overheard him the day before, having a passionate argument with someone, only to discover that he was alone. That his father's voice still plagued him was only too clear. From her eavesdropping, she had also realised that for Gabriel, this was only a happy interlude. His job was to destroy Edward's good name, and delivering his wife's sister home with his bastard child in tow had to fit into that category nicely.

To say that Crecy was devastated was perhaps to simplify her feelings. She didn't blame Gabriel, though, she couldn't. His father was to blame for this. For everything that Gabriel had become, that man was to blame, and she had never hated anyone more. For she knew, without a shadow of a doubt, that Gabriel loved her, that he wanted their child and feared for both of them … and that knowing he could not keep them was tearing him apart. That was why he became increasingly unsettled as the time passed all too quickly, because he did not want to let her go.

It was August now, and the days were almost too hot to bear. They stayed indoors most of their day, either locked in their bedroom and each other's arms, or in the sanctuary of the library, which was clearly Gabriel's favourite room. After dinner that evening, however, the temperature had been more moderate and Crecy desperate for some air, so she had persuaded Gabriel to take a walk with her.

The gardens here were exquisite and, of course, another thing that Gabriel had controlled with precision. The design was his own, after having studied a number of books on the subject, and Crecy was delighted and fascinated that such a natural and gently beautiful garden had come from his own hand. She might have expected mazes and tightly clipped box hedging, but not the profusion of colour and variety that was to be found here.

They settled themselves on a bench not too far from a small river that wound through the property towards the bottom of the gently sloping grounds. Close enough that they could hear the soft murmur of the water, but not so near that they'd get bitten to death by the wildlife. Crecy liked sitting and talking to Gabriel in the dark. Outside of their lovemaking, it was the one time that he let his guard down a little and would speak more freely. It was almost as though the darkness shielded him somehow.

"Why doesn't it bother you?" Crecy began, voicing a question she had long wanted to pose.

Gabriel turned his head, the slight glint of his eyes visible in the moonlight.

"It probably does," he replied, his tone dry. "But what precisely are you referring to?"

"When we make love," she said, smiling as she knew he still wasn't used to her directness. "It's wonderful and joyous and … well, simply the best thing in the world," she added, knowing it would amuse him even if he said nothing. "But it's also messy and disordered and out of control and ... well, all the things you can't abide."

He was quiet for a long while before he shook his head.

"No, it isn't," he said, his voice quiet. "It's perfect."

Crecy was quite certain she could melt at his feet at that moment, but contented herself with raising his hand to her lips and kissing it.

"I love you," she said, knowing he wouldn't reply and feeling quite at ease with the fact. She knew how he felt. That was enough.

"You were right," he said, his voice a little tense now.

"That sounds unlikely," she laughed, squeezing his hand and snuggling closer against him despite the heat.

He let out a huff of laughter, but shook his head. "About the night Aubrey Russell was shot. I didn't order it."

Crecy smiled in the dim light. She'd been sure that had been the case, but she was simply happy that he felt like telling her the truth.

"I knew that, Gabriel," she said, watching as he turned his head.

"Why do you have such faith in me?" he demanded, sounding angry all at once. "I don't deserve it, you know. I may not have ordered Edward's murder, but the man who did it knew I wanted rid of him, and he wanted to be free of his debt to me. He thought if he solved the problem of Edward returning and taking back the title that I would owe him instead."

Crecy held his hand tighter, knowing that he would retreat from her if she let him.

"But you didn't order his death, Gabriel. I know you've done some bad things and I can't condone them, and I hope, in time, that you will find a happier way to live your life. But I do forgive you for them, and I understand why you did those things."

"How?" he said, the word almost a snarl of anger. "How can you possibly understand? I killed a man in a duel, did you know that?"

Crecy took a breath, but nodded. He was trying to drive her away like he had many times before with his angry words. He would push and push, all the time waiting for the moment she would leave, as she knew he believed she would, whilst all the while praying that she wouldn't. Surely, sooner or later, he would have to believe that he was stuck with her for good?

"Yes. I knew that, Gabriel. Though I don't know why you killed him. Tell me, please?"

He fell quiet then, and she didn't need to see his face to imagine the mutinous expression that was on it now.

"Well?" she pressed him. She knew for certain that Gabriel never did anything without a good reason, no matter how tangled that reasoning might be. But she felt in her heart that he would not have taken a man's life for nothing.

"It's of no matter," he snapped.

Crecy sat up, turning towards him. "Oh, but it is," she said, her voice firm. "You want me to believe you the very devil, Gabriel, well, prove it, then. Tell me why you killed him, and don't you dare lie to me, for I shall know it."

"I didn't like his face," he retorted, sounding so much like a sulky boy that she had to bite back a smile.

"Liar," she said, her voice tart as she let go of his hand and folded her arms.

"Did you know I own a whorehouse, too?" This one had been designed to make her jealous, but Crecy didn't rise to it. She knew him too well to believe he would ever give anything of himself to a woman he had no feelings for. Whatever he had done before she had arrived would have been out of physical need, and perhaps simply a desire for some form of human contact, no matter how sordid. She pitied him for it and could only feel gratitude to the women there if they had brought him some comfort in the years before she'd come to him.

"I knew that, yes," she said, her voice placid. "Are the ladies pretty?"

"For the love of God!" he exploded, getting to his feet, though to her relief, he did not walk away.

"Gabriel," she said, getting up and walking to stand beside him. "You cannot shock me into not loving you and you cannot drive me away, so you may as well tell me all of your darkest secrets. I will keep them safe for you, and you will feel all the lighter for it."

He let out a breath and stared up at the stars. His body was taut, and she knew he was fighting a war in his head. He wanted to tell her everything, but his father's voice was determined to undermine them. If she could only make him see that it wasn't his father he heard at all, just his own conscience because he didn't believe he deserved to be happy. He sabotaged every opportunity he had for happiness because he didn't dare take it.

"I killed Lord Aston because he nearly killed one of the girls."

Crecy let out a breath and smiled in the darkness, but she said nothing, hoping he would say more without her forcing the words from him.

"I didn't know at first, they contacted the law, but of course no one was interested in helping a woman like that." The anger in his voice was obvious and she moved closer to him, holding his hand within both of hers. "He beat her, oh, God, so badly, and then … he cut her face. She'd been beautiful before, but she knew she couldn't work after that. The bastard had stopped short of killing her, but taken her ability to support herself. So I killed him."

"Good."

Gabriel gave a laugh, but it sounded almost as though he wanted to cry.

"You're madder than I am," he said, his voice rough as he covered his eyes with his free hand.

"In the first place, you are not mad, Gabriel," she said, staring up at him and willing him to believe her. "You have a beautiful soul." She ignored the sound of ridicule he made to that comment and pressed on. "You do, but you're damaged, too, and in everything you do, you are always fighting your past. But you win out so often, my love. If only you could see that."

Crecy wished the moonlight was stronger so that she could see his face clearly, but he would not look at her. She tugged at his hand, pulling him back to the bench and sitting herself in his lap this time. Leaning into him, she placed his large hand against the fullness of her stomach and covered it with her own. "Someone who could not protect themselves was badly hurt and you couldn't bear it. So you took action. That is not the work of a bad man, but a compassionate one."

"And you don't care that your child's father is a whoremonger?" The words were crude and designed to shock her, and Crecy sighed.

"When was the last time you visited them?"

"Just before Christmas," he said, sounding satisfied in the fact that it had been after they'd met.

"And did you … did you take anyone to bed while you were there?"

She saw his jaw stiffen, even in the dim light, and knew her suspicion had been correct.

"Not that time," he admitted, but implying there had been plenty of other times.

"When was the last time?" she pressed, needing him to see she didn't care. It was now that mattered, not then.

He let out a frustrated sigh and she knew she'd won. Whenever it had been, it was before she arrived. Long before, if she was any judge.

"Why own a place like that, anyway?" she asked, not really expecting an answer and not in any way judging him, simply curious. That was it, of course. A place where no one judged him. For surely, if there was a place where the most base of human nature could be found ... it was there. "They were kind to you," she guessed, and Gabriel dropped his head forward, resting it against her, his big hand still splayed over her stomach.

"How do you do that?" he asked, sounding raw and unhappy and afraid. "It's like you get inside my head, and believe me, that is somewhere you do not want to be."

Crecy stroked his hair, leaning her head upon his.

"There's nothing in there that frightens me, Gabriel."

"Oh, there is," he said, a dark threat lacing through his words. "Believe me, Crecy, if you knew ..."

She raised her head and looked at him, putting her finger to his lips before he could say more. "I do know."

"You can't!"

He was tense and angry again, all at once, and he began to withdraw his hand from her stomach. Crecy grabbed his wrist, holding on tight.

"Your father wants you to return me to Edward once the child is born, so that he is forced to raise your bastard. Isn't that it, Gabriel?"

He looked away from her, making a choked sound.

"But here's the thing, my love," she said, her voice soft. "I know you, and I know that it's killing you. You don't want to do it." Crecy watched as the emotions chased over his face, revulsion and self-loathing, guilt and sorrow, they were all there.

"Why don't you hate me," he demanded, and she could see the glitter of anguish in his eyes as the words tumbled out, harsh and desperate in the darkness. "Can't you see how vile he is? He's in me, Crecy. He *is* me. He's in my head and under my skin. Sometimes I think I can even see his face behind mine in the mirror."

"Hush, love, hush," she said, feeling heartbroken by his agony. "It's all right." She held him close, rocking him like a child even though he was stiff and angry and unbending, refusing to allow himself to grieve. "Tell me about that night," she said, realising that if she was ever to truly understand him, she needed to know the horror of it, needed to hear exactly what had happened.

"I told you already," he said and she heard a weary note to his voice now. He would retreat into himself and lock himself away with his compulsions unless she could get him to talk.

"You told me about finding your mother," she said gently. "You said that you'd never seen so much blood." He flinched, and she leaned her head against his once more, holding him closer against her. "You said your father had beaten her, and then gone back to confront Winterbourne. When he returned home, she was dead."

He nodded, but said nothing.

"What happened then, Gabriel?" She kept the words soft but firm, he would tell her, he had to.

He drew in a breath, but it was a long moment before he spoke again.

"His grief was ... Shakespearean," he said with a snort of disgust. "I think he'd have done well on the stage. I always felt he was acting, always acting, always lying, professing how much he loved her ... *'I only get so angry because I love you so deeply and you hurt me so much'.*" He shook his head. "He didn't know the meaning of the word. He'd punish her for simply speaking, for expressing an opinion; good God, if she disagreed with him, there'd be hell to pay."

Crecy waited as he gathered his thoughts, feeling as though she was bleeding inside for the pain he was in, wishing she could take it from him.

"He wept and screamed and lost his mind for … I don't know, a long time," he said at last, and she could hear the tension in his voice now as he tried to keep himself calm. "His shirt was soaked in her blood. I remember that. I remember thinking how strange that Father was wearing a red shirt, and then realising it was her blood." He swallowed and she clung to him, only too able to imagine the horror of it. "He turned on me, then. He said it was my fault. They were happy before I was born, it was all my fault. He should have drowned me, thrown me in the lake before I had the chance to come between them."

Crecy sobbed, and Gabriel put both arms around her now, pulling her against him, covering her stomach with his body and his arms, as if protecting the child within from the monstrous words. She held her tears back as best she could, knowing he would stop if she became too distressed.

"He said Mother's death was on my conscience, and his would be, too, because he had to follow her. He could not live without his love. The only way that I could make amends was to destroy the Greyston line." He looked up at her then, his eyes full of tears and confusion. "I was ten, Crecy. I didn't know how to do what he wanted and ... and I said so." His voice broke, and Crecy could do nothing but hold him, stroking his hair and whispering that she loved him. "He went downstairs in a rage, and I thought perhaps he'd changed his mind, but when he came back, he had a pistol." Gabriel sucked in a breath and she could feel his big shoulders trembling now. "He held it to my head. He said that I had to swear, upon my life, that I would destroy Edward's father and everyone that followed, or he'd shoot me before he killed himself."

"Oh, my God." Of all the things that Crecy had imagined, she had never realised how very black it was. That Gabriel had survived at all, let alone become a man capable of such love and compassion, was nothing short of miraculous. "Oh, my love, I'm so sorry. I'm so desperately sorry."

"I did it," he said, the words forced out now, though his voice shook with emotion. "I swore that I would do it, and he said that he would haunt me until the day I succeeded, that I would never be free of him unless I kept my word." He swallowed, then, hauling in a breath, the next words halting and so vile that he clearly didn't want to say them aloud. "He ... he was standing right in front of me, pointing the gun in my face, pressing the barrel against my forehead, and then ... and then he shot himself instead."

Crecy buried her face in his hair, rocking both of them now, weeping for the poor, frightened boy and all the horror he had experienced. They stayed like that for a long time, until Gabriel had composed himself a little.

"He won't let me be, Crecy. He'll never let me be." The words broke her heart completely as she heard the exhaustion behind them, the defeat. He was so tired of fighting.

Crecy drew in a deep breath and took his head in her hands, forcing him to look up at her.

"You just listen to me, Gabriel Greyston. I'm not afraid of your wretched father, and I won't let him hurt you anymore. We are going to get rid of him. You and me, one way or another. *Do you hear me, you bastard?*" she screamed, raising her voice to the skies, knowing it was ridiculous, but shouting into the darkness all the same. "I won't let you have him. He's mine now, and I'll fight you until you're burning in hell where you belong!"

Gabriel gave a startled laugh, staring at her with wonder, and they stayed there until the dawn came up, safe in each other's arms.

Chapter 29

"Wherein a surprise and a return to England."

If Crecy had hoped that the events of that night would mark a turning point, she was sorely disappointed. On the one hand, Gabriel was changed. When they were together, he was more attentive and loving than he had ever been, more demonstrably affectionate than ever before, as though he had given up fighting his feelings and accepted them. Though he refused to divert from the blasted doctor's instructions - much to Crecy's frustration - their lovemaking was a joy and a time where she knew they were both as happy as two people had any right to be.

Outside of this, however, there were times when she could feel him withdrawing into himself. With increasing frequency, he seemed to be lost in the dark, so full of sorrow and despair that she found it hard to reach him. He spent long periods of time alone in his study, writing letters and dealing with things he would not tell her about. There was an almost feverish quality to his work, whatever it was, and he was forever jotting notes down in a small leather bound book which he kept in his coat pocket. Try as she might, Crecy couldn't get him to explain what the book was for, and the one time she dared to try and take a peek, his anger had been quite something to behold. On top of this, his compulsion to arrange and tidy and straighten was no better, and he would struggle to keep his temper if Crecy tried to persuade him to leave things be.

This morning, she sighed as she stretched in bed, wondering if she dared to ask him again what he was going to such lengths to arrange, as surely he had something in mind? She suspected it was preparations for the baby, but he had done so much already that she couldn't fathom what else could possibly be required. At this rate, it would be the most indulged child in the history of England.

Crecy smiled at the idea, stroking her hand over her belly and feeling the twitch of a tiny foot pushing against her skin. Turning over on her other side, she reached for Gabriel and looked up, blinking in the morning light as she discovered he wasn't there.

Gabriel slept very little, but he was always beside her when she woke. Flinging the covers back, Crecy got out of bed with a groan, rubbing the small of her back and fetching her wrap, neatly folded and put away, of course.

The day was already warm, but at least not the sticky, sultry heat of the past week, which had made her feel so uncomfortable. Padding on bare feet, she headed back to her own room to discover Beth crouched beside a large chest and surrounded by more open chests as she packed Crecy's belongings. Crecy stared for a moment, a strange and unsettled feeling of foreboding stealing over her.

"What on earth is going on?" she demanded of Beth. The girl looked up, blowing a dark lock of hair from her face, which was already rosy and shining with perspiration. Judging from the scene around her, she must have begun at dawn.

"Why, miss, you're goin' back to England?" Beth sat back on her heels looking up at her with a frown. "Didn't 'e say nought to you?"

"No," Crecy replied, feeling suddenly cold and frightened despite the warmth of the day. She turned around, needing to see Gabriel, to discover what on earth was going on. Hurrying down the stairs as fast as her now generous proportions would allow, she looked up as Gabriel appeared in the hallway.

"Slow down," he ordered, looking furious with her. "How many times do I have to tell you to be careful on the stairs?"

"Gabriel!" she exclaimed, ignoring his words completely and throwing herself into his arms. "Tell me you're not sending me back," she said, fear a bitter taste in her mouth as she wondered if his father had won after all. She realised she was trembling, tears pricking at her eyes as she grabbed at his lapels and held on tight. "Please, Gabriel?"

She stared at him, seeing sorrow in his eyes even as he smiled and shook his head.

"Don't be foolish. Of course I'm not sending you back, you ridiculous creature." He gestured for her to follow him into the library and away from prying eyes, where he pulled her into his arms. "Crecy, you're trembling," he exclaimed, holding her tight and rubbing his hands up and down her back. "Come now, stop this nonsense. You'll upset the baby."

Crecy gave a hiccoughing laugh, looking up at him and not feeling as reassured as she perhaps ought by his words.

"W-why are they packing my things, then, and not yours?"

Gabriel smiled at her, one big hand cupping her face. "Because I didn't want you to be disturbed. John will do mine now you're up. We've a long journey ahead and I don't want you to get tired."

"But where are we going?" she demanded, feeling more perplexed than ever. "I thought I was to have the baby here?"

A look of guilt crossed his face and he didn't meet her eyes. "I know. But I am going to put things right, Crecy. I'm going to do what I should have done months ago."

Crecy stared at him, bewildered and anxious, as he too looked like he was scared to death.

"I don't understand," she whispered, turning her face into his hand and covering it with her own. Why did she feel so frightened?

"Well," he said, his voice suddenly taking on the rather gruff tone that always meant he was anxious. "Assuming ... assuming that you'll have me, I'm going to marry you."

Crecy blinked as the words seemed to float around her, but her brain didn't seem to be able to catch up. The hand that was still clutching his now ruined lapel held on tighter as she felt suddenly a little dizzy.

"W-what?" she stammered, needing to be certain she really had heard him correctly. "What did you say?"

Gabriel frowned, his blue eyes troubled now. "Dammit, Crecy, you heard me," he growled, looking so tense she thought he might bolt from the room at any moment. "Will you marry me or not?"

She gave a startled laugh and threw her arms about his neck, getting as close as her stomach would allow her, and pulled his head down for a kiss.

"Yes," she said against his mouth, smiling as she kissed him. "Yes, yes, yes, yes, a thousand times yes, Gabriel."

He snorted, but looked rather pleased all the same. "Well," he said, leaning down a little so she didn't have to strain to reach his lips. "That's all right, then."

Crecy sighed with relief, leaning her head on his chest. "But why England?" she said, looking up at him again. "We could marry here."

Gabriel shook his head. "I want to marry you at Damerel, and ..." He let out a breath, looking a little shifty.

She stared at him, narrowing her eyes. "Gabriel, what have you done?" she asked, wondering what he was hiding.

He scratched his head, not looking at her. "I ... may have bribed the reverend there into putting a false date in the register."

Crecy's mouth dropped open in shock. "You never did!" she exclaimed, gasping at his audacity. "How ever did you manage it?"

He snorted, looking relieved that she wasn't cross with him. "I think the fellow believes he's made a deal with the devil, but ... well, the village church will have a new roof before Christmas, put it that way, and no one will be able to say anything to you, Crecy," he added, his voice growing stern all at once. He stroked her face, staring at her with such a look that she felt utterly cherished, and for some reason still very afraid. "The register will show that I married you before we left England. You can hold your head up and our child will be legitimate."

She blinked, wondering what it was that felt so wrong when he was trying so hard to do everything right.

He frowned at her, perhaps sensing her unease.

"Does this not please you?" he asked, the anxiety returning to his eyes.

"Yes," she said, trying to smile as tears fell down her cheeks. "Yes, you've made me very, very happy, my love." Swallowing, she clutched at his arms, staring into his eyes. "But I feel like you're hiding something from me."

Gabriel's gaze slid from hers and he let her go.

"Don't be foolish," he said, his voice harder now. "It's just you being overemotional. You know how you've been at times with this child." He looked around then, a rather fond look in his eyes. "You've become a regular watering pot."

"I have not," Crecy objected, despite the fact she was wiping her face dry with the sleeve of her wrap.

He snorted, clearly disagreeing with her on that point.

"Go and get dressed, love," he said, sounding softer all at once. "I don't want you rushing about. We'll take our time getting back so you don't need to spend so long in the carriage, but I would like to leave by mid-morning."

"Very well," she said, smiling at the very rare use of an endearment for her, despite the sense of unease that wouldn't leave. She walked to the door and then hesitated, turning back to him. "You're really not hiding anything from me?"

"Of course not," he said, though he didn't meet her eyes, and she knew he was lying. "Now run along and get dressed. You know how cross I get when people don't follow the plan."

She smiled, aware that he was making a joke at his own expense, but quite unable to shake the feeling that she was missing something.

Chapter 30

"Wherein a homecoming and a wedding."

The journey back was, at least far better than the one coming had been. Gabriel was a good as his word, and despite his distaste for public inns unless strictly necessary, they took their time, breaking the journey often so that Crecy was only in the carriage for short periods. This inevitably made Gabriel tense, however, and there was nearly a very ugly scene when the proprietor of the place they stopped to eat in realised that they had *quality* dining with them. He proceeded to sweep away the wine and the glasses with shouts for the staff to bring the best stuff. As Gabriel had spent longer than Crecy cared to remember getting it all to his satisfaction, his display of fury had been inevitable. It had taken all of Crecy's persuasive skills to make him see that the man had been acting kindly and not with the sole intent of driving Gabriel to distraction.

The seas were still and their crossing uneventful, as they were followed by blue skies and a lovely breeze which took the heat from the sun. Try as she might, however, Crecy could not help but feel it was the calm before the storm. Gabriel seemed at times more tranquil than usual, as though he'd made peace with himself, and at others more uptight and anxious … and sadder than she had ever seen him.

She could only hope that it was simply his worries over getting married and the coming child that were playing on his mind. Crecy knew well enough that the baby terrified him. He'd said little about it, but the few remarks that he had let slip led her to believe that he was frightened out of his mind. She could guess why. It was difficult to raise the issue with him, but she had tried to reassure him that there was no reason the child should be plagued with the same problems as he was. It would not be the least bit out of the ordinary in that regard. Unless the poor thing took after her, she'd added, trying to lighten the mood. The look that had crossed his face, however, told her that she had struck a nerve. His self-esteem was so low that she didn't doubt for a moment that he thought he would make a poor father, and she knew that she must do everything in her power to reassure him.

As the carriage began to roll over familiar territory, drawing them closer to Longwold and Damerel, Crecy began to feel nervous. How would Belle and Edward receive them? She must endeavour to see them alone before they met Gabriel, for she could only imagine the horrific scene that would ensue. With Gabriel in such a fragile state of mind, that was the last thing he needed. So she would try and be brave and face them alone, and then try to explain. The idea was not a happy one, despite her longing to see Belle. She wondered if she had a niece or nephew yet, and hoped she did. Then Belle might be able to advise her about the coming birth, as she'd not understood a word the French doctor had said. A very uncomfortable Gabriel had translated for her, but she'd still rather hear it from her sister.

If Belle would even see her.

She would, of course she would, she scolded herself. But although Crecy had written regularly to Belle, at first simply to explain a little and to confess about the child, and then to try and assure her of her happiness, she had no idea of her sister's feelings. Because no one knew where they were and Crecy never gave them the address, aware that Edward would be dispatched the moment their whereabouts had been revealed to fetch her home.

The closer to home they got, the darker the mood Gabriel sank into. He'd barely spoken a word since breakfast. Crecy turned to him, trying to keep her worry from showing. "Are you so dreadfully unhappy at the prospect of marrying me?" she said, keeping her voice light and teasing as she smiled at him. But Gabriel didn't smile back.

His expression was intense as he looked at her, his eyes serious and melancholy.

"Never think that. I've never wanted anything more, I promise you." He reached out and touched her cheek with the back of his fingers. He paused for a moment and she waited, sensing he was struggling to say something. "I love you."

Crecy felt her breath catch. Gabriel rarely said anything of a romantic nature, but even when he did, he'd never yet managed to say the words ... not out loud. She gave a little laugh, but her throat was tight with emotion. "I know that, Gabriel," she said, praying that Belle and Edward would try and see the wonderful man he was and forget everything that had come before. "But thank you so much for saying it. It ... it has made me very happy."

He opened his arms to her and she moved into the space without hesitation.

"That's good," he said, his voice low. "I want you to be happy, Crecy, so much. More than anything. You and the child."

Crecy took his hand and kissed it, looking up and seeing his face become blurry as she blinked hard. *"You* make me happy, Gabriel, and you will our child, too. You'll see."

He fell quiet, then, and she could only hope that he would heed her words.

***

It was hard to approach the private chapel at Damerel. Gabriel took a breath and walked up and down again, feeling like a fool. Crecy was waiting for him as patiently as ever. *For God's sake, man, just move your feet and walk to the bloody chapel.*

But his parents were buried down there. Not within the grounds, since as suicides, they had been denied that right, but close enough that you could see the graves. Perhaps this had been a bad idea. He swallowed, bile rising in his throat at the idea of seeing the graves. Though he paid to have the chapel and the graves tended, he hadn't been there himself before. Not since the funeral all those years ago.

He couldn't do it. He couldn't do it.

Gabriel glanced over at Crecy, seeing the concern in her eyes and feeling a jolt of sorrow. *Yes, you damn well can. You do it for her. God knows you've given her little enough.* Every head of the DeMorte line had been married here for centuries. He was damned if Crecy would be any different. She would be Lady DeMorte, and once the gossip had died down, she'd be able to hold her head up. There would be no question of illegitimacy for the child, either. He hauled in a deep breath and began to walk down the path. There was a dreadful, harsh prickling feeling up and down his spine as though he was being prodded over and over with a sharp stick, and he was sweating, too. *Fine husband material, you are*, he muttered inwardly before pushing the idea away. He'd not think on that. It was irrelevant.

Crecy smiled as he finally managed to put his foot on the path that led to the chapel, beaming at him and taking his hand. God, it took so little to make her happy, he thought in despair. She deserved so much more. He took another breath, feeling nausea roil in his stomach as the chapel came into sight. Crecy's hand in his was firm, sure, and he knew she was willing him on. Gabriel glanced down at her to reassure himself as they approached the chapel doors. His heart expanded in his chest, filling him up and making him desperate to be worthy of her, even if only a little bit. Every instinct was screaming at him to turn and bolt, but he had to do this. He would do this, for her.

He paused on the threshold, wondering with a wry smile if he'd be struck by lightning the moment he set foot inside. He wouldn't be entirely surprised. Refusing to think about it a moment longer, he stepped inside before he lost the nerve, and all at once they were there. The reverend who served the DeMorte family and had never actually seen Gabriel face to face, despite the poor man's best efforts, looked just as anxious as Gabriel. White-faced and sweating, Gabriel was certain that the fellow believed himself in the presence of evil. It had taken a deal of money, a fair amount of persuasion, and finally a touch of blackmail to get his own way.

Piper, may the Lord bless him, had informed him that it was rumoured the fellow had been rather indiscreet with a young lady from a local pub, The Lamb. After a bit of digging, Piper had returned the information that the young lady had a small boy, the spitting image of the reverend. So in return for Gabriel not informing his superiors of this dreadful behaviour, the Reverend Haley would marry him to Crecy, put a false date in the register, and swear to anyone who asked that the ceremony had taken place in January. He would also give a generous monthly allowance to the poor woman whom he'd left to fend for herself and her son without so much as a farthing from him. All in all, Gabriel was rather pleased with the arrangement.

Piper and his valet, John, were witnesses, both of whom could be relied on to confirm the couple had been married months ago. And then, all at once, the ceremony had begun, binding him to the woman at his side.

If the reverend's voice trembled a little and he found it hard to look the extremely blushing bride in the eye, Gabriel neither cared nor noticed. The words were all he focused on, making promises before God that he knew he could never keep. But if there was such a thing as a god, he must know that Gabriel was a liar, so there would be no surprises.

Piper, who was giving the bride away and looking vastly proud of it, said his piece, and then the reverend turned to Gabriel, who repeated the words, feeling his throat grow inexplicably tight as he spoke.

"I, Gabriel Rochester Francis Greyston, take thee, Lucretia Jane Holbrook, to my wedded wife, to have and to hold from this day forward, for better or for worse, for richer or for poorer, in sickness and in health, to love and to cherish."

Gabriel paused, holding onto Crecy's hand too tightly.

"Till death us do part, according to God's holy ordinance; and thereto, I plight thee, my troth."

***

There had been a small wedding breakfast prepared for them, though it closely resembled Gabriel's usual fare on his part. Gabriel did his best to say the right things, to smile more than he had done in his lifetime before, and then to give all of the staff the rest of the day off. Once they had endured the interminable, if well-meant, congratulations, they were finally alone.

Crecy sighed and sat herself down beside the tea tray Piper had insisted on bringing before he left for the day.

"Did you see Piper during the ceremony, Gabriel? I think he was actually weeping."

Gabriel snorted, shaking his head. "The tears were for you, I assure you. The fellow wanted my head on a pike after …" He trailed off, not quite certain how to put it into words without being crude, and so gestured at Crecy's stomach.

Crecy laughed at him as she always did when he failed to be as blunt as she so often was. He could only ever manage it when he was angry, and he was far from that. Gabriel turned to look out of the window. He wanted this. He wanted Crecy and his child, despite the fact he would be a horrible father. God help the child, it would likely be as mad as he was, and then what? Crecy would hate him for it. What if there were more of them, all of them as strange and black-hearted as him?

He shivered at the thought, fear prickling over him.

You know what to do.

This time, it was not his father that spoke to him. Gabriel had made his decision. He would no longer do the man's bidding. Edward could live his life in peace, Gabriel no longer cared. He could hear his father's rage, condemning him as a coward, a failure, a madman, a pathetic worm, but it was nothing he hadn't heard before, nothing he didn't already know. Crecy was all that mattered to him now, though, she and the child. There was nothing more than this, no other thought in his head. They must be safe. They must be happy. Two things that he could not give them.

But security, a certain future, a name - albeit a tarnished one - that he could give.

"Let's go to bed," Crecy said, grinning up at him in a way that made his heart feel like it was caught in a trap, the spikes digging in, tearing through the tender flesh.

"It's the middle of the day," he said, filled with longing to forget his plans, to do what she said. Perhaps he could try? He could try, couldn't he? Just for a little while.

"So?" she retorted, sounding indignant and making him smile though he wanted to weep, wanted her to hold him and tell him nothing bad would ever happen. It would all be all right.

"I thought perhaps you'd want to see Belle," he said, knowing that, in truth, she wanted to see her sister more than anything.

Crecy's face fell and she looked up at him. "I do, very much. I ... I'm just nervous, I suppose." She huffed and shook her head. "Though I don't know why, as Belle is the most loving, forgiving person in the world, and once she sees how happy I am ... I know she'll love you, too, Gabriel."

Gabriel refrained from comment. Well, there was another reason. Crecy would forever be torn between him and her sister. Belle would never forgive him, that much was certain. He would hardly expect it of her, either, after everything he'd done. Edward would likely call him out. Ironic, really, after trying to provoke the man into it for so many years, he might actually get his wish.

"If you're going to see her, you should go now," Gabriel said, hearing the words stick in his throat. "You should stay the night there, too, I think."

"What?" Crecy looked up in outrage. "Gabriel, it's our wedding night!"

Gabriel steadied himself against the flood of emotion that overcame him, swelling in his chest and squeezing his lungs so tight it was painful to draw a breath. He turned his back until he had gained control again, smiling at her as best he could, one eyebrow raised. "I rather think that ship has sailed."

Crecy pouted at him, looking so adorably sulky that he had to go and sit beside her, to kiss her and hold her to him. He placed his hand on her stomach, still finding it hard to believe that he had a child, despite the overwhelming evidence. He gasped, astonished as the child moved, pressing against his palm.

"She knows her daddy," Crecy said, her voice quiet, staring at him with such love that he didn't know how he could bear it. He pulled her to him, feeling overwhelmed with love, with the need to do the right thing, and such desperate sorrow.

"I love you," he said, hearing his voice quaver with emotion, but quite unable to stop it. "You won't ever forget that, will you? I love you both, so much." He blinked hard, knowing he had to hold on a little longer, relishing the feel of his wife in his arms, wishing so very much that it was forever.

"Of course I won't forget," Crecy said, resting her head on his shoulder. "We shall be together every day, and I will nag you to tell me every morning and every night, so I couldn't possibly forget."

"I don't think it would require much nagging," he said, his voice quiet now as he was keeping hold of his emotions by a thread. "Come along, you've had a long day. If you're going to see your sister, you should go now."

Crecy sighed, but showed no signs of moving. "Won't you come with me, Gabriel?"

"I don't think that's a good idea, do you?"

"No," she admitted. "I don't suppose it is. But when I've explained ..." She looked up, then, her lovely eyes shining with such hope that he thought the pain of it would kill him there and then. "You'll come, then, and they'll see, Gabriel, they'll understand. Not right away, perhaps, but they will, you'll see."

He forced a smile to his lips, smoothing a curl from her beautiful face. "You are a hopeless and foolish optimist, wife."

She grinned at him, a sly look in her eyes. "Well, of course I am. Otherwise, I might have given up on you."

"But you never did," he whispered, wondering why this woman had loved him so hard, had been so determined to save him. God knew he didn't deserve it.

"I never will," she amended.

Gabriel choked, covering the sound by pretending to laugh. "I have something for you," he said, trying to divert her attention as she was looking at him a little strangely. "John was turning out some old clothes and he found this in one of the pockets." He lifted out the Jay feather, still as dazzling blue and black as it had been the day she'd given it to him.

"Oh, my goodness," she cried, delighted. "How funny, I wondered where it was when you'd kept everything else so carefully." Gabriel raised an eyebrow and she blushed. "Oh. Well, after you left here, Piper let me into your study to write you a letter. I ... I may have been a little nosy."

Gabriel smiled and leaned forward, kissing her forehead. "No, you weren't. It's all yours now, so you can be as nosy as you desire."

She returned his smile, and then her face fell. "Can I look in that little book you've been writing in, then?"

His blood ran cold and he shook his head. "No." Realising he'd unsettled her, he let out a breath, forcing himself to relax. "At least, yes, you can, but not yet."

"Tomorrow? When I come home?"

Gabriel swallowed, his throat too tight to speak, but he nodded. Crecy relaxed, looking relieved. "Very well, then," she said, her tone that of a long-suffering spouse. "If you're so eager to get rid of your wife, I suppose I must go."

Gabriel helped her into her pelisse, doing up the buttons for her and smiling at how even this latest one strained over her stomach. "You're getting fat, wife."

Crecy snorted. "And whose fault is that?" she demanded, her voice tart as he tied the ribbon under her chin and bent down to kiss her.

"Mine," he whispered. "All mine."

She sighed, a wistful look in her eyes. "I shall miss you dreadfully, you know, are you sure you won't come?"

Gabriel shook his head. "I must go to Bath tonight on business. Bainbridge has some documents that I must sign without delay."

"You'll return here tonight, though?" Gabriel nodded as she took his arm, and he escorted her out to the carriage. "Very well, then, I shall see you tomorrow," she said as he handed her inside.

She sat down and Gabriel leant in, quite unable to resist one last kiss.

"Until tomorrow," she whispered.

Gabriel kissed her again, but said nothing, closing the carriage door and watching until she had driven away, out of sight.

Chapter 31

"Wherein Gabriel puts his final plan into action."

"Crecy!" Belle ran into the hallway of the great castle, her eyes alight with both joy and distress. "Oh, love, oh, I've been so worried."

Any anxiety that Crecy might have felt at being shunned or at least scolded evaporated as Belle threw her arms around her. She was hugged and squeezed and kissed until she was forced to protest, and then Belle put her hand on her stomach.

"Oh, Crecy, love," she said, her voice so sad that Crecy felt a burst of anger.

"Don't say it like that, Belle," she said, unable to keep the irritation from her voice.

"How else can I say it, love?" Belle asked, holding her hand and looking so utterly miserable that Crecy gave a tut of impatience.

"We're married. Happy now?" she said, with the quirk of one eyebrow. To her disappointment, Belle didn't look much happier at all.

"Well," she said, and Crecy could tell Belle was being careful with her words. "I am glad, of course, for the child's sake, but ..." She could apparently not keep her thoughts to herself a moment longer. "But to such a man, Crecy? Why? Why DeMorte, of all people?"

Crecy gritted her teeth. She should have more patience, she knew she should, but there had been something raw and fragile about Gabriel when she'd left him, and the more she thought on it, the more worried she became.

"What, why stay with a man who beats me and drinks and gambles and visits whores?" she said, feeling a stab of satisfaction as Belle turned a deathly shade of white.

"Crecy?" she exclaimed, obviously taking her words at face value. "Well, you're safe now, love. He'll not touch you again, I promise. You need not be frightened anymore."

Crecy threw up her hands and stalked into the parlour, leaving Belle to hurry behind her. "Did you actually read my letters, Belle?" she demanded as her sister closed the door behind her.

"Of course I did," Belle replied, sounding affronted.

"And?"

Belle held her arms about herself, and Crecy suddenly realised Belle had delivered her child. She must have a niece or nephew somewhere about the place. She felt a rush of sadness that she didn't even know the child's name, and her heart softened a little.

"And …" Belle hesitated.

"You thought perhaps I had to say such things? That Gabriel forced me to tell you that I was happy, that I'd gone with him willingly, is that it?"

Belle said nothing. She didn't have to.

Crecy sighed, suddenly exhausted. She sat down and patted the seat beside her. Belle came to her and Crecy took her hand.

"This is the truth, Belle," Crecy said, looking directly in the eye the woman who had been more mother than sister. "Gabriel is the most loving, kindest, most wonderful man. He's not who you think he is, he never has been." Crecy swallowed, feeling a lump rise in her throat. "But he is damaged, Belle. Oh, if you knew what he'd gone through." She blinked back tears and Belle squeezed her hands tighter.

"Don't cry, love. You're back home now and ... and if Gabriel is everything you say, then ... well, I'm sure we can work things out. Together."

Crecy burst into tears and Belle gathered her up, rocking her like she'd done as a child when she'd scraped her knee or some ugly pet that she'd loved to distraction had died. She knew Belle didn't believe her, not yet. But she knew that she'd try, and sooner or later she would realise that Gabriel was everything that Crecy knew him to be.

***

Gabriel looked up at the elegant façade of the rather infamous house he owned in one of the more scandalous neighbourhoods of Bath, away from the more fashionable thoroughfares. He entered to be greeted by the lady of the house, who beamed at him, holding out both hands in greeting.

"My lord!" she exclaimed. "What a lovely surprise."

Gabriel bent and kissed the woman on both cheeks. "Hello, Mary," he said. "You're looking well."

Mrs Wilkins - though she'd never been married a day in her life - grinned at him. "Come and have a drink," she said, leading the way to her office. Gabriel passed a couple of scantily clad young women, who giggled and blew him kisses.

"Hello, Lord DeMorte," they chorused, affecting a shy demeanour that neither of them owned.

Gabriel nodded to them, closing Mary's door behind him. "I'm not stopping, Mary. I just have something to give you."

"Oh?" She looked around at him, her expression curious. Gabriel thought she was still a handsome woman, despite the ugly scar that marred her left cheek, perhaps even because of it. She was a strong woman, a fighter, and she wore her scars with the pride of one who had looked into the abyss and survived. Gabriel envied her.

"Here," he said, putting a thick envelope on her desk. She looked at him, frowning a little as she reached to take it. "It's the deeds to this place, Mary. It's yours."

The woman before him stared, gasped, and then sat down heavily in her chair, still staring at him, and for once beyond speech. That was amusing, at least.

"You'll also find an annuity in your name. There ought to be enough for you to be comfortable and to help set the girls up doing … well, something else," he added. "If that's what they want. You'll know what to do, I'm sure."

Mary's eyes filled with tears, her hand covering her mouth as she gave a sob, and Gabriel looked away, uncomfortable with such a show of emotion.

"Why?" she asked, her voice thick now.

Gabriel shrugged. "Because it's the right thing to do." He gave a twisted smile as he glanced back at her. "I was curious to know how it felt."

Mary got to her feet and crossed the room, holding out her hands to him, and then paused as Gabriel didn't move. "In the first place, you've been nothing but kindness to us, my lord. You gave us a safe place to be, and as for what you did for me …"

Gabriel waved his hand, an impatient gesture that clearly showed he had no desire to hear any more thanks.

"A business venture, nothing more," he said with a shake of his head. "Any good businessman protects his assets," he added, his voice hard now.

Mary snorted. "I'm pretty good with numbers, my lord, and I know full well that most of the profits have been used on improving the building, doctor's bills, those two big fellows who keep order, heating this huge house in the winter, clothing and feeding us, and sending the kids to school."

Gabriel frowned and wondered how he could leave now without offending her.

"How is Sarah's child?" he asked, hoping to get her off the subject so he could make good his escape.

Mary's face softened and she smiled at him. "The doctor said he'd make a full recovery."

Gabriel nodded. "That's good." He turned away, moving to the door.

"I heard you'd run away to France with some beautiful blonde chit," she said, and Gabriel's head snapped around, fury rising at hearing Crecy spoken of in such a manner.

"Have a care, Mary," he said, his voice a growl. "That's my wife you speak of."

Mary's mouth fell open, her eyes wide. "Well," she said, the word little more than a whisper. "That explains a lot." She smiled at him with such warmth that Gabriel felt the desire to just run from the room and slam the door as he went. The last thing he wanted right now was kindness or gratitude. "It's about time. I'm so happy for you." Her head tilted as she regarded him. "Is she very beautiful?"

Gabriel frowned, not wanting to discuss Crecy with her but quite unable to not reply. "Yes. Very," he said.

A broad smile curved over the woman's generous mouth now as her eyes lit up. "You love her."

It was more an accusation than a question, and Gabriel took a breath, the ache in his heart so intense he could hardly breathe.

"Yes," he agreed, his voice rough. He turned, looking Mary in the eyes. "More than life."

***

Frederick Bainbridge had been Gabriel's man of business, and his father's before him. He was getting on in years, now, but was a jovial-looking man - for a lawyer - with a heavy jowled face and thinning grey hair. Today, however, his ruddy countenance was filled with concern.

"I don't understand the hurry, my lord," he said, pushing the papers towards Gabriel. "May I enquire if you are in good health? You've not received any … any bad or worrying news?"

"My health is no concern of yours," Gabriel said, his tone sharp as he signed the papers. "You're sure this is enough to tie things up?" he demanded, knowing he could not act until he was quite certain.

Bainbridge sighed, obviously knowing Gabriel well enough to realise he'd not answer any questions that he did not wish to answer.

"It is a most unusual arrangement, and it has taken me a great deal of difficulties, but, yes, I believe so. Your wife will inherit everything on the event of your death, and even if she marries again, the wealth and properties will remain in her hands and then go to your child, be it male or female."

Gabriel let out a sigh. Crecy and the child would be safe. They had everything they needed to live a good and happy life, without his toxic presence to taint everything.

"Thank you," he said, his gratitude so obviously heartfelt that he earned himself a look of surprise from the man before him.

Once all of the papers had been signed, he got to his feet. There was no point in delaying.

"Goodbye, Mr Bainbridge."

Bainbridge stood, hurrying to open the door for him, but paused, his hand resting on the door knob.

"My lord?" he said, his voice hesitant and full of concern. "I've known you for a long time now, and it has been my privilege to serve you."

He ignored Gabriel's grunt of amusement at that. Gabriel well knew he'd been a thorn in the man's side on many occasions. Bainbridge shook his head and carried on.

"I know much about you that most do not," he continued, apparently determined to say something, whatever on earth it might be. "The good you have done alongside the ..."

"Wickedness?" Gabriel supplied for him, his voice deadpan.

Bainbridge smiled a little. "I can't help but think that most who fell foul of you got exactly what they deserved, but nonetheless, perhaps after so many years, you will allow an old man the privilege of sticking his nose in where it's not wanted." To Gabriel's horror, he moved forward and clasped his hand between both of his. "Don't do anything foolish, young man. I know that your life has been a hard one, but you have a child now, a wife ... Do you really think all the riches in the world can replace a father and husband?"

Gabriel withdrew his hand from the man's grasp, shaken by the affection in his voice, the concern in his eyes. "You are right, Bainbridge, it is not your affair, and as for that ... it rather depends on the father or husband. Speaking for myself and my mother, we would have happily buried my father in the ground and danced on his grave. Now, if you'll excuse me, I have things to attend to."

Gabriel left before the old man could say anything further. It had occurred to him that his intentions might have been suspected, but that the fellow would actually care one way or another had been a surprise. He hurried back to his carriage, lost in thought, mentally checking off all of the items he'd had to accomplish that had been written so carefully in the small notebook he'd been guarding. All that remained was to write some letters of explanation, as best he could, at least.

Gabriel was so lost in thought that he almost didn't hear the furious voice that rang out across the street.

"DeMorte!"

Gabriel looked around, in no mood to be delayed, and gave a snort of amusement as he saw his cousin, Edward, striding towards him with murder in his eyes. He, too, had inherited the Greyston stature and breadth, and looked a little like a raging bull as he advanced. If there really was a god, he had a damned twisted sense of humour. Gabriel didn't doubt the fellow wanted his blood and would call him out now. After so many years of wanting it, now he could not allow it. For with him gone, he needed Edward to protect Crecy and the child. So Gabriel could not kill him even if he wanted to, which he was startled to find he didn't in the least. It would be an easy way out, too, to get Edward to kill him. Nice and neat, but then Crecy would never forgive Edward. No. He couldn't do it.

"You bastard!" Edward growled, giving Gabriel a hard shove. "You filthy, evil bastard. You just had to have her, didn't you? I don't care what you do to me, but to use an innocent like Lucretia …"

"Keep your bloody voice down," Gabriel hissed, aware that they were drawing curious looks from passersby.

Edward gaped at him, his green eyes incredulous. "Now you think about her reputation? When it was shredded months ago? People have done nothing else but salivate and chew over the story of how you seduced and ran off with my sister-in-law."

Gabriel flinched but said nothing. There was no time now. There was too much to be done and too little time to do it.

"Go and speak to Crecy," he said, feeling suddenly all used up and worn to a thread. He had no energy to deal with Edward. His anger had left him, and all that remained was a bone-deep sorrow what for he had to do. He moved away, but Edward's big hand grasped his arm hard.

"No, you'll answer for this," his cousin growled, fury vibrating through him. If it wasn't for the people thronging the streets of Bath, Gabriel didn't have the slightest doubt that he'd try and murder him with his bare hands. His alternative was hardly a surprise, however. "Name your seconds."

Gabriel laughed, but it was an exhausted sound. "Go home to your wife, Edward."

"You bloody coward!" Edward raged, his face more filled with hatred and fury than Gabriel had ever seen it. Edward had always been the golden son, beloved by all, hail fellow well met. Until after the war, of course, but even then, everyone had loved and admired the fellow, despite his temper and glowering looks. He'd never been reviled or hated or shunned. Gabriel had envied him for that. "You'll meet me, tomorrow," Edward snapped. "The lake at dawn."

"For God's sake, Edward," Gabriel said, shaking his head. "If you think me afraid, then you really don't know me at all, but you have a wife and a child to think of now."

"Like you care?" Edward snapped, his fury palpable; the man was alive with tension and anger and it rolled off of him in waves. Gabriel felt suddenly relieved by it. This was a man driven by the desperate desire to protect those he loved. He would do the same for Crecy and the baby, for the only two people Gabriel had ever loved since his mother had died.

Gabriel nodded, knowing it made no difference now. "You are right, of course, Edward. I don't care," he said, too aware that time was slipping away from him. "Very well. Dawn tomorrow."

Edward gave a taut nod before turning away. Gabriel watched him go, feeling a sudden sense of regret that he hadn't known Edward better. He wondered what his life might have been like if Edward had been a friend rather than an enemy, but Edward's father had taught his son to shun his cousin, just as his own father had blackmailed Gabriel into destroying his.

Well, it was too late now, and his time was up. Gabriel turned away and hurried back to his carriage.

Chapter 32

"Wherein sunrise brings terror and the threat of bloodshed."

Crecy woke in the room she had called her own at Longwold, feeling disorientated. After an emotional few hours with Belle, she had been exhausted and gone to have a nap, and now it was dark, apart from the bright moonlight that flooded the room through the open curtains. She lit the lamp beside her and hauled her heavy body upright. She was hungry, she decided, and Edward's wonderful cook, Puddy, was bound to have something delicious in the kitchen if she hunted about.

With a yawn, she shuffled out of the bedroom door, realising it was later than she thought, as the castle was in darkness and none of the staff about. Pausing in the corridor, she felt a stab of alarm as she heard a furious argument coming from Belle's room. Feeling like an eavesdropper, but anxious for Belle, she moved closer to the door just in time to hear a baby's high-pitched wail. Ah, that would be Eli. The little baby boy certainly had a fine set of lungs, though he had been all smiles for his aunty Crecy earlier on.

"Now you've woken the baby!" Belle's exasperated voice snapped.

"I wasn't the one shouting," Edward retorted, though he sounded rather chastened in Crecy's view, which was quite amusing.

"I wouldn't have been shouting if you hadn't ruined everything, Edward. You must go and see him, call the whole thing off!"

"Damned if I will!" Edward shot back. "After what he did? Besides, it's a matter of honour now."

"Honour be damned! Edward Greyston, if you kill Crecy's husband, she'll never forgive you, and if he kills you ..." At this point, Belle's voice broke and she began to cry as hard as Eli. Crecy couldn't hear anything past a loud buzzing in her ears, though. Belle had said Edward had gone to Bath that day to meet an old army friend. He must have run into Gabriel. Oh, no. Oh, no, no, no. She had to stop this.

She raised a fist, about to pound on the door, when the front door bell began to ring and didn't stop, accompanied by someone hammering on the door.

"What the devil is that?" Edward exclaimed, pulling open the door and nearly running into Crecy.

The two of them started in shock whilst the ringing and banging continued unabated.

"Promise me you won't do it!" Crecy said, not giving a damn who was at the door, only that Gabriel was safe. "Promise me, Edward. Gabriel isn't who you think." The words tumbled out, one after the other, so fast she didn't know if she was making the least bit of sense. Edward looked a bit astonished by her outburst on top of the cacophony downstairs, but she pressed on. "He's a wonderful, kind man and he loves me, Edward. You have to believe me." She was crying now, and Belle came out, still sobbing and holding the wailing baby.

Edward looked between the three of them as Garrett hurried to the front door downstairs. "Good God, this is a bloody mad house," he exclaimed, throwing up his hands. "Fine, fine, I'll find a way to call it off, though I still don't understand why, but I tell you this, if the fellow calls me a coward, I'll have his blood one way or another."

"He won't, I promise he won't," Crecy said through her tears. Though the idea that Gabriel had agreed to it was a cold feeling sliding beneath her skin. Of course, the way men's stupid ideas on pride and honour worked, she supposed he couldn't very well have said no. Her thoughts were side-tracked, however, by a woman's voice from downstairs and Garrett's indignant tone as he tried to eject her from the house.

"Garrett, what the devil is going on?"

Garrett looked up as they all hurried down the stairs. "There is a ... *lady* who is desirous of speaking with you, my lord."

When they got closer, Crecy saw a rather vulgarly dressed woman standing just inside the door. She had been beautiful once, but an ugly scar marred one cheek.

"Oh," Crecy exclaimed in surprise as she realised who this was. "You're Mrs Wilkins."

The woman's eyes opened in shock. "Lady DeMorte?" she said, staring at Crecy's bulging stomach. "He told you about me?" She looked more than a little scandalised, which, in other circumstances, Crecy would have found amusing.

"Yes, of course," Crecy said, beaming and holding her hands out to the woman. "And how he fought a duel for you. I was never more proud of him. How do you do?"

Mrs Wilkins looked really stunned, now, and barely managed to stammer a reply. "V-very well, thank you."

"Fought a duel for her?" Edward exclaimed, staring at Mrs Wilkins with suspicion.

"Yes," Crecy said, nodding. "Lord Aston. He badly hurt this lady and..." She hesitated, not wanting to be indelicate.

"He gave me this," Mrs Wilkins supplied for her, pointing at her scar.

Edward frowned, clearly surprised by this. "That's why he killed Aston? I heard it was gambling debts."

"Of course you did," Crecy said with disgust. "Because no one would ever consider Gabriel could do anything honourable." Her words were so full of accusation that Edward stilled, looking a little uneasy.

"Never mind that, now," Mrs Wilkins, said, sounding impatient all at once. She grasped Crecy's hand. "Why are you here? Why aren't you with him?"

"Because he knew I wanted to see my sister," Crecy said, an increasingly uneasy feeling prickling up her spine.

"Oh, God," she said, sounding horrified. Before Mrs Wilkins could say more, however, another ring came at the front door.

"What on earth ..." Edward said as Garret stepped forwards again to reveal an elderly-looking man on the doorstep.

"Lord Winterbourne," he exclaimed without delay, hurrying inside. "Tell me I'm not too late?" he gasped, looking around with wild, anxious eyes. "I didn't know where else to come."

Edward's mouth dropped open, his expression utterly dumbfounded. "Too late for what?" he demanded, looking like he thought the entire world had run mad.

"Viscount DeMorte," he began as Crecy felt a wash of terror hit her like a ragging sea.

"What?" she said, hurrying forward. "Oh, my God, what has he done?"

"Are you Lady DeMorte?" Bainbridge asked, his face full of concern. "I'm your husband's lawyer. Please forgive me for this strange visit. I'm so sorry to cause you distress, only ... his lordship was with me today and he ... he has tied up his affairs in a way that led me to believe ... to suspect ..." He trailed off as Crecy's worst fears were realised.

"No!" she gasped, her heart leaping to her throat in horror. "Oh, Gabriel. I must go to him at once."

Crecy was forever grateful to Edward, who might not have understood what the devil was going on, but realised time was of the essence. "May we use your carriage, *mister...?*"

"Bainbridge, my lord, and yes ...Oh yes, at once."

***

Gabriel sealed the last of the letters and laid it upon the pile on his desk. That one had been for Piper, asking forgiveness for the unpleasant task he was asking of him. He could not have Crecy seeing the evidence of his last act, however. He didn't want her to remember him in such a way. He hoped that in the past few weeks, he had brought her some happiness, at least. She had seemed happy, though he often thought that she pretended her pleasure in his company just to make him feel better. She was too good, too generous for such a dark soul as his. But she would have a brighter future now.

Hopefully, the truth of his death would be buried, as he had given detailed instructions and left money for the necessary bribes that might be required to do so. So after the initial scandal had died down, it could only ever be speculation, and after that she would be clear of his taint. A beautiful young widow with a child would always gain sympathy, and she would be as popular as before. Perhaps she'd marry again? He pushed that thought aside as fast as he could, the pain of it too great to contemplate. That would be her affair.

As methodical as ever, he checked off each letter against the list in the notebook, his hand lingering over the one that bore Crecy's name. He had thought he'd be at peace with the idea of leaving her now, knowing that he was doing it for the best. The idea of his ... his obsessions and vile reputation bringing harm or ridicule to his child in the future was more than he could bear. What if they escaped the taint that the Greyston blood so clearly bore, only for him to contaminate them just by his presence? The child would be taunted for having such a father. A boy would find himself condemned to follow in his footsteps, as he would never be accepted by his peers, a girl untouchable as the young men feared her father or feared their children would bring another generation of madness in the world.

But if he was gone, the memory of him would fade over the years and they could start afresh. People would see only Crecy's bright smiling face, and surely that would find acceptance anywhere?

It was right. It was the right thing to do. He must do it. But, oh God, he didn't want to. He didn't want to leave her, couldn't bear the thought of her loving another even as he told himself he wanted only her happiness. He wanted to see his child born. Crecy was certain it was a daughter, and the thought of it, the thought of some pretty little child with blonde curls was enough to make him put his head in his hands.

Stop it, stop it. If you want to be a man, a good man, if you actually want to do something decent for once in your miserable life, do this.

Gabriel dashed away the tears on his sleeve. He placed the little diary he had promised Crecy she could read beside his letter to her, hoping she could see the pains he had taken to ensure that both her and their child were safe and secure. All of his less reputable interests had been sold off and everything else put in Crecy's name. He prayed he'd thought of everything. For a moment panic overtook him, but then he let out a breath. Edward would know what to do; he would protect them. Gabriel knew that was true.

He took a moment to rearrange the items on his desk, even knowing it was ridiculous, but finding at least that it was easier to walk away from it now. Piper always checked his desk for correspondence to be sent first thing in the morning, knowing his master often worked into the early hours, so he would find the note in his own name long before Crecy was due home. Hopefully, early enough to send word to detain her and keep her at Longwold. She would do well to sell Damerel; this godforsaken place had seen nothing but misery - well, except for when she'd been here, he amended.

He moved to open a large cupboard under some of the bookshelves, reaching in and taking out a beautiful and ornate wooden box. Gabriel unlocked it and looked at his father's duelling pistols. He could still hear him, that despicable man, raging that Gabriel was a coward and a failure, a disappointment and a disgrace. The only thing that had changed was that Gabriel no longer cared. He knew there was truth enough in the words, but not because he hadn't destroyed Edward, but because he had listened at all.

Gabriel loaded the pistol with care, the same one his father had used. It seemed fitting, somehow. Carefully, he stripped off his coat and waistcoat, finding the idea of covering the fine cloth in blood unacceptable, and headed out of the house. He wouldn't subject any of the servants to the kind of mess his father had left them. It was too cruel.

The first tentative fingers of light were creeping over the sky as he walked, the day already warm. The air was sweet and Gabriel weighed down with the realisation that he had never before wanted to live so very much. For so many years, he had longed for someone to call him out and put a bullet to his brain, to save him from the constant battle that life had become, against his father, against Edward, against himself, and now that he was giving himself permission to give up … he didn't want to do it.

He reached a large outcrop of stone that jutted out over a steeply sloping field. From here, the land fell away, an expansive view stretching out for mile upon mile of fields and forests. Gabriel had come here often, when things were at their worst. He had found comfort in the peace and beauty of the place, and in the idea of how small and insignificant he was in the scheme of things. If he died, the earth would not stop revolving, the sun would still rise, and soon enough his body would return to dust, as did everything else. There had been a strange sense of serenity in that.

Gabriel sat down, his long legs swung over the edge of the rock, the pistol lay in his lap, as he waited for the sun to rise. He had promised himself one last sunrise. He could only hope it was time enough to find the courage to do what he must.

***

The carriage ride to Damerel was horrific. Crecy was beside herself with terror, trembling and sick with fear as Belle tried to comfort her and hold her tightly, begging her to be calm for the child's sake. But Crecy could not be calm; if Gabriel did this, she did not know how she would go on. That she would, she didn't doubt, for his child would be loved and cherished as no child before or since, but how she would do it, she just could not imagine.

"I don't understand," Edward grumbled for the fifth time as the carriage jolted them over the road, the horses going at breakneck speed and giving them a very rough ride. "You're telling me Gabriel is killing himself for your sake?"

"Yes, yes," Crecy sobbed, wishing Edward would just realise that his cousin was far more troubled and broken that even he could understand. "Edward, do you not know what his father did to him?"

Edward returned a blank look. "I know he saw him kill himself," he said, frowning a little.

Crecy snorted in disgust. "You have no idea, do you? He found his mother dead in a pool of blood, and then his father put a gun to Gabriel's head. He told Gabriel it was all his fault she'd had an affair with your father. He'd come between them. They'd been happy before he'd been born, and he should have been drowned in the lake," her voice became angrier and louder as she spoke, as she saw Edward's face pale, and she realised he didn't have the slightest clue. "He said that Gabriel had to promise to destroy your father and you, or he'd kill him there and then, and even if he agreed, that he would haunt Gabriel until he got what he wanted …

then he turned the gun on himself." Crecy choked, her heart too full of fear and sorrow. "He was ten, Edward. What if that had been Eli? Could you do such a thing to your own son?"

"No!" Edward looked dreadfully shocked, horrified at the very idea. He shook his head. "No, of course not. You're right, I ... I simply had no idea."

"He was all alone, Edward, all alone in that big house and your father, *and you,* the only family he had, shunned him. How do you think that felt?"

Belle was sobbing beside her now as Edward just swallowed, his green eyes troubled.

"I can't imagine," he admitted, his voice low and troubled.

By the time the carriage drew up at Damerel, the sun was breaking over the horizon. Crecy flew out of the carriage as fast as she was able to, despite Belle's protests, as Edward ran ahead of them, all of them shouting for Gabriel.

Piper came running out of the study, ashen faced as he held a sheet of paper in his hands. "Oh, my lady," he said.

"Where is he?" Crecy screamed, feeling as though she would lose her mind at any moment.

"He's gone down to the rocks ... I know the place," Piper said. "But perhaps ..."

Crecy ran forward and grasped his arms, shaking him hard, absolutely out of her mind with terror. *"Show me!"*

They hurried outside, following Piper and cursing his slowness as he could not go at much of pace. "Down there," he gasped, gesturing to the south. "He'll be down there."

Edward ran ahead, but just as she crested the rise, she saw Gabriel, silhouetted against the sun as he raised the pistol to his head.

"Gabriel!" she screamed, as her legs finally gave out beneath her. *"Gabriel, no!"*

Chapter 33

"Wherein everyone holds their breath and prays for deliverance."

The sun had finally slid past the horizon, painting the skies in a glorious, opulent sweep of colour that dazzled his eyes. Gabriel took a breath, tears streaming down his face, for once crying for himself, for his own loss, for everything he was giving up. He closed his eyes, shutting out all of the beauty and the colour, and he raised the pistol. The metal was cold against his temple, and suddenly he remembered his father's snarling face, threatening to kill him ... at least he need not see that again.

"Gabriel!"

Gabriel jolted, his finger had been about to squeeze the trigger and he barely stopped it from carrying through the action. He lowered the gun, swinging around in horror to see a cluster of people rushing towards him over the rise of the hill and ...

"Gabriel, no!"

"Crecy?"

She collapsed, falling to her knees, and Gabriel's heart felt like it had turned to ice in his chest. He was on his feet in an instant, throwing the gun down and running to her.

"Crecy, Crecy, love, are you all right?" He fell to his knees beside her, gathering her into his arms as she turned on him and slapped him hard.

"No!" she shrieked, crying and shaking so hard that he didn't know how to calm her. "I'm not all right, not at all, not at all." She hit him, then, over and over, crying hysterically until Gabriel pulled her so close that she could no longer move, rocking her and crying himself.

"I'm sorry, I'm sorry," he whispered. "You weren't meant to see, love. I didn't want you to see."

"How could you?" she said, sobbing as she reached up, holding his face between her hands and looking so hurt and heartbroken that he felt like the worst kind of brute. "How could you leave me?" she demanded.

"I ... I didn't want to," he said, the words broken and thick with emotion, knowing he needed to explain, but not knowing how. "Never think that, only ... I'm no kind of father for our child, Crecy," he said in a rush, wishing he could get the words out, could make her see how much better their lives would be without him. "I'm afraid," he said, the admission hard to make, but knowing he owed her the truth.

"Why?" she asked, such confusion in her eyes, now, and such sorrow that it hurt him all the more to know he had put it there.

"What if I hurt it?" he said, his voice low. "What if ... if it makes a mess and I get angry? What if I'm jealous? What if I'm ... *like him?*"

Crecy shook her head, tears streaming down her face. "Oh, my love, you could no more hurt me or your child than ignore a bully. When will you see that you are nothing like your father, but that you are a good and kind man?"

Gabriel gave a desperate bark of laughter, tears glittering in his eyes, and Crecy put her hand to his face, making him turn his head. "Look over there," she said, her voice harsh. "Do you see all those people?"

He blinked, looking confused all at once. "Good Lord, is that ... Mrs Wilkins? And ... *Bainbridge?*"

"Yes, Gabriel," she said with such frustration in her voice that he looked back at her. "And Piper, who's beside himself, and look, John is there, too, now, and do you know why Mrs Wilkins and Mr Bainbridge left their beds in the middle of the night to come chasing across the countryside to find Edward?"

Gabriel frowned, he could find no reason whatsoever for them to have acted so, unless ...

"Because they couldn't sleep, you'd unsettled them so and they were afraid of what you might be about to do, *and they wanted to stop you, you fool!*" she snapped at him, sounding really quite angry. All at once, the fight seemed to go out of her, though, and she just stroked his cheek, looking so sad that Gabriel knew he needed to make sure such a look never crossed her face again. "They care for you, my love," she whispered, smiling at him now in a way that broke his heart. "They know the truth about you, you see. You've tried so hard to keep it a secret, but some of us have worked it out. You are a good man, Gabriel Greyston."

"You'd be better off without me," he said, stubborn to the last.

"Don't you dare," she hissed, sounding so utterly furious now that he looked up with caution. "Don't you dare tell me what is best for me, Gabriel. I have loved you my whole life and worked so hard to be with you. I gave everything up just for the chance of loving you. You are *all* I have ever wanted, do you hear me, and if you take that away from me, I swear I'll never forgive you."

Relief that maybe ... just maybe he could stay. He could try and be a husband and a father. Sorrow for all the pain he had caused and would likely cause in the future, and joy ... He would live, he would live with the woman he loved, and who for some inexplicable reason loved him, too. He would see his child born and be there to protect it from anyone who dared disparage the DeMorte name.

He'd put the fear of God into anyone who tried.

Gabriel buried his head in Crecy's hair, breathing in the familiar scent of her and finally letting go of so much of the fear and hurt he had held onto so long. For once in his life, he had hope ... and something to look forward to.

***

It was a dazzling late summer's morning by the time they got up and made their way inside. Gabriel had not wanted to face everyone. In his opinion, it would have saved everyone a deal of embarrassment if he had just slunk upstairs and Crecy had seen them out. But his wife was having none of it.

"You will go and see them, Gabriel. You will thank them for what they've done for you face to face, or you'll never bring yourself to see them again, and then we'll be back to square one." She had crossed her arms on top of her large belly with such a look of determination in her eyes that Gabriel was torn between amusement and chagrin.

"If you're going to bully our children like this, I'll ..." he began, seeing outrage flicker in her eyes with amusement.

"You'll what?" she demanded, her lovely eyes filled with the kind of worry and suspicion that he knew would take a long time to rid her of. He leant down and pressed his lips to hers; no time like the present, after all.

"I'll have to try very hard to keep you sweet-tempered and happy, I suppose," he said, smiling at her and finding his heart swell as she returned it.

"I love you so much, Gabriel," she said, shaking her head. "Please, please, don't ever frighten me like that again.

Gabriel shook his head. "I never will. I swear it. I didn't want to, I ... I just thought ..."

"I know what you thought," she said in disgust. "But you were more wrong than you can know, and I'm going to prove it to you."

They entered the parlour to which everyone else had discreetly retired to and where Piper was serving tea, as though he had a marquess, a madame, and a lawyer in the house every day. To Gabriel's amusement, Mrs Wilkins and Bainbridge, who was a confirmed bachelor, were deep in conversation. Everyone fell quiet as Gabriel came in. He felt heat and anxiety creeping up his neck, making his throat feel like it was clogged with a tangle of roots as all eyes turned to him. Crecy slid her hand into his, however, and suddenly it wasn't so bad.

"My lord!" Mrs Wilkins was first, launching herself at him and crying all over his shirt, which was horrifying and unsettling and admittedly rather touching, too. It seemed she hadn't been able to get his parting words out of her head, and had worried herself to death to the point that she'd had to do *something*. Even though the animosity between him and Edward was well known, she'd rightly assumed that his cousin wouldn't want yet another suicide tarnishing the Greyston name further.

Bainbridge was next, so obviously emotional in his relief that they'd been in time, that even a cynic like Gabriel had to concede that it might have been more than disappointment at losing his best client. Piper took a moment to clasp his hand, saying nothing, but with such warmth in his eyes that Gabriel had been at a loss to form a reply.

And then Edward walked towards him.

"I think perhaps it's time I apologised to you, Gabriel," the words were rather gruff and stilted, but Gabriel could not but hear the sincerity of them. He felt his eyebrows rise, utterly astonished, not only by the words, but by being addressed by his Christian name.

"What on earth for?" he managed, though his voice was rather hoarse. Surely, it was he who ought to be apologising?

Edward cleared his throat and looked at the floor before casting an imploring look at his wife, who glowered at him. He cleared his throat again. "I had no idea of ... of the circumstance of your father's death, and I ... *regret* that we have never been better acquainted," he said, finally looking up and meeting Gabriel's eyes. "I must confess that I took my father's opinion of you and your own father as the truth, and never troubled myself to discover if there was any other side to the story."

To Tame a Savage Heart

"I don't blame you for that," Gabriel said with a shrug, meaning it. "He wasn't so far from the truth."

"Gabriel," Crecy said, scolding him for his words as Gabriel let out a breath.

"Come now, love. We can hardly pretend I have done no wrong in my life, but …" He looked up and met Edward's eyes. "I intend to change that. I promise you need have no fear for yourself or your family. I mean you no ill will. Not any longer."

"A truce, then?" Edward said, offering his hand.

Gabriel nodded and took it, the two men shaking on a more peaceful future.

"A truce," Gabriel agreed.

***

As soon as everyone had gone, Gabriel took his wife to bed. He would have liked to make love to her, but she was so clearly worn out and uncomfortable that he kept the idea to himself. Besides, lying with her in his arms after so much sorrow was heaven enough alongside the depths of darkness he had faced over the past hours.

She stiffened in his arms and he felt her stomach tighten as she held her breath.

"What is it, love?" he asked, feeling panicked all at once. "Is it the baby?"

Crecy smiled and shook her head. "She's just practising. Belle said there would be lots of spasms like this before the actual birth."

Gabriel let out a sigh of relief. Now that his own death had been taken from his hands, the danger that his wife faced in childbirth was in the forefront of his mind.

Crecy looked up at him, quite rightly interpreting the look in his eyes as terror.

"I'll be fine, Gabriel. Don't worry. Everything is going to be quite wonderful."

Gabriel swallowed, wanting to believe, her but knowing all too well how many women died during or after a birth.

"Gabriel." Her voice was stern, now, and she stared at him, giving him that look which always made him feel his soul was on display. "You must promise me something. If anything ever does happen. You must look after our child. Don't let them be alone like you were. Let them know how loved they are, how much we both wanted them. Make them know they are everything we ever wanted."

Gabriel shook his head, horrified by the idea of a life without her. "I can't ..." he rasped, panic flooding his chest. "I can't ..."

"Yes, you can," she snapped. "I have no intention of going anywhere at all for a good long while, Gabriel, but I will feel a deal happier knowing that I can rely on you for this. You are a father, and you will act the part." She paused, forcing him to look her in the eyes. "Promise me."

Gabriel closed his eyes, the words were beyond him, but he nodded. Praying that such a day never came, for he had no idea how he would survive it, he gave her his promise. After that, they just lay together, happy to be alive, to be together, until Crecy decided she was restless and needed some fresh air.

The heat of the day had mellowed now, and the countryside had that familiar faded look of late summer. There was a pleasant breeze rustling the leaves and the birds were singing. It felt good to be alive, to be able to appreciate it.

It was awhile, then, before Gabriel realised they were heading toward the chapel and his parent's graves. "Where are we going?" he asked, feeling his chest grow tight with anxiety.

"We are going to speak with your father," Crecy said, her voice quite calm.

"What?" Gabriel stared at her and began to back up. "No. No, Crecy, don't ask me to."

"Gabriel, after what you've put me through this morning, I will ask and you will give," she replied, her voice soft but firm. She stared at him, those unusual lilac eyes daring him to disagree further.

Gabriel found he could hardly argue the point, but still felt like he wanted to vomit. "Why?" he croaked, wondering if this was punishment for frightening her so.

"To forgive him."

He caught his breath and Crecy smiled at him, moving forward to take his hands. "Not for his sake, my love, for yours. You've carried so much anger and hurt inside of you for so long, you need to make peace with it, and you can't do that until you forgive him."

Gabriel stood stock still, concentrating on breathing in and out with difficulty. "I can't do that."

"No," Crecy replied, her voice soothing. "I don't suppose you can. Not yet, at least. But we will keep coming until you find you mean it, and then we need never come again." She moved beside him once more, holding his arm. "Come along, then."

By the time he reached the graveside, Gabriel was sweating and tense and he wanted to turn and run and lock himself in his study. But Crecy was looking at him with such expectation that he couldn't do it. He could not let her down.

He swallowed, clearing his throat and feeling foolish in the extreme as he addressed the ornate headstone.

"Hello, Father. I have come to tell you that ... that I am married." He covered Crecy's hand with his own, comforted by her touch. He looked around, knowing anyone observing them would believe he'd finally run mad. Seeing no one, he turned back to the grave. "I will be a father soon, and I wanted to tell you ... I will do everything in my power to ensure that I am nothing like you. You were a bully and a despicable man and I hate you. I have always hated you." The angry words fell from his lips faster now, more easily, and though his fury and hatred was harsh and raw, he felt strangely liberated as he spoke to a long-dead man who had haunted him for nearly two decades. He took a breath, trying to calm himself, to say the words Crecy wanted him to give the man. "I don't know if I can forgive you for everything you did to me, and to my mother, but … I am going to try. I am going to forgive you, and then I shall forget you, and I pray that no one in this family ever speaks your name again."

He exhaled, feeling as though he could breathe all at once. Gabriel looked around to see Crecy staring at him, full of such pride that he could do nothing but smile.

"I love you," he said, feeling the most ridiculous grin curve over his mouth.

"I love you too," she whispered, before sucking in a sharp breath and clutching at her stomach. Gabriel put his arms around her, supporting her until the pain passed. She leaned into him, breathing hard as he rubbed circles on her back.

"That is another practise spasm?" he asked with trepidation, feeling suddenly terrified at the ordeal she must face to bring their child into the world.

Crecy gave him a sheepish grin as she looked up at him. "Actually, Gabriel … I'm not entirely sure it is."

Epilogue

"Wherein the Greyston family goes from strength to strength."

A little over six years later ...

Crecy watched Gabriel cradling the tiny bundle in his arms as he sat on the bed beside her, and felt her heart swell. She had given him a son this time, and he looked about as proud as any man could. Though if anyone knew the way their little daughter, Hope, twisted the man around her tiny thumb, she doubted anyone would believe it.

He had proved himself to be a wonderful father and a devoted husband, though that wasn't to say it was always plain sailing. He still had to fight against the desire to obsess over details, but mostly he had it under control enough so that it didn't completely control him. He was still rather overbearing at times, and had a tendency to put his foot down over things that frightened him, like allowing his daughter a small pony so that she could learn to ride. Gabriel was horrified by the idea that she could fall and be hurt, and so he wouldn't move an inch. So Crecy still hadn't won that one, but she'd started early, knowing full well it would be a battle royale. She hoped by the girl's seventh birthday, she'd have cracked him.

"What shall we call him?" Gabriel asked, looking up at her, his indigo eyes shining with happiness.

Crecy pursed her lips, and pretended to think about it. "Frank?" she suggested, sighing happily as she admired her handsome man cooing over their baby.

Gabriel scowled, looking up from his son and tutting at her. "We are not naming our child after that blasted book," he protested. Crecy grinned, knowing full well he'd noticed that she'd been reading Frankenstein again. She always cried for the monster, which caused Gabriel to mutter that it explained a lot about their relationship. Crecy laughed as she saw him realise she'd been teasing him. Gabriel gave a huff of laughter, shaking his head.

"It's my turn," she reminded him with a smile. "I let you name Hope, didn't I?" Gabriel nodded, turning his attention back to his son, who Crecy had to admit was handsome, just like his father. "How about Henry Edward Gabriel Greyston?" she suggested instead, watching as the idea took hold in her husband's mind.

"Henry is a good strong name," he said, nodding, as the little boy clutched at his finger. "He likes it," he added with a grin. "And Edward would like that, too, I think."

"He'll be a playmate for Eli and Leo," Crecy said, beaming as she reached to stroke her son's downy head. "Belle's boys have been praying it wasn't another girl by all accounts."

Gabriel grunted. "Well, better him than Hope," he muttered, which made Crecy laugh. Her daughter had inherited every bit of her mother's daring and curiosity and love of adventure and all the things girls ought not to like. The sweet-looking little girl adored her two male cousins, and constantly led them into mischief. Crecy still cringed as she remembered Belle screaming over the frogs in the fruit bowl. Indeed, little Hope frightened her poor father to death on a daily basis.

"Here," he said, giving his son back into her arms with a look of regret. "Belle will be here soon."

"That doesn't mean you have to go, Gabriel," she said with a sigh, though she knew it would make no difference.

"I know, but you'll enjoy your visit more if I do," he said, leaning over to kiss her before he got up off the bed. "Well done, my clever, beautiful wife, I was never more proud." He straightened and paused to look at the picture of her holding his son with obvious pleasure. "Besides," he said. "I have an engagement with a very beautiful young woman." He left her with a smirk and she laughed with amusement, knowing full well he'd promised to play with Hope.

A moment later and Belle came in, cooing and delighted with baby Henry. It was strange, really, how Edward had given Gabriel a second chance, but how Belle was finding it the hardest. Belle simply couldn't forgive him for the heartache he had brought her sister, and though she was always scrupulously polite, there was never more than that. She said she pitied him terribly for his past and wished him well, but no matter how happy Crecy was, Belle could not seem to let go of her anger.

After allowing her sister a generous cuddle with her son, Crecy decided she had one last trick up her sleeve.

"You should visit Hope before you leave, Belle," she said, hiding a sly smile. "You don't want her to think you love Henry more than her."

"Oh, no, of course not," Belle exclaimed, looking horrified. "And as if I would," she added, her tone a little smug. "I have a present for her."

Crecy nodded, beaming. "Well, you'd best run along and give it to her, then."

With a smile, she watched as Belle left the room. If there was one thing guaranteed to melt the hardest of hearts, it would be the intimidating figure of Gabriel Greyston playing with his six-year-old daughter.

***

Hope sat patiently beside him as Gabriel arranged all of the tiny cups and saucers and plates, ensuring that each one was placed directly in front of the various dolls and wooden creatures that she had invited to tea. She never interrupted him when he was tidying or rearranging, and though it broke his heart, she would try and keep her toys tidy when she played, somehow aware that it distressed him even though he tried hard to hide it. Crecy, of course, was determined to help both of them overcome any tendency to worry, and encouraged her daughter to play in the dirt and climb trees and do all sorts of things that made Gabriel sick with worry all the same.

"It looks lovely, Daddy," Hope said, beaming at him as he tweaked the teapot a little.

He looked up for a moment, thinking that he'd heard a footstep outside the half open door, but then turned to her as no one came in.

"Sorry it took so long," he said, wishing he could overcome such foolishness. He was better than he used to be, but his compulsions were a hard thing to be rid of. He had not heard his father's voice for over a year, though, and had finally been able to tell the man he forgave him and mean it. He had no desire to remember him, or to visit his grave, but he felt his anger at least had been buried in that grave along with his father's bones.

"Good things are worth waiting for, that's what Mummy says," Hope replied, repeating faithfully a phrase he had heard Crecy say on a number of occasions. "Besides, Sarah Rotherford's daddy doesn't *ever* play with her. She didn't believe me when I said you did, *and* even when I told her that you give the best tea parties, too."

Gabriel cleared his throat, wondering if Sarah would repeat that to her mother, who was the biggest gossip in the county. With chagrin, he found he didn't much care if she did.

"And what did you say when she didn't believe you?" Gabriel asked with a little niggle of misgiving.

"I punched her on the nose," Hope replied calmly as she lifted a tiny teacup to her doll's mouth.

Oh, Lord.

Gabriel cleared his throat, straightening and attempting to give his daughter a stern look. It was a difficult thing to do. "You really ought not to hit other children, Hope, it isn't nice."

"I know," she replied, her blonde ringlets bobbing as she nodded at him. He looked down at her, feeling such a swell of love and protectiveness as he looked into eyes that were just like his own that it quite took his breath away. "But she said I was a liar, and that's not nice, either."

"No," Gabriel replied, wishing Crecy had unearthed this little nugget, as he didn't know what to say. "But, it is perhaps a little hard to believe." He paused, watching as Hope fed the dolls their imaginary dinner. "How about we ask Sarah to come to one of the tea parties?" he offered, wondering if he had completely lost his mind. God alone knew what they'd say about him if this got out. He found that didn't matter, either, however, as Hope beamed at him and threw her arms around his neck.

"Oh, yes, please, that would be wonderful."

Gabriel hugged her, making his voice stern again with difficulty. "But only if you promise that you won't hit anyone else."

His daughter sighed and scowled a little before giving a shrug. "All right, then," she muttered, sounding as though it was a very unfair bargain to have struck.

"Good girl," Gabriel said with a sigh, pleased to have cleared that hurdle. "Perhaps we'd better get it ready before she arrives, though," he added as an afterthought.

"Yes, you'd prefer it if she didn't watch you," Hope said, getting back to her dolls.

Gabriel smiled, amazed and overwhelmed by his daughter as he always was. "I love you, monkey," he said, getting a grin before she pulled a face at him.

"I'm not a monkey, I'm a wolf, grrrr," she shouted, baring her teeth and turning her little fingers into claws. "And I'm going to eat you up."

She threw herself at Gabriel, who pretended to shout in terror as she tickled him until both of them were crying with laughter, and then he became aware they were being watched.

Gabriel looked up to see Belle staring down at them, one eyebrow raised a little.

"Auntie Belle!" Hope cried with delight, rushing to hug her.

Gabriel cleared his throat, a flush crawling up the back of his neck. "Hello, Belle," he replied, feeling a little awkward as he got to his feet. He looked down at Hope with regret. "I'd better go, darling. Why don't you invite your aunt to your tea party?"

He felt a stab of guilt at her obvious disappointment, but he knew Belle didn't like him around. "Oh, but Daddy, you promised to stay." Hope tugged at his hand and pouted at him, making him feel torn and unsure of what to do.

Gabriel looked at Belle and was surprised to see her looking at him with warmth in her eyes. "Oh, I'm sure Daddy will stay, if we ask him nicely, won't you, Gabriel?"

Gabriel hesitated, wondering if he'd mistaken her look or her tone, but Belle reached out and took his hand, giving it a brief squeeze. "I've just met your son," she said. "And Crecy looks so very happy."

He smiled and nodded, and Belle gestured to the tea party as Hope was tugging impatiently at her hand, too, now. So the two of them got to the floor as Hope served them tea. Gabriel cast his sister-in-law a look of chagrin as he lifted the tiny tea cup obediently to his lips and pretended to drink it, but Belle just grinned back at him. She reminded him so much of his wife in that moment he could not help but chuckle.

"Oh, Hope, I almost forgot, I have a present for you," Belle exclaimed, pulling a small wrapped package from her reticule. Hope bounced on the spot with excitement as she carefully opened the parcel, handing the paper to Gabriel to fold.

"A snake!" she exclaimed, waving the carved wooden creature in the air like a prize. "Look, Daddy, isn't it wonderful?"

Gabriel looked at the carved and painted snake, with wicked black eyes and a painted red, forked tongue. Personally, he thought it looked a revolting creature. "Wonderful, darling," he agreed with a grave nod.

"I'm going to show Mummy and the baby," she shrieked, holding it above her head and running out of the door.

"I couldn't resist it," Belle admitted as she left. "It's the sort of thing Crecy would have loved as a child."

Gabriel nodded, his eyes full of worry all at once. "I know. She's so much like her mother. I sometime worry that ..." He trailed off, turning his attention back to folding the paper into a neat square, not wanting to voice the fact he was terrified his daughter might be drawn to a man like him one day. He looked up in surprise as Belle laid her hand on his arm.

"Have faith in her, Gabriel. If she's anything like my sister, she'll be absolutely fine. Better than fine," she amended with a smile, her voice warm. "She'll be happy."

Gabriel let out a breath, knowing that he'd been forgiven at last, and feeling that his future was full of hope, in every sense of the word.

Keep reading for a peek at the next riveting tale in the Rogues & Gentlemen Series. Out June 1, 2018.

Persuading Patience

Rogues & Gentlemen Book 8

Lord Percy Nibley needs a wife, preferably before his mother's nagging on the subject drives him to distraction. But being more comfortable with his rock collection than flirting, he's not having a lot of luck.

In desperation, the shy nobleman enlists the help of Baron Marchmain - Lord August Bright. August is nothing short of dazzling. Charming, witty and amusing, he's the darling of the ton, and a notorious heart-breaker.

August selects a suitable young lady for Lord Nibley; Miss Patience Pearson, a cool, level-headed woman, close to being on the shelf and with the reputation of a blue-stocking, meanwhile setting his own sights on capturing the heart of her vivacious younger sister, Caroline.

But Patience is not easily charmed, guarding her sister with the tenacity of a lioness and August must be at his most devastatingly charming to get past her defences.

Having finally done so, however …

August isn't at all sure he's chosen the right sister.

Pre-Order your copy now!

Persuading Patience

Chapter 1

"Wherein we speak of fallen idols, lost slippers, and lion-tamers."

17th May 1818

Lord Marchmain, otherwise known as August Bright, stared at the man who had been his idol for so many years and shook his head with remorse. That the fellow had been reduced to this; it was shocking, and rather terrifying, too.

The object of the young man's pity was none other than the Duke of Ware, otherwise known as Beau to his intimates. To be fair, August had to concede that Beau didn't seem the least bit regretful at the loss of his freedom and his decadent lifestyle. In fact, truth be told, the fellow seemed to revel in his new way of life. One might even say he was ... *happy.* Yet as August watched him juggle one of two newborn babies with surprising ease and confidence, he could only wonder at how this was possible. His duchess, Milly, was a good sort, too, rather fun, in fact, but that poor Beau was quite firmly under her thumb was only too obvious.

This was the man who'd had half the women in London falling at his feet, and one that August had tried hard to emulate. To be perfectly truthful, he'd done a damned good job, too. Bearing in mind he was neither a duke, nor even a marquess - as Beau had been at the height of his fame - but a mere baron, August thought he'd succeeded rather admirably in taking up the man's crown as darling of the *ton* and the most notorious rake in town.

"It won't do, August," Beau continued, handing the mewling baby to his wife, who was scolding him about feeding times. "By all accounts, your mother is at her wit's end, and believe me, I know, as she was here all of Monday afternoon, thank you very much." Beau's tone was terse now, though August didn't blame him, a visit from his mother was enough to leave anyone feeling blue-devilled.

He was embarrassed, however, so he just glowered and rolled his eyes to the ceiling as Beau kissed his wife and actually looked regretful to see her take the horrifyingly noisy twins from the room. "Dammit, Beau, you know that was none of my doing. I'm mortified that she came to you."

"No more than I," Beau replied, his tone dry as they were finally left in blessed peace. "I've heard more about you and your scandalous affairs than I needed to know, I assure you, but the only way I could get free of her was by promising to talk to you." To be fair, Beau looked just as disgusted by the turn of events as August, but they both knew his mother was a hard woman, and one that you crossed at your peril.

August glowered harder nonetheless. His mother was a dreadful snob, and one of the only things he had ever done that she had approved of was making friends with the duke of Ware. That she'd had the audacity to come to Beau herself to discuss her son's sordid behaviour …

August shuddered with the humiliation of it.

"So tell her you did your duty and leave me be," he said, crossing his arms and feeling increasingly indignant. "Just because you're happy being a poacher-turned-game-keeper, I don't see why you have to try to spoil my fun," he added, more than a little aggrieved at the duke's interference, bearing in mind the man's own reputation had been every bit as black as August's.

Beau snorted and shook his head. "That's exactly why, you fool. Believe me, I have every sympathy with you for your mother." August flushed, mortified at Beau realising what a dreadful bitch she really was. God alone only knew what she'd said to Beau about him. Beau's face softened with pity and August felt ill as his worst fears were confirmed. "But she does have a point," Beau continued, "and I'm not talking about providing the heir she's so desperate for, either. You need to take an honest look at your life, August, because I know all of that fun you're having will begin to pall soon, if it hasn't already." Beau's intense blue eyes turned on him with rather too much force and August looked away. The devil always seemed to see through him, and it was disturbing.

August got to his feet, determined that he bring this interview to a close as soon as possible. "Look, I've brought most of what I owe you, I just need a few weeks to find the rest, but you'll have it, I promise. So there is no need to punish me any further with this father-figure speech of yours. You can tell Mother you did everything you could with a clear conscience." He reached for the thick wad of notes in his pocket, the result of a timely win on the horses, and held it out to Beau with regret. It was all the money he had in the world at the moment, and if his mother had been here complaining about him, well, an advance on his allowance wasn't looking likely.

Beau shook his head. "No."

August blanched, wondering if Beau was going to insist on the whole lot. He'd been very patient, after all, allowing him to pay off his debt over the course of a year, but this last instalment was already a month late.

"Oh, don't look so horrified," Beau replied, shaking his head and smiling. "I've just decided on another way in which you can repay me."

August's eyes widened and he knew well that he really must look horrified now. He was in debt to the man and late with payment and Beau had him over a barrel. Honour demanded he do as he was asked. He waited in trepidation to discover what on earth it was he was in for.

Beau chuckled enjoying his discomfort enormously. "You remember Lord Nibley? He was up at Eton with us, my year so older than you."

Frowning as a tall, gaunt man with spectacles came to mind, August nodded. "Dull fellow, academic, always on about rocks or something?" He watched as Beau grinned at him.

"That's the fellow. Well, as it happens, he's a good friend of mine and he needs help, and you're going to give it to him."

"What?" August demanded, wondering if Beau had taken leave of his senses. "What the bloody hell could I possibly help him with?"

Beau turned away and poured them both a drink, carrying the crystal glasses over and handing one with a generous measure to August. There was a rather amused glint in his blue eyes that didn't bode well.

"You, my dear August, can help the man learn how to charm the birds from the trees ... and find him a wife."

***

"It's got to be here somewhere!" Patience threw the cushion back onto the armchair as though it had offended her and put her hands on her hips. Her younger step-sister, Caro, quailed a little and bit her lip.

"Well, I suppose I might have come home without it," she offered, as Patience rolled her eyes to the heavens and prayed for more of what her name implied she had in abundance. It was ironic, really, a more impatient woman you'd be hard-pressed to find. She wondered if her parents had known it all along and had merely named her so to remind her daily of what she most lacked.

"Caro, even you cannot be so utterly bird-witted to come home with only one shoe," Patience retorted, getting on her hands and knees and looking under the sofa. "I refuse to believe it."

"Well, I don't know why," Caro replied, flopping into the nearest chair with a flurry of muslin skirts. "You have to admit, it's the sort of thing I *would* do."

Patience snorted and then gave a lusty sneeze as the dust under the sofa got up her nose; they really ought to get another housemaid, but their mother - Patience's step-mother - was economising again. That was a laugh, too, her darling step-mama had no more idea of economy than she did how to lie through her teeth. It was really too much when you couldn't remonstrate with the woman for spending the entire week's grocery allowance on a pair of kid gloves because the colour matched her eyes, when she was so utterly guileless.

"Whilst I'm prepared to concede that you would do such a thing, surely you would remember coming home on Friday night with one shoe?" Patience demanded as she fumbled for her handkerchief. "It was raining, for heaven's sake." She blew her nose with gusto and looked up, watching as Caro screwed up her own nose, deep in thought. She was really a very pretty girl. Black hair fell in thick ringlets around a heart-shaped face, and her blue eyes were perfectly angelic. Her nature was just as sweet, and despite being only a half-sister, she was devoted to Patience, as was her mother. Patience's own mother had died young and her father had quickly married Cecilia, or Cilly as she was known to her friends. It was an alarmingly apt name for her. Neither Caro nor Cilly had an ounce of common sense between them, and Patience had become the one they both deferred to. Her own father had died not long after marrying Cilly, and it was her step-mother's unwavering kindness to Patience during this difficult time that made it all the easier to bear with her rather frivolous nature.

Cilly had naturally married again, but her new husband had died of tuberculosis after only two years of marriage, leaving Cilly to bring up little Caro alone. Cilly had been distraught, as she truly had loved her husband, and it fell to Patience at the tender age of twelve to take over the running of the household. It was not a role she minded exactly; after all, she couldn't bear to see the two of them get themselves into such ridiculous situations and do nothing, but she did occasionally experience a pang of regret for what her youth might have held if not for them. Now at the ripe old age of twenty-eight, she had accepted that any thoughts of marriage were behind her, but didn't mourn the loss of it as hard as some might have believed. After all, she was used to being in charge, used to her independence, and she was damned if any man would take that away from her.

"Of course!" Caro exclaimed, jumping to her feet. "It must be in the larder."

Patience stared at her sister and refused to bite. There really was no point in asking how one - not both, mind - but one of her best satin dancing slippers had ended up in the larder. "Of course it is," she muttered, getting to her feet again.

"Well, Rufus was trying to eat the rosette off it, you see," Caro continued as Patience followed her down the stairs to the kitchen. Rufus was Cilly's obnoxious little pug dog. It was spoiled and bad-tempered and Patience despised it. The feeling was most certainly mutual. "He didn't want the left one, for some reason, only the right, and I was hungry after that party so I went to the kitchen …"

"Yes, yes," Patience replied, holding up a weary hand. "I do see."

She waited whilst Caro trotted off to retrieve her missing shoe and looked in the parlour where her step-mama was sipping tea with a distracted air.

"Is your packing all done, Mama?" Patience asked, though it always seemed odd to her to call the woman Mama. Her step-mother was only thirty-seven and looked younger. She could easily pass for Patience's older, and far more lovely, sister. It was just as well Patience didn't care for such superficial things as looks, or she might have been just a little put out. As it was, Patience was perfectly content to have taken after her father. He may not have been the most handsome man in the world, but he had a good brain in his head, a great deal of common sense, and had even wit enough to educate his daughters. As Caro would only too quickly point out, it had only been of use to Patience, as she herself was quite stupid. This comment would quickly dissolve into a row as Patience knew quite well that Caro was not stupid at all, only rather lazy and more interested in pretty frocks and parties than anything that taxed her perfectly capable brain.

"Mama!" Patience repeated, as the lovely woman before her jumped and nearly dropped her teacup.

"Oh, Patience, dearest," she said, flushing a little. "I didn't see you there."

"I asked if you had finished packing. You know we leave early tomorrow morning?"

Cilly bit her lip and shook her head. "No, not yet. I ... I did start, only ... Oh, Patience, it's so fatiguing. Mary will keep asking me questions about whether I want to bring this or that, and I needed a moment to get away."

Patience folded her arms, narrowing her eyes. "You only began after midday, Cilly," she said, her tone rather severe now. "Despite promising me you'd do it this morning, and as it is only now two o'clock, I find it hard to believe that you have over-exerted yourself."

She watched as Cilly huffed and pouted and then made a sound of objection as Patience took her cup and saucer away and hauled her to her feet. "Just think, though, Cilly, what will happen if you don't oversee things. You know, I think I saw Mary pack that shocking violet outfit you bought in London that makes you look positively hagged, *and* that old sprigged muslin you wear out in the garden to prune the roses."

This, far more than any other remonstration, had the desired effect as Cilly gave a cry of alarm and hurried back up the stairs. Patience snorted and shook her head, making a mental note of all the other things she must do before they left in the morning. She must take a moment and sit down and pay the last of their bills before they left, and give instructions to the gardener, help Mary put the Holland covers over the best furniture, as the poor woman would drop with exhaustion after dealing with Cilly and her packing - oh, and make sure they had a picnic, as Caro and Cilly were bound to attract unwanted attention if they stopped at an inn, no matter how respectable. She could only pray that the lodgings she had found them were every bit as elegant and well-placed as she had hoped from her correspondence. Not that she could do anything about it now. Patience was torn from her thoughts, however, as Caro appeared from the kitchen.

"Found it!" she crowed, dark curls bouncing as she ran towards Patience, triumphant as she held the blue satin slipper aloft.

"Well," Patience murmured as she gave a heavy sigh. "That is a weight off my mind."

***

To Patience's great relief, the three-story town-house on Henrietta Street was everything she had hoped for. One of a long row of identical houses, built of Bath stone, it was everything that was quiet elegance. Not at the height of fashion, perhaps, but a good and very respectable address that should speak well for them as a family, and that was what mattered.

Patience had little time for the *haut ton* and their notions of what was and was not of the first importance. There was no denying, however, that for Caro to make some good connections, and, God willing, a suitable marriage, appearances had to be maintained. In truth, this didn't ought to be difficult. Her father had left them all very comfortably off if only Cilly would try to remember she was a widow and couldn't spend and gamble as she had whilst her darling husband was alive. In fact, her second husband had been a very wealthy man and the bulk of his fortune had been left to Caro. This was both a blessing and a curse, since her come-out as a pretty, young heiress meant every fortune hunter in town was nosing about after her like asses after the last carrot. Patience snorted, rather pleased by the appropriate mental image that conjured. Still, it was her job to ensure that Caro did not get taken in by rakes and libertines, but married a good and kind-hearted fellow that would treat her well and not squash her enthusiasm for life.

As Cilly was as ill-equipped to deal with such men as Caro herself, it fell to Patience to be the grown-up, and the lion-tamer. Any man who set his sights on Caro had better be worthy of her, or face the consequences.

Want more Emma?

If you enjoyed this book, please support this indie author and take a moment to leave a few words in a review. *Thank you!*

To be kept informed of special offers and free deals (which I do regularly) follow me on *https://www.bookbub.com/authors/emma-v-leech*

To find out more and to get news and sneak peeks of the first chapter of upcoming works, go to my website and sign up for the newsletter.
http://www.emmavleech.com/

Come and join the fans in my Facebook group for news, info and exciting discussion...

Emmas Book Club

Or Follow me here......

http://viewauthor.at/EmmaVLeechAmazon
Facebook
Instagram
Emma's Twitter page
TikTok

About Me!

I started this incredible journey way back in 2010 with The Key to Erebus but didn't summon the courage to hit publish until October 2012. For anyone who's done it, you'll know publishing your first title is a terribly scary thing! I still get butterflies on the morning a new title releases, but the terror has subsided at least. Now I just live in dread of the day my daughters are old enough to read them.

The horror! (On both sides I suspect.)

2017 marked the year that I made my first foray into Historical Romance and the world of the Regency Romance, and my word what a year! I was delighted by the response to this series and can't wait to add more titles. Paranormal Romance readers need not despair however as there is much more to come there too. Writing has become an addiction and as soon as one book is over I'm hugely excited to start the next so you can expect plenty more in the future.

As many of my works reflect I am greatly influenced by the beautiful French countryside in which I live. I've been here in the

South West for the past twenty years though I was born and raised in England. My three gorgeous girls are all bilingual and the youngest who is only six, is showing signs of following in my footsteps after producing *The Lonely Princess* all by herself.

I'm told book two is coming soon ...

She's keeping me on my toes, so I'd better get cracking!

KEEP READING TO DISCOVER MY OTHER BOOKS!

Other Works by Emma V. Leech

(For those of you who have read The French Fae Legend series, please remember that chronologically The Heart of Arima precedes The Dark Prince)

Rogues & Gentlemen

Rogues & Gentlemen Series

Girls Who Dare

Girls Who Dare Series

Daring Daughters

Daring Daughters Series

The Regency Romance Mysteries

The Regency Romance Mysteries Series

The French Vampire Legend

The French Vampire Legend Series

The French Fae Legend

The French Fae Legend Series

Stand Alone
The Book Lover (a paranormal novella)
The Girl is Not for Christmas (Regency Romance)

Audio Books

Don't have time to read but still need your romance fix? The wait is over…

By popular demand, get many of your favourite Emma V Leech Regency Romance books on audio as performed by the incomparable Philip Battley and Gerard Marzilli. Several titles available and more added each month!

Find them at your favourite audiobook retailer!

Girls Who Dare– The exciting new series from Emma V Leech, the multi-award-winning, Amazon Top 10 romance writer behind the Rogues & Gentlemen series.

Inside every wallflower is the beating heart of a lioness, a passionate individual willing to risk all for their dream, if only they can find the courage to begin. When these overlooked girls make a pact to change their lives, anything can happen.

Ten girls – Ten dares in a hat. Who will dare to risk it all?

To Dare a Duke

Girls Who Dare Book 1

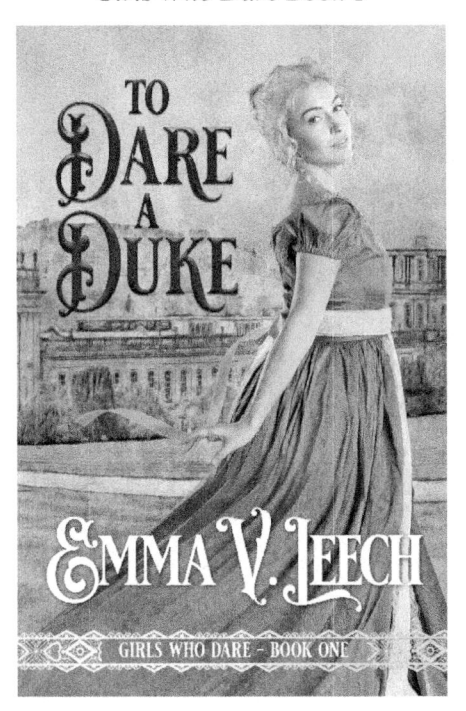

Dreams of true love and happy ever afters

Dreams of love are all well and good, but all Prunella Chuffington-Smythe wants is to publish her novel. Marriage at the price of her independence is something she will not consider. Having tasted success writing under a false name in The Lady's Weekly Review, her alter ego is attaining notoriety and fame and Prue rather likes it.

A Duty that must be endured

Robert Adolphus, The Duke of Bedwin, is in no hurry to marry, he's done it once and repeating that disaster is the last thing he desires. Yet, an heir is a necessary evil for a duke and one he cannot shirk. A dark reputation precedes him though, his first wife may have died young, but the scandals the beautiful, vivacious and spiteful creature supplied the ton have not. A wife must be found. A wife who is neither beautiful or vivacious but sweet and dull, and certain to stay out of trouble.

Dared to do something drastic

The sudden interest of a certain dastardly duke is as bewildering as it is unwelcome. She'll not throw her ambitions aside to marry a scoundrel just as her plans for self-sufficiency and freedom are coming to fruition. Surely showing the man she's not actually the meek little wallflower he is looking for should be enough to put paid to his intentions? When Prue is dared by her friends to do something drastic, it seems the perfect opportunity to kill two birds.

However, Prue cannot help being intrigued by the rogue who has inspired so many of her romances. Ordinarily, he plays the part of handsome rake, set on destroying her plucky heroine. But is he really the villain of the piece this time, or could he be the hero?

Finding out will be dangerous, but it just might inspire her greatest story yet.

To Dare a Duke

From the author of the bestselling Girls Who Dare Series – An exciting new series featuring the children of the Girls Who Dare...

The stories of the **Peculiar Ladies Book Club** and their hatful of dares has become legend among their children. When the hat is rediscovered, dusty and forlorn, the remaining dares spark a series of events that will echo through all the families... and their

Daring Daughters

Dare to be Wicked
Daring Daughters Book One

Two daring daughters ...

Lady Elizabeth and Lady Charlotte are the daughters of the Duke and Duchess of Bedwin. Raised by an unconventional mother and an indulgent, if overprotective father, they both strain against the rigid morality of the era.

The fashionable image of a meek, weak young lady, prone to swooning at the least provocation, is one that makes them seethe with frustration.

Their handsome childhood friend ...

Cassius Cadogen, Viscount Oakley, is the only child of the Earl and Countess St Clair. Beloved and indulged, he is popular, gloriously handsome, and a talented artist.

Returning from two years of study in France, his friendship with both sisters becomes strained as jealousy raises its head. A situation not helped by the two mysterious Frenchmen who have accompanied him home.

And simmering sibling rivalry ...

Passion, art, and secrets prove to be a combustible combination, and someone will undoubtedly get burned.

Order your copy here Dare to be Wicked

Interested in a Regency Romance with a twist?

Dying for a Duke

The Regency Romance Mysteries Book 1

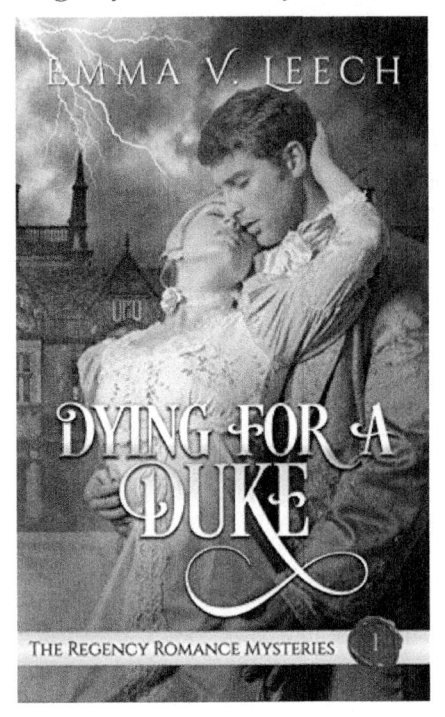

Straight-laced, imperious and morally rigid, Benedict Rutland - the darkly handsome Earl of Rothay - gained his title too young. Responsible for a large family of younger siblings that his frivolous parents have brought to bankruptcy, his youth was spent clawing back the family fortunes.

Now a man in his prime and financially secure he is betrothed to a strict, sensible and cool-headed woman who will never upset the balance of his life or disturb his emotions ...

But then Miss Skeffington-Fox arrives.

Brought up solely by her rake of a step-father, Benedict is scandalised by everything about the dashing Miss.

But as family members in line for the dukedom begin to die at an alarming rate, all fingers point at Benedict, and Miss Skeffington-Fox may be the only one who can save him.

FREE to read on Amazon Kindle Unlimited.. [Dying for a Duke](#)

Lose yourself in Emma's paranormal world with The French Vampire Legend series.

The Key to Erebus

The French Vampire Legend Book 1

The truth can kill you.

Taken away as a small child, from a life where vampires, the Fae, and other mythical creatures are real and treacherous, the beautiful young witch, Jéhenne Corbeaux is totally unprepared when she returns to rural France to live with her eccentric Grandmother.

Thrown headlong into a world she knows nothing about she seeks to learn the truth about herself, uncovering secrets more shocking than anything she could ever have imagined and finding that she is by no means powerless to protect the ones she loves.

Despite her Gran's dire warnings, she is inexorably drawn to the dark and terrifying figure of Corvus, an ancient vampire and master of the vast Albinus family.

Jéhenne is about to find her answers and discover that, not only is Corvus far more dangerous than she could ever imagine, but that he holds much more than the key to her heart …

Now available at your favourite retailer

The Key to Erebus

Check out Emma's exciting fantasy series with hailed by Kirkus Reviews as "An enchanting fantasy with a likable heroine, romantic intrigue, and clever narrative flourishes."

The Dark Prince

The French Fae Legend Book 1

Two Fae Princes
One Human Woman
And a world ready to tear them all apart

Laen Braed is Prince of the Dark fae, with a temper and reputation to match his black eyes, and a heart that despises the human race. When he is sent back through the forbidden gates between realms to retrieve an ancient fae artifact, he returns home with far more than he bargained for.

Corin Albrecht, the most powerful Elven Prince ever born. His golden eyes are rumoured to be a gift from the gods, and destiny is calling him. With a love for the human world that runs deep, his friendship with Laen is being torn apart by his prejudices.

Océane DeBeauvoir is an artist and bookbinder who has always relied on her lively imagination to get her through an unhappy and uneventful life. A jewelled dagger put on display at a nearby museum hits the headlines with speculation of another race, the Fae. But the discovery also inspires Océane to create an extraordinary piece of art that cannot be confined to the pages of a book.

With two powerful men vying for her attention and their friendship stretched to the breaking point, the only question that remains...who is truly The Dark Prince.

The man of your dreams is coming...or is it your nightmares he visits? Find out in Book One of The French Fae Legend.

Available now at your favourite retailer

The Dark Prince

Acknowledgements

Special thanks must go to my wonderful sensitivity reader Amanda for her help with making Gabriel a real and imperfectly perfect character. Thank you, my friend. I could not have done it without your insight and generosity in illustrating all the myriad ways OCD and PTSD impact people's lives every day.

Thanks as always to my wonderful editor for being patient and loving my characters as much as I do. Gemma you're the best!

To Victoria Cooper for all your hard work, amazing artwork and above all your unending patience !!! Thank you so much. You are amazing !

To my BFF, PA, personal cheerleader and bringer of chocolate, Varsi Appel, for moral support, confidence boosting and for reading my work more times than I have. I love you loads!

A huge thank you to all of Emma's Book Club members! You guys are the best!

I'm always so happy to hear from you so do email or message me :)

emmavleech@orange.fr

To my husband Pat and my family ... For always being proud of me.

Can't get your fill of Historical Romance? Do you crave stories with passion and red hot chemistry?

If the answer is yes, have I got the group for you!

Come join myself and other awesome authors in our Facebook group

Historical Harlots

Be the first to know about exclusive giveaways, chat with amazing HistRom authors, lots of raunchy shenanigans and more!

Historical Harlots Facebook Group

Printed in Great Britain
by Amazon